Julie P. Smith

His Young Wife

A Novel

Julie P. Smith

His Young Wife
A Novel

ISBN/EAN: 9783337001308

Printed in Europe, USA, Canada, Australia, Japan

Cover: Foto ©Andreas Hilbeck / pixelio.de

More available books at **www.hansebooks.com**

HIS YOUNG WIFE.

A NOVEL.

BY

JULIE P. SMITH,

AUTHOR OF

"WIDOW GOLDSMITH'S DAUGHTER," "TEN OLD MAIDS,"
"CHRIS AND OTHO," ETC., ETC.

"Marriage is the nursery of Heaven. The state of marriage fills up the number of
the elect, and hath in it the labor of love; the delicacies of friendship; the blessing of
society, and the union of hands and hearts. She that is loved is safe, and he that
loves is joyful."—JEREMY TAYLOR.

NEW YORK:

G. W. Carleton & Co., Publishers.

LONDON: S. LOW & CO.

MDCCCLXXVII.

JOHN F. TROW & SON,
PRINTERS AND BOOKBINDERS,
205-213 *East 12th Street,*
NEW YORK.

To

GEORGE W. CARLETON,

MY FRIEND AND PUBLISHER.

AND MAY NOT "THE YOUNG WIFE" BE SAFELY AND

CONFIDENTLY CONSIGNED TO *HIS* CARE,

WHO WAS NEITHER ASTONISHED NOR DISMAYED

BY "A WIDOWER," "TEN OLD MAIDS,"

OR A "MARRIED BELLE."

PREFACE.

Lux and I had just finished a story by which we were well entertained.

"Dear old woman," said Lux, "I wish you would try your hand at something in this vein. There's Sam Slaughter he ought to have a gift from the Lord, that is, a wife."

"Of a truth good Lux thou sayest well: I am minded to set about it straight, and twelve moons shall not wax and wane before the man Sam is mated."

The position of the center figures toward each other has been a favorite one among novelists. I have myself found a like couple in one English tale, two French, two German, and one Swedish. The working out of each, following, of course, the bent of their creating minds; for how sayeth old Ben Johnson: "A man is not better known by his face than by his written works, if so be he draweth his discourse from his own braine, and be not a book-botcher."

CONTENTS.

HIS YOUNG WIFE.

CHAPTER I.

"HE RECEIVES COMFORT LIKE COLD PORRIDGE."

RS. SLAUGHTON had been watching her son, "off and on," for five minutes or more without speaking. Although he was well worth her scrutiny, it was quite evident she got little pleasure out of it.

He was the pride of her eyes, but not the joy of her heart at this precise time, because she saw plainly that his thoughts were not with her; that when he did reply to any of her remarks, he seemed to come out of a world of his own, peopled with strangers whose names and inclinations towards him he never disclosed to her, and he retired into it again with the shutting of his lips.

It was nothing new either. She was often conscious that his preoccupation held him aloof from her, having some cause she was not able to fathom.

In June he had returned from his last journeying, California this time. The absence before that took him to Egypt, and so through the gone years since he was twenty-one, always a wanderer.

To be sure his profession afforded sufficient reason for his nomadic life, and his pictures were in good demand.

But Mrs. Slaughton had a purpose in her mind which words had failed as yet to help on, and which was an ever-present source of trouble because it would not arrive at completion. And she turned it over in her thoughts and wishes, while she fretfully rocked herself to and fro in her swaying chair, and drew her thread across and across the little star of white wax she took from the pocket of her work-basket, till it was stiff and firm enough to hem through a sail-cloth. And finding she only tore the heels she wished to mend, she pulled it out of her needle and laid it aside, and threaded a fresh piece, letting the wax alone this time as an unnecessary aid.

"Samuel!" she said at length, seeming to come to the expression of her desires with the last darn and the folding up of the last pair of socks of the week's mending. "Samuel, my son, you *must* get married."

Mr. Slaughton broke up his meditations, and abruptly took leave of a group of memories he had been conjuring amongst his smoke-wreaths, and enjoying with the sedate tranquillity conferred upon the votaries of nicotina, and turned his gaze, which had been fixed upon the airy dance of some golden maple leaves away down by the gate, towards the speaker, and a queer smile played over his features.

His light brown hair and eyebrows, his very fair mustache, and full rolling lips gave him an air of effeminate softness, which his clear eyes, penetrating and thoughtful, wide forehead and firm lower jaw, entirely contradicted. He looked like a man slow to arouse to any overt action, needing powerful motives to induce him to any decided step involving either his own weal or other people's. Evidently endowed by nature with a most equable temper, and much forbearance ; but in studying him closely you would not have liked to pronounce with certainty as to the exact point at which he might cast aside his *laissez faire*, or the speed he might make in the pursuit of a prize attractive enough to set him in chase, or the violence his manifestations of love or hate might reach if he were once shaken out of his apathy, and kindled with all the life he had capacity for.

Still it was patent that he had nothing aggressive in his character. In fact, smart managing people often thought they had imposed upon Mr. Slaughton, and were hoodwinking and leading him by the nose, when he merely permitted them to grind all their little axes and chuckle over his dulness, because he did not care enough for them and their plots to get up and circumvent them.

His voice sounded a trifle careless as he replied to the startling announcement just made to him ; it seemed that the subject had little interest, or as if it might be a repetition of an appeal with which he was familiar.

"What, mother! are you still determined to cut the thread of my bachelor freedom as you snip your yarn with those bright scissors ? I thought I gave you the other evening so many reasons for declining the duties and obligations of a Benedict that you could never reach the end of them ; and look now, here you break out at the old starting-point as fresh as a west wind from Summit Mountain, or the lark which sings at Heaven's gate. Truly, if the stay in women could but be attained in our horses, what enduring steeds we might rear ; it is beyond belief—marvelous ! "

" I don't know what you mean by ' stay,' Samuel. I don't think it is proper, or dutiful, or respectful, for you to compare the mother who bore you to a dumb beast."

" Far be it from me, mother, to belie you by an association with any *dumb* creature."

" I am glad to hear you say so, Samuel," replied the old lady, without noticing the slightly malicious emphasis her son had rested on the adjective. "And I do declare ! there *is* a kind of stay I want to find in you, and that is, stay at home."

" But, mother, you must allow—now, mustn't you ? *that* is a sort of stay which comes especially in woman's sphere. You remember what your beloved St. Paul says, ' Let *women* be keepers at home,' " replied the gentleman, in a tone of good-humored banter.

" Yes. Men are always willing to quote the apostle when he happens to meet their views. It is true, indeed, that all through the toiling and moiling, woman must tarry by the stuff. When her children are little she can't leave them, and when they grow out of her arms they leave her. Right here, on this farm, I've seen the sun rise and set ever since before you were born ; but that is nothing to the purpose now, Samuel. And I feel hurt and disturbed that you will always jest and quibble whenever I try to talk earnest on this subject. You can't help seeing how much I have it at heart. I consider it a vital necessity—of the most serious importance."

" But I fail to find any such necessity, mother. I am satis-fied to take care of you, and keep myself out of mischief. Marrying a wife is too stupendous an undertaking for a fellow of my small capacity. ' Art thou loosed from a wife ? Seek not a wife,' says St. Paul. I should have to confess my sins and get shrived, for ' such shall have trouble in the flesh.' I cannot find the courage. ' I say, therefore, to the unmarried and widows, it is good for them that they abide even as I.' "

" There was an apostate angel who used to quote scripture, Sammy," said Mrs. Slaughton with a smile of grim amusement, "and he got it just about as near right as you do ; and remem-ber, there is a curse pronounced on those who pervert the Sacred Writ, wresting it to their destruction. So I'd leave St. Paul out, if I was you. He was an old bachelor, any way, and could not be expected to understand all about a life he had never tried."

Mr. Slaughton threw back his head and laughed heartily at this heterodox statement ; but seeing his mother gathering up her forces for a fresh argument, he hastened to pull a sober face, and say in a tone of assured conviction :

"And really, mother, I value far too highly *your* importance, to say nothing of my own, to put my hand on my heart and make my best vow to any other lady. You surely do not covet the name of old Mrs. Slaughton ?"

"Coveting don't count ; it neither helps nor hinders. I *am* old, I get feeble too ; I feel it every day. I haven't half the strength or endurance I used to have. Why, I can remember when I didn't know what 'tired' meant, and I never left doing anything I wished, because it might hurt me. I didn't know as I could be hurt ; but now, Samuel, the days have come when the grasshopper is a burden. In my youth, I went whither I would ; before long, a day will darken for me when I shall be carried whither I would not. Life is short, Samuel."

"Nonsense, mother ! I don't like to hear you talk like the old vanity preacher. It is conceded on all hands that you possess the ablest executive ability of any woman in Blithebeck. Who but you heads all the donations and missionary boxes, ordering the deacons and driving up the sexton, and keeping things in order generally ? You know what Farmer Slowgo said of you after you had watched his work—or rather, his idleness in the barn, in the hay-field, at the stone wall, appearing when he least expected, keeping him up to it when he wished to loiter and lounge."

"I don't know what he said in particular, Samuel ; of course it was something teazing, or you wouldn't bring it up now. However, you can go on and tell it, if you want to. There, my boy ! if you would look that way at a girl and ask her to marry you, she'd be sure to say 'Yes'—and I'd get a daughter, and you a wife in this lonesome old house."

"Mother, I keep my best expressions for you ; it is my duty and my pleasure to do it, and I do. So you don't care to hear what Slowgo said about you ?"

"If it will relieve your mind to repeat it, pray go on. I know I shall never get any serious talk out of you till you do."

"Thank you, mother. Mr. Epaminondas Slowgo says he

likes Widder Slaughton well enough, only she is a little too
owly."

"Owly indeed! That means that I see more than he likes, I
suppose. Well, I do say it wants the eyes of a lynx to get a
day's work of that shiftless fellow, jogging and poking as mod-
erate as the oxen, and dodging under cover with the least patter of rain, as if he expected to melt like a lump of sugar. I
won't be put off with any of your nonsense ; you shall listen to
me."

"Attentively, mother, and most respectfully. You can't say
I'm not a tolerable son, as sons go ; now, can you ? I remember Chandy Goldsmith remarked to Johnny Hauxhurst and me
that we three were ducks brought up by mother-hens. You've
stood on the bank and watched me swim off on the great pond
of life ; but I've paid pretty good attention to your clucking,
haven't I, mother ? "

"Well, Samuel, you *do* surprise me! First you compared me
to a horse, and now it's a hen ; perhaps I shall be likened to a
cat next, or a turkey, or a goose."

"Or a dove, mother ; yes, I really do think you resemble a
nice little dove, in that soft-tinted dress. I feel truly thankful that my mother never gave in to the common folly of
womankind, and drenched her locks with filthy brimstone and
other bad-smelling things. Your gray hair is so pretty! You
are a nice-looking old lady altogether. I'm very proud of you,
very proud indeed."

"I'm sufficiently buttered, thank you, Sammy," answered
the widow dryly, twinkling her eyes at the speaker ; "and now,
if you please, we will return to our subject. It is quite time
for you to settle respectably, and raise a family, manage the
farm, keep Slowgo in order, take hold in the parish. Your
father was deacon of the church at your age, and had charge of
the town poor besides. He was a public-spirited man, your
father was, Samuel. Now, here you are thirty years old, and
you have never voted! It is not the way for gentlemen to do—

American citizens! If *men* would busy their heads with the affairs of our country, rogues and aliens would be held in subjection, and we should have less defaulting, less repudiation, less bribery and corruption!"

"What a wise little mother!" exclaimed the listener, in real or pretended admiration. "What a sagacious, well-posted observer of passing events!"

"I read the newspapers, Samuel, and I know that there was never a time when good, honest men were so much needed as now. I should like to see you in Congress, Sammy."

"Congress, mother! Heaven forbid! I should rather get married than go to that bad place."

"Get married first, Samuel, and you will be on a good road to all kinds of usefulness. *Do* get married, Sammy, there's a nice boy."

"But, mother, suppose I should go and tie myself up. Suppose I could bring a wife to the old homestead; what kind of a life should I lead, between two women, both wanting to rule! Don't you candidly think such a prospect for a quiet man is appalling? And I could not take your side, you know, in any strifes or conflicts which might occur. 'For this cause shall a man forsake his mother and cleave to his wife.' And again, 'He that is married careth for the things of the world, how he may please his wife.' So you see your chance is small if I once get married."

"As if I was quarrelsome! as if I could not live in peace with people! I see quite plainly through your silly banter. You are amusing yourself, making fun of me, putting aside carelessly what you know are my true and real desires, for the sake of a life of lazy, irresponsible ease. You had rather roam up and down the earth purposeless and aimless, than to stand in your lot at home. You are selfish, and you are unkind to the poor old woman who has been only too willing a slave to you all her days. But, thank Heaven! I have not many left; and after I am gone, I suppose you will bring somebody, enough to make me turn in my grave to see in the old house. Perhaps that is why you wait, so that I shall give no opinion of your choice, find no fault, nor speak my mind. Dead folks are well out of the way, and the living can do as they like."

"Mother!" interrupted Mr. Slaughton, in a voice of most unpleasant surprise, "selfish! unkind to you! Come, take that back. You shan't say I am either of those. If you have any really cogent and sufficient reasons for the queer determination to double me up you seem to have taken, bring them on, and we'll see what can be done in the light of them. I must confess to having been a rover (and I thank Heaven, he thought, nobody knows what a sore heart I have carried with me); but I forewarn you, if you get your will and I get a wife, —whom I consider a most inconvenient and unnecessary incumbrance—if I do this to please you, you will have to stand whatever racket you pull about your devoted head by the arrangement. I give you fair warning—I will not lift a finger to help you."

"I am not afraid of any trouble, Samuel. I feel so sure of getting ease and comfort, that I shall take the risk."

"But the good reasons, mother. Don't go too fast; I must be convinced first that it will be best for you."

"I should think it would be plain that I need young eyes, young hands, young feet, to do the work I shall soon be unfit for, since you put it on the ground of my happiness," replied the widow fretfully, tossing her spools about, and puncturing the darning-ball with her big needle. "There's all Sallie's children have got to come here right away. *I'm* too old to undertake to bring up another family, and too feeble. I shan't last out the job."

"Have a governess, then, and a housekeeper; get more servants—that's easily settled," spoke up Mr. Slaughton, quite briskly for him, and he waved both hands indefinitely enough to include all Ireland in his idea of unfailing supplies.

"I won't have a fussy, troublesome thing of a governess here

making eyes at you, and taking up your time ! A pretty way
that would be to bring me ease ! And as for more servants, the
more you get, the more bother and vexation you pile on to
yourself. That is just like a man, Samuel ; you positively make
me think of your father. He'd come in and find me all twisted
up with housework ; fifty things to do, and only one pair of hands
to push them with ; and he'd stop and look at me, and say :
' Let your *cares* be your pleasures, Patience.' Positively, I used
to feel as if I'd like to throw something at him, he provoked me
so ; and once, I had a dreadful boil which would not let me
sleep, and he waked up and found me crying with the pain, and
what do you suppose he said to me ? ' What is the matter,
Patience ? I am very sorry, can't you make a poultice of some
cold water and something?' and off he snored again as fast
asleep as a dormouse in January. Such absurd, useless creatures as men can be, with their ridiculous suggestions to help a
woman out of her difficulties ! You are as bad as any of them,
Samuel, with your trumpery governesses and servants. Yes,
and worse."

Widow Slaughton suddenly dropped her voice, which had
fast risen to a scolding pitch, being warned by some symptoms
that her son might presently slide out of ear-shot if she persisted ; it may be *that* was also a trick he inherited from the
paterfamilias now at rest in the city of the deaf and dumb.

"Besides, Sammy, I want you to have an heir to my property. Don't laugh at your poor old mother ; but I do want to
hold your son in my arms before I fold them above my heart in
the coffin—I do. I should like to be grandma to your beautiful
boy ; that's the way I feel, and you see if I don't make a good
grandma. I know I failed often and often in being just such a
mother as I ought to, but I can do better now, and I'll make
up all you lacked to little Sammy ; you see if I don't."

The old lady was weeping by this time, and she picked up a
pair of the darned socks, and dabbed at a couple of tears which
were slowly trickling down her cheeks, getting caught among

the wrinkles, like a rivulet among gravel, and then coursing on afresh till they dropped on her hand, from which she wiped them, having been unsuccessful in her first endeavor to stay their journey ; and she sat rubbing her fingers hard, and looking at them, and sniffing dismally, till her son spoke again.

Mr. Slaughton gazed at her in a silence which was half curious, half pitiful, thoroughly convinced that she was in deep earnest, and that it would be difficult to turn the current of her thoughts from the marriage scheme she was evidently nursing and cherishing in her soul, altogether monstrous and impossible as it seemed to him.

He rose at length from the bamboo chair he had been occupying, and walked slowly the whole length of the wide piazza, to toss away the cigar which was only half smoked, among the tangled rose-bushes at the south end.   The ripening leaves over his head were practising the airy dance they meant to take as soon as they could cut loose from parental bondage, and he listened a couple of seconds to their "tinkle, tinkle, tinkle," and the grand sweep of the wind-harps among the pine branches, —as he loitered, looking down where his habana had lodged in a clump of red hips, as if its tiny breath of useless smoke held some spirit of his past—before he turned about and approached his mother, still mournfully busy with her faded hands, and he came so deliberately that he had time to hum the whole recitative which begins : "Now lead me to the rack or to the flames. I'll thank your gracious mercy," and the chagrin and disgust in his face gave the burden an odd adaptation to his own case.

It being, however, always easier to be led than to stand up and resist, he put his conclusion into words calculated to soothe and please the only woman to whom he was at present in the least degree accountable for his actions.

"Well, mother!" he began, kindly placing his hand on her shoulder, "it appears you are fully resolved to be old Mrs. Slaughton ; you are anxious to assume the title and state of dowager. So be it, then. I don't know who it is my business to

gratify and indulge, except you, and I'll strike a bargain with
you. If you can settle upon a candidate for the place who
suits you, I will make no more objections, and I'll pay the bills
like a man ;· but I will not be a *spooney*, even to suit you, my
mother."

"Not a spooney, Samuel, of course not. But why should you
not fall in love as well as another man ? You are good-looking,
you are personable, you are nice, and you are rich—any girl
might be proud to get you."

"Do not let us discuss the subject of my possibilities,"
answered Mr. Slaughton in a light tone, while a quick shadow
of pain darkened his face. "I can't, and I won't, that's all."

"You oughtn't to say won't to your parent, my son," spoke
up the widow hurriedly, "although it is all just as I say. I
won't talk about it if you are so modest. And of course, how
should you know how you appear to the women ? There, now,
don't bluster. I thank you for the will you show to please me.
You won't be sorry when I am dead and gone. You won't,
Sammy ! You mark my words, and may thy days be long in
the land."

She forbore to press him further, fearful of losing the concession she had gained, and quite satisfied in her own mind
that she wrought for his good, and that once tied fast he
would pick up the duties of the married state honorably and
respectably, and settle down in the old homestead, where she
should be sure of his company and cheer for her declining years.

"Much obliged to you, I'm sure," replied Mr. Slaughton
aloud; and he mentally added, "They will not be *many*, long
or short. I shall leave this land double quick, if you *do* carry
your point. Yes, I'll go and kill tigers in Timbuctoo."

"You are a good boy, Sammy," the old lady went on.
"Good sons make good husbands. And I'll leave the painted
egg-shell china that Grandmother Pritchard brought over with her,
to little Sammy in my will, and the cuckoo clock, and——"

"*Festina lente*, mother. That means make haste slowly.

Don't look cross. I will not disturb your agreeable anticipations. I leave my fate in your hands. You are a smart woman ; but if you can manage a wedding without any wooing, you are a deal smarter than I give you credit for."

Mr. Slaughton did not take any anxiety among his reflections after his mother left him ; in fact, he rather smiled, thinking he had been remarkably diplomatic in his arrangement of concession. "It will amuse the old lady to think about it, I dare say. I was dutiful and affectionate, and I am as safe as a toad in a hole. ''Tis much to tread the ooze of the salt deeps, to run upon the sharp wind of the north, to do me business in the veins o' the earth when 'tis baked with frost,' sayeth old Prospero ; but mother hath undertaken, to my mind, a harder task than these. I can't see how any girl can get to be my wife unless I ask her ; and that, I swear by the roes and the hinds, I won't do. I asked once, and I got a plain " No ! " from the sweetest lips that ever smiled. Heigho ! let me see, that was ten years ago. There are not two Sabrinas in this miserable world ; the consequence is, I must go to my grave unmated. I'm sorry to disappoint mother, but it can't be helped."

CHAPTER II.

THE DESPISED FORNARINA.

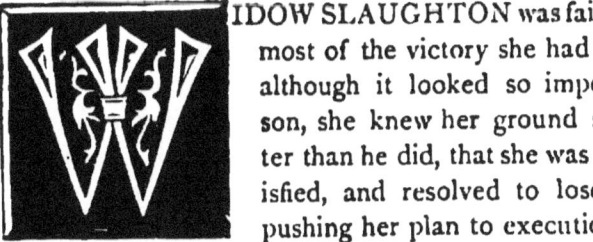IDOW SLAUGHTON was fain to make the most of the victory she had gained ; and although it looked so impossible to her son, she knew her ground so much better than he did, that she was tolerably satisfied, and resolved to lose no time in pushing her plan to execution.

She carried indoors her work, and finished putting away the

week's wash, which she carefully looked over, making certain that each garment was in perfect order.

She walked hither and yon, dreaming a dream she was fond of. She saw a bright, healthy youngster clinging to her skirts, calling her "Grandma"—a memory of her past; a hope of her future—her son's son; the object and recipient of her savings, cares, and foresight; the inheritor of her husband's good name, and her own good estate.

She opened her store closets, and peeped in with her housekeeper's eyes.

Filled to fulness with fine twined linen, gay bed-covers, and beautifully quilted spreads—the patterns of her own designing, the execution of her own handiwork, the garnering of an industrious womanhood which had wasted little time in idleness. She passed from room to room, dusting here or there, replacing what was out of the order she liked, and thinking: "*Now* I shall know who is to take care of all my nice things after I am done with them. I shall be safe from leaving mismanagement and waste among this handsome furniture, when I shut my eyes on life. My son's wife will have my son's interest at heart, as I have."

Mrs. Slaughton had reason to be proud of her home; it was roomy, commodious, well planned, well finished, and as nice as nice could be. One of those grand halls which our forefathers liked for the entrance to their houses, ran the whole length of the mansion, opening into large parlors on one side, and on the other into a library filled with low book-cases of dark wood, holding many elegant and costly volumes of architectural designs among their treasures.

Her husband had been a successful builder of bridges, aqueducts, churches, and state edifices; and had amassed a fortune in a short life. A falling timber from one of his half-completed structures had put an end to his labors, and left her without any last words of advice or counsel, to the lonely responsibility of his only son and his heaped-up riches.

Above the carved cases hung many pictures—some gathered by Samuel from Old World collections, some painted by a dear friend of his early youth, named Chandos Goldsmith, and others the fruit of his own study, the production of his own pencil.   Back of this rather sombre apartment, was a tiny dining-room—so tiny that the family had been in the habit of considering it a most inconvenient defect in the house plan, its size having been encroached upon by its neighbor, the library, so much that it could scarcely hold the necessary furniture.

It was sniffed at by the widow as a " tucked-up little bother," and was a constant source of discomfort to Sam, who hated being crowded, he being one of those gentlemen who like to find plenty of elbow room in the places they most inhabit, as well as comfortable appliances for what they call "lying off."

The rear of the mansion overlooked the garden, and had a roomy piazza, which, in fact, ran around three sides of the building—the front, south, and west ; supported by light pillars railed in by fantastic iron-work of wheat-stalks, corn-ears, and grass-blades, of which the builder had himself designed the pattern.   The cane-seated sofas, arm-chairs, and bamboo tables, looked as if this airy, commodious gallery might be a favorite lounging for luxurious people.

Mrs. Slaughton had a reason, known only to herself, for insisting upon her son's speedy marriage.   She was a sensible, practical lady, well informed enough, a little homely and old-fashioned in her dialect, which was quite apt to draw its illustrations from the untrimmed simplicity of the life she knew best.   She was sufficiently proud of her position among her neighbors, of her husband's untarnished memory, of her son's artistic skill and good looks, of Blithebeck, and in fact, of whatever belonged to her ; proud, of course, in a humble, pious way, " For what we have now received, etc."   She was a good Christian, an active member of her church—whose communion service she had been careful to keep shining bright during the deaconship of her husband—to whose benevolent societies she steadily contributed. But with these matter-of-fact qualities and habits, she kept hidden out of sight and ken a vein of superstition, which was so absolutely interwoven among her beliefs as to become an essential element of her character, and which insensibly influenced not only her secret thoughts, but her words and plans of action. She believed in a family omen. There was a white horse which was sure to appear in dreams to her kindred at particular crises of their lives, and his coming had been persistently fatal to the individuals so warned, always presaging and preceding disaster or death.

Twice within a year she had seen the baleful steed. The first time she rode him, fording a clear stream of running water; she saw his milk-white mane lying in silky profusion on his neck, which shone like silver in the cold moonlight, and his flashing eye, as he turned to look in her face, had such a glare of supernatural intelligence and power, that she shivered into frighted wakefulness, to find great drops of sweat on her brow and her palsied tongue cleaving to the roof of her mouth.

The next time she saw him coming from afar, free and wild, over her native hills, and on his back a lovely child, which he cast at her feet bloody and mangled with its fall, just inside the great gate of the old homestead.

The evil visions were often in her mind, and she scarcely ever laid her head on her pillow that she did not say to herself: " Perhaps to-night he may come for the third and last time, and then I shall be assured that I am called to go speedily away, so that the places which now know me shall know me no more forever."

Without ever giving her convictions voice, which would enable her friends to combat them, they were positive and settled, and she felt an overweening desire to set her house in order, being warned that she should die and not live ; and who so likely to maintain that order after her demise, as a prudent, sensible wife for her son ?

If she had explained her hidden motive to him, he would

2

have ridiculed it, or tried to convince her of the absurd impossibility of any sequence following an airy, baseless dream, produced by an extra piece of apple pie, or a bit of cheese, which would be more injurious to her than the fit of nightmare it provoked.

As she had gone on begging, pleading, and insisting; putting forth no reasons except such as belonged to life and its needs, he gave her credit for immense will and the wonderful stay which held fast to her purpose with untiring perseverance, and would have been startled and astonished to find a fetish among his respected mother's Christian beliefs.

However, having obtained the rather doubtful promise above stated, she donned her gray silk and nice fine hat of platted straw, trimmed with a bunch of natural ostrich feathers, and the costly Indian shawl her son had fetched from the east the same time he brought her the crape from Canton, and the box of wonderful tea, whose delicious flavor and inspiriting effects she only permitted herself to enjoy on very rare occasions.

Being fitly attired, she came down looking as she always did, the very perfection of nice, *neat* old-ladyhood, which has done with gauds and fripperies, and does not change its costume to suit any breath of fickle Fashion; which no more desires to dodge its status, accepting with dignity the sober tints and ripeness which hallow and embellish autumn.   And really and truly, my dear readers, is there a more pitiable sight than an old woman absurdly young, or one more agreeably comely and pleasant than a matron who majestically wears her years and her gray hairs with undismayed satisfaction, enjoying the harvest time of her life in a rich ingathering of the fruits of her early toils and cares? " So say we all of us."

Sam was proud of his mother.   He was proud of her smartness, her executive ability and business faculty; and he walked by her side down the path to the gate, and opened it for her exit, with a compliment on her new fall bonnet, and a gratified survey of her attire.

"How well you look," said he, smiling. "Really, mother, I do not discover any signs of the feebleness you would fain make me believe in."

"You can't see into the future, Sammy? Well to-day may be dead to-morrow! I mean to live as long as I can, and that I may get as much comfort as possible out of my last days, you should wish me success in my errand."

"What is it this time, mother—a Dorcas or a donation?" asked Mr. Slaughton, into whose mind a certain suspicion began to creep as he observed the brisk crispness of the old lady's manner.

"Me no Jackey now; me Kalingalunga," said the savage, when he donned his chieftain's war-paint and feathers. Jackey's assumption was faint meekness compared with Dame Slaughton's resolute determination.

"I shall let you know all in good time, Sammy," replied she, shutting her eyes tight and nodding, as he closed after her the gate. "All in good time, my son."

He watched her stepping quickly away, as if on an errand which was full of interest and importance.

"Mother means business," thought he; "it can't be possible she is out on a wife-hunt already. Thank heaven! the damsels are few and far between among these old houses. I don't know any eligible ones. Let me see. There's Almira Pratt, she squints; Jane Batt, she limps; Mary McNulters, she horribly stutters; or Jemima Wade, the fearful old maid; all the others are little things. It isn't Dickey Pritchard she's after this morning, because she's out on foot; nor Martha Rame.stone—she's just my age and we never could agree; no, mother's got some missionary business on hand. I'm safe enough, I'm sure; because, when she comes really to look at any woman as mistress here, she will shrink from the preposterous notion, especially as I have given her carte blanche. Yes, I expect that master-stroke of policy which squelched all opposition and argument, will finish the matter. It is my opinion that women like to have a grievance to harp on and knock around a man's head; and when you cease to oppose, why, down drops the grievance, you see, dead as a mummy.   An odd idea of her's; how it could have got lodged in her head just at this particular epoch, I can't imagine.   A wife!   Well, time was when I might have lent both my ears to the suggestion; but that time is drowned in oblivion.

While ruminating in this wise, Mr. Slaughton had mounted to his studio.   Sauntering slowly (he was not much given to hurry), his hands jingled some loose coins in his pockets, his head was bent, his face overcast, and his eyebrows gathered together in a frown, which was so habitual as to have stamped itself in a light perpendicular line upon his forehead, ineffaceable even in his best humor.

An easy-chair occupying its own place, as was proved by the worn spot in the carpet in front of it, was so convenient to his entrance, that he dropped into it almost unconsciously, raising, as he did so, his eyes to a picture on the wall opposite to him. His action and look were as much a habit as the homage a pious Catholic offers at the shrine of his patron saint.

It was an auburn-haired Ruth, not oriental, not Hebrew, except in costume; a beautiful, majestic creature of noble traits and serene individuality; a face full of fidelities; sweet and strong; such a woman as might choose to turn her back on ease and home, and elect to follow the fortunes and attend the old age of a childless widow who needed her loving care, and find daily joy and satisfaction in the hardships and sacrifice included in her exile and devotion.

Mr. Samuel Slaughton painted the picture many years ago at Craigenfels, when the house was full of Christmas gayeties, which he helped and enjoyed, till a certain day, when he was no longer able to find any gayety in the world.

Every one of the sittings was fresh in his memory.   Every tone of voice, every eye-beam the Ruth had given him, every "golden-netted smile" was his then, now, always.

Beneath the large picture, in a much tarnished Venetian frame, was a smaller one of a girl bearing a pitcher in her hands. The wonderful face of the baker, the Fornarina, who enthralled the young painter Raphael, had been ejected from it to make place for the golden-haired American, because she seemed to Sam worthier of worship than the Madonna could have been at her best; and yet Raphael had poured his whole soul into the one love of his life. "The eyes of the Fornarina," said he, "are my eyes; without them I see nothing but horrible darkness."

In miniature the face was a reproduction of the Ruth. There were the carnelian-hued eyes concealing subdued fire beneath their half-shadowed brilliance, the luxuriant tresses of dead gold, the purple robe, and even the rich velvet violets caressing the lovely neck.

He remembered well the discussion he had; with his beautiful sitter over the incongruous flowers he would persist in placing on the breast of his Ruth, and how she said mockingly, "A wild cockle is as purple. We know it flourished among the grain your Moabitess gleaned.

> " Look how the cockle red,
> Alone on its wistful bed,
> Turns up its dark-blue eye to thee.'

Boaz gathered it with his sheaves, its perfume clung about him when his day's work was done. Ruth was a wild cockle herself." And how she had paused suddenly when she had caught the glance he could not help giving her, and how the beauteous blush had stolen over her face, mantling it with rose-bloom; and he felt sure she had half divined the secret of his persistence, and why the violets lay in almost odorous perfection on the exile's neck. Because Sabrina would not be Sabrina without the flowers of her daily choice, and oriental consistency was of minor importance to him, who saw only the woman he loved on his canvas, as he saw her breathing and glowing before him,

who wished to see only her among all the women of the whole
world.

Mr. Slaughton meditated while the fire of love still burned
on the altar of his soul.   It had never gone out all these years,
during which he had not tired of secretly feeding and fanning
the flame._ Secretly, I say, because in those days, before the
last touches had been put to the Ruth, he had gotten by heart
a couplet which he chanted in desolate loneliness while he completed the work he had so hopefully commenced :

> " What care I how fair she be,
>   If she be not fair for me ? "

He had asked the question on which his happiness depended
at a fête one pleasant evening, when he had found and worn
the scarf to her apron, one famous neck-tie party.   He asked
it in so light a tone that she scarcely guessed the deep darkness
which obscured his life when he got his answer.   He had left
her with a smile on his lips, but such a dull pain in his
heart as nothing had ever healed ; and all through the following years, in his wanderings up and down the wide world, not
a single daughter of Eve, no matter how beautiful or excellent,
had ever won from him a look of admiration or a thought of
fondness.   Thirty of his years were gone now, and the old
refrain had changed a little in his rendering :

> " What care I how fair they be,
>   Not one of them shall be fair for me."

CHAPTER III.

"SHE HATH MANY NAMELESS VIRTUES."

EANWHILE no grass had grown beneath Mrs. Slaughton's feet, and before her son had half dreamed out his vain dream of what might have been, she came back, and after glancing through the lower rooms she pattered hurriedly up the stairs and entered the studio.

Sitting down close by the artist, she laid her hand on his knee and looked in his face with an expression curiously mingled of apprehension, determination, uncertainty, and flurry.

" Well, Sammy," she began, " I've set about it, and it goes nicely so far. I've got her picked out ; in fact, I've had my eye on her for a good while, and I have talked over the probabilities and fitness with her mother, who always agreed with me ; but of course couldn't say too much—it wouldn't do, you know. No woman likes to seem over-anxious to get rid of her daughters, however much she may wish to see them settled. And this is a changing world, and girls are such forlorn things to be left unprotected and knocked about at everybody's beck and call ; and her health is so poor, and there's such a family, and I don't suppose there will be any provision for them, that you can't wonder she was pleased, as indeed why shouldn't she be ? Such luck don't come to every girl, and I consider it as good as settled ; and very glad I am, to be sure, and the sooner we get it over the better it will be for all of us. I declare, I've walked like a steamboat. I feel very tired, the east wind is so strong in September on these hills, and I didn't stop to breathe hardly. I'm all *tuckered* out, and *so* warm."

" Well, Samuel, haven't you anything to say to my news ? " she asked, after a minute's silence. " And me fit to drop."

"Not much, mother," he answered a little bitterly. It was a rough waking from the joyous vision which had visited him, a swift and unwelcome dissipation of his memories.

He wheeled about in his arm-chair so as to shut from his sight the two pictures, and his face wore not the faintest shadow of the smile the old lady wanted to see there, as he went on :

" You post expeditiously to your consummation. You are taking much trouble, if you are in earnest, which seems hard yet to believe. You are piling up great stores of worry for your future, if you are able to succeed, which I regard as impossible. I've done some tall thinking, mother, since you went out, and I cannot understand your object or motive."

" I'm sure I made it plain enough, Samuel." Mrs Slaughton pulled out the gold pin which held her India shawl, and threw it back, and fanned herself with her handkerchief ; she *did* look terribly flushed. "I can go over the whole ground again, I suppose——"

" No, no, mother, don't. I shall get no fresh light, I dare say. So the mother-in-law to be thinks well of the match, does she ? But does the daughter-in-law think well of it also ? "

His manner, half incredulous, half mocking, irritated the widow, who was in a very nervous, excitable state, as it seemed from her fidgeting and panting, and her crimson face, usually so composed and pale ; and she failed to see that her son was really making an effort to be indulgent and forbearing, though something as if he treated a weaker vessel whom he more than suspected of having a bee in her bonnet.

" Of course," she answered tartly, "why shouldn't she ? That is, I have not seen her. I left that part of the negotiation to the proper time and the fit parties ; I have not a particle of uneasiness on that score. It would be very odd indeed if she was not only willing, but thankful and anxious to marry my son. I should say, very ! "

"The best and noblest woman God ever made thought other-wise. She saw no good parts in the miserable fellow; she would none of him," remarked he, with such a smile on the points of his lips as looked as if he was not very proud of himself. He kept his gaze steadily aloof from the two pictures on the wall while he spoke thus lightly, but he saw the royal girl-hood which had not been fair for him, as if he were living at that precise moment the second of time in which she had said:

"Never! dear friend. I am ashamed that you have asked me, because I ought so to have behaved that you must have seen that I did not love you," and the music of the waltz he had danced with her afterwards seemed anew to knock at his heart with its steady time-beats, in the dull refrain tiresomely repeated:

" She never can be fair for me."

"I should have to see that woman, Samuel, before I believed such a ridiculous statement. Your white swan would prove a silly goose, after all. I used to feel troubled to hear you say such things. I didn't know one while but you had fallen in love with some actress; but I comforted myself that my boy was the child of many prayers, and would be kept out of such temptations, and I thought six or seven years ago that you had a sort of a sneaking notion after Martha Ranestone; you were always sparring so, whenever you happened to meet. At any rate, I am certain now that the wonderful creature you rave over sometimes is just a myth, as much as that handsome Arabella was in the "Prue and I" book you read out loud to me the other evening; and if *he* had kept his sweet looks for the poor Prudence who mended his old duds, I should have thought better of him, for my part. Nobody ever marries their ideals, Samuel. When I was sixteen I meant to be united to a tall, slender, beautiful man, who would adore me, and I took your father, who was rather fat, not to say clumsy,

2*

and did not adore me ; on the contrary, he was particular about
his meals, and apt to find fault with the neck-bands of his
shirts.   He said I always got them too long, or too short, or
too wide, or too narrow ; and he used to swear dreadfully if
he happened to miss a button anywhere on his clothes, before
he joined the church.   Of course he enjoyed his mind after that,
and left off all his bad habits.   I believe it is a certain truth,
my dear son, that if a man makes up his bent never to love
any but a slight, ethereal fairy, he is sure to get tied to a
chubby dumpling, all fat and dimples ; so you may as well
settle to the certainty that your wife will be the exact opposite
of what you thought you wanted, and she will suit you to a
charm.   I flatter myself I am a tol'able judge of my sex, and
I assure you I am more than pleased.   Such a quiet, sensible,
reasonable child as she has always been.   Her mother tells me
she recited seventy-five verses in Genesis before she was four
years old, and has read a chapter in the Bible she got from
her Sunday-school teacher as a reward of merit, every day
since."

While the dame rambled on with her diffusive remarks, Mr.
Slaughton turned over in his thoughts the probabilities as to
the performer of this pious feat.   Is it Almina Pratt, or Jane
Batt, or Mary McNulters, or Jemima Wade ?

The widow, not observing his disgusted face, continued :

" Yes, Sammy, and we've settled on the day for the wedding
—private.   Only the two families, and a few neighbors ; and I
think I shall have the Vance children home right away that it
is over."

"Humph," muttered Sam.   "She speaks of my nuptials as
if she arranged for an amputation, or a hanging, or a funeral ;
upon my word, this *is* cheerful, and the Vances are wanted to
devour the remains of the marriage-feast.   They will make
them dreadfully ill—that's some comfort."

" I don't suppose you will care about any trip.   You have
been running up and down in the earth, and to and fro in it,

like Job's three comforters. No, I believe it was not the friends, it was——"

"The devil!" ejaculated Sam with some emphasis.

"Hush, my son! don't explain in such a loud voice, it sounds too much like swearing, and I know you never *do* swear. And as I was saying, a quiet, regular life will be good for you, and I could not stand the hubbub of those Vance children myself; so I made up my mind to wait till I could get settled with a likely girl to take them off my hands and keep them in order; and she's used to children, and I shall feel easy."

"And you really mean to bring a luckless female into such an abominable position? Put her among a lot of noisy, roystering brats in whom she has no interest. But it seems to me you are projecting a torture daily renewed for the daughter you have elected. Of a truth, I could find it in my heart to feel sorry for her."

"Sorry, Sammy! You needn't, then. It is a piece of luck they never looked for, nor expected, to marry one of their folks to a Slaughton. They must all feel it so. I am sure they do."

"She wants me to take a wife beneath me, it seems, in order that she may get a housekeeper," thought Sam, and he scowled as the idea suggested itself. "It must be the Batts; their name is legion, and they never did amount to a general issue." "You have not laid aside your family pride, I hope, mother."

"Oh, no. I think a good deal of blood—blood will tell."

"To have a young woman about you who squints, or limps, or stutters, would be far from pleasant, would it not?"

"Now Samuel, if you mean to put me off and dodge the question with any of your nonsense, I can tell you it is entirely too late. I've set the ball rolling, and you need not try to stop it, because, if you get obstinate, I shall be firm."

"Go on, mother," answered Samuel dryly.

"I am going on, Samuel, and you'll have a wife in spite of your teeth."

Sam groaned in the spirit. "Oh, cursed sprite! that ever I was born," muttered he. "Yes, mother, that was what a fellow said, named Hamlet. It was his *mother* who got married, though. I wonder you never took a second; wouldn't it suit you just as well now as to get me doubled?"

"For shame, Samuel! to jest on such a serious subject!" exclaimed the widow, bridling up. "Not but that I could have got married a dozen times, but I wouldn't—once is quite enough."

"Yes, mother," rejoined Sam, shaking his head in mock despair, "and too much, I think. Look here now: what if this lady should develop a temper. I'm told the best of women are liable to it. Hadn't you better stop and think while on the brink. I am afraid you are preparing for a leap into a bramble-bush that will scratch out both your eyes."

"Nothing of the kind, my son. Do, pray, give me credit for *some* shrewdness, *some* insight into human nature. I am not buying a pig in a poke; far from it, I know just what I am about. Why, I tell you her mother assures me that the girl never did a disobedient thing in her life without being well whipped for it; her will was broken before she could speak plain. Quite a terrible scene, and cost her mother a good many tears. She refused to say 'Pa,' and it took a whole afternoon to bring her to it, but she was conquered then and there. Her father is a perfect disciplinarian; his children obey the nod of his head."

"A nice, tyrannical old party you are for making me son to. I should like to inquire, just from curiosity, when you get to a good place to rest a little, who these people are? these last delicious revelations are so inspiring. I begin to feel symptoms of extreme interest. A bride who has been well whipped; how much more desirable than one who has been badly whipped—who, mother, tell me who?"

"I have been waiting for you to ask that question, Samuel. I was determined not to mention any names till you did. But I *do* wish you would not talk in that voice—I don't like it; nor the quizzical, disagreeable smile on your mouth. Even your *mustaches* can't hide the disgustedness of it; and it is far from becoming. It reminds me of the way your father's upper lip used to go up in the middle and down at the corners when you upset all your victuals onto the table-cloth, and the bread and milk sploshed his clean shirt-bosom; children *are* so careless! There! That's right; now you look like my own good boy, who means to make his mother happy for the little while she has got to be with him in this poor, perishing world. It is not as if I wanted you to give away a treasure, or afflict yourself. It is a nice girl, Samuel—a wife, that I'm talking about; every man ought to want a wife, and look chirp and pleasant over the prospect of getting one: and I know Perdita Hethwaite will make this house tidy, and do her best— her mother says she will. Only promise that you will take her, and I shall feel that I have done a good day's work, and feel easy in my mind."

"Perdita Hethwaite! The old parson's lean, scraggy daughter! A half-starved, pinched little object, hardly out of short frocks! Well, this *is* a choice. This *is* a day's work."

Mr. Slaughton threw up his chin and laughed, and he looked in such a provoking way at the dame out of his half-shut eyes, that she almost wished he was again small enough to be well spanked for his impudence. Her little boy being lost, and her six-footer being beside her, words, not deeds, must serve her purpose—words which must be carefully picked and chosen, too.

"Perdita is *not* scrawny, Samuel; she is nice-looking. You must allow that it is a good long time since you saw her. While you have been hazing round the globe she's been growing; she's plenty big enough and fat enough. We don't want a doll to lock up in a glass case; we want usefulness. "Handsome is that handsome does." She understands housekeeping, Perdita does. Her mother says she's made all the pies and cake they've eat for more than a year."

"Which isn't much, if Slowgo speaks the truth. I heard him telling Stephen, only a day or two ago, that when they pulled down the old shed, they found a pile of codfish-bones three feet high, which looked like a battle-field in Liliput."

"Don't men enjoy a bit of gossip, and roll it as a sweet morsel under their tongues," retorted the old lady. "Plain living is no disgrace to any family, and it's better to eat gruel than get in debt. Perdita runs the machine beautifully; she does most all the family sewing. She's just the one to pull on poor Sallie's children, and she's able to teach them besides; she has three hours' school at home every day."

"And do you mean to tell me, mother, that this well-chastened paragon can be brought here unmoved? Is she willing to acquire such a commodity as a husband, without being allowed a choice—without a civil word from him? Is she so eager to provide for herself, that she will waive *all* her rights? —make no objections? Mother, I *cannot* believe it!"

"But, Samuel, let me explain. Parson Hethwaite is a very peculiar man. He has never allowed his children to have any minds of their own, or his wife either, for that matter. I undertook to broach *this* subject to him; she could not get courage to do it. I must allow she is afraid to say her soul is her own. I don't see how she can be; for my part, I found him quite agreeable, quite much pleased, in fact. His wife likes it, and the girl is so well trained that she will do precisely as she is bid. *She'll do it in this house too!* Besides, her mother assures me that she looks forward to a very pleasant time with us; she had her into the bed-room while I was there, and said a few words to her, and she came back and told me (her mother did) that everything was satisfactory. She has never had any lovers or flatterers; she does not expect anything of the kind. Now, Sammy," continued the widow, not liking the

look in her son's eyes, which began to grow dark and angry—
"now, Sammy, you told me to pick her out and you'd take
her.   I have picked her out, the best I could, and it was not an
easy job either, under the circumstances; and I am sure you
didn't get much bothered over it."

"Bothered !—no; you have managed thus far to suit
yourself, but I am afraid you will not be able to proceed much
farther without meeting a barrier.   You know the old proverb:
"You may lead a horse to water, but you cannot make him
drink."

"There you go again, Samuel !—when you promised only
this morning." Widow Slaughton raised her voice to a plaintive
pitch, and began to pull fretfully at her shawl-fringe.   "Yes,
only this very morning, and I do hope you don't mean to back
out now, and make me ridiculous."

"There ! there, mother, we won't pursue that branch of
the subject.   You need not fear; I won't fail you.   Some men
get fine turnouts to please their women folk; some invest in
dry-goods; some buy jewels.   I am about to acquire a trifle
called a wife.   A mad scheme it is; and I shall be as mad as
a March hare to content you.   That is, you understand,
always supposing you are able to carry out the conditions."

"That is the way to talk, Sammy.   I mentioned to them I
would be down to the parsonage this evening, and of course you
will speak pleasantly to them all, Perdita especially.   She isn't
much of a talker—never was, her mother says; but she is an
efficient, capable, stirring, industrious girl, and that, you must
allow, is what we want in this house, the most of anything."

"Don't you think it will be a good plan to have the interview
conducted on the Chinese plan ?   You might place the bride-
elect behind a screen, and let me walk up and down before it,
where she could peep at me, and let her clap her hands three
times if she finds me to her taste."

"Oh, you can have all the fun you want, Samuel, provided
you act your part like a good boy.   Now I must go down and

see about your rooms. I suppose you will like to have one
turned into a kind of sitting-room ; luckily there's folding doors
between them. I shan't hardly have time for that, either. I
guess I'll wait till she comes, and let her fix them herself. There
will be some lifting and moving, and I don't feel hardly equal
to it. I'll have Hannah make all the cake and the jellies and
those things, and I haven't much time to lose."

The widow was half-way down the stairs before she finished
the summing-up of her projected labors, and her voice came
back to her son in fitful gusts, even after she had reached the
kitchen, where she immediately set about giving orders.

CHAPTER IV.

TWO HORNS OF A DILEMMA.

R. SLAUGHTON meditated a long while
on the queer *rôle* he was pledged to play
in a drama called " Marrying in Haste."
Very little time, it appeared, would be
allowed him to study his part, and he
could scarcely expect to appear to advantage in a *début* with a bride of whose
capacities and peculiarities he was totally
ignorant ; but as he was undertaking the *rôle* neither for his
own pleasure or aggrandizement, that was perhaps of minor
importance, so he acquitted himself to satisfy the managers.

The affair certainly had a ludicrous side ; but he did not feel
inclined to laugh—far from it. In fact, such a consummation
of his fate seemed a sorrowful ending to all his youthful hopes.

He had no right to be dreaming of Sabrina Bradshaw. She

was irrevocably lost to him—separated by an invincible barrier, "Thou shalt not covet." Sam had no intention of breaking the tenth commandment. The Sabrina who came to him in his musings was the superb maiden clothed in violet, and majestic in her youthful, pure loveliness, whom he had known ten years ago, when he had good hopes of winning her to be his wife.

A banging of doors and a shrieking among the poultry aroused him, and dissolved into thin air the old-time fancies which had been floating around his easy-chair—impalpable, voiceless visitors, but always dear and welcome. Perdita Hethwaite to be brought to Blithebeck through his means ! His mother wished to use him for a cat's-paw, to help herself to a young worker and companion. Well, what of it ? It is so much easier to float with the current of other people's wishes than to swim up stream against wind and tide of everlasting nagging and entreaty. "I dare say," he thought, "if I had married Sabrina, she would have led me in a string, like a tame bear."

The summing-up of the position in his mind seemed to be that the Parson's daughter must be either a poor-spirited creature, to let herself be traded off by her elders, or a sharp, cute one, having an eye to the main chance, tired of the stingy grinding of the poverty of the parsonage, willing to better her condition on any terms. "And a mere child, too ! Why, she was not three feet high when I saw her last, a little, puny broomstick of a thing, as thin and pale as a workhouse slave. A child fed on codfish can't be expected to be presuming, or positive, or high-colored. Stringy, I suppose, and pallid, 'well whipped,' afraid of her shadow. A most delicious prospect for a man whose tastes tend towards domestic joys—'the pleasures of home.' It won't make much difference to *me*, because as soon as mother has completed her little arrangement, I shall leave the country. I had a sort of idea of turning Slowgo adrift and amusing myself with farming ; but that notion is up in a balloon now. 'A man who is .wived has need to get shrived.' I don't feel ready to go to Heaven yet, so I'll post as far from the disagreeables which menace me as I can.   Mother, mother, what a manager you are ! "

CHAPTER V.

PARSON HETHWAITE AT HOME.

" Samuel Slaughton, so they say,
    Went a-courting one fine day,
    Sword and pistol by his side,
    And asked Miss Hethwaite for his bride."

 LONG, low, dingy room, lighted in day-time by four windows of seven-by-nine panes ; faintly illumined this evening by a couple of tallow candles which stood on a table in the centre, around which were gathered the young Hethwaites, doing their lessons.

Teddy, the eldest boy, a pale young-ster, with hollow cheeks and eyes set in a deep rim of purple, leaned on his elbows and stopped his ears with his forefingers, while his gaze was fixed and his faculties were centered in a book of travels, of which he was appropriating the pith and marrow. His shoulders were level with his chin, and his head stuck for-ward, for poor Teddy had the common American defect, near-sightedness.   In his case the cause was a habitual use of his vision in insufficient lights and at improper times ; but as can-dles were luxuries hard to come by at the parsonage, and his hours for culture few and mostly after the sun was down, the lad was rather to be pitied than blamed.

Teddy was the laborer of the family—indeed, he scarcely escaped being its drudge.   What little farming was done on the worn-out land which had been plowed and harrowed for generations by the Hethwaites, he accomplished, and he did it always at a disadvantage, with old-time tools, which took much strength out of him.   His hands were spread, brown, and notched and seamed with scars and bruises, and on either wrist he had the unsightly protuberance called by the country folks "a weeping sinner," the effect of lifting too heavy weights ; and his back was fast curving into a stoop, which it is a pity to see in a boy not yet out of his teens.   His clothes were homespun, home-made, patched and darned.   Teddy's outside was of little account, and Teddy's hair was cut very short.   Parson Hethwaite was his family's barber, and Malcolm said, "Father could never leave off snipping while there was a hair on their heads he could catch hold of."

But, in spite of all hindrances, the pains-taking, industrious lad had hoarded up much knowledge, and he was all the while digging.   Whenever he wished for money, it was to buy books. If by great luck he got a shilling, it went for some eye-destroying paper-covered copy of a work he could never hope to look into in decent type.   So the poor fellow fed his mind, at dear expense of his eyesight.

He had one ruling desire, one goal of all his aspirations—a professorship in a college.   That life, secluded, studious, undisturbed by farm drudgery, and surrounded by the best works of master-thinkers, appeared to Teddy to be the good place to get into.

Such a culmination of vain longings and useless dreams seemed impossible, even to his elder sister, who would have bartered her life to make them realities, and could only fret and chafe in secret rebellion at her powerlessness, while she listened to the poor fellow's talk ; but the hope was always ahead of *him*, making his distasteful present endurable.

Dolly had no such volumes beneath her eyes as sixteen loves

—no poetry, no romance, no thousand and one tales, to kindle her young fancy and enthrall her mind.   Oh, no ; she was knitting her brows over a Latin task, and her constant reference to her dictionary kept up a rattling of its leaves which tormented Teddy's quiet-loving ears.   Dolly was trying to read what Malcolm called her " Kikero."

Malcolm, who would have been a merry-hearted, frolicsome lad in a more genial atmosphere, was often sullen and ill-tempered.   He was hard at work on a problem, and certain tear-stains and dirt-splashes on his cheeks hinted that he might have failed in his lesson, and borne the punishment of failure.   In fact, the irritating, provoking gestures of Billy, the ten-year-old, who acted a pantomime, behind his father's back, of a wriggling sufferer writhing under the rod, in the pauses of the buzzing whispers in which he conned his geography, presently drew from Malcolm this threat, also in pantomime :

" I'll punch your head when we get upstairs."

The baby of this household, little Bettine, or Betty, as she was commonly called, leaned against her sister Perdita, who showed her pictures in an old Pilgrim's Progress.

The clasp of the elder sister's arm around the little one was close and fond ; the voice in which she spoke to her as she turned the pages was soft and loving ; the looks she poured into the small learner's uplifted eyes were such glances of absorbed and absorbing fondness as a slave mother might give to a helpless child at the mercy of a cruel master.

Betty belonged to Perdita by a wrecker's right, who claims flotsam and jetsam.   She saved the waif from the billows of death which swept her to her very feet, a mite of humanity scarcely large enough to hold a soul.   All the dreary while that the worn, exhausted mother lay just pulsating between time and eternity, Perdita attended the child whose birth had laid her so low ; and when at last she rose again to the duties and self-denials of her hard lot, Perdita held fast to her waif.   On through helpless babyhood and delicate budding, had the tiny childlet clung close to her preserver, who watched over her, worked for her, shielded her when she was able, and suffered treble tortures when parental authority fell with a strong man's heavy hand on the tender thing so soft and harmless and beautiful, in which she had garnered her love.

Every article of clothing the mite ever wore was the work of Perdita's fingers. If she could have had her will, choice, lovely fabrics would have adorned her; and though she was only able to manage ordinary stuffs, odds and ends, often pieced and seamed, she put so much of her woman's skill into patterns and color-blending, that her darling was always wondrously dainty, as are the fringed gentians and anemones of the wood.

There was a repressed, subdued, chastened appearance in the group around the table this evening, including even the frail nestling, only a baby yet in size, for all her five years of growth. Such a timid, fragile, slender slip of a girl as a rough father might crush in his grasp. She looked as if a small infliction of his "good bringing up" might send her so high among the angels that he would never be able to reach her forever.

Behind the old-fashioned mirror were tucked a couple of whips—lithe, elastic apple-branches. The end of one was fringed and worn. Little Betty's eyes often turned towards them, and a shudder passed through her as she included Malcolm in the involuntary glance. She had also been weeping bitterly, and a sob shook occasionally her small form. She was vicariously suffering for her brother, who had endured the blows in her presence—a terrible sight for a weak, timorous child; a frightful memory to give her; a night-mare for a life-time.

An old-fashioned chair stood in a corner by the fireplace, having a rude table on one of its arms, with a drawer beneath, and in it sat a bent, thin-haired man, whose head was covered with a cotton handkerchief. This was Parson Hethwaite, the law-giver of the household, and also its executioner. Hard,

relentless, unforgiving as any secular tyrant who had not been
ordained to proclaim the gospel of mercy and peace.   It could
not be said that his government was "a word and a blow;
the blow coming first," because he was by no means niggardly
of his words, and his blows followed no stated order in their
coming, except that they generally dropped too thick and fast
to be pleasantly counted, either by his victim or any chance
witness; and his arms were kept in good muscular condition
by frequent practice.   His children well understood what he
meant by a "sound drubbing," or a "smart flogging."

The pale, pinched, crushed thing who sat on the other side
of the chimney, footing a blue yarn sock, was the wife and
mother, who years ago promised to obey the slumbering autocrat opposite her. *He* also swore to cherish her. *She* had
kept thoroughly her promise ; *he* had long ago lost sight of his,
in the wear and tear of a life which had mangled him sorely.

A very learned man was Parson Hethwaite, but not apt to
teach, not acceptable in the pulpit or parish.

In his youth he had nourished high hopes and expectations,
and had completed his college course creditably, plodded
through the University, taken in all the dogmas and doctrines,
all the traditions of the elders, and laid them up as the staple
of his sermons ; and he ground away at them in the most orthodox manner, giving himself no leisure to use his own brains
beyond his patterns and teachers, so that he was an eminently
safe preacher, never off the platform, and it seemed that the
absence of danger from heresy and schism, lulled his hearers
to sweet repose during his discourses, for they often slept the
sleep of the just, even while he was demonstrating to them
that hell-fire was the certain destiny of a very considerable
portion of the human race.

Mr. Hethwaite married a wife intending to take care of her,
' if he had any definite intentions on the point.   At any rate, a
wife being a necessity to a minister, he picked out one; and
he had his little romance over the selection too, and talked

honey and "rained kisses" with the best of them. A grocer's clerk couldn't have been more "spooney" over a milliner's apprentice, having no fear of perdition before his eyes.

Being settled with a helpmeet, he looked about for a field wherein to exercise his calling. But the laborers were not few ; that scarcity was over long ago, and the young men who did not want to work with their hands had been for years slipping into the ministry, so that the vineyard was, so to speak, glutted, and nobody wished to listen to Mr. Hethwaite. When he preached his ordeal sermon as fifty-second candidate for the Merry Bank stone church pulpit, he was voted "slow, dull, tiresome." Miss Walsingham said he could not reason, Bianca Ashcroft said his sermon ought to be set to Windham and chanted at funerals. The young folks complained that he talked through his nose. Nobody was suited ; so they waited for candidate number fifty-three, and Mr. Hethwaite looked farther.

He did get a parish at last, and held it, or rather it held him a year, and no efforts could ever get him another ; and the upshot of it was, he was soured, out of conceit with the world, which used him so hardly, and discouraged, before he had fairly had a chance to develop into any usefulness.

A few years' teaching in a boys' school gave him a meagre support, but even there he was not wanted.

The lads hated him ; they cut up his whips, stuck him to his chair with shoemakers' wax, rubbed his desk with poison-ivy, locked him out, and fastened him in, and made his life a burden to him in a thousand other of the ingenious ways delighted in by vivacious and amiable boys. And when he could no longer endure their pleasantries he resigned, and as he was leaving the village they hooted, and bawled, and screeched after him, till their lungs gave out and their throats were hoarse.

Next Mr. Hethwaite went out as a missionary to the Choctaws, and he tarried long enough among the noble red men to feel that shooting was the only christianizing they were capable of. He acquired a full and accurate knowledge of the flora and fauna of the country, and being recalled and dismissed by the Board on the charge of incompetency, he brought home a healthy boy, born to him in exile, and a box of Osage orange-seed, with which he planted a hedge all around his old home-stead, and he retired behind it in disappointed seclusion, mak-ing no fresh efforts for the good of mankind, and beyond an occasional supply of some of the neighboring pulpits in cases of absolute emergency, his preaching was finished.

He was too poor to hire a horse, and the nearest meeting-house was a couple of miles off. Therefore his long walks of.en made him late, and he had an embarrassed, perturbed habit of consulting his watch after entering the pulpit, and mopping his face and saying,

"There appears to be a discrepancy in the time." A thoughtless girl, who got tired of the repetition, dubbed him " Old Discrepancy," and somehow the name got fastened on him, so that after a while it reached his ears, and it added gall to his cup already bitter enough.

His eyes, jealously sharpened by past experiences, observed that the young people were apt to slip away at his approach, and the elders yawned or slept through his discourses ; and he really felt heart-sore enough to weep, when a certain well-to-do farmer, who had been comfortably awaiting the expected coming of his own pastor, jumped up at sight of *him*, and seized his hat, glancing hurriedly out of a window near his pew, as if he saw a fracas among the horses under the long shed, and must hasten to adjust it, and he plainly heard him say in the porch as he went :

" No buzzing from Old Discrepancy for me. I'll go over to the Universal, and get myself comfortably put into glory."

A disappointed man is not as a rule the jolliest sort of father, and Mr. Hethwaite's treatment of his children was calculated to take the cheerfulness out of them in his pres-ence. Not one of them ever thought of addressing him, even

to ask the simplest question. Dumbness being the rule when
the solid clump of the paternal boot was heard approaching,
even the wife and mother got a habit of saying,

" Hush, children, your father is coming."

Fun being made a crime, it took all the violence of reckless
debauch in his absence, and was severely punished when discovered.

As the young folks grew up, they made sorry jokes over
their dreary childhood. Teddy said his father used to take him
out into the orchard for a pleasant stroll, when he went to cut
the weekly whips, and make him carry them home, and that
the afternoon was mostly his pleasantest time, because he had
usually got his diurnal flogging then, and felt that it was over.

Malcolm being up for punishment one day, when the supply
of rods was exhausted, his father bade him wait in the kitchen,
while he cut a twig ; the poor lad stood trembling with dread,
when Billy appeared. Suddenly the spirit of self-preservation
led Malcolm to procure a substitute.

" Billy," said he, " father wants you to stop here till he comes
back," and darting away, he made good his escape.

Presently the excellent divine returned, trimming his stick
and peeling it to his mind, and he seized Billy by the arm, and
lashed him till he howled again. It was not till he stopped to
bestow the withering look which always topped off his discipline,
that he discovered he had been thrashing the wrong boy.

" Oh, it's you, is it, sir ? Well, well ! If you don't deserve
it now, you will some other time ! "

With this consolation, he stuck the rod in its place behind
the looking-glass, and stalked away in a most stately and dignified manner, leaving his son to rub his bruises and wipe his
tears, and swallow his indignation at his leisure.

Perhaps it is as well to add the sequel of the story, in which
wicked Malcolm got his reward.

Teddy, the peaceable, was so much roused by the injustice of
the action and the mean selfishness of the proper culprit, that

3

he drubbed him soundly, and thus brought the glee and frisk and chaffing with which he was triumphing over Billy, to a sudden conclusion.

Parson Hethwaite taught his children with accurate method and painstaking labor; but half the benefit of his instructions, and all the pleasure they might have given, were taken out of them by the dreary grind and ever-recurring punishments.

As his eldest daughter, Perdita, grew towards womanhood, he gradually imposed the daily drill and drudgery upon her, so that, while other girls of her age were likely to be thinking of merry-makings and carnal pleasures, she was digging amongst the roots of the dead tongues, and puzzling her young head for some effectual methods of imparting to the others what had cost her so much toil and weariness to get, so that they might escape the ferulings and ear-pullings she had endured; and all of them looked forward with dread to the weekly examinations, when the teacher often shared with her pupils the punishment of mistakes or failures.

As the years wore on, the Parson spent more and more of his time in his bare, dreary study, writing bare, dreary sermons on the doctrines his theological school had taught him, and which got no softness or smoothing with his increasing age.

Ripe thinkers, well-balanced, soundly developed men, who lead pleasant, profitable lives, often come to apprehend and feel more love in their Christ as the fleeting days bring them closer to his many mansions.

Mr. Hethwaite had hard lines for everybody. "Wrath! wrath!" The thunders of Sinai, and the terrors of the law till the bitter end, insomuch that it appeared to his household that the principal object of bringing them into the world must have been to keep everything away from them which they could enjoy, pile on as many disagreeables as possible, and after this life of privation and constant endurance was finished, to drop them into a per-dition which they had had from the first no chance of escaping, try as hard as they might, because they felt in themselves a wicked, rebellious dissatisfaction with their lot, which proved that they could not be of the elect, who are thankful for everything.

Poor Mrs. Hethwaite, pretty Violet Wemple that was, followed her husband among the Chocktaws, dreadfully afraid of every redskin she saw, keeping as much out of their way as possible, and plagued with nightly visions of seeing her children scalped before her eyes.

She used to tell stories to them of that period, and her hardships and perils, to which they listened with eager ears.

"One night," she would say, "when your father had gone away from the settlement, leaving me in the house with only Teddy and Perdita, there came four great stout Indians, wrapped in their blankets, and planted themselves before the kitchen fire. They asked me for something to eat, which I got, and then they lay down on the hearth. I dared not tell them to go, and was afraid to stay; so I took my two babies, and slipped into my bed-room and locked the door. I did not go to bed, but sat beside them as they slept, listening to every noise, and feeling my blood creep at the falling of a brand in the fireplace, or the chirp of a cricket, till midnight, when your father came home.

He looked in at the window and saw by the light of the embers, the savages sound asleep. And then he came around and tapped on my sash and called softly, "Violet," and I guess, for once in his life, he was glad to hear my voice; at any rate, he was as white as a ghost when he came in."

From the wooed to the drudge had been a swift transition, and the wife droned on in the everlasting rut; pinching, saving, making do; footing stockings, piecing out garments, feeding many mouths on little; always ill-nourished, ill-clothed, kept down to the barest possible allowance of everything. What wonder that her prettiness soon faded, and premature age stamped her face and form with lines and angles, defacing and deforming her upright, beautiful youth?

Once in a while the neighbors would rally and give them a

donation party, on which occasions she had to come to the fore, and do all the cringing and thankfulness, to which her husband would not stoop ; and her constant habit of concealing transgressions which were not sins, as well as faults which were, permitting things forbidden whenever she was able, standing between the culprit and the executioner, gave her an uneasy, apologetic way not at all pleasant; and if she had not been the most patient and gently-kind of mothers, her own children must have despised her, so rebuked and lectured, and made to obey, were they accustomed to see her.

Whatever Violet Wemple might have become under sunnier skies and genial warmth, Violet Hethwaite was certainly a poor-spirited, nervous, thin, feeble woman, just what her husband and his treatment had made her.

This was the household to which Mr. Slaughton and his mother were admitted, when they accepted the " Come in " which followed their knock on the side door, and entered the keeping-room of the minister's family.

" Oh, good evening," said Mrs. Hethwaite, gathering up her ball and pulling her needle out of its sheath, as she hurriedly rose with a humble bow to her visitors; "most happy to see you, I'm sure. Husband, here's Mrs. Slaughton come to call ; Perdita, get up and speak to the friends."

The divine pulled down his extinguisher and disclosed a head as hard and round as a granite bowlder, and a face full of untimely lines, all bearing downwards, such as only an unsatisfied, meagre, mortified life, full of disappointments and bitter set-backs, could have chiselled there, but a face set with obstinacy, with overbearing, arbitrary will not broken by adversity.

He rose with a "what-have-you-come-for ? " kind of manner, and barked out a sort of welcome, while his wife fidgeted and smiled, and repeated " Glad to see you, very glad," and nodded and frowned at her daughter with a face as nearly threatening as such a poor-hearted creature could assume.

Perdita stood up quietly and did as she was bid. If she had been forewarned of the visit and its meaning, she gave no evidence of such knowledge by agitation or trepidation. She took the hand which the dame offered, or rather she touched the tips of the fingers; and she accepted the kiss which was proffered, but she turned her cheek to the saluting lips, and she wiped it off as soon as she could afterwards.

She bowed and curtsied to the gentleman, who was introduced by his mother, with her eyes upon the middle button of his waistcoat; and then she went and sat down in a corner, taking Betty with her, and followed by Teddy, who flamed up red and angry, as if he had been insulted by the visitors, who had, however, spoken courteously enough to the group around the table.

Sam Slaughton could scarcely see the girl who was selected for his wife, through the gloom of the shadowy room. An erect figure she seemed to him, stiff and awkward, a dark face made more sombre and forbidding by masses of black hair.

Sam's ideal of female loveliness had a beautiful head covered by braids of dead gold, and features as fine and pure as chiselled marble. Sam never in his life saw anything to admire in a brunette. Even that specimen of Spanish loveliness named Dolores, or the breathing brightness called Peace Pelican, had no charms for him; and while he listened to the crabbed growl which the Parson considered conversation, he remembered how Lord Pembroke had styled Dr. Johnson's talk and manner "a sort of bow-wow way;" and he also felt an amused resentment at his mother and a plain statement which she had set forth quite positively to him.

"A man *never* marries his ideal." He looked at the girl selected for him, that brow of Egypt in the corner. He took the lappels of his coat-breast in his two hands and adjusted his collar with an aggravated pull and a duck of his head. "Not that it makes any difference to me, while there are countries left to explore, new scenes to visit."

Once or twice he caught splashes of talk, but that was Teddy,
who spoke in a low tone to his sister, sitting so close to her
that his imperfect eyes could study her face.

Scraps of the conversation of the two old ladies also reached
him. "Three kinds of cake, with the bride's loaf, quite sufficient; hum hum; frosting; hum hum; burnt almonds; good
bake; hum hum——"

Presently there came a loud knock at the front door, which
Malcolm was sent to answer.

"The tax collector, father; he's in the spare room," he said
when he returned; and Parson Hethwaite begging to be
excused, went out, making his hard face harder while he
counted over his available dollars.

The two mothers exchanged winks; or rather, Widow
Slaughton cut her eye at her neighbor, who could not be bold
enough to venture on such a liberty as returning the signal;
taking the hint, which was made plain by some pointing at the
young people, and the single word "out," pronounced in a
wide-mouthed whisper, she arose and sent them to bed; nearly
trembling as she did so for fear of the scolding she might get
from her lord and master for her presumption; and then the
arch-plotters left the room together. Outside the door they
paused for a conference, and presently Mrs. Hethwaite put in
her head.

"Hadn't you better go down and make sure that you locked
the hen-house, Teddy? Mr. Batt lost twelve of his best hens
last night, and they think it is Teagle; he was caught lurking
about. Hadn't you better, Teddy?"

"Hen-house be hanged," muttered Teddy. "They want to
get rid of me, that's all. Perdita, I shall have to leave you to
the Goths and Vandals."

"I am able to take my own part, if necessary," replied the
girl in a low voice. "Ridiculous, is it not?"

Dame Slaughton came pattering in while the young man was
gathering up his books; and with as bland a smile as she could

have bestowed on a *second*, she whispered in her son's ear, first saying in a preternaturally audible voice,

" Oh Samuel, my son, is this your glove ? " showing him one she had just drawn from her own fingers for the purpose. "Now, my dear boy, talk a little—there's a dear ; just a little to please me. You won't have any trouble, the ground is all laid out—she understands her part. Speak out, now, Sammy —do ! "

Mr. Slaughton had no idea of speaking out, and the information he had gotten that " she " was up in her rôle did not any more incline him towards the girl in the corner ; but it was abominably awkward. He felt as if he was back into youth and roundabouts, when his mother washed his face and bade him " behave in meeting." The ludicrousness of his position so forcibly struck him, that he could have laughed if he had not been so angry.

A couple of minutes of dead silence followed the exit of the ladies—silence which made the snores of Rose, the yellow dog, who lay in a corner of the hearth, absurdly distinct and audible ; while Perdita's eyes rested on her visitor with a glance entirely free of curiosity or interest.

Little Betty climbed on her sister's knee, and snuggling into her arms, settled herself with a contented squirm, and she too scanned the guest with her clear baby-eyes, which seemed able to fathom his inmost thoughts.

Sam felt nettled and provoked with the dumbness of the girl, but he also felt obliged, as a gentleman, to make a remark.

"Your little sister seems quite fond of you, Miss Hethwaite."

" She is fond of me—she has good reason. I am her best friend," was her reply in a sort of unchanging monotone, as cold and indifferent as human voice could be.

" You make a great pet of her, I dare say," continued Sam, not much relishing the rôle of a snubbed individual.

"We have no pets in this house. I wash and dress Betty, and I make her clothes and hear her lessons."

"She studies Mother Goose and doll-babies, I suppose," said Sam, looking at the mite.

"We never had any such nonsense. We are not allowed. I did once make her a rag-baby, which father burned up; and as I hated to see her cry her eyes out over her loss, I never tried it any more."

"How extremely unpleasant!" thought Sam. "I wonder why mother plunged into this family of all others, and picked out this icicle, this stock, this stone, this frozen thing."

He was still ringing the changes on the unpleasantness when the arch-plotters returned.

"Well, Sammy, did you pop the question?" inquired the dame in a cheerful whisper, patting his head with her hand and smiling benignantly at him. "Is it all arranged?"

"Mother, this is not fair," replied Sam in a subdued growl. "You remember what I told you. I shall stick to the letter of my bargain; but I won't go an inch beyond."

As he finished his speech he laughed and pulled away his head from the encouraging caress it was getting. He could not help laughing at the absurdity of the whole proceeding; it was *so* ridiculous. "Come, mother, I think we have stopped long enough; let's go home."

"Not yet, my son," replied the dame decidedly. "I have not finished my business yet. Perdita, come here."

"Yes, Perdita, come here!" chimed in Mrs. Hethwaite in a cringing way. She had been rumpusing with the poker and tongs during the dialogue between the guests, and she enforced her order by thrusting the poker towards the distant corner where the girl sat, as she spoke. "Come right here, when Mrs. Slaughton is so kind as to call you."

"Here's my son Samuel, come to ask you to marry him. I suppose he feels a little bashful, and so I help him along," the dame finished, maliciously twinkling her eyes at her victim. "Sammy always was rather bashful with the girls. He's afraid of women; but he'll make you a first-rate husband."

"And a high honor he confers on you, I'm sure," chimed in Mrs. Hethwaite, frowning and grimacing at her silent child. "Speak immediately, and say 'I am much obliged, and thank you kindly.'"

"I am much obliged, and thank you kindly," recited Perdita, as if it had been a lesson. She had risen when bid to do so, but had not stirred from her place; and she clasped a little closer the small hand she held in her firm grasp.

Sam glowered at his mother, but he bowed to the girl. He could do no less, and he would do no more.

"Next Wednesday, three o'clock," said Mrs. Slaughton. "That is what your mother and I have settled to. Does the time suit you?"

"As well as another, ma'am," was the concise answer. As she spoke, she looked down at Betty, who was clinging to her in a frightened way. They could not fathom the tumultuous thoughts which had been raging beneath her outward stillness; they had no idea of the motives which impelled her; they only saw her dark, quiet, indifferent.

"Yes, Wednesday, the thirtieth of September," said Mrs. Hethwaite; "a very nice time of year to get married—very, indeed! It is very thoughtful of you, and we are grateful that you have come to our poor house, and picked out our poor girl, when you had rich folks to choose from, with nice clothes and everything. Well, if she don't bring any money with her, it is all the more reason why she should make a good, obedient wife; and I am sure she will, Mr. Slaughton, she has been well trained."

"I shall not be exacting, madam," replied the gentleman, and his tone and manner said plainly, "all I wish is to be left alone."

"And we think you had better come right home after the ceremony. My son has travelled about all over the created world, and he needs quiet. I did not take any journey after my wedding. I don't approve of the fuss and the expense, and

3*

I don't suppose you care about going anywhere, do you ?
remarked the widow.

"Not in the least, madam."

"That is all settled, then. Now I am ready to go, Sammy.
We shall have to be pretty middling busy to get ready ; but
when I have any plan on hand I like to drive it through, don't
you say so, Mrs. Hethwaite ?"

, Of course Mrs. Hethwaite agreed with the wealthy lady ;
and she made great haste and show of saying that she did.

"So far so good," continued Mrs. Slaughton to the other
arch-plotter, whose hand she lingered a moment behind her
son to shake impressively. "So far so good. We'll hurry
up and have the knot tied, and they can take all their lives to
get acquainted in afterwards, if they want to."

"I suppose so," replied Mrs. Hethwaite with a weary sigh.
"My Perdita is a good girl ; she deserves to be as happy as she
can. Life is a vale of tears—we journey to the tomb."

"She will have a good home, and plenty to do, and that is
the best way to be happy *I* have ever found," replied the dame,
rather tartly.

"I know I ought to be very grateful to you, and I trust I
am. I do get a little low in my mind, sometimes. Yes, yes,
I shall make haste as fast as I can. Wednesday will soon be
here. Dear, dear, only to think !"

Mr. Slaughton turned to offer his adieux to his affianced
bride ; but she seemed to have forgotten his neighborhood.
She had picked up little Betty, whom she held close pressed to
her heart, and her head was bent so that her cheek touched the
child's forehead, and a strange, defiant gleam shot from her
eyes. The two, standing in the half gloom, apart from the
others, made a group which impressed itself unpleasantly on
Sam's mind, and he left her without attempting to say so much
as "Good-night."

All the way home, the dame talked of the rest and ease and
comfort in store for her ; of the Vance children, and the changes

to be made in preparation for their arrival; and when they reached their own door, she stopped and took her son's hand in hers.

"You will never be sorry for your giving in to my wishes, my dear Sammy. I shall not be long here, and I shall be able to get everything settled to my liking, and have *her* broken to my ways, and I shall feel that I have indeed set my house in order, so that it will stay put; and you will be married and respectably fixed at home; and you will tidy up the farm, and look after Slowgo, and make him attend to his business; and I shall see your boy—my little grandson, before I go. That is the best thought of all—my dear, beautiful grandson. You are a good lad, Samuel. God bless you!"

While the old lady talked, holding his fingers in hers and patting them softly with her other hand, Mr. Slaughton was thinking of the girl he had left holding the child in her arms, as a priestess might hold the victim she has consecrated, and is about to offer upon the altar, pouring out her own soul in the precious gift; and he let the half-formed intention which had been gathering in his mind, of rising to the effort of combating this woman's scheme, recalling his promise, and refusing to go any farther, slip away from him. With his mother before him, talking as if it were already finished, and commending his goodness for the excellent action, and her great consolation in the same, he said nothing, kissing her and going away to his room, though with rather a rueful countenance, and as "measured tread and slow" as might have done for a funeral procession.

CHAPTER VI.

"THE EYE OF PRUDENCE IS NOT SHUT."

ONDAY morning Mr. Slaughton left for Toptown, where he proposed to remain till the wedding-day. He had planned to start Saturday, but finally concluded to stop over Sunday and accompany his mother to church, as she begged him to do. He might have had a secret reason for his ready compliance, for aught I know. Neither can I tell what was passing in the dame's mind; but instead of attending her own place of worship at Blithebeck village, she went in another direction and walked up the aisle, on the arm of the tall fellow she was so proud of, and seated herself in a pew of the old South, where the Hethwaite family were accustomed to assemble beneath the droppings of the Sanctuary.

They were directly in front, a couple of slips off, and Sam looked them over, with eyes not quite as willing to see them at their best as they might have been, had they not been so strangely and unexpectedly thrust upon his notice a few evenings since.

Pinched poverty, which strives and strives to be decent! Such small patterns and eked-out material! Dolly's hat had dyed ribbons, and the mother's gown had been so often turned that the seams were quite worn and threadbare. Perdita sat in the far corner, with her mother; and little Betty leaned against her. He could only see her profile, which he was unwillingly obliged to admit to himself was "well enough," and the thick braids of long jetty hair, which hung below her trim shoulders.

She held down her head ; not looking at the minister, or any person or thing around her, though she kept closely clasped in hers the small hand of the child.

A motionless slip-full they were. Even Billy scarcely moved his head ; and Betty was so free from the natural restlessness of children that she looked like a little waxen baby in her perfect repose.

When they rose for the long prayer, the Parson stood up in his place, bending his shoulders and grasping the pew-rail before him in his hands, and keeping his eyes shut till the "amen." Malcolm sat down an instant before the old gentleman, folding his arms devoutly ; but he reached out just one point of time before he placed them, to the part of the cushion • his father was about to occupy ; and when the pater dropped earnestly and solemnly into position, he popped up again very quickly, and his face grew extremely red while he furtively reached under his coat-tails and produced thence a long carpet tack which had been standing on its head ready to salute him with its "business end." He turned his gaze slowly upon his son, who was looking at the minister with his soberest Sabba-day countenance on, oblivious of all about him—as blank and innocent as if he had never smiled in his whole life.

Those near who had seen the performance laughed, and Mr. Slaughton was intensely tickled with the boy-prank.

"There is something in that lad," he thought. "Why, he can't help playing tricks, even on his pompous old father."

The truth is, Malcolm had a little grievance to adjust. That morning, at family prayers, he had knelt down as usual next Teddy, with Billy on the other side of him. When the petition was about half over—that is, while the Parson was busy among the South Sea heathens, whom he mentioned as excellent sub-jects for a thorough reform (he had read that morning, in the *Herald*, of a case of missionary eating, which had filled him with indignation), Billy had moved softly on his knees around to Teddy's place, and had given his hair so smart a pull

that he had bent over to keep in a cry of pain—and he hastily
and quietly closed a book he had been perusing to wile the tedi-
ous hours. His first thought was that the check had come from
his father, who must have had his eyes open, and he did not
stir for half a minute. When he did look up, the boys were
each in his place, and the Parson going on so steadily that he
had evidently not seen the book, or known his offence.   Of
course, then, it was Malcolm.   Yes, of course it was ! else why
was his face buried in his arms that way, pretending to be so
quiet and proper ?

Malcolm rose from his knees, his thoughts still running on a
sled he meant to build for coasting that winter, the shoes for
which were the theme of meditation which had given him so
devout an outside.   Being sent to the wood-house for chips as
soon as the orison was ended, he was closely followed by Teddy
in a flaming state of wrath, who pitched into him right and left,
and punished him quite thoroughly before he had time to collect his forces of defence, or inquire what it all meant.

The young Hethwaites were accustomed to say that " when
Teddy did get mad, he got as mad as fire ; " and so it appeared in the present instance, and as he dropped the blows he said
by way of punctuation, " Now, then, pull my hair again if you
think best, in prayer-time.   There, and there ! "

A chuckle behind them, and a hop and skip of delight made
them both look around, and there stood Billy dancing and
clapping his hands.

" It was me ! it was me ! Goody ! goody !   Give it to him,
who got me whipped in his place.   Now we are even, I think,
Mr. Malcolm.   Go it, Teddy ! "

Teddy made haste to apologize, though he could not help
laughing, and he had used up all his anger ; but the feelings of
the innocent sufferer were too much injured to see any joke, and
when he returned to the keeping-room with his chips, his under-
lip was hanging and his face was as sullen as possible.

The Parson saw his son dash down his load with a grunt,

and he rose and gave him a sound box on the ear for his cross-
ness over his chores.

"Look pleasant, you, sir," said he. " I'll have no grumbling
and growling here. Who feeds and clothes you, do you suppose, when you can't earn the salt you eat? Look pleasant, I
say."

Malcolm forgave Teddy's mistake, and shook hands with him
before meeting ; but not his father's blow, and the carpet-tack
was his payment of what he considered a just debt.

Perdita found the Bible chapter, and followed the minister's
reading of the lesson ; she sang all the hymns, and bent her
head in the prayer, decorous and irreproachable, but with such
a dreamy manner—so spiritless, so uninterested, so preoccupied, that the bridegroom-to-be caught himself wondering what
she might be thinking of, and whether she was really willing to
be made a wife of in such precipitate haste—in such an uncanny way ; and the result of his reflections was a resolution
which he put into effect as soon as he reached the Toptown
House, Monday evening. He wrote her a letter, recommend-
ing that she should think twice, or even thrice, before submit-
ting to the will of the managers who had been so busy about
her future, and suggesting that if she refused *him*, she might
have a chance to find a man who would make a wooing before
the wedding.

"It matters little to me," he thought as he finished the mis-
sive. "*I* am a free man, I can go where and when I like ;
but it is rather a dreary lookout for her, if she does not incline
to it from interested motives. There! I have washed my
hands of the responsibility," he concluded, as he sealed and
stamped the letter and tossed it from him. It was a queer sort
of epistle on a queer subject, and Sam lit a fresh cigar after he
had got it off his mind, while he hummed the refrain :

"What care I how fair they be?
Not one of them can be fair for me."

CHAPTER VII.

THE BARMECIDIAN FEAST.

ERDITA HETHWAITE went about her duties as usual during the days which followed the important evening when she had been asked and promised in marriage.

Nothing was said to her concerning the important change which was arranged to take place in her condition. She often caught her mother's eyes dwelling wistfully on her, and many times she saw her wipe away tears which had filled them to the brim ; but that was nothing unusual—the poor old lady's eyes were habitually weak and watery.

Sunday her father preached at Quaker Four Corners, and she and Teddy were detailed for service, to help swell the congregation, the Parson's audiences being apt to be rather thin ; so the brother and sister walked over together.

And Teddy enjoyed that walk, although he did scarcely any of the talking. He often thought afterwards of Perdita as she looked that bright, breezy Sunday ; of the brilliant tints in her face, made more freshly blooming by the exercise and the cool west wind which was blowing across the hills ; of her dress of sombre stuff, plain, meagre, devoid of ornament ; her chip hat, with only a band of sad-colored ribbon around its crown ; and he remembered also the bunch of crimson leaves she culled and fastened into it ; and how impetuous and defiant she looked while busy with them, and of the speech she had made about her work when it was completed, and she admired it at arm's length ; and how affrighted he had felt at her and her bold action, and the tremendous destiny before her.

" There !" she said, "God made them, His forests painted them, and I've got them ; now I will wear them to meeting, and father may help himself."

It was as if,. in the act so simple and trifling, she was seizing a precious right from the hand of a hard tyrant, which she was ready to defend with her life.

Such a sudden uprising as it seemed to Teddy—such a dangerous, desperate rebel as she appeared to him !

Oh, yes, he enjoyed that walk ; such a many new thoughts and feelings as she let herself disclose to him.

Seeing always the same faces, occupied by a round of monotonous pursuits, staid and sober in the presence of her elders, this girl had unconsciously ingrained a deep inner culture from the sweet serenities and bold wonder-work of Nature, in close harmony with whom she lived her unspoken life. The nameless spectacles which pageanted before her eyes of summer sunsets and moon-risings ; the resonant organ-tones of the majestic thunder-storms, rolling their deep diapason among the mountain-tops ; the merry tinkle and " tireless play " of the pure brooklets she was so fond of following in their devious windings ; even the many-pointed snow-flakes falling softly, softly before the window-pane, gave her rich, sweet thoughts, which she carried with her to the study of the old books of the library, and which were intensified and harmonized by the master-sway of the noble minds she daily communed with there.

Teddy only rarely got glimpses of what was passing in his sister's soul. She was shy of speaking her best conceits, because the home influence was depressing ; and besides, she often felt her ideas and conceptions monstrous, because they were so out of the narrow bound she was taught to set for herself.

This day her tongue was loosened, and she talked so fast and so wonderfully that the long miles seemed as nothing to Teddy, who was sorry when they reached the church door, and she shut in and composed her face to the Sunday gravity which was a part of the parsonage religion.

Fortunately the preacher was in sufficient season to save any "discrepancy," but it seemed to his children that the cast of his discourse was even more gloomy and lugubrious than usual.

He had chosen for his text the declaration of Paul: "For all things are yours, whether of the world, or life, or death, or things present, or things to come ; all are yours."

After the terrors of the law and threatenings were dealt out to the non-elect, the preacher proceeded to prove to his own satisfaction that all things in the universe belonged to believers. If they had them to enjoy in abundance, of course they were theirs by possession ; if they had them not, it was because they were not good for them, and were held in trust as minors wait for their estates ; and he wound up in quite a frenzy of exaltation.

"I claim that we ought to enjoy all things that are withheld equally with those which are bestowed. Castles, thrones, principalities, luxuries, wealth ; perhaps I might have liked all these, but my Father owns them ; I am His son, and they are all mine. I enjoy them, though I want all things. Though I starve, I am filled ; though I am houseless and despised, I am rich, because all things are ours."

"Well," said Teddy, on their way home, "how do you like that sort of doctrine ? Can you feel that you have been all your days rolling in the lap of luxury ? "

"I feel as if I had been to a feast of the Barmecides ; and really, if father was not a preacher, I should say he gives out curses with astonishing vehemence and enjoyment."

" That is a fact, Perdita. They say he used to swear like a trooper before he was converted, and I suppose it comes natural yet. I believe the reason ministers put so much damnation into their sermons is, that they never get any other chance to let off the hard words."

" That sounds rather wicked, Teddy ; but I'm not sure there is not sense in it," replied Perdita, laughing.

" How I shall miss you next Sunday, Perdita," said Teddy,

after a short silence. " Did you see the Slaughtons in church ? It must be pleasant to ride to meeting."

" It is pleasant to walk with *you*, Teddy," said she, turning quickly towards him. " No, I did not see those people ; I should not have looked at them if I had."

" I should not wonder if they came on purpose to look *you* over ; they always go to the village meeting, you know."

" I hope they got paid for their trouble, if they did," observed Perdita, contemptuously.

" Mr. Slaughton is a handsome man," said Teddy in a regretful voice ; " he wears beautiful clothes."

" What of that, Teddy ? So do professors wear beautiful clothes ; so will you some day. As for his looks, do you know I should not be able to pick him out of a crowd ? And it is not of the least consequence to me whether he is handsome or ugly. Don't let's talk about *them*. Let's gather some of these pretty leaves ; come help me, Teddy. I mean to use a good many of them ; I never had a chance to adorn my room. I'll do it when I get free."

She shut her lips on her destination after this remark, and would not let her brother discuss it, and he was quite willing to leave it, and follow her lead ; for she launched out into his future—the college he would join, the multitude of books he would have, the delicious leisure for study ; and as she talked, a sort of self-devoted elevation shone in her face.

" Teddy !" exclaimed she as they reached the parsonage gate, " you are worth everything ; I couldn't do too much for you ; I shall buy you the pebble glasses you have been longing to have, and Betty shall go fine as the Princess Delight who married Almanazor."

CHAPTER VIII.

"THE DEVIL BEHAVES TO US EVEN AS HE FINDS US."

ONDAY morning Perdita came upon her mother counting some bills which she had spread out on the lap of her check apron.

"Only ten dollars," said she, with a hopeless sigh. A silk is out of the question, poor child ! She will have to be married in a pongee, for all I can see, and Heaven only knows what Dolly is to do for her winter things. Well, Perdita, I am sorry I can't fix you up as I should like to," she added, seeing her daughter near her ; "but when folks can't do as they would, they must do as they can, and try to be thankful."

" Is it for me that you are lamenting the paltriness of that pile of filthy lucre ? I hope there is not the small-pox in it. Truly, it has an ancient and fish-like smell."

" Of course it is for you, child ; there isn't anybody else going to get married Wednesday, is there ? I wouldn't mind how they smelt, if I only had enough of them ; chicken-money, rag-money and all—such a pitiful trifle !"

" What is the difference, mother? According to father's doctrines, we own vast possessions ; all we lack is fertile imaginations."

" I am glad to see you so chirk," said Mrs. Hethwaite complainingly. " Why couldn't you smile so when Mr. Slaughton was to see you, instead of looking as glum as if it was a funeral."

" It might have been, with me for chief mourner, for all cause I found for cheerfulness. Come, mother, put up your hoard, I don't want any of it ; and Dolly must have her new

cloak and the beaver bonnet she would long for, if she dared.
She is young and pretty—she loves finery ; she says all the
heaven she wants is plenty to wear, and a visit every day in
the·year. 'I think she may get just that, or its equivalent,
somewhere in this life or the next ; maybe she will start as
a rich man's daughter, with silks and jewels, and servants and
horses and carriages, when she's got through being Dolly
Hethwaite, the pinched child of a poor minister."

"What *are* you talking about, Perdita ? It's lucky your
father don't hear you."

"Father has not been able to hear me think, since I found
out how ; for which mercy let me be thankful."

"Oh, dear me ! what's that ? " exclaimed Mrs. Hethwaite,
looking over her shoulder in a dreadfully frightened way.

"It's a thing in a red coat prancing after your money. Hide
it up, quick ; he smells of brimstone. Don't turn so pale,
mother. If the Old Scratch should come, he wouldn't dare
touch you ; and I don't feel afraid of him just now. Put up
the chicken-money and the rag-money, and come and show
me how to darn Teddy's best coat ; it is broken on the elbow."

"But I must stop to consider ; you can't be married in that
shabby calico, can you ? "

"As soon as any. There, don't scold, don't cry. I'm going
away too soon. If you had the finest silk in the store, you
could not get it made, you know. The time is short—not many
working hours before the awful day shall come—the appointed
time which makes haste."

"I thought of getting Polly Marner to come and cut it out.
She's swift with her needle."

"We can't cut out what we have not, though we are often cut
out of what we most desire. Shall I tell you the sort of gown
I would like to wear for my wedding ? "

"Oh, dear ! as if liking would bring it ! "

"Mother, what sort of a dress did you wear when you married father ? "

"I had a white silk—a pretty dress it was. I dyed it and wore it out years ago."

"I am glad I cannot have a white silk, then. You've had a hard life, mother ; a hard husband, an overbearing, selfish tyrant to you and to us all. I cannot be much worse off than you have been. Don't look so scared ; don't reprove me. I've said it out loud now. I've felt it always. You cannot suppose I have been blind and deaf and insensible all these years. Oh, no ! I learned to suffer as soon as I began to breathe, I think, and I've had no chance to forget the trick of it."

"Hush, wicked girl ! Hush, I say ! " cried the wife, pale and trembling. "Why, what is going to happen ? I feel so strange —as if you was elected to be a castaway. Oh, Perdita ! I hope you have not sinned away the day of grace."

"Which particular day of my existence was that, mother ? Grace, 'tis a charming sound, and means much the same, I suppose, as pity. The one most likely to show pity to a helpless child he has full power over would be her father ; as I never found any grace or pity in father, it don't seem worth while to look away off to an indifferent essence of a God who can't be capable of pity, since he made beings on purpose to damn them, when he was able to ordain happiness just as easy."

"Shut your lips instantly, Perdita ! Remember, God hears you. He *does* pity his children. *I* put my trust in him."

"He ought to pity *you*, mother, if anybody. Your hard times ought to be made up to you some time. I trust they may. As for father, I should just like to be *his* father a little while, that's all ! "

"Perdita, beware ! ' The eye that despiseth its father, the young eagles shall pick it out, and the young ravens shall eat it.' "

"I don't believe that story, mother. If the young eagles take the trouble to pick them out, they are great fools not to swallow them themselves ; that is, if they are fond of eyes. There, there, mother ! The heavens are not going to fall, nor

the earth open and bury me. Remember how many years my
tongue has been tied, and you cannot wonder if it runs riot
when it is loosed. I wish you would take me up-garret—not
with a stick in your hand, as father used to do; but with a key,
and let me look into that old iron-bound trunk that has got a
till to it. It is full of the things you had when you was a girl,
which were too fine for a poor minister's wife, and had to be
put out of sight to save scandal in the congregation. Aunt
Prudence showed them to me when I was a child, and told me
that was why they were shut up there. I never forgot it. You
wore them, I know, before you took up with father, when you
was a gay young lady with lovers. What a pity you hadn't accepted one of them! My father's money did not buy any of
the nice, costly fabrics. You never wore them in his company.
There's where I want to look to find the dress which I will
wear."

"Mercy on me! Prudence did very wrong."

"But what she said was true?"

"Yes, all true. I went to New Orleans and spent the winter—a gay winter, which seems like an impossible dream, it was
so filled with worldly pleasure. I had grace given me to choose
the better part, which can ne'er be taken from me."

"You mean father, perhaps," said Perdita, scornfully.

"No, my child; I mean religion. I took up my cross."

"I should say so, and cross enough he has been. A bear is
amiability itself compared to him," muttered the girl, looking
curiously at the faded woman, who was rocking herself to and
fro, and fingering the bills on her knee with trembling flutter.
She was trying to muster courage to say something which she
felt would be ill received by the daughter who had so suddenly
found her tongue and used it so brashly.

"Perdita, stay a second, child. I want to mention to you—
you can have a beautiful gown, if you will consent to take it."

"How, mother?" asked the girl, wheeling about with her
head up and her eyes flashing; "tell me how."

" Mrs. Slaughton appeared ; she proposed, she asked me——"
Poor crushed creature ! she could get no farther. She was
almost as afraid of her child to-day as she habitually was of her
husband. The child, too, who had been so passive and obedient ! She could scarcely credit her senses, there was so remarkable a change in her every way—words, looks, and actions—all
strange.

" You refused, mother ; of course you refused. Say yes.
Say yes quickly, or I——"

" Yes, yes, Perdita. I did put aside the offer, though I don't
know what is to be done. Only ten dollars. I can't raise any
more. I've nothing to sell——"

" Not even your child ! You are ready to *give* her away.
But one humiliation is spared me—I'd go in such rags as
served Patient Griselda, before I would put on a thread of
theirs. I thank you for saying *NO*. Come quickly now, and
fetch your key."

Perdita ran swiftly up the garret-stairs, and when the old lady
came panting after her, she found her seated on the floor before
the great chest, leaning her chin in her hand, buried in thought.
After the lid was lifted, she silently watched her turning over
the relics of her own by-gone pleasures, with a strange throb of
pain in her heart. Pretty Violet Wemple had been so gay
in those days ! It seemed a pity to think about it, now that
Violet Hethwaite had forgotten how to be blithe—a mockery
almost of her weary age and heavy burdens.

Nothing was left which could be altered or any way suited
to her changed estate. There were laces, ball-dresses, tumbled
flowers. There was a spencer of amber satin trimmed with
feather bands, but the moth had corrupted the plumes and the
fabric was faded and stained. Violet Wemple had eaten ices in
that garment at the planters' ball ; and a bashful young fellow,
who trembled at sight of her, he worshipped her so, had spilled
a whole saucerful into her lap, and been so overwhelmed with
mortification at his awkwardness, that she had been fain to

comfort him, and so had made matters worse, by being obliged
to refuse to marry him. Cruel Violet Wemple! There was a
pelisse of quilted silk, dark red and heavy, which would not
bear dyeing. That had also a history. There were gauzy fabrics,
such as suit the tropics.

"There, mother! I knew I could find my need," exclaimed
Perdita, pulling out a white muslin dotted all over with crimson
rose-buds embroidered in silk floss. It was a pretty, dainty
robe; scanty, simple, and as quiet and quaint as it could possibly be. "Now let me try it on."

"But you can't wear that old-fashioned thing, and there's not
a piece to alter it with."

"I will wear it as my mother wore it when she was my age.
See how it fits me! There! look close. Am I not like the
girl who had lovers, who went to races, who sat in her box at
the opera, who danced the stars out and saw the day dawn
before she had enough of the pleasure?"

"Oh, deary me! What dreadful talk! Where *did* you get
it?" exclaimed the poor woman, who felt as guilty as a crim-
inal. "It was so long ago, such a dreary while back, it don't
seem as if it ever was. I have repented since then."

"Yes, I believe you—in dust and ashes," thought Perdita,
looking askance at her mother, who went away and sat down
on an old chest and wept silently, covering her face with her
thin, hard hands, spoilt out of all their symmetry by years of
rough usage among coarse household labors.

While the daughter lost herself in strange musings, the worn
wife's memory strayed unbidden among the circumstances of
her youth. The tender petting of her parents, the multiform
kindness of her friends; the sweet, innocent enjoyments of the
old days; the kisses of girl-companions, the fond hugs and
hearty caresses of her schoolfellows; and farther on, the gay
scenes from which she had so hopefully turned to a life full of
promise with one, forsaking the many.

She lifted her eyes to Perdita, who stood erect, proud, defi-
4

ant, gazing off into space, already so far from her monotonous home experiences, from the customs and manners she had been reared into ; so unlike the silent, uncomplaining machine her father's training had striven to make her. The swift retrospect poor Mrs. Hethwaite had just indulged in made her feel with bitterness how happy *she* might have been if she could have been allowed to let her tenderness bubble and play around her family. She had been rebuked and reproved for every such outgo. "Bestow not so much love on the child which may be dead to-morrow—taken away to punish you for your idolatry," had her husband said when he caught her caressing her baby. "God is a jealous God ; fear and tremble before him."

She had been coerced and commanded before them, as they grew up, till she learned to submit to everything, if she might so avoid daily mortification ; and she bent her will, lost it almost, dumbly thankful to escape harshness for herself as well as for them.

"Mother, don't cry !" said Perdita, swiftly turning towards the drooping figure. The soft touch which she laid on the bent shoulder, well used to stoop under heavy burdens, was so unusual and so unexpected, that the poor wife quivered and trembled, and could not at first look up into her daughter's eyes. "Don't cry, I did not mean to hurt you. I feel everything so strange that my world might easily return to chaos. My speech was too rude and fierce. I will not offend again. Will you forgive me, mother ?"

She had never kissed either parent, or been kissed by them, and it did not occur to her that such a caress was possible. Absolute astonishment took possession of her when the crushed, faded woman rose and fluttered up to her, and throwing her lean arms around her neck, pressed her in a close embrace.

"God bless you, my daughter ! Your life cannot be a greater failure than mine has been. God in Heaven bless and help you !"

Perdita's cheek burned with the kiss her mother had left there, even after she was shut up in her room, among her reflections. How mixed, tumultuous, and chaotic they were, I cannot tell you, or what resolutions and purposes she had evolved from them when she put them aside and went down stairs to her daily round of multiform occupations.

CHAPTER IX.

THE NIGHT BEFORE THE WEDDING.

HE lessons were recited for the last time before the great event in the Hethwaite family, and to very little good, notwithstanding the sure-coming examination, when poor scholarship was certain to suffer its penalty. All the young heads were full of the grand doings of the morrow, and it proved how pinched and parsimonious had been their rearing, when so much of their talk ran on the good things they expected to get to eat.

Malcolm had gone to bed, tired out with his half-holiday of bean-threshing in the barn (he had been ordered to do all his lessons in the morning so as to make time for the recreation), and he was sound asleep, dreaming that he had a beautiful pony of his own ; and he had not yet reached the part of the vision where the animal was taken away from him with a high hand by his father, which would have been a natural sequel if he had followed his dream far enough, when he was aroused by a thundering racket, which brought him up wide awake, still weary, and possessed with the unwelcome idea that morning had dawned before he was half rested. It was his father, who rapped on the staircase with his cane, and shouted to him to come down directly. The clatter disturbed little Betty, setting her into a fit of nervous trembling and weeping, which the mother surreptitiously hushed for fear the autocrat might hear her, and come up and hush her after his own pleasant fashion.

While the Parson had sat toasting his feet before the embers, he had espied his high-lows in the corner, having on them "very much land," as the Dutchman said of his muddy shoes. Now, he had ordered the lad to clean his high-lows before he retired, which order had been neglected in the stress of the afternoon work. He very properly required the culprit to dress and appear before him armed and equipped with brush and blacking; and he also rated him soundly while he did the job.

Malcolm scrubbed away, and his face scowled with the rebellious anger he was full of to overflowing. He also muttered and "slatted things" a good deal. His improper behavior earned him a profuse allowance of cuffs and blows, and promises of a "sound flogging" the next time he was caught napping, and his "chores" not done.

His duty to his son thus well performed, the old gentleman retired, and the lad crept back to his bed, but I am afraid he did not say any prayers for his father after he turned in.

Teddy and Perdita, who had been witnesses of this highly proper exercise of parental dominion, and had exchanged significant looks, were left alone at last, being permitted this once to sit out their elders and betters, because of domestic necessity in the shape of apples to pare for the weekly pies. They were silent for a long time, sharing the labor, and each busy with troublesome thoughts.

" It is a cruel thing for you, this marriage," said Teddy at last. " You have hindered me from saying my mind, but I knew it would have to come out."

" No, Teddy, not more cruel than the lives I leave behind me. Poor Malcolm is in a sweet state to get refreshing repose and comforting dreams, is he not? I know right well t.ere have been sore hearts under this roof all these years, and I begin to see things very clearly. Don't trouble about me, Teddy; remember, there will be one less mouth to fill, a smaller amount of codfish to buy. I have a healthy appetite, you know. I want to eat a great deal; I love meat."

She smiled while she talked, but the youngster's eyes filled with tears.

"Yes, I hope and expect," she went on, "that my going to that place will be better for you all. I can speak my mind to father when I am independent of him, and you will find he will listen to me. I look to set you loose from the farm drudgery, and to place you in the good life you dream of. I don't know how it is to be done, but I shall be able to find out. When one has the will, one can do much, I am quite sure, if father is not around to sit down on everything. And, Teddy, do you realize it? I am going to get rid of father! Dolly will be old enough to teach a school next year, and she'll grow steadier when I'm no longer here to mend her tatters and gloss over her scrapes. Malcolm will be ruined with a little more of the treatment he has to bear. I mean to hunt him a clerkship; I had rather he were apprenticed to any honest trade than subject to such indignities as he has just gone through. He is bound to run away, or sink into a sneak before long. Billy ought to be among lads of his age, having good times, and I intend he shall be."

"But you think all for the others, and not a mite for yourself," said Teddy, mournfully studying her face and trying to guess the source of its strange expression.

"No need for that. *I* have been thought for by others," replied Perdita bitterly. "I am not such a machine as they suppose me. I might have rebelled, if I had not seen something ahead which I meant to accomplish."

"But Mr. Slaughton must be a queer man. He must know you do not in the least care for him."

"Care for *him!* why should I? He wants a housekeeper,

a woman to pour his tea and wait on his friends, and be a
governess to those Vance children. All that has been carefully
set forth by his mother. I am well trained as teacher, you
know, and really, it would have astonished you to hear how
many questions have been asked and answered as to my ability
in cooking, clear-starching, brewing, making beds, sweeping
rooms, and so on. If I wanted to find out a servant's capacities, I should know exactly what to demand."

"It's a burning shame! If I had a daughter, I would not
let her go to any man's house on such terms. I wonder father
don't forbid it."

"Forbid it, Teddy! You should have heard the voice in
which he expounded his sovereign will and pleasure. If I had
stood a slave in the market, and he the Great Mogul, he could
not have assumed a more despotic demeanor. Oh, no; father
has been all his life writing sermons to prove foreordination
and predestination; but I notice he don't scruple to give events
a push to speed them to his liking, when he sees a good place
to get hold. Outside my teaching, he will be only too glad to
be quit of me. It does not occur to him that I lighten mother's
burdens; he never seems to think she bears any. He must
see, if he has half sense, that I should get up some day and
throw off the hard yoke he has pressed upon my neck."

"Mother ought to know better, anyhow! Women should
stand up for each other."

"Poor mother! her life is all such hard lines, she never
learned to stand up for herself. If she had, we might have seen
better times. She feels glad to think I shall be rich and grand,
and I can't help thinking she is thankful for the chance to put
me outside of this house, when we have witnessed her thousand
humiliations. Teddy, mother kissed me yesterday!"

"Kissed you, Perdita! how did it feel? A mother-kiss!

"It burns on my cheek, right there, Teddy! If I had been
ever so rebellious up to that instant, I would not have raised
another word of opposition—no, not for the world. It felt

like the seal of my freedom. Oh, yes, she talks all the while about the better days in store for me. I cannot find the heart to interrupt her. I can't help thinking what a good life Violet Wemple had a right to, if only she had had the luck to marry a *man*, and had never set eyes on father!"

"But father is not cruel to mother," said Teddy reflecting. He was retrospectively considering, and failed to find the causes of intense grievance which inflamed his sister's mind.

"I don't know what you call cruel. *I* call it cruel to make a drudging slave of a woman, never giving her a kind word, nor a tender look for all her hardships; to make her feed a lot of children on nothing; to kill herself mending old clothes, and scrubbing bare floors, while he is shut up scribbling away at what he calls sermons, that are only fit to light the fire with when they are done. If *I* was a man, and had picked out a woman and promised to cherish her, I'd take off my coat and go to work, and I'd earn white bread for her to eat. I wouldn't starve her on rye stuff not fit for pigs, and codfish; and I'd leave off scribbling till I had won the right to amuse myself. I wouldn't have a family if I was not man enough to make life endurable for them. Owner of all things, indeed! we might have decent clothes, at least, if he had had the courage of a flea!"

"Perdita, I think the man who has picked you out had best be smart."

"I have not been picked out by a man, Teddy. I have been bargained for by a couple of old women."

"I don't like to hear you talk so. You don't seem like yourself."

"I am telling out loud what has been fretting and angering me, all these years, ever since I was old enough to see the meaning of things. I say father is a coward, afraid to face the world; he's lazy! he's not willing to work with his hands; he is a sneak, willing to owe his comforts to the hardships and self-denials of a frail woman. I despise father! Yes, I despise

him !   I don't see any single trait in him to respect or admire.
He never loved one of us ; he never did anything to make us
happy ; and he thinks we ought to be very grateful to him for
our existence ! a tremendous blessing to be born into
his house, to be sure !   Why, he whipped you with a raw-hide
not five years ago, as no man ought to beat a dog, and had
family prayers after he got through."

"So he did, Perdita.   The old gentleman has a heavy hand
with a stick.   I remember I threw up my arms in agony ; and
he thought I meant rebellion, and he did lay it on.   He
called it 'lacing my jacket !'   I could count the laces when
he got through.   But I don't hold malice ; his intentions were
good.   Oh, yes, he meant well."

" He meant to work off his unpleasantness on a defenceless
boy !   And he did it, because there was nobody to prevent
him.   Yes, I *hate* father !   I am glad to go out of his house ;
and I'll never rest till I set the others free.   When he whips
Betty, I feel boiling hot all over : I could tear him to atoms !
It makes my head swim, I hate him so."

" Why, Perdita, how you look.   I am glad you don't hate me.
You are too hard on father.   He is a just man ; he thinks that
is the way to bring up children.   The fact is patent to *my*
mind ; he does by us as *he* was done by.   He had just such
hard licks as he gives us ; he believes firmly in the oil of birch
for dressing down young hides."

Teddy laughed ruefully.   " I won't deny he is severe.   I've
felt it in wheals all over my body.   I seem to feel them now.
Though lost to sight, to memory dear ; but you musn't hate
father, Perdita ; think how much he knows ; what a linguist he ·
is ! what a botanist ! there isn't a plant in the country he can't
name ; and what a thorough grounding he has given us."

" Yes, Teddy, he has educated our heads at the expense of
our hearts.   And do you know where he got all his books ?
He bought them with mother's money, which she was so weak as
to give up to him as soon as he married her.   And she packed

and unpacked his library every move they made, out to the Chocktaws and back again ; and that is all the good she ever got out of the little bank stock her father left to her."

" But what good we have got out of the volumes ! If we had been amused and petted, do you suppose we should have ever learned almost by heart all that old history and poetry, and cosmical lore that we used to dive into ? Our hearts are all right, as witness how you, our elder, are planning and hoping for us, and forgetting herself."

" Yours is, anyhow, Teddy. I don't know just now as I have any, I feel so disturbed and unmoored. You see I am not able to help going over my child-life here under this old roof, as I am about to turn my back on it, and I get a little wrathy thinking over the dreary grind it has been : when we might just as well have had good times. It is not the poverty, Teddy ; a dinner of herbs, or codfish, where love is allowed to show itself, might be the dearest, pleasantest meal in the world. There, cheer up, good Teddy ; don't look as if all things were going back to chaos, as if the last link was broken that bound me to thee ; I am more closely linked to the brothers and sisters I am going to leave, than ever before. Good-night, Teddy. What a bright yellow moon ! how the slanting beams glint and gleam among those noble oaks, mighty and broad-armed, making their dark crimson leaves shine like gold. 'Tis a grand old grove. Mother says the twentieth of September is a good day to be married on. Don't you think great Sol ought to pour down his glory to-morrow, if there's any truth in the old saying, " Blessed is the bride whom the sun shines on " ? I am a unique sort of bride, about to be united to a unique sort of suitor in *holy* matrimony, by a most unique priest. I wonder how I shall feel to be blessed by father, and married to the man of his choice."

" I have a great mind to cry, Perdita, to hear you run on so," said Teddy, wiping his eyes.

" Oh, no, good brother, don't cry. Laugh, as I do."

4*

CHAPTER X.

MALCOLM'S DANCING BEAR.

T was indeed a bright and beautiful day. Whatever benison there might be in joyous sunshine, which kindled the ripening foliage into flame and bathed the old parsonage in a flood of effulgence, was the glorification of Perdita Hethwaite's bridal morning.

The mother and wife was out of favor. She had been discovered by her lord and master hiding on the cellar stairs, bitterly weeping, and had been rated for her weak, silly behavior, and told that if it had been Dolly he had caught acting so, he would have severely punished her.

She had not the heart to sit at the head of her table when the morning meal was ready, and had absented herself from that family reunion, remaining absent till summoned by Billy.

"Father says come to breakfast, mother."

" Tell him I don't want any, Billy."

Presently the boy returned. " Father says he shan't have prayers till you've eaten your breakfast."

The poor lady knew what that meant, and hastily composing her features, she appeared in the room, sitting down on the nearest chair, like a culprit.

" Mrs. Hethwaite, you have eaten no breakfast," announced the Parson in a pompous voice, gripping and ungripping his great, horny hands, and grimacing horribly as he surveyed her.

" I do not want any."

" I desire you to partake, Mrs. Hethwaite. I shall not proceed with family worship till you do."

The wife looked at him an instant, and then cast her eyes

down. She knew he was quite obstinate enough to keep his word; she had been humiliated and coerced for years and years, and was used to it; but somehow it came hard on this day, when her eldest-born was to be taken away from her, and a dreary loneliness of heart mingled with her mortification. She rose and stepped to the table and ate, standing, a few mouthfuls—enough to give sign and token of obedience; and, with her children's eyes upon her, she retreated to her corner and sat down and folded her arms, while the Parson read the daily chapter. And then they all sang *at* the hymn, and knelt for the prayer; and then they separated, after this fresh lesson to the young people on the value their father set on his wife, and also on himself.

Perdita went to the door and looked out over the hills glowing and flushing in the beauteous sunshine.

"'He maketh the sun shine on the just and the unjust,' so there is no reason why *this house* should be in darkness," said she aloud.

"What are you saying?" asked her father.

"I was drawing a conclusion from the lesson we got this morning; and I am going upstairs now to say a private prayer to follow yours that the year of jubilee may come when all the oppressed shall go free."

She did not wait to be questioned further; and though the Parson was too much bound up in his own importance, and too little in the habit of troubling himself about his children's thoughts or feelings to take the full weight of her thrust, he was astonished and displeased at her tone and attitude, and looked after her and snorted, with his mouth open and his thick underlip hanging, till she was out of sight.

Dolly and Malcolm had gathered a host of gay leaves, with which they planned to build a nuptial bower in the best room, after the pattern of one the girl had found described in a novel which she had borrowed from Almira Pratt, and kept hidden under her pillow for secret devourance.

Dolly did a wicked thing, of course, to disobey her good papa, and enjoy slyly such forbidden pleasures, and her naughtiness did not end there either, because she sat demurely by and heard her father tell a brother clergyman that not one of his children had ever read a romance, and she did not contradict his statement, although she had that very day finished a third perusal of "The Children of the Abbey," and had on hand two more she was longing to get at—"Thaddeus of Warsaw" and the "Three Spaniards."

The mother had not given them permission to fashion the bower, neither did she tell them they might peruse fiction; but she passively allowed them to go on, saying nothing; and in fact she had stealthily peeped at the pretty bell cunningly made of moss and white feverfew, and admired it very much.

The best part of the structure was completed before the Parson discovered what they were doing, having gone to his study after Perdita left him, and commenced a sermon suggested by the text she had uttered in his hearing, which clearly proved that the more rain there was wasted on the unjust in this life, the less refreshing coolness they would get in the next.

Whether it was the sound of their hammers and voices, or the suspicion of a good time somewhere on the premises which he had not sanctioned, something disturbed the dreary flow of his dreary arguments, and he felt moved to descend and investigate.

"A pretty piece of work, truly!" exclaimed he after a survey of the leafy arbor. "What sort of a place do I inhabit? Is it Vanity Fair, or the home of a sober Christian minister? Pray let me know what this rubbishing fuss is all about."

"We thought we could make a pleasant look for Perdita's wedding, father," said Dolly in the humble drawl with which the Hethwaites were apt to speak to the paterfamilias. "It don't cost anything," she added, thinking this a clinching argument.

" Did your mother give you leave to commit this folly ? "
" No, sir ! " chorussed both hurriedly, and the haste they showed
was a sorry comment on his husbandhood.

"I ain glad to hear it ! Now pull down the stuff, and throw
it out on the dirt-heap. *My* daughter will take upon her the
marriage vows as befits the solemn promises she will make
before her God, and not with vain shows and profane music,
like a child of Belial. Make haste, I say ! Fall to, both of
you ! and when next you desire to erect a booth fit for monkeys
or dancing bears, you had better get my permission first."

Shamefaced and disheartened, the young workers despoiled
their temple under his severe scrutiny, which bored into them
till the last bright branch was dragged away, and every stray
leaf swept out of sight, when the Parson departed with his
heavy clumpy tread. It was lucky for them that he did not look
behind him at their rebellious faces, nor hear their wrathful
mutterings.

"Dancing bears ! " growled Malcolm. "I know one old
bear I'd like mighty well to make dance on a hot plate."

Their defeat and drooping downheartedness so dampened
the spirits of the young ones, that they could hardly for a time
admire the beautiful cakes which Mrs. Slaughton had sent
down, nor the ham, nor the jellies.

As for the Parson, he strided about in his black clothes
when the few guests were arrived, and "bow-wowed" at them
and looked askance at everybody, as f somehow his great
possessions had got distributed among them by mistake, and
he was trying to identify his property.

He arranged the little table at one end of the room, with the
Bible and hymn-book atop of it as if there was going to be a
funeral, and he made Perdita get ready a whole hour before the
time, and sit down in front of it as if she was the corpse.

Mrs. Hethwaite, in her best gown, looked worried and
anxious, and her worn face flushed as she walked noiselessly
here and there, placing and replacing the chairs, and dusting

the furniture ; too uneasy to sit still, too flurried to converse
with the friends.   The corners of her mouth trembled, and she
wiped her watery eyes, as she glanced from time to time at the
man who had promised to love and cherish Violet Wemple.

Perhaps she was thinking of the breakfast she had eaten ;
perhaps she was recalling her own wedding with the young
minister, full of hope and strength, and of how he had said and
said again that he loved her above all things.

That was the man ! that sour-faced old Parson, stalking
about half bent, with frowning visage cut into a series of paren-
theses which enclosed his mouth :

He did not look any more like her *lover* than the pinched,
grizzled, faded creature the old looking-glass showed her,
looked like the rosy bride he took.

She felt sorry for the children too, who had all been called
in and ordered to sit down, as if it was a meeting.   She wished
they could have had a frolic out of the wedding.

She looked at her daughter sitting so silent and still, so uninterested and indifferent, till the Parson scolded Betty and
bade her go and take her place among the others, and not be
hanging on to her sister like a silly baby.   She was quiet even
then, and kept her eyes on the floor ; but the mother knew a
little what a storm was raging under the outward calm.   She
knew it by the anger she herself felt and dared not show.

She heaved a deep sigh.   What if, after all, the girl should
be worse off for this marriage ?   Only exchanging one tyrant for
another, from whom there could be no escape while life lasted.
But no ; all *her* unhappiness, all *her* discomforts had been born
of poverty.   If her husband had been well off and easy in his
mind, he would have been kind and indulgent, so she believed,
remembering how his misfortunes had soured and changed
him.

Perdita would be rich and have enough of everything.   Comforting her poor heart with this certainty, she tried to be brisk
and look pleasant, and jerked Dolly by the shoulder, bidding her

sit up straight and not make an ampersand of herself, and added :

"Try to behave pretty, and may be your turn will come some day, and you'll get a rich husband too ! "

CHAPTER XI.

LOOKING AHEAD WITH A VENGEANCE.

R. SLAUGHTON did not arrive at the mansion house more than a couple of hours before the time fixed for the ceremony. In fact, an anxious thought had flitted through the dame's mind—"what if he should not come at all ?" and she seized on him almost before she had made him welcome.

"Come here, my son. I have something particular to say to you."

He suffered himself to be led by the arm (Sam was so easily led) to a small nook over the dining-room—the scene of his youthful exploits and experiences ; and as he went, he inly wondered if his letter had after all taken effect, and the old lady was making preparations to break it gently to him, the contract having fallen through.

"Samuel ! this is the place where you used to sleep. I've come up here many a night to tuck you into bed and hear your little prayers, and you used to fetch in every living thing on the farm into 'em—Bose and the steers and the old speckled hen. You was a real kind-hearted little boy, Sammy ; and if you thought I felt bad, you'd take on and hug and kiss me

mighty sweet and affectionate.   Now, here are all your little
toys and your books and your first drawings.   I kept them
every one.   I've swept and dusted the place myself, because I
could not bear to let anybody in among these precious things ;
and I used to visit this room every day while you was wander-
ing around the world, and ask God to take care of you and
keep you out of temptation.   I want all to stay just as it is
here, till little Sammy is old enough to have it.   I want you
to bring him up in the nurture and admonition of the Lord—in
the faith of his fathers.   Have him learn his catechism, and
' Though I am young, a little one,' and all the pretty hymns you
used to say at my knee ; and I hope his hair will curl as yours
did.   I may die before he gets to understand much—very
likely I shall.   I fully expect to—my summons may come any
night ; but I want you to tell Sammy that his grandma quilted
this spread, and braided this rug, and kept all these things together on purpose for him."

The dame was so solemn and serious, and so fully occupied
with her explanations and instructions, that her son could not
laugh at her, nor toss back any of the teazing speeches which
rose to his lips.

" Mother, why will you talk so much about dying ?   Such a
brisk, lively lady !   You are likely to outlive us all, Slowgo
included.   Yes, yes ! you will be too many for everybody,
years to come.   Why, you are hardly in your prime."

" This is a beautiful world, Samuel, and there's plenty of
work to keep me busy as long as it is allotted for me to stay in
it ; but I felt like speaking my mind about little Sammy to-day,
because this seems to be the proper time.   I have finished
now, and you must make haste, or you will be too late for your
own wedding."

" Father used to say, ' Late to breakfast, late to heaven,'
when I did not get up in time.   He never admonished me
about this other affair."

" Yes, I remember, he did have to make that speech pretty

often. Men don't generally want much hurrying up when
about to approach the altar, I expect."

Mr. Slaughton turned and glanced at her, but he did not
speak what rose to his lips, she looked so eager and expectant.
He went to his room and locked his door, and proceeded to
the business of dressing—thinking about his mother, and his
pictures ; anything but the approaching ceremony of which he
was to be centre figure, and which he desired to consider
nothing in particular to him.

His room was well stored with curious and rare treasures,
such as bachelors are apt to collect. Elaborately cut meer-
schaums, nargilehs, cigar-holders, cameos, carved work, and
canes. On a hook in one corner hung a Sciote dress, and over
it an ancient helmet. A Persian rug, hallowed by the bended
knees of devout fire-worshippers, lay before a Turkish divan.
On the mantel was a little whitewood model of the Norwe-
gian carriole in which he had made the Ava Saxa journey to see
the midnight sun, and beside it a beautiful cabinet of uncut
gems. Some pictures adorned the walls ; but among them no
women's faces, not even a Magdalen.

Mr. Slaughton's dressing-case was open before him—a costly
thing, as rich and complete in its appointments as possible—
the gift of his travelling companion, one Chandos Goldsmith,
upon whom his thoughts had been much running since the
queer complication of his affairs. "What would Chandy say ?"
"How would Chandy look at such and such epochs of the
transaction ?" being questions often suggested to his mind ;
and the mental replies which presented themselves, as based on
the absent gentleman's character and habits, caused him to
smile in sympathy with the broad grin he seemed to see on
that merry face, which mirrored mirth so readily. Rather grim,
'tis true, the smiles became on Sam's countenance when he
took in the fact that it was *he himself*—Samuel Slaughton !
who was billed to play the fool or bridegroom (synonymous
terms they appeared to his mind) in this absurd comedy about to

be put before a select and appreciative audience, down at the
old parsonage.

Mr. Slaughton's personal appointments were of the very
choicest; his suspenders of embroidered silk were held to their
office by gold buckles; his sleeve-buttons and bosom studs
were of diamonds; two neck-ties lay on his table—one of
creamy white, the other that shade of rich violet which the lady
he loved had been used to wear.   He had laid them out for
selection, both being hues he was accustomed to don for festive
occasions, and his eyes rested on them ever and anon while he
stepped about; and as they did so, he was certainly *not* thinking of Perdita Hethwaite.   His stockings were of silk, as was
the vest on the bed, and the black suit he was about to assume
was as handsome and modish as possible.

Mr. Slaughton had a hair-brush in each hand.   The handle
of one was ivory, and the other ebony inlaid with pearl.   Judg-
ing from the way in which he was scrubbing his devoted head
with them, it seemed that he was fighting some disagreeable
subject of cogitation; and when he paused his face was red,
and his light hair was tossed every which way, while he laid his
fists, armed with the brushes, on the table before him, and
leaned forward, looking attentively at them, and he uttered half
aloud what seemed the focussed result of his physical and mental manipulations.

"I shall be obliged to have a little talk with the young
woman the very first opportunity, and let her plainly understand
that the romance of *my* life is over, and it won't be of any use
to try to get up the smallest sort of a tenderness for me, because I cannot return it, and I don't mean to try."

Although his vanity had gotten a terrible blow, his self-love
a severe shock several years since, when he had wished for the
woman who did not wish for him, there was still enough of the
leaven of manishness to leaven quite a lump of conceit, and
make him apprehend the certainty of positions and scenes
where he might be the victim of attentions—perhaps also of

reproaches mingled with tears, from the maid who was about to assume his name and state.

I don't suppose any kind of experience could shake the idea out of any man that the wondrous spell of his daily presence is not certain to be dangerous to the peace of any woman.

Samuel certainly looked very handsome when his toilette was completed, and he finished his preparations as elaborately as if it had been Sabrina Bradshaw who awaited his coming down at the old parsonage. In fact, he could not help stopping to dream one short dream—of how they two would have looked, standing hand in hand before the altar—and he rolled the towel with which he had been drying his face into a hard ball, and dashed it into a corner, as he growled :

" Jove ! what ever possessed me to let mother push me into this abominable predicament ? I'm too easy by half, that is what is the trouble. I'm always letting people knock me about to suit their plans. I'm just like a shuttle-cock, now here, now there. Such a bore as it is to stand out and make a rumpus ! But I never in my life expected my complaisance to carry me thus far ! I did not really suppose she could take me by the hand and walk me up to matrimony as she used to lead me to school ! It is so confoundedly absurd that I could find much food for mirth in the performance, if it was any other fellow who played first fool. What a tale Chandy would make out of the circumstance ! And besides, who shall be able to compute the loss to the farming community which this affair shall entail ? because I really did intend to study :

> " What makes the richest tilth ?
> Beneath what signs
> To plow, and when to match my elms and vines ?
> What care with flocks, and what with herds agrees ?
> And all the management of frugal bees."

Although Mr. Slaughton purposed to be magnanimous towards the other actor in the approaching ceremony, in so far as to give her fair and timely warning, he rather doubted whether or no she was worth much thought or trouble. She had paid no heed to his letter, and must be deliberate in choosing, or at least accepting the place in his house on such terms as would be extremely distasteful to a sensitive girl ; and as he recited the couplet from old Melbourne's lines, he dismissed from his mind his agricultural plans, and also all responsibility for the future of the Parson's daughter, so repugnant and distasteful to him in every way.   He shrugged his shoulders, and made a disgusted grimace as the scene in the keeping-room— when Perdita had stood silent and apart with Betty in her arms, rose before him ; and he also gave his white glove such a vicious pull that he divorced the thumb from the fingers, and disabled it for service.   A good deal of muttering ensued while he selected a fresh pair, and he went down stairs with the perpendicular line between his eyebrows deepened into a most unseemly frown, for a happy bridegroom.

" Come along, Sammy !" called out the old lady, as soon as she caught sight of him.   " We are none too early."

" To my mind we could not be too late ;" and he looked hard at her as he added : " Mark my words, now, mother ; I tell you you will not find the play worth the candle."

CHAPTER XII.

"LOVE ME IF I LIVE, LOVE ME IF I DIE."

HE marriage service was short. The two stood up before the old Parson, who cleared his husky throat and pronounced them husband and wife.

Perdita lifted her eyes in positive affright. She could scarcely believe what she heard and saw. Kindness, almost tenderness, in the voice she was accustomed to know hard and harsh; and benevolence which nearly amounted, to love illumining the stern face; and—could it be? Yes; there were tears in the eyes deep-set and forbidding, where she had seen reproof and displeasure, but never love; never sympathy; scarcely the forbearance of the judge who hesitates to pronounce sentence on the culprit.

A flood of burning crimson dashed over her cheeks with the strange sight, and she threw a swift glance at Teddy. He had thoughts only for the friend he was losing, and was gazing sadly at her. He had not seen the incredible phenomenon; and when the Parson took his daughter's hand in his, and said in a solemn voice:

"The Lord bless you, my daughter! The God of your fathers be with you and make you a good and faithful wife." She shuddered. A blessing from those lips sounded so unfamiliar, it felt almost like a curse, and her thoughts rebelliously flew towards her poor mother, who had been a good and faithful wife to him. There she sat in a corner. What a pitiful wreck the goodness and faithfulness had reduced her to be!

As soon as he loosed his grasp she stepped away from her husband without a word or look in his direction. Their hands had been joined, but no electric thrill had passed from heart to heart—dead fingers could scarcely have been colder or more irresponsive than hers as she placed them in his, extended to receive them by the order of the clergyman. And he surrendered the little hand without the least pressure, although he had just promised to love and cherish its owner. Such idle words were scarcely ever uttered, as that marriage vow, conveying no meaning to either of them ; speaking no purpose of their wills, no compact even of their understandings. The husband offered no salute to his bride ; she did not observe the omission. She would have been shocked and indignant if he had kissed her. It would have appeared to her a public insult, an outrageous presumption. She was in no such danger, however ; and the bridegroom's lips, drawn up in the centre and dropped at the corners, were in no shape for tenderness, or even politeness ; and his head was lifted stiff and stubborn, while his " eyelids looked straight on and his eyes right before him." He did not seem to observe the swift and eager motion with which his bride turned away from his side, nor the hasty tread of her light feet as she hurried towards the object, source, and centre of her thoughts and longings—little Betty, who had been quite chatty and gay in the early part of the proceedings, fluttering about her sister, chirping in her ear, and nestling close to her, and had been sternly ordered to go away and " keep still."

Such a festive and cheerful admonition ! so suited to a wedding occasion ! Parson Hethwaite's youngest nearly wilted under it ; she crept to a far corner and crouched there, palpitating and grieving, apart from her best friend, and watching with eager and affrighted eyes the stranger who stood beside her. No man had ever stood by her Perdita like that before, and the sight filled the trembling mite with terror and dread ; and when at length she saw the face she loved and trusted bending over her, and heard the lips which always spoke truth whispering to her, she began to weep.

" Betty, stand up," said Perdita quietly ; "don't sob ! don't cry! hush! Father's mouth is open; he is looking over here at you, and he will send you upstairs, and then you won't have any of the nice ice cream. Come out with me. I am not father's slave any more; he can't hinder my going where I choose, and I choose to get away from these people as fast as I can."

As she passed from the room, holding the child's hand, the Parson eyed her severely, but he did not call her back; and as soon as she was in the open air under the oaks, she picked up the mite and held her fast locked in her arms.

"Betty, listen to me," said she; "pay attention to what I say. I am going to leave you for a little while. I shall soon come back again; and till I do come, you must be brave. Keep out of father's way all you can. Mother will dress you, and you must not trouble her much; she has enough to do. And when I am here again, I will tell you something very nice."

The child clung to her, pale and affrighted. "Don't go, Perdita, and leave Betty," she whispered; "don't go."

"I must—only a little while. There! they are calling me. Remember now! Be quiet, and don't make any fuss when I go. You know what father does when you make a fuss. Now come, and Dolly shall give you some cake and things."

When she returned to the guests her husband was standing among them, looking bored and disdainful, and his mother was bustling about, helping the refreshments in such an ubiquitous style that Mrs. Hethwaite was quite thrust aside and left out; but she did not seem to mind; she was used to being undervalued and suppressed. And when the widow came with a plate full of eatables and asked her if she would have some, she meekly took it and said "Thank you," and ate the cake as unassumingly as if it had been somebody else's daughter's wedding, in which she had no interest.

The married pair tasted nothing; and as nobody was very talkative or cheerful, it was even more lugubrious than weddings generally are, and no one was inclined to linger long among the festivities.

"A very handsome couple; indeed they are," said Mrs. Pratt to Mrs. Batt; "as good-looking a pair as ever I saw."

Perdita heard the remark, but she did not apply it to herself; why should she? Nobody had ever told her she was pretty. She—a "vessel of wrath born under sin, totally depraved." Of what consequence were looks to her father's child? As to her husband, she had not once lifted a glance to his face; she was not in the least troubling herself about him. Swiftly as her thoughts were whirling, not one of them stopped upon him. She caught sight of a lonesome, dreary, forlorn woman in the corner, and she went and bent over her, putting out both her hands and seizing the trembling arms which lay close locked above the poor heart which had suffered so much!

"Good-by, mother," said she. "You kissed me Monday; may I kiss you now? If you had kissed us oftener, we might have had better times; but I know it was no fault of yours. Don't lay up my badness against me, if you can forget it. There's Betty! watch her as close as you can. Can't you smile once, mother? I'm sorry 'I——"

A sob was gathering in her throat, tears were ready to burst from her eyes; but she forced them back, and at the sound of Dame Slaughton's brisk voice, she wheeled quickly around, and stood in quiet silence, while she waited for further orders.

"We are all ready to go now, Perdita; don't you see my Samuel holding out his arm for you to take?"

She looked scornfully at the arm, which certainly was not as yet offered her; but she placed the tips of her fingers upon it, when her husband approached with an indifferent bow, and she stepped out of the old room by his side, turning her back on her girl-life without regrets for its past or hopes for her future. At least none appeared in her dark, set face, her still, emotionless manner; no tears, no smiles, no flutter; only dumb, uninterested obedience, which submitted to the sway of others.

CHAPTER XIII.

A TIME TO LOVE AND A TIME TO HATE.

HERE'S a gentleman in the library," said Hannah to Mr. Slaughton, as the bridal company reached the door of the mansion-house. "He's just this instant come."

"Yes, old boy, I am arrived at this identical point and period of time," exclaimed a familiar voice, which had always been welcome to Mr. Slaughton's ears up to this moment; "and hours too late at that, it seems."

And handsome Chandy came out, and offered his hand to his boyhood's friend, the companion of his youth, the sharer of his travels—through all which years they had been like Damon and Pythias, David and Jonathan, and others.

"Chandos Goldsmith!" exclaimed the bridegroom, with a slight shade of chagrin or annoyance beneath his cordial welcome. "Well, this *is* a surprise!"

"I should say so! Why didn't you let a fellow know? You might have knocked me down with a feather when I found you had gone to be married. Pray present me to your bride."

"Of course," said Mr. Slaughton, getting red, and turning very slowly and unwillingly towards Perdita, who stood in the doorway, not yet having crossed the threshold. Perhaps she meant to stand there till she was bidden to enter.

"Yes—ahem! Mrs.—ughf—ughf—Slaughton, Mr. Goldsmith. Make yourself at home, Chandos, old chap."

"Thank you; I will. Most happy to see Sam's wife, I assure you, madam," answered Chandy, in his frank, pleasant voice.

5

" I am lucky to be just in the nick of time for congratulations, Sam ! Of course it is *en règle* for me to salute the bride.   My gracious ! to think of kissing Sam's wife !   That is a happiness I never expected."

Taking the permission for granted, he tasted the girl's lips before she knew what he was about, while the husband stood back, quite as red and embarrassed as the recipient of the kiss.

Perdita was utterly abashed and astonished, and knew not what to say or do, being entirely ignorant that such a custom obtained, or such a liberty could be thought of, much less seized on as a matter of course.   She looked at the offender as if she thought somebody ought to kill him on the spot, and she had two minds to do the deed herself, only waiting to see how the others would behave ; and she inly wondered if a truly chosen and well-beloved wife could have been so treated before them all with impunity.

"I call it unkind of Sam," remarked Chandy easily, " to steal such a march on me ; but you see my good fortune favors me in spite of his churlishness, and I feel that we may be excellent friends.   What say you, Mrs. Slaughton—will you enter me on your list?   I never needlessly set foot on a worm ; so you perceive I am eligible, according to Cowper."

Even while he was running on thus, Chandy could not help observing that something was out of joint, and he tried to divine what was the subject of discord, and what lay beneath Perdita's stillness.   Was she shy, or furious ?   Was she angry with his presumption, or out of temper with her husband ?   And he scanned the group curiously, while he blandly chatted as if he saw around him the most commonplace of wedding parties.

Mr. Slaughton threw open the parlor door, and waving his hand towards Perdita with a sort of compulsory politeness, invited her to enter, which she did, followed by the guest, and walked towards the window, before which she placed herself, turning her back upon them all and gazing down the road which she had come.

The dame pattered away, and presently returned intent on business.

"Come, Perdita," said she with a gesture of hurry. "Come, and I will show you the rooms and the presses and things, and you can take off your bonnet and get ready for supper. I don't suppose you feel very hungry. I don't, after eating cake, and ham, and all that. But the men-folks will want their tea— they always do. I think men are continually hungry; they live to eat, while women eat to live, which is just the difference between them and us. They are devoted to creature comforts, and it seems to be our principal business to pamper them. Well, we must let our cares be our pleasures, as Mr. Slaughton used to say to me when I had so much to do that I felt fit to drop. Yes, I've worked hard in my day; but I mean to take a rest now, *that* I do."

They had ascended the stairs while the dame was talking, and she pushed open the door of the front room before she had finished all she had to say about her expectations.

"Here you are, my dear! and welcome home! This is the scene of your future cares and labors, and you will not find time to hang heavier here than down yonder. Solomon praised up capable women; though I dare say he had a good mess of lazy ones amongst his sixty thousand wives. We've all got to work; the odds of working in one place or another don't count much. You've got to work here after this, and I shall see that you have all that you can do on your hands, I promise you. I know you will be pleased to be busy. You have been an industrious girl, and now you are going to be an industrious woman. I shall send immediately for Sallie's children, and I forewarn you, you will find your minutes full. Such healthy, active young ones as they are, overflowing with life and spirits! Here are the presses, and these are the closets. I will give you a list of their contents to-morrow. You see they are well stored with handsome things; they need good care; and I will talk over my method with you. I like to

have the house move like clock-work, and your mother tells
me your habits are order itself. This room back of yours has
been my son's ever since he got to be a man—though, to be
sure, he hasn't used it any great deal, being all the while travelling about. He'll stay at home now, and settle down. You see,
it is full of costly notions." She stepped forward and pushed
open the door, and went in with an air of pride as she spoke.
"Some of them, money foolishly spent, to my mind ; but, as it
was spent, they have got to be taken care of. You will have
to dust and sweep in here yourself. I always did. I was
always afraid Hannah might break something. I think it is a
good plan for a woman to take care of her own room. I know
you are used to it; so it will come easy to you. Now, out
here in the north wing, are some rooms for the children ; you
may fix them up as you have a mind to. I shan't interfere.
You will have to teach them—the children, I mean—and dress
them and see to them. Your mother says you pretty near
brought up your little sister, and did a good deal of teaching
for the others ; so it will make it seem quite like home to you.
Well, I shall have to go down now and see to the supper. I
suppose you won't feel like helping to-night. So you can put
up your clothes and tidy round ; and then you had better go
and sit down in the parlor. You don't need to begin *too*
smart."

After the dame pattered away, Perdita took off her wraps,
smoothed her hair, and looked about her. It was a very pretty
room which she had been told was hers, over the front parlor,
opening southward into the garden, and east on the shrubbery
and trees, and beyond giving a vista of the road up which she
had just come from the parsonage. It was nicely furnished, and
every way complete and handsome. But though her eyes roamed
over the chairs and tables, though she stepped to the window
and gazed out upon the wide prospect—"the orchard, the
meadow, the deep-tangled wildwood "—there was no pride of
possession in her face ; no visions of grandeur and ease rose

before her mind. She was busy with a purpose; her steady
eyes showed it, her firmly closed mouth, and the defiant poise
of her head, full of will and resolution.

A tale she had heard once, came to her memory, of a man
who turned to his bride as soon as the ceremony was finished,
and said, "Yesterday you was a poor seamstress! to-day you
are Mrs. Johnson Jones." "*This man*," she reflected bitterly,
"said to me—*nothing*, though it is quite likely his thoughts were
busy enough. He certainly looked almost as disagreeable as
father. *She* greets me, not as mistress here, not as wife to her
son ; but as a servant to receive her orders and do her bidding.
She does not link my life with the man's down stairs by a
thought; neither do I, as I shall make them both understand."

While she was brooding, she heard voices advancing along
the upper hall, and footsteps which paused at the door opposite. Mr. Slaughton was conducting his friend to his apartment. They entered, shut themselves in, and presently from
the interior there came a sound of chatting and merry laughter; the unbidden guest was making himself at home. She
frowned, and tapped the sash with her fingers; she recoiled
from the certainty that they were *able* to make her, *the bride*,
a subject of their conversation. That they had glib tongues
was evident—as fleet and swift as women's ; and what so likely
to occupy them as the most recent occurrence of Mr. Slaughton's life? She chided herself immediately, however, for the
suspicion; because as yet she knew nothing absolutely to the
discredit of either. Neither she nor Teddy would be guilty of
such meanness ; and as she had no standards of comparison,
she rested on what she knew. She stepped out while they
were engaged, and retracing her road she waited at the stair-
head until Mr. Slaughton should appear.

Pretty soon he came, alone, having left his friend to the business of dressing. He hesitated when he saw her, as if unwilling to encounter her face to face ; seeing which, she deliberately approached him.

"Mr. Slaughton," she began in a low voice, of which every tone was clear and sweet, "Mr. Slaughton, permit me to say a few words to you, just here—before we two are one minute older."

"Now it is coming," thought Sam. "She is going to throw herself on my mercy, and try to make me say something spooney."

Perhaps the bored and supercilious expression on his face helped her to speak plainly; and she needed some steadying force, for her heart beat fast, and she trembled so much that she grasped the stair-rail, clasping it firmly in her fingers.

"God has not joined us together. It is but a contract for a housekeeper which you have signed—a contract agreed upon by two women. I do not learn that you have sanctioned or approved it by a single word. Your mother has already explained to me the duties of the place, and set my tasks. I am to labor in the school-room—I am to be the Slaughton housekeeper. I consider it *your* business, as master of this house, to assign me the proper rooms for the service ; that I may have the privacy out of hours, to which every servant is entitled. I intend to be faithful. I know it is no light thing I have undertaken. The Vance children are not promising ; I am young ; but I am used to hardness and crosses. I have been placed here without my consent ; my inclinations were not consulted——"

"Pardon a moment's interruption. I understood you were quite agreeable to the arrangement ; you have entered no protest ; you left my letter unanswered——"

"What letter, sir? You surprise me ! I have received no letter from you—have heard of none."

"That is strange, because I wrote you from Toptown last Monday, begging you to make sure that you wished to be——"

As Sam rather hesitated for the proper word, she quickly and impetuously interrupted him.

"So you endeavored to decline the bargain your mother was

making in your behalf," she said with curling lip. "Why couldn't you have *said* as much? that would have saved you at once. I assure you no epistle of yours ever reached me. I was told that you preferred to leave the affair in the hands of the parents, being too sensible to be sentimental, and that it was my pious duty to be deeply thankful that the leadings of Providence were so plainly marked in my behalf as to be unmistakable."

"I trust you were not *forced* to this step."

"I was not whipped! though there's no knowing what might have happened to me if I had stood out. If you comprehended better the internal economy of the Hethwaite family, you would know there is but one will there—one autocrat—one Sublime Porte."

"I am extremely sorry," began Sam.

"Not so sorry as you may be, probably. As for me, I have only a feeling of pure amazement that a grown man should allow himself to be disposed of like a boy in short jackets. If I were a man, I would select to my pleasure."

The gentleman listened in wonder. Indeed, he felt as if he had somehow lost the initiative, and that it was *she* who was having the little talk with *him*; and very plainly and pointedly was she conducting it, marking out her ground and saying to him, as King Canute said to the waves, "Thus far shalt thou come, and no farther." A curious idea those parsonage people must have, if disciplined obedience, which never spoke up, "had its will broken at four years old, was meek and quiet, and accepted all things without a murmur."

He looked her unpleasantly over, standing there straight as an arrow, as proud as Lucifer himself, at her coal-black eyes kindled into blazing scorn—her jetty hair, clearly-lined brows, a trifle too much arched, which gave her face a mocking expression, just now, at any rate; and he felt that she had been weighing him in her mental balance, making a judgment of his strange conduct from her stand point, which must of course be anything but favorable to him. He might have known she would do it; and still it had not before occurred to him that she could; and he was to the full as embarrassed in this first interview as she ought to have been during the explanation *he* had planned.

Her position there—an unwooed wife—might summon the haughty intensity to her countenance, the cold scorn to her manner. Alone among strangers who had, so far, been scarcely civil to her. And she looked so hostile, that he felt no desire to ascertain whether there might lurk any soft tenderness in the hidden depths of those lustrous eyes, any kindness behind the disdain of the unfriendly face. On the contrary, he experienced extreme bitterness and rising pique—not to say enmity, against this woman with the brow of Egypt, who confronted him with a mien so fearless and even menacing.

"Here is a fine ending to all my youthful fancies! Tied to this creature forever, whom I could not love if I tried—the opposite of all I ever desired. Married before I knew the color of her eyes, or the sound of her voice (not a dissonant voice, I must acknowledge that); and here I stand like a great, lubberly boy, brought to book for my folly in getting so rashly mated. I deserve it too. Oh, write me an ass! I will be written an ass!" His full under-lip dropped, and he wore a most rueful visage as he arrived at this culmination of his reflections.

"Madam," he began, "what you say is true. Your taste is questionable in saying it. I did take a wife to please my mother; I have no doubt she will realize from the transaction all the advantage she counts on. As for me, I am proverbially a quiet man. It seems most evident that you expect little from me, and rest assured I shall take excellent care to cross your path as seldom as possible. Since you have assumed my name, I trust you will try to behave so as not to make my private affairs a theme for gossips. I do not relish the idea of being laughed at. You will find me uniformly civil when I am called on to be so, and decent appearances may be preserved."

Sam's instincts led him to be habitually gentle to women ; but he was determined to say that much, and he said it with a good deal more vim and rasp, it may be, than he might have used had he not been forced to be a target for her glances, a victim to her sharpness ; and he felt uncomfortable as he said it too, and foolish. That was probably the effect of a scarcely perceptible shrug of the well-turned shoulders opposite him, and an almost inaudible sniff with which his proposition was received.

" Do not feel the slightest alarm, sir. Should you do me the honor of a remark at any time, on your basis of appearances, you may be sure that I shall reply humbly and properly. I shall do my best to make my deportment such that your friends will not be able to find in it a flaw to hang a thought on. I shall be a painstaking housekeeper; I shall jingle my keys conspicuously (housekeepers carry keys, I believe). I shall keep the obstreperous children in such order that your after-noon nap shall not be disturbed. Oh, yes, I have a full schedule of the pleasant tasks which are to fill my hands ; and I mean to do them. But—I will not serve for nothing. I demand an equivalent for the teaching, which, with the housekeeper's business—if I am to give my opinion—I should say was roll-ing the proper work of two girls into one. Still, I do not object, on one condition—I must have my sister Bettine to share my life. Had it not been for this intention, I tell you plainly I might have braved the paternal wrath. I am twenty, and in another year I could have gone out from the home bondage to earn my living ; but in that case I must have left this timid, tender child to the experiences of my own youth. Grant me this favor, and I will do my best to please. Whatever you may demand to keep up appearances in public shall be attended to, and you may be assured that I shall never in any way intrude upon you anywhere."

" Do not ask my permission, madam ; pray carry forward any schemes you may have formed, independently. I have no intention to dictate to you on any subject, or interfere with

5*

you. Perhaps I ought to have told you—at any rate, I shall tell you now, in justice to my own consistency—that the romance of *my* life is over, my dream dreamed out. If you choose to accept this as a reason for my easy compliance with my mother's wishes, at which you were just now pleased to express wonder—'pure amazement,' I think you said—you will see that this arrangement of your life assumes less importance in my mind than you might have supposed."

"You are altogether mistaken, sir. I never for one instant flattered myself that you were thinking of me. You might have told me! oh, yes, you might have done several things which you neglected. This bit of gratuitous information, which certainly intensifies the charm of my position, is intended, I suppose, to crush any little aspirations I might have, and to warn me that no efforts of mine, were I eager to make them, could ever win for me a place in your regard; or perhaps you mean to be interesting in the character of a blighted being (I have read of such in the novels we used to borrow). In either case, rest perfectly easy, Mr. Slaughton ; I shall not miss, fortunately, what is called *love*. I never saw anything worthy the name, either at home or elsewhere, among married people, and I do not believe it is readily to be had for the wishing ; and I must congratulate you on having gone through the malady so that you are cured for life, as from scarlet fever or measles. Ah, let me assume my proper expression. I must purse my lips thus. Your friend approaches. You see our conference has a most natural seeming, and I hope this sort of smile and courtesy will do for a leave-taking ; it is the best I have at present. I will endeavor to improve."

She left Sam in a dazed state. Such a glib tongue ! such spirit ! such fearless daring in so difficult a place, among such mortifying conditions. He watched her out of sight, to all appearance undaunted, independent, and he muttered to himself :

"Poor mother ! she will have the worst of it, because she cannot possibly go and kill tigers in Timbuctoo."

CHAPTER XIV.

"HE TEMPERS THE WIND TO THE SHORN LAMB."

AYBE you feel too tired to pour the tea, Perdita," said Dame Slaughton, coming into the supper-room to find the two gentlemen conversing by the window, and the bride standing near the head of the table, evidently waiting for her appearance to assume her duties as hostess.

"Oh, no, madam. I flatter myself I am entirely equal to the occasion ; we are quite ready, gentlemen," she added, turning to the friends, who approached at her summons ; and then she seated herself at the tea-board.

"You don't find getting married so very fatiguing?" asked Chandy, laughing. "Such a lazy dog as this Sam is! I hope you will be more successful in keeping him to hours than I have ever been ; a regular slow-coach, is Sam!"

"I shall undertake no responsibility of that kind," she answered, looking at the guest and not at her husband. "I assure you it is entirely out of my part."

"*I* always like to pour the tea myself; I can make it just to suit. I'm rather particular," remarked the dowager, dropping discontentedly into the chair which Chandy placed for her.

"I intend to concentrate my faculties on the task, and I am confident of success. Shall it be one or two lumps?" asked Perdita, poising a piece of sugar in the tongs above the cup she held, and looking at the dame for instructions.

"I take mine clear, and pretty strong. Samuel likes his weak," replied the old lady disconsolately.

"Nothing more simple. I am able to go by the card : plain and strong for you, sweet and weak for your son. Now, Mr. Goldsmith, shall it be strength to the strong, as well as sweets to the sweet, for you." .

"Oh, thank you, yes," said Chandy. " Sam ! your wife is a lady of rare discernment, I perceive. See how aptly and readily she reads my character," he added, with a face full of merry mischief. "And don't you think this will be the appropriate moment for the little recitation I am accustomed to make to newly-married people ? "

As the bridegroom only glowered without opening his lips, he went on, taking silence for consent :

> " ' In peace Love tunes the shepherd's reed ;
> In war he mounts the warrior's steed ;
> In halls in gay attire is seen,
> In hamlets, dances on the green.
> Love rules the court, the camp, the grove,
> And men below, and saints above,
> For love is heaven, and heaven is love.'

Therefore, friends, let me congratulate you on your arrival in Paradise."

"A very pretty song of Byron's, indeed," mumbled Sam, who felt that he must break the dead silence which followed Chandos's recitation. " I seem to recollect your spouting it on Dolores' balcony several years ago. I compliment you on your wonderful memory."

"Yes, of course. But is it Byron's ? what do you say, Mrs. Slaughton ? " asked Chandos, looking pleasantly at the young girl, whose eyes rested on her plate, but whose face, it seemed to him, showed a glimmer of amusement beneath its quiet.

"There was 'Scott' in large gilt letters on the back of the book where *I* saw your rhymes," she replied simply. " It was an old college prize of my father's. I am sure I cannot be mistaken, because Teddy is fond of repeating that poem, so that I had it often in my ears."

"I think your wife is right, Sam ; in fact, I know she is. And, by the way, I should like to propose a question to this highly intelligent group, beginning, of course, with the eldest and wisest," said Chandy, bowing to the dame. "I've had it asked me a couple of times. Whereabouts in the Bible do you find this passage, madam, ' God tempers the wind to the shorn lamb ' ? "

"I should say Job," answered the widow, reflectively.

"What do you think, Sam ? "

"It sounds like Job," replied the bridegroom, who was unconsciously listening to hear what Perdita would say.

"Now, Mrs. Slaughton—a minister's daughter—I expect to get chapter and verse from you."

"Opposite to the words, I remember the picture of a pretty girl sitting under the trees, holding a string in her fingers, which was fastened around the neck of a little dog who slept at her feet, and her name was ' Maria.' "

"And there isn't any Maria in the Bible, is there, madam ? " asked Chandos of the dame, who was sourly eying her new daughter.

"Humph ! I don't really suppose *you* know whether there is or not," answered the old lady.

As for Sam, he looked across at the young girl opposite him. He could not choose but look, though he found small pleasure in what he saw : a slender creature, in a simple, quaint dress, with low, full body, and dainty little sleeves. Her long, heavy hair, plaited in thick braids which reached below her waist, was tied with crimson ribbons which the hue of her fresh cheeks outrivalled. Her dark, clear skin was soft and smooth, having the down of youth upon it, as on a luscious peach just ripened in the warm sunshine ; her lips were richly colored, deeply blooming. Such a childish, bright young thing she looked, so simple, so unfrizzed, so natural ! she might have just stepped out of a frame, quaint and picturesque, with the wreath of sumach leaves glistening like satin around her head—(which poor Dolly had placed there, in fear and trembling, after her most signal defeat in other wedding adornments), and Teddy's tea-roses upon her breast.

Mr. Slaughton frowned, as he contrasted this girl who had spoken so cuttingly to him upstairs—who was talking to Chandos in such a pure voice, low and clear—who behaved to his mind so *pertly*. This mere child, who had seen no society, knew no worldly ways. What right had she to be so sufficient to her new place, when he felt as if she ought to be embarrassed and awkward? And he half wished she would make some *faux pas*, which might justify the aversion and repugnance he felt towards her. What a contrast she was every way to the ivory-white, golden-haired beauty his reveries and musings were always bringing before him, adorned and glorified with the thousand nameless graces which had made her the one and only woman-delight of his whole life.

The amused, interested expression on his friend's face vexed him. He well knew how clear-sighted and discerning was this friend, who so easily chatted with the stranger with whom he might almost be said to be *flirting ;* in fact, who observed also the old lady eying apprehensively over her tea-cup the bride who came recommended as "silent and obedient," and who looked not exactly resolute, because her face was not aggressive, but who was assuming the dignities of the position into which she had been thrust, as if she knew her rights and was able to maintain them.

He writhed under it all, and he sailed into the talk, secretly intending to keep it away from the women, a project in which he was signally defeated by Chandos, who constantly included " Mrs. Slaughton" in his remarks, dwelling on the name and often producing it, as if it had a fascination for him, which, indeed, I think it had.

Modest ? Oh, yes, Perdita was modest, but retiring ! No,

I cannot say she *was* retiring. She accepted the topics which Chandy offered her with tolerable ease, and much more self-command than could have been expected of her, and she showed some knowledge of nearly all of them. She looked candid and sincere. Once in a while her large eyes suddenly sparkled with vivacity, and the jetty brows which arched them no more helped to show scorn and defiance. Her small mouth was the only feature which betrayed uneasiness; it drooped at the corners, and trembled in spite of her sometimes, as she began to speak.

When supper was over there was a bright red spot on each of the bridegroom's cheeks, and the perpendicular line in the middle of his forehead was more marked and deeper than usual.

Had Perdita been anybody else's wife, he must have acknowledged her not only pleasing, but engaging. Her figure was so symmetrical that it needed not the aid of corsets, even in this plain muslin, and her arms and hands were certainly faultless in shape, although 'tis true they were browned by exposure to the sun and wind, and her fingers were a little hardened with use, and there were plenty of needle-marks on them. Had they not done the family sewing, made the family bread, and cooked the family meals?

Had he been an outsider, like Chandy, he might very likely have found amusement in the querities of the tea-table and the strange attitudes which the party assembled held towards each other. As, however, it was his own life which was in question, it is not surprising that he not only saw no food for mirth, but was sorely vexed that his old friend could see any.

He experienced not a jot of pity for his mother, so speedily and certainly set aside and dethroned, and her rueful appearance awakened no sympathy in his breast. Had he spoken out what he felt, he would very likely have said, "Good enough for her!" One thing above and beyond all impressed him in his bride's behavior. She concerned herself not in the slightest degree about him. His approbation or his displeasure carried no weight to her mind. They modified not in the remotest particular her appearance, her words, or her conduct. Although that was the very positive position he had indicated to her by his remarks upstairs, it nettled him that she was so ready to assume it, and it is quite true that the close of the evening meal found him as much out of harmony with the wife he had taken as it was possible for him to be with any woman living.

CHAPTER XV.

"LET US SIT ON THE GROUND AND TELL SAD STORIES."

S soon as they rose from the table, the gentlemen walked into the garden to smoke a social cigar, and Perdita went straight to her room.

While she stood by the open window, gazing into the moonlight, yellow and serene, which bathed her in its soft effulgence, thinking such strange thoughts as made her brain whirl, she heard voices below her, and caught distinctly her own name.

Poor human nature would not permit her to leave the place till she found how she was getting treated by the talkers. Indeed, I am afraid she rather craned her neck that she might catch the exact significance of every word they uttered.

" Well, Sam, this is a queer world ! Here you, who raved over auburn tresses and milk-white maids, who saw only Sabrina divinely fair, who sniffed at black-browed beauties, counting even my Bertha too dark to please you, and Peace Pelican's brunette dash and flash unpleasant and repugnant, have at last selected a lady with hair and eyes which out-Ethiop even poor little Dolores."

"Selected!" repeated the new benedict testily. "Yes, so it seems;.a clinging little vine, is she not? A patient, pains- taking, obedient child, who never had any will of her own—at least, that was the character which came with her."

"What an odd expression, Sam!"

"Not odder than beseems the odd subject. The fact is, I am likely to be at odds with the lady you saw opposite to me this evening, and whom you gave yourself such infinite trouble to entertain, for the whole of the balance of my life."

"You surprise me! You positively alarm me!"

"I know you are surprised, Chandy, and I know that you are also devoured with curiosity to find the clue to what you have seen and heard; and I am going to tell you all about it. There is not another living being to whom I would open my lips but you; and I have shared our lives too closely to have many secrets. At all events, I want to talk it over with you, and I'll speak once for all. It is not a theme to which I ever desire to return, I assure you. I married my wife as kings get theirs ; the royal relatives arranged the alliance, and much good may it do them."

"What, Sam? What, old fellow? You surely do not mean me to understand that you have wedded a woman without courting her ; that you don't care for your wife!"

"You do your remarkably clear penetration injustice, Chan- dos, to pretend that you have not already discovered that patent fact ; you found it out the same instant that your eyes lighted on her."

"I certainly did observe something unusual, Sam, I won't deny that ; but I know there do arise clouds on the matri- monial horizon ; they ascend in haste, their currents move by no fixed laws. But, Sam, a man of your sound sense and ex- cellent ideas, and above all, your abominable laziness! You are the very last in the world whom I should expect to find out of perpendicular with yourself."

"That's just it. Sense gets muddled with eternal dropping,

and ideas go for nothing ; and laziness has quite finished me. The fact is, my mother became possessed of a most unaccountable whim—she would have me married ! And as I got weary of the din and clatter over it, I finally told her, if she could pick out a girl to suit her and manage a wedding without any wooing, I would not refuse any longer ; you have seen the result of her efforts—they culminated in yonder. By Jove ! Chandos. I did not think I could by any means get tied for life to a woman I never asked to have me, to whom I never spoke seven sentences, nor looked at seven times. But, I'm fast ; I'm caught in the net of matrimony just as sure as you stand there. Absurd, isn't it ? "

" Sam, I believe you are admirably mated. She is a most lustrous creature ; a strong character, too, quite able to interest you if you make it worth her while to try. I'll wager anything that, queerly as you have begun, a whole month won't pass before you are head over ears in love with your wife."

" Chandos, Sabrina Bradshaw is the only woman I ever saw worth loving. You know I am a constant man in my friendships ; I am constant also in my love. I gave my heart to a lady ten years ago—she has it still. I never meant to say so much as that to any living being. I loved not wisely, as I found out ; but I loved for all time."

To the listener's ears her husband's voice took a deeper tone, and it seemed to convey to them an unmistakable truth, which must have been also a bitter sorrow, if she had ever for a moment turned towards him her heart or her wishes. As it was, her cheeks burned, and they kindled deeper still when he spoke again.

" My spouse does not much resemble that beauty, does she ? As much as darkness resembles light. However, it matters but little. My mother, who never rested till she pushed the young woman into this. house, must get what comfort she can out of her investment ; as for me, I shall try if I can't kill tigers, and maybe myself, in Timbuctoo."

"She is of good family, I know," said Chandy musingly ; "she proves that by every motion, every look, past doubt."

" The blood is well enough, for all I know. The mother is a poor, timid creature, afraid of her shadow. And as for Papa Hethwaite, I believe the devil owed me a grudge, and paid me off in a father-in-law, for a more dogmatic, abominable old bear I never met in my life."

. "Sam, my dear old friend, you shock me. It sounds a deal worse to hear you go on like this than it would anybody else ; you are such a genial, live-and-let-live old chap ! I don't like it. Your life is spoiled unless you take a bit of advice I'm going to give you. No, no, don't shrug your shoulders that way. You are too valuable a man to lose. We can't spare you. Stay at home, Sam. Be a family man. Woo your wife, win her ; she is richly worth your while, I do honestly believe. I have been more than astonished at her this evening. There is not one girl in a thousand that in her place would have sustained the rude ordeal so well ; and, upon my soul, Sam, there's no other course left you as a man of honor.' If you had not allowed her to come here, some other fellow might, very certainly *would*, have taken her and made her happy."

" Exactly the argument I used, Chandy ; I made plain to her that very thing. No, I will do her the justice to say she never got my letter. There is rigid truth in her face, if it don't suit me. She told me she did not ; and I believe her. But you are mistaken in your premises, Chandy. She has taken some trouble this afternoon to make me understand what she wants. She left me no chance to act for myself ; and if I was dying of love for her, I would not alter my course by the estimation of a hair. Console yourself, the young woman craves none of my affection ; she declines all attentions."

"Who can blame her ?" said Chandy (secretly amused at his friend's evident irritation and chagrin, and imagining how proud and perhaps contemptuous Perdita might be able to show herself under her very provoking and mortifying circumstances), "and as she had proper spirit to withdraw from trespassing on you, it is your plain duty, and ought to be your pleasure, to pursue her with your most winning smiles."

" Winning smiles ! Not if I know myself. No, Chandy. I am disinclined in that direction ; but if kind Fate had given me Sabrina Bradshaw, I would have been the most devoted slave woman ever had. As it is, I have no interest here except to pay the family bills."

" But, Sam, that old love ought to be dead and forgotten. Sabrina—— "

" Oh, yes, of course. I understand all that. Millions of words won't render it any plainer. I lost my chance ; never had any, in fact. But that does not make me ready to pick up a new love—least and last of all, such an one as this which has been pushed and dragged into my notice. If I ever could fancy a girl, I'd have my little romance over it. I would not select a wife as I would a cow, for her good points. I would be as sentimental as any other fool. I'd make eyes, and sigh, and talk nonsense ; give gifts, and glean the most from the situation. Even that possibility is blotted out. I mustn't dare to dream that I could be spooney on a pretty girl. I've got a wife, Lord bless her ! Do you remember the ' Ruth' I painted up at Craigenfels ? "

" Indeed, yes. Bertha sat to me also. Yours was a picture of rare merit and finish, and an admirable likeness. I should be glad to see it again."

" I'll show it to you, and another of her as she looked at the Christmas Eve supper, when she waited on the mission choir."

"Yes ; I remember the evening well. She had a spurt of a quarrel with my brother-in-law. Sabrina had a temper which was not the ' very dove and blessed spirit of peace.' Well, Bertha's ' Ruth' hangs in our best parlor ; she thinks the world of it."

" There is nobody who thinks the world of my poor efforts ; so I keep them in my den. I've got the Amy Robsart there

too, Chandos!" broke out his friend with sudden vehemence.
"What a life I might have had with that woman. How rich
and full and complete might have been all these dull, flavor-
less days, which have gone on just dropping and dropping without any worth. You got your Ruth for the asking; why
couldn't I have got mine?"

"Sam, I really must protest. This dwelling on the memory
of a lady who never could be your wife is really monstrous."

"Do you remember her on that famous horseback excur-
sion?" continued the speaker, as if he had not heard the interruption, as very likely he had not. "Such a figure! Such a
regal head! Such glances of fire! Such smiles, such perfection in riding! Such a delicate, true hand, altogether superb!
I am very fond of horses, Chandy," he ended, with a sigh.

"I have a happy thought, Sam; you shall teach Mrs.
Slaughton to ride; that will be an admirable opening for a
better understanding between you."

"No, thank you, sir; excuse me, if you please. I could not
think of teaching that girl anything; I don't fancy playing
Petruchio to such an Ethiop Kate. You remember I wanted
to play Benedict to Sabrina Bradshaw that Christmas, and I got
cut out of the part."

"Now, my dear boy, don't be offended, but such rhapsodies,
such perverse and continual harping on that theme, is far from
pleasant. I hate to see you show this wilful disregard and
studied and intentional neglect of what you can have. It is a
bitter wrong to the poor child in there. It is not like you,
Sam! Dear, true-hearted old chap. I can't bear to think of
it."

"Don't preach, Chandos; or if you must hold forth, I advise
you to take Solomon's wisdom for your text: 'Vanity of
vanities.' My pipe and I must be better friends than ever,
that's the upshot of it all."

"Well, Sam, here's my hand. I sincerely hope you will live
to the time when you'll promenade up and down your apart-

ment in your roaming toga, with your child in your arms, as I have done often and often, and get *solid* enjoyment out of the goodly possession which is testing the muscles of them."

Mr. Slaughton's thoughts turned involuntarily to the little room upstairs, which his mother had showed him, and as he remembered her words and instructions, he shrugged his shoulders.

"Timbuctoo, or No Man's Land, or the antipodes, or anywhere but here, Chandos. Another month will find me a wanderer."

"A month is thirty days ; that is thirty chances for you to change your mind."

"Let's walk down to the pond, Chandy, and change the subject."

CHAPTER XVI.

ONLY HOUSEKEEPER AND GOVERNESS.

ERDITA stood still at the window long after the friends had vanished from her sight.

Anger and mortification filled her soul to be thus discussed, and disavowed, and dismissed, as too poor in charms or qualities to awaken even esteem. It was a phase of the subject upon which she had not dwelt during the few days which had been allowed her before the consummation of her fate. Marriage was a very hum-drum affair to the best of her knowledge, and no expectation of it for herself had ever come to her, till suddenly one day she was told to be ready. Betty was her object in the enforced bargain to which she had been a silent party. Her mother's talk had dwelt, not on the man, but the place; *her* thoughts had centred in the *child*, the confluence and focus of her passionate ·devotion. Betty's safety, Betty's comfort, Betty's future, were constantly before her, and furnished sufficient motives for any sacrifice or suffering she was capable of.

Now, for the first time, she let her imagination wander among the delights of a home she might have shared with a true man who truly loved her; she could see her husband while he talked, down there in the garden; the yellow moonlight was shining on his face so that its features were distinctly beneath her vision. Tall, muscular, graceful, he carried about him a certain consciousness of finished manhood which has tested its powers and has full faith in them. Such a gentleman as might be worthy a woman's admiration. Why should he have failed in securing that wonderful creature called Sabrina? *Men* who have all the right of choice should be successful; through what vital error had he missed his happiness? Her thoughts forsook herself in their play about those two. "Ivory-white, with golden hair." Every word of the conversation was burned into her memory, ineffaceably branded there. She had sat for her picture as Ruth, as Amy Robsart. Then and there she had been beautiful. She had presided at a feast, this Sabrina, (how well she remembered the name as it sounded when spoken by *her* husband!) There she had been gracious. She had a matchless form, and a regal head, glances of fire, adorable smiles; she was altogether superb. That had been the tenor of her husband's praises, such his summing up. What a loss to lose such a rare creature!"

She recalled his observations on *her* own family as well as herself; they had been undervalued *en másse*.

When she retired from the window she took with her more bitterness and unrest than she had ever felt in her old home at its bleakest; and above and beyond every other emotion was resentment against the man who had, through inertia and selfish carelessness, allowed himself to be fettered to her. His conduct seemed wicked and monstrous in the new light she had received on probabilities and realities among men and women who do love each other, and choose each other for better, for worse.

" He has not kept to the spirit of our agreement," she thought. "There is not a woman living with whom I would discuss our mutual relations, sorry as they are;" and yet he could cooley talk them over with this other man, as gossips prate over their knitting. Now, to-morrow I must show myself to them—I, the despised wife, to the master who bought his slave and finds her so poor a bargain that he will travel to the ends of the earth to get out of sight and hearing of her. I must walk before them with an untroubled face, and then the stranger will carry the pitiful tale home to his wife whom *he* loves—Bertha, who is not ivory white or golden-haired, and is a happy wife in spite of such shameful defects. Some man might have taken me ; he . said so. Have I made a blunder in keeping silence ? Ought I to have stood out and fought for my life ? No. I will have my Betty. I will shield her and keep her safe from father. That will pay me for everything."

She walked about the chamber, examining its furniture, handsome, solid, even elegant, her home for the future. She had no bridal finery to arrange or admire ; the pomp and circumstance of glorious weddings had no part in her thoughts. She opened the little old trunk which had travelled to the Chocktaw settlement and back again, and put away her few simple garments in the stately bureau, laying out the plain gingham and white apron trimmed with the tatting she had made in winter evenings, stealing for it the time, because it seemed necessary to gratify in small measure her love of ornament and finish.

She carefully removed the sumac wreath, and as she held it a moment in her hands, caressing with gentle touch its bright leaves, she sighed.

" Poor Dolly ! maybe *she* will get a husband who will praise her a little, and not shut the door of his heart against her, so that, if she desires to enter, she cannot."

She laid Teddy's roses away after a smell at their fragrance. It seemed to her a pity that their freshness was so fleeting ; because they were the one treasure he had been able to sacrifice to her, and she would have been glad to have it immortal.

A misty shadowing of new knowledge had dawned dimly upon her.   The life of books might be a real life under certain favorable conditions.   It was nearly certain, in the light of recent revelations, that all wives were not drudges or machines ; there were fortunate ones who came into the world to be approved, commended, admired, even worshipped ; but it was an existence in which *she* had no share.   The ceremony of the day made her a housekeeper and a governess.

The folding-doors between hers and the bridegroom's rooms stood open.   She quietly closed and locked them, and stepped softly about hither and thither, thinking, trying to steady her purposes and mark out the line of conduct she would take ; trying to know herself and feel her strength, so as to be ready for what the morrow, and on ahead of that other morrows, might bring her, and what she had got to meet and face alone, unfriended, seeking neither advice nor sympathy.

After a while she heard the two gentlemen come up stairs. They lingered a while in Chandy's room, still chatting.   She caught herself in a bitter surprise that men could have so much to say to each other.   When Teddy talked, it was to her.

They exchanged " good-nights " at last, and Mr. Slaughton walked slowly back to his own door, which he entered, closing it behind him ; and this was the end of the wedding-day which the sun shone on.

6

CHAPTER XVII.

"A BEAUTIFUL WOMAN COMMANDS THE GODS."

HE next morning, at the breakfast table, Chandos broached the object of his journey : certain views among these high-lying counties which he desired to put on canvas.

"Under your peculiar circumstances, Sam," said he, "I can't think of bringing out a proposition I had in my mind when I started from Roaring River.   It says in the Bible, a newly-married man shall stay at home one year and comfort his wife.   I will not be so barbarous as to ask you to join in my wanderings.   I won't, I assure you, Mrs. Slaughton," he continued, with a bow to the head of the table.   "I do perceive you bear a gentle mind, and heavenly blessings follow such creatures ; a husband *should* be a blessing ;   therefore he ought to be your very shadow."

"I do not know fully what kind of thanks 'tis meet that I should render for your good opinion, sir ; more than my all is nothing, my prayers are words not duly hallowed, my wishes are but empty words.   Yet prayers and wishes are all I can return."

Perdita made her answer with her hands busy among her cups, and her eyes intent upon the amber stream of coffee she was drawing from the silver urn.   She made it in a soft, smooth voice, easy-flowing and natural.   She was rather pale and had light circles of purple around her eyes, as if she might have been weeping ; but she was quite composed and mistress of her motions, attending to the business of the table with careful consideration and modest politeness.

Dame Slaughton stared openly at her, while she spoke to Chandy, as if she suspected her of mental aberration. Her son's color rose as he listened, and he *nearly* stared at mischievous Chandy, who was extremely urbane and bland, and evidently contemplated amusing himself further with experiments on the self-control of the couple whom he was treating as if he considered them the ardent lovers the recent nuptials ought to have found them.

The host cut rather pointedly into the conversation before his guest had time to bring out any more quotations from his faithful friend and ally "Billy Shakes," by expatiating on the beauties of scenery abounding in their neighborhood.

"You seek autumn tints; we have them in perfection; there's the old mill just in the picturesqueness of ruin, bittersweet climbing all over its rafters, green moss dotting its roof, and a little brook trickling down the rotting race; we'll go there this very morning."

"Have I Mrs. Slaughton's gracious permission? I am too well trained a benedict to venture far till I know the mood of my hostess."

"Of course, Mr. Goldsmith," spoke up the dame, "do stay, we shall be delighted, I'm sure."

Chandy had a great mind to make Perdita speak; his question had been addressed to her. It might have been pity for her blushes which withheld him. It certainly was not compassion for his friend, whose dissatisfaction was patent, which induced him to change the subject.

"What delicious fish-balls," he exclaimed. "I never ate any so good in my life. When I was in Paris with Johnny Hawxhurst, he used to walk five miles of a morning to get an American breakfast of these things. He tried to coax me to go with him. Upon my word, such plump, delicate, brown pats, are worth a tramp of double that! I never have been much addicted to the use of codfish, but I confess I did not know what excellence it was capable of. Give me another, please,

Sam. Mrs. Slaughton, I am glad you find so good a cook all ready to your hand. I believe I am familiar with the trials of housekeepers. Bertha pours them into my devoted ears sometimes."

A very peculiar expression flitted over Perdita's face. Her talk with Teddy came to her mind, and the absurd reason she had given him for not rebelling against this marriage.

"I'm weary of keeping lent, Teddy. I have an excellent appetite, I want *meat.*" A vision of her father's family sitting down that very morning, probably to a meal of the same comestible Mr. Goldsmith was so highly lauding, and the various signs of lean, grinding poverty in its partakers which made it necessary, arose before her. As she looked up she caught her husband's eyes studying her; but she had no idea how her reply would gall him, and she made it without malice prepense.

"Thank you, sir; I am pleased that they suit you. They are the result of steady practice, I assure you. Where cheapness is the prime object of life, it becomes important to understand cooking inexpensive dishes in the most palatable manner."

"Yes, Perdita, they *are* nice," said Dame Slaughton, taking the compliments to herself. "Oh, I knew you was a good cook. Your mother told me what you could do," she went on, as if praising a new servant. "I asked plenty of questions, and I got first-rate answers."

Mr. Slaughton was exceedingly displeased. Although he was indifferent to the woman opposite to him, it did not suit his ideas of his own dignity that she should descend to the kitchen and cook his breakfast on her first morning in his house, as if she was the purchased slave of an Ashantee chief; and he felt his mother's manner to her an insult which included him, especially in Chandy's hearing, in whose elegant home he had been a frequent guest. Chandy, whose lady-wife presided over her costly appointments as a rich man's wife should, mistress, director; setting tasks, not performing them; and it was an effort for him to hold fast to his resolution not to interfere with the internal economy of the household his mother had chosen to institute.

"I must take home to Bertha an elaborate account of your housekeeping, Mrs. Slaughton. I shall hold you up before her as a bright and shining light—a model for her imitation."

The host really could not make up his mind whether his friend was trying to make things pleasant, or was mischievously amusing himself at the expense of his entertainers. He looked as bland and amiable as a Dutch doll, and ate away at his fish-cakes and sipped his coffee with as appreciative gusto as if it had been a breakfast at John John's, the prince of caterers, whom the travellers had been used to patronize and praise when they were roving bachelors.

"Oh, yes," spoke up the dame, "oh, yes, indeed. Perdita takes right hold. This is Hannah's scouring day, and unless she gets at it early she is apt to be late, and that clutters up things towards night so. I told Perdita about the way I liked to have a girl do, and she said she could make good fish-balls ; so I had her do them."

The young wife saw how her husband was writhing under these revelations of domestic economies and smart thrifts, which burst on him in such an abominable light, with exquisite Chandos for fellow-listener, and she restrained her inclination to stab him in a fresh place, as she had an opportunity to do by further interesting developments of the service and duties which had been already laid upon her ; but she refrained, not from patient acceptance of the dame's patronage, or out of regard to her husband's feelings, but simply because she meant to hold her resolution to move quietly in the path she understood herself pledged to, by the talk and explanation at the stair-head when little Betty's future life had been tacitly decided.

She saw also as plainly as Mr. Goldsmith saw it, that the bridegroom winced every time her new name was brought out. She wondered at the audacious daring which went on so needlessly repeating the "Mrs. Slaughtons" in his talk; and which adopted such a manner towards them, ignoring anything strange or trying in *her* position; treating all parties as if the marriage had been a love-match; and she almost felt as if he must be drawing her out for his amusement right under the husband's nose, and in defiance of his very evident uneasiness and the expression of undone infelicity every reminder of his fresh ties brought to his face.

She wondered how the guest could be so gay and chatty among such incongruous people. Very handsome and entertaining she found him, to be sure. (What woman, young or old, ever failed to like our spoiled Chandy?) And she was the least bit in the world secretly amused, *naïve* and inexperienced as she was, with the lazy grace and careless ease with which he put himself on a friendly footing with her; until a certain look she had caught in his eyes—just as he stooped to kiss her on the threshold—teazing, saucy, merry, flooded them afresh with a laughing remark he addressed to her, sent the blood to her cheeks in a painful blush and tied her tongue with silence.

She acquitted herself very tolerably, however, through the first breakfast. She talked, and listened, and smiled a little; Mr. Slaughton also listened and he did not smile. He sat stiffly, getting redder and redder, recalling with every tone of her voice what she had said to him yesterday; and how dark, and positive, and unfaltering she had looked; and how vivid like a rose; how straight like a reed she was; how still-black her eyes had been while she said, "It is for my sister Betty that I am willing to be true; for her I am ready to count all things valueless, and myself as nothing."

He was not able to cease looking at her either, even while he felt with concentrated bitterness that his mother could not by any means have lighted on a more disagreeable choice.

CHAPTER XVIII.

"HOUSE GOES MAD WHEN WOMEN GAD."

 HERE are you going, Perdita?" asked the widow, who met the young girl in the hall with her hat on.

"Only for a walk, ma'am," she replied concisely.

"Indeed? how queer! That don't seem to be necessary, does it? I never think of stirring out of the house till the work is all done up, and Hannah is so dreadfully busy to-day, and there's company besides. I thought maybe you'd see to his room the first thing after breakfast.

"I did, ma'am; it is all tidied, as are the other chambers."

"Oh, I want to know! Well, you have been spry! Did you dust and pick up?"

"Yes, ma'am."

"Don't you think it seems a little kinder shiftless to go *trillicking* off in the morning so? I mind me of the old proverb, 'House goes mad when women gad.'"

"Perhaps it may; but as I have an especial reason for going, I shall not allow specious appearances to influence me."

"You are married now, you know, and keeping house. You are not a free maid any more, to run about and do nothing. Women have to settle down and be steady when they get married."

"I do not feel inclined to be riotous. I fully intend to keep this house; that is what I came here for."

"Well, don't be away long. I lotted on going through the presses and closets with you before dinner," continued the dame sourly. "I didn't expect you'd be leaving me in the lurch like this."

"The inspection will keep, I dare say ; to-morrow will be as this day, probably, and much more abundant."

"It is a bad plan to speak so trifling about what's in the Holy Bible. I don't think your father would approve to hear you."

"My father's authority over me ceased yesterday," said Perdita quietly.

"Yes, and your husband's began," replied, the dame, with quite a smart accent.

"When I receive his commands I shall endeavor to be obedient. Would you advise me to ask his leave to go out this morning ?"

"Why, no ; I don't know as it is necessary. I should think my wishes would be enough," said the old lady, looking grim and disturbed at having so soon come in contact with a will belonging decidedly to the young person who had been highly recommended as possessing no such encumbrance.

"I feel quite like being a law unto myself at present, ma'am." As Perdita made this announcement, she added a good-morning, and shutting the door, ran swiftly down the steps and out into the wide road, which was a thoroughfare and belonged to everybody alike. The little wordy contest had not tended to calm her ruffled spirits, and she walked on very fast, trying to keep pace with her tumultuously hurrying thoughts, which flew fiercely and wild, defying her control.

When she arrived at the parsonage she found her mother alone. The doubtful, scared glance she gave her child was like the look the Irish mother sent to the girl whom she had married to the brown man who came to the shealing courting one stormy night, on a brown horse, followed by a brown dog—the eerie, fearsome gentleman who left his bride o' nights to feast in the churchyard among the ghouls :

"Whist, Nora, how does he trate ye, an' has he hit ye over the head wid the poker yet ?"

She searched Perdita's face, as if dreading and almost expect-

ing to find in it already some of the disappointed, sorrowful
lines her own had assumed so early. They were not there,
however. The girl glowed with her rapid walk, and no signs
of self-depreciation or abasement were visible. She stood
erect. She looked purposeful, and spoke with decision.

"Mother, where is father?" were her first words.

"He's gone up to the study. I haven't seen him since
breakfast. He's got a chance to preach next Sunday, and I
suppose he is looking up a sermon."

"I hope he will stay there, because I want to speak to you.
I had something on my mind, mother, when I let myself be tied
to that man"—she jerked her head in the direction of the Slaughton mansion house—"something I meant to gain by it."

"Oh yes, Perdita; and now that you have got such a nice
position and plenty of money, you must try not to be proud
and vainglorious; you must remember the hole of the pit from
whence you was digged, and be humble and thankful."

"Pshaw, mother! Leave that kind of talk to father. Betty
is the subject I have come down to see you about; she is my
object, she is my motive."

Mrs. Hethwaite listened in open-eyed astonishment while her
daughter went on with earnest rapidity, unfolding her plan and
furnishing the key to her passive obedience.

"Oh, deary me! how beautiful it would be!" said she.
"Well, sure enough, we don't know much what is in other folks'
minds, even those closest to us. I never dreamed of such a
thing being in yours, I'm sure. I'm most afraid you won't be
able to manage it. It seems too good to happen. What a
comfort to me, if I was to be taken away, to know that two of
you was safe! She belongs to you, and it really makes my
heart sore to see how she pines for you, poor little creature!
moping in corners and gazing out of the window by the hour.
I almost wish she would cry out loud, like other children; but
you know Mr. Hethwaite never would allow that. And she
doesn't dare to whimper, hardly, when he's 'round; she's dread-

6*

ful 'fraid of him. I can't comfort her ; I forgot years ago how to comfort anybody. Your father is so terrible queer, Perdita ; I don't feel as if there was much harm in telling you so, now that you have set up for yourself; but he does make me think of the pig that they drove east, so as to make him go west."

"I believe you, mother. Aunt Patience said she knew he'd got a row of bristles all up and down his back."

"What a curious speech for Patience to make ! She meant he was a little set in his way. Well, he is. If he thinks he starts a plan he'll follow it freely enough, no matter who goes against it ; but if he surmises that I lean any particular way, he is more than likely to declare my wish is improper, and shan't be carried out anyhow. Why, Perdita, when we were not married one year, he took up the stair-carpet with his own hands and tramped over the bare boards all winter, because I happened to say it wasn't wearing very well, and we'd soon have to get a new one. I've had a deal of trials ! and I do believe there would not be a surer way for you to get Bettine, than for me to cry and take on and insist that I couldn't spare her. Oh, yes, Perdita, it is very comforting to know that you are provided for."

"I've got a bone to pick with you, mother. Why did you let Mr. Slaughton's letter remain unanswered ? Why did you keep it a secret from me ?"

"Oh, dear ! you don't say you've found that out so quick ?"

"A pleasant bit of information you saved for me ! a nice greeting in his house, you may think ! Why did you expose me to such degradation ?"

"I didn't dare to do otherwise," cried the poor woman, desperately. "Your father would have been so hard on me if the plan had failed. He would have said I was to blame somehow, so I burnt the letter and didn't tell anybody. It was a good letter, though, Perdita. Mr. Slaughton must be a nice gentleman, generous-hearted and amiable, to say what he said, I am sure."

"You need to think so," replied Perdita, frowning, "when you pushed me into his house after he had declined me. You ought to have considered me a little as well as yourself."

"I did, child, I did! I could not bear to let such a chance go by to set you free. I could not endure to think of long years of such slavery as I saw before you; don't blame me. I meant it for the best, I did, indeed."

Perdita looked at the thin, crushed, spiritless woman, whose eyes were faded to a dull brown, whose skin was sallow and shrivelled, whose shoulders stooped as under a perpetual burden, and unconsciously contrasted her with the girl she had stopped to think about and observe for a half minute opposite to her in her mirror that morning, and was prompted to ask a question.

"Mother, did you look like me when you was young?"

"I believe I might."

"Black eyes and hair like mine?"

"Oh, yes, black enough. I remember one day your father came in from hunting with a crow he had killed, and he matched its plumes to my braids, and he said he could not tell which was the darker or more glossy."

"Father!" repeated Perdita, with incredulous accent.

"Yes, father! I got plenty of sweet words when I was Violet Wemple. You would hardly believe it; but I've some verses up-chamber that he wrote to me that spring, praising my eyes, and setting me up high. I thought them ever so pretty then. I used to read them a dozen times a day. I had seasons afterwards when I pulled them out and meant to toss them into the fire. That was when life went hard, when I was young and had a temper. I never get into a passion now; it don't pay," she went on, sighing wearily. "I might as well run my head against a stone wall as to try to stand out against your father's wishes. I could not bend; so I broke down.

"Mother, show me the verses! give them to me. I'll forge a weapon from his muse, if he is contrary about Bettine," she

thought, smiling to herself; " I'll confront him with his courting nonsense, and make him so ashamed that he will be glad
to give in to get rid of the sight of me.   Do fetch them,
mother," she added, " father's poetry must be something so
soothing and delicious!   I should as soon expect to hear a bull
sing psalms as father talk sweet.   How *did* he look?   did he
smile, and squeeze your hand, and go down on his knees as they
do in books?   Father in love!   What a strange idea!   so
impossible!"

" Your father was a very fine young man, or I should never
have fallen in love with him.   All the girls were after him."

" It appears incredible, mother; and yet it should be true,
because you were a pretty girl, were you not."

" A little compliment to yourself," answered the mother, with
a sort of smile the daughter had never observed before on that
face—and which had a gleam of youth in it.   " I hope you are
not going to be vain."

" Me vain?   Could I be, do you think?" and then queerly
enough she began to wonder if Sabrina or Bertha were vain.

" Come upstairs, mother," she said quickly, " I have nothing
to do with such ideas as might suit other women.   I am busy
with Bettine; get me the verses."

" Well, I'll let you see them.   After all that is said and done,
he's had a hard time, poor fellow!   They say adversity is good
for people.   I don't believe it.   If he had lived in easy plenty,
he would have been as pleasant as anybody.   I feel almost
guilty to talk so to you about him.   I have not ever spoken
my mind to the children, or anybody else, for that matter."

A new conception of the shut-in loneliness of her mother's
life, which had no confidences, dawned on Perdita.   The need
or possibility of such an outing presented itself as a revelation,
and a wish and hope began to spring within her that she might
be in some sort a friend to her.

While she went on thinking, she unconsciously watched her
mother's hands, which turned slowly over the contents of an

octagon box, pasted on its outside with pictures—a receptacle evidently of mementoes of joys that were wasted. An ancient ring, in jeweler's gold, bearing for a device two clasped hands, and worn thin and small till its linked fingers had parted at last ; a couple of broken brooches ; some locks of hair cut from the heads of the children, flossy and babyish, and hoarded in secret ; an old locket, a packet of letters yellow and faded, and a "Daily Food" in crimson and gilt, much worn and tarnished, whose texts had been often conned for comfort during the starved years so empty of worldly consolations.

"Mother, did not Violet Wemple wear jewels with those ball dresses up-garret ?" asked Perdita at last, picking up the ring and trying to join its severed emblem.

"Yes, a few. I had a set of garnets. Those your father sold one hard year to buy him a coat. I had a diamond pin ; we used that to live on once when the folks could not raise our salary, and we should have famished without it. I did hate to part with that ; my father gave it to me when I was sixteen. But it had to go. My watch your father carried after he had sold his, and he finally gave it to the Missionary Society and made himself a life member."

"How selfish ! how mean ! Why did you let him ? "

"He did not ask my consent ; it was at a synod, when all the ministers were giving, and I suppose he did not feel like being singular. And he had worn it so long that he sort of felt as if it was his. I think he must have been a little ashamed, though, for he was so cross when I asked him where it was. I could not help showing that I was sorry, and I cried about it. That made him so angry that I didn't know but he was going to shake me. I never mentioned it afterwards, nor did he. As to the other things, necessities pressed us so hard that I was quite willing they should go—I had no longer any use for ornaments, except a meek and quiet spirit ; and that I've tried hard to cultivate."

Listening to these queer revelations, it seemed as if a new

light from her mother's past illumined the daughter's future. A vision of herself in the time to come—old, humble, cringing, pale, sallow, arose before her.

"Never!" she exclaimed half aloud. "I'll neither bend nor break. Have you found the love-verses? Ah, yes! now let's read them quickly," she added, as she heard some papers rustling in the old lady's fingers.

The ancient bead-bag, such as had been the fashion of Violet Wemple's youth, lay on her knees, and she reluctantly brought from their long hiding the tributes to her faded charms—all crumpled and soiled and worn, like the beauties they praised.

"Don't read them out loud, Perdita," said she. "Take them home and keep them. If I should die first, give them to *him*, when this old face is out of his sight. They might recall Violet Wemple to him as she was when he took her."

"Mother! Oh, mother! I see it—I feel it; you have a soft, tender heart; I never dreamed it! There is one more reason why I am glad I did not rebel. I can be good to my mother. I can help you over some of the rough places. You will let me, won't you? You'll tell me when you feel bad? You'll talk to me about your troubles? Kiss me once more. Give me the mate to that one I got up-garret beside the old chest."

The poor woman was quite overcome, and wept profusely till a well-known step on the stair brought her back to the dreary necessity of concealing her emotion. She arose quickly, huddled her treasures into the box, wiped her eyes on the corner of her apron, and composed her features into their customary expression of patient endurance.

"There's Mr. Hethwaite. He don't like to see women cry. Put it in your pocket, Perdita (she gave the girl's hand which held the poetry a hurried little push). Now, be very careful how you go about Bettine. I do hope you'll get the little thing; she isn't *cut out* for hard knocks."

"Father's gone down the road," said Perdita, peeping from

the window. "I don't know but I am glad of it. I'll wait till another day, till I have read his verses. I'm coming every morning to see you. Pluck up a heart, mother; don't mind what father says—he isn't everybody."

"It is too late. I'm like on old machine, good for nothing but house-work. If anything could cheer me, it would be a sight of you healthy and doing well. You will be a good subject to think about, and I shall think about you all the while. Good-by!"

CHAPTER XIX.

QUI AIME BIEN, BIEN CHATIE.

HEN Perdita stepped out of doors, she stopped to look up and down, hoping Betty might be in sight. The child had been sent over to Mrs. Batts on an errand with Dolly, and she knew by her own longing how sorry she would be to miss the visit.

Yes, there she was, stepping along, with her head bent. At the first sound of the voice she turned. She lifted glad eyes, and hurried eagerly on to meet her sister. Walking was too slow; running could not suffice for her joy. She bounded and frisked like a kitten. But alas! her passage was speedily checked by a hard reproof which was shouted after her.

"Stop that there skippin'! stop, I tell you! walk. Do you think I've got nothing to do but buy shoes for you to *stomp* out?"

The Parson unintentionally adopted the style of speech current among his homely neighbors, and his child instantly subsided into a crawl, looking scared and unhappy.

"A nice father you are, to snarl like that at the tender creature ! Don't you see God's warm sunshine caressing her ; don't you see the merry breeze lifting her curls? Can't you feel this fresh air, which ought to make her young blood play warm and bright through her dear little heart ? Don't you know she is coming to *me* ? Yes, she has stopped her skippin' ; she creeps on, shame-faced and still ; she would weep if she dared. That pace suits you, it saves leather. There go a family of birds ! they can hop and skip all they please ; there are no shoe-bills in that crowd. Here comes a dog leaping on all his four legs at once ; there goes a sportive kitten, kicking up her heels. They are Nature's children—they can use their limbs at their sweet pleasure ; but the offshots of a minister have no such liberty.

"What a lean, lank, hungry existence is before this child, if I leave her here ! no games, no sports, no joys ! There's mother—his wife ; she stopped her skippin' long ago at the church door, when she took his name. Fie ! father. Go and write a sermon on depravity, and leave my Bettine to me."

Such swift thoughts chased each other through Perdita's mind as she returned the "bow-wow" good-morning of her parent, and watched him out of her sight, before she stooped and picked up her pet, who nestled into her arms with such a contented face that she hated to put her away again from the shelter she loved. Feeling that the time for her appeal was not fully ripe, however, she chatted with her and Dolly ; and promising to come run down again to-morrow, she left them.

She did not desire Betty to come up to the mansion house till the Vance children should arrive, so that she could begin her life there with playmates and companions ; and she was fully resolved to carry her point, and braced herself for the battle she anticipated.

CHAPTER XX.

"PAS À PAS ON VA BIEN LOIN."

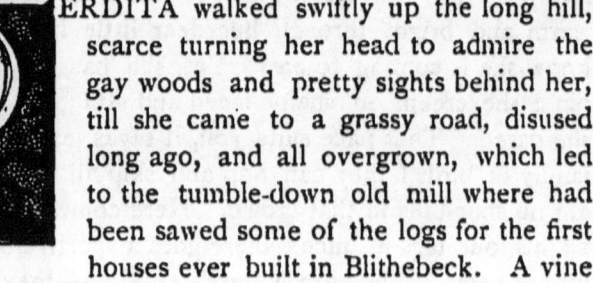

ERDITA walked swiftly up the long hill, scarce turning her head to admire the gay woods and pretty sights behind her, till she came to a grassy road, disused long ago, and all overgrown, which led to the tumble-down old mill where had been sawed some of the logs for the first houses ever built in Blithebeck. A vine of bitter-sweet hanging from a tree far within the overbending arch of gorgeous foliage caught her eye and tempted her to follow the lonely path by the fern-bordered brook till she reached it, and after plucking all she could carry, she wandered on towards the ruined dam, over one end of which plunged with much foam and fracas a rapid torrent, falling into the deep pool below in yellow eddies around the boulders bedded in the stream, and leaping with crest of foam to her very feet as she stood on the bank watching the stately play of a couple of wild geese who sailed right into the spray, clapping their wings and squalling among the mist-wreaths, like gray spirits of the flood.

Voices above her mingled with the turmoil, and looking up, she espied the Pratt boys standing on the dam, and holding between them a dog which yelped and struggled in their clutch.

They were fastening to the poor brute's neck a stone, and while she was observing them they secured it to their liking and tumbled him over into the dark water with a whoop and yell fierce and discordant enough for wild Indians. She saw the mad plunge of the victim, and presently he came swimming towards her, the rope trailing in his wake. The knot around the sinker had slipped, and given him a chance for his life, which he was frantically using; and he patted struggling out of the stream, and crawled to Perdita's feet, where he lay down, turning on his back, and whining for pity and succor. Dropping her berries, she knelt on the bank beside him; she caught him all dripping to her arms, and poured out a flood of sympathy and caresses, well understood by the dog, who thanked her at his best, licking her hands and face, and industriously wagging his bushy tail.

The Pratt boys came scrambling down the rocks presently, and claimed their prey, which she refused to surrender. The dog, also taking courage from her protection, showed them his teeth, and snarled and tried hard to bite, when they seized his tail and began to pull him by lateral force.

Perdita held him fast, and parleyed with them, to no good, and would have been obliged to give up had it not been for Mr. Slaughton, who laid his hands not gently on them.

"What are you about, boys? how dare you touch the lady?" demanded he sternly.

"How dare the lady touch our dog, if it comes to that, then? Just leave go now; we're goin' to drownd him! Father said how't we must, and we will."

"But stop a minute; why do you wish to drown him? what is his offence?"

"He's a trouble; he's a lost dog, don't belong to nobody; he's always 'round, he howls all night; mother hates him, and father said how't we should kill him this arternoon."

"Suppose I were to buy the creature of you."

"What'll ye give?" asked the elder Pratt, with true Yankee appetite for driving a bargain.

"I'll give you five dollars, on condition that you are out of sight up that road in three minutes, and go straight home!"

Astonished at the magnitude of the offer, they suspiciously eyed its maker while he pulled out his wallet and took from it a crisp new bill bearing in one corner the magic V, and the spokesman of the pair very nearly snatched it as soon as held towards him, for fear it might be a hoax, or that the gentleman would change his mind; and they ran on nimble legs, leaving Perdita in possession.

Before they were well gone, she awoke to the awkwardness of her position, sprinkled from head to foot with the plentiful wetting her new friend had given her from his enforced bath, her gingham dress all limp and draggled, her hat off, and a pile of scarlet berries at her feet; to be left in this shape, tête-à-tête with the man who despised her at her trimmest and tidiest, was hard; and she sprang up with crimson cheeks, and turning her back, she began folding her apron into a bag in which to recover her wood spoil, vainly trying to ignore his presence.

"You can no longer say you have no pets, I think," said he, looking curiously at her. "Of course you will keep what you have so willingly protected."

"I cannot consider mine a thing *you* have just paid *your* money for, and a ridiculous price too.

"In that case I shall call back the boys. I have no use for this brute; shall I present him to you, or offer them another five to toss him into that black pool, which looks like churning ink? I wait for you to decide."

"You could not be so cruel," said Perdita, dividing her glances between the suppliant at her feet and the smileless man before her. "Surely you would not give those unfeeling wretches a second chance to torture a helpless creature."

"Assuredly I shall return them their property, if you will not accept and acknowledge an ownership in him; a dog without friends is better dead than alive."

"If it is your pleasure that I take care of the animal, I will add that to my other duties."

"It is not my pleasure or intention to arrange either your duties or occupations," replied the gentleman coldly. "I rescued the miserable puppy from a fate which threatened him. I know that *you* meant to do it, but you had not the strength;

because I saw that you failed in power to achieve your charitable desire, *I* stepped in and used my strength, which was sufficient.   Unless you are very inconsistent, you must feel pledged to continue your good offices, at least till he runs away from you, which will of course be before long."

"Oh, indeed!   You mean to say that anything or anybody would run away from me?   You had better make your statement good by going at once."

"Not till this matter is disposed of.   To be, or not to be, is a serious question for that fawning creature at your feet."

"I do not incline to gifts, unless I like the giver.   I should get fond of the dog, and I don't choose to be fond of anything which——"

"I understand.   Pray don't take the trouble to amplify," said Mr. Slaughton, scornfully.   "He has lost his chance of a good old age.   Hillo! you Pratt, hillo."

The lads turned at the shout, and hesitated whether or no to come back, evidently fearing that the gentleman had changed his mind, and would demand his money.

"I shall keep him," said Perdita quickly, stooping and putting both arms around the crouching dog.   "Send those horrid little imps away; they shall not touch this poor brute; they shall not torture him; he is mine!"

"What you want?" shouted the Pratts, who kept at safe distance.

"Nothing; you may go," cried Mr. Slaughton, waving his hand impatiently.   "I was about to say, that if you were not out of sight in one minute more, it would be bad for you, do you understand?   Now, then, if you will loosen your frantic clasp of that animal for a moment, I should rather like to see where he belongs in dogdom," said he, turning to her with a provoking half-sneer.   "Ah! golden-brown coat, long and shining; drooping ears like softest silk; flossy fringe under all his paws; and a smart, sharp knob on the top of his head. Your puppy is a setter; tolerably pure blood.   Charge, sir!

very good! He knows what he is about. If you want to go out shooting, I think you will find him an active helper."

"Oh, dear," thought Perdita, ruefully listening, "what a beginning I have made! This will not do. I shall be as meek as mother, at this rate." She picked up the end of the rope as she rose to her feet. "Come, Sam," said she, "let's be going."

"I beg pardon! did you speak to me," asked Mr. Slaughton, coloring and stepping back.

"To you? Oh, no! far from it. I called my puppy. Sam is a very good name indeed for a dog; it is so short and so easy to speak. Sam! Sam! Sam!"

She lifted her voice to a musical shout, awakening the echoes, which sent her back a number of small Sams in return, while the setter dropped upon his haunches in front of her, and fixing his eyes on her face, gave out a volley of shrill barks in reply.

The gentleman looked into her sweet, rosy mouth, well opened for the tone she wanted, and observed how white were her regular teeth, even on their inner surface, how well-tinted and healthy her small tongue. Nothing unsightly or unpleasant there; the breath coming thence could not choose but be odorous as balm.

"You see I can send my call ever so far, in case he should justify your opinion and run away. Perhaps I ought to beg your pardon, for I do remember it is the name your friend gives you."

"It was not suggested or made applicable to the dog, I trust, by any puppyism you may have discovered—in me, for instance?"

"No, sir; I assure you, you are as bare of suggestions to me as a blank wall; you don't even cast a shadow."

"Oh, in that case the name is yours in common with all the world, from Bible Hannah down, and I beg you will not consider it mine in the least."

"I won't, then. Little Sammy is an excellent, suggestive

title. He was *also* a good boy ; *he also* minded his mother, answered when he was asked, did as he was bid. I begin to recognize these gifts as characteristic of the Sammys."

"Your choice certainly has a kind of poetical association with the escape of your prize, and will rhyme well in an epitaph ; as, for instance :

> " ' Here lies poor Sam,
>   Once saved from a dam.' "

"That is quite true too ; or Samson might be a proper name, for your Samsons were strong dogs from the beginning."

She glanced up towards the heavens, in which the day god was careering high.

"I see by the sun it is almost noon, and time Sam and I were at home an hour and a half ago. The point is what I am to do with the white elephant of a gift I have got. Father would kick him out of the parsonage, and I more than suspect that his advent will not be greeted with effusion up yonder."

Mr. Slaughton laughed in spite of himself. "As he has a taste for roving, I think you will do well to rope him in once more, or fasten him up for a while, which will probably afford you an opportunity for listening to the melancholy moaning of the tied."

Perdita glanced at him, and entirely failed in keeping the amusement she felt out of her eyes; but she would not smile, so she turned about quietly and jerked at the rope, saying, "Come, Sam!" and she and her joyous companion were soon out of sight.

"Bravo, old boy!" exclaimed Chandos, who had been a silent and unseen witness to the meeting and colloquy. "'Tis said when Sir Miles McKillgrist wished to break with Mistress Tabitha Bramble, he kicked her cur. You are reversing the order in a masterly stroke of policy, and turning the old proverb most admirably into ' Love my dog, love me.' The poor beast has stemmed for you the billows of aversion, and may convey you safe into the harbor of tenderness."

"Pshaw!" ejaculated Mr. Slaughton sharply; "how long have *you* been here?"

"Oh, I followed close on your heels. I must applaud your behavior during the interview, you were so amazingly affable."

"'Affable?' Why should I snarl at a young female I meet in a wood? I'm not a tiger, you know. I hope I *was* decently civil; but I do not admire or approve the girl for all that."

"Smart, though, Sam—is she not? You have a spouse who quotes Congreve, and most glibly and appropriately does she make it serve her turn."

"So it appears," grimly rejoined Mr. Slaughton. "She might have gone a little farther and added, 'Have a care, for the strongest Samson of them all pulled the old house over his head at last.'"

"I perceive you are much in the temper of the big chap who was brought into the house of Dagon to make sport."

"Pho, Chandos, those villains wrote nothing fit for the perusal of young, innocent girls. I wonder how far this parson's daughter has dipped into their filth."

"Education comprises all literature, ancient and modern, and you know noble ladies went night after night to applaud the Mourning Bride and the Old Bachelor."

"Granted; but neither you nor I would take our friends to sit out such stuff. If the world is not purer in our day, it is at least more decent."

"Perhaps. You have begun well, Sam. Go on this way, and you'll soon tame your Kate. You did quite right to insist on her accepting the dog *you* had offered."

"A worthy gift, truly—my first! a half-starved, half-drowned puppy."

"You have demonstrated in some small measure a fact I have always held to; in spite of your easy ways, you have will and power enough even to rule a fractious woman."

Presently Sam burst out laughing.

"What is the joke?" asked his friend.

"I was thinking how mother might relish the little Sammy I've sent home to her. You must know she desires a grandson who shall inherit the family name."

"I trust you were not malicious in your seeming kindness."

"Oh, no ; but I foresee squalls, and I confess to a little curiosity to find out which of the two will win."

CHAPTER XXI.

"SERMONS IN STONES AND GOOD IN EVERYTHING."

 SUPPOSE you are all going to meeting, this morning," said the widow, when they were seated at the breakfast table, Sunday.

"Oh yes, indeed, madam," answered Chandy. "Sam proposes to take me out to the Holy Saint Roofus, Dr. Woods rector, the Right Reverend Bishop Forest presiding. Quite a respectable congregation, and a most perfect service. The church is a venerable cathedral, ancient-gothic, designed by Mr. Stone, carved by one Mason ; the choir is led by Prof. Bird, assisted by Mr. Robin, Miss Nightingale, Miss Martin, Miss Finch, and young Breeze, who does the tenor solos. The usher who has care of the naughty urchins is old Badger ; and among the congregation are the most distinguished names in our country. There are the Beeches, the Oaks, the Maples, Dr. Birch, Esquire Brooks, Deacon Rivers, and Judge Groves; then there is Mr. Green, the celebrated carpet-weaver; Mr. Brown the trunk-maker; Mr. White, the artist, who paints such beautiful arbutus blossoms and dogwood flowers; Mr. Marble, whose record is as clean as his face; also the beautiful Miss Plum, whose habits are a little wild, 'tis true, but whose purple dresses are the very perfection of color. Colonel O'Wheat, a bachelor, who does not live among his relations; quite a large family of Foxes, who are said to be intimate with the spirits of just men made perfect; and those slender Aspen girls, who cannot keep quiet one moment of their lives."

"You are leaving out the Colts," said Sam, laughing.

"They are not regular attendants of Dr. Wood's church; when they do come, they are generally in too shaggy coats to be quite genteel, and often barefooted. Then there are the Larks (Sam used to be fond of a lark, Mrs. Slaughton) and the Deers. I've known him to slay many a dear, but that was before he knew you. Quite a family of De Wolfs; they only appear occasionally, when they expect to meet the Lambs, of whom they are so fond that they can never get enough of them. There's the Hogg family; they are to be found among the Fields and the Penns. They are also intimate with the Roots, who are a low connection, well known as underlings to the Trees and Branches."

"Mr. Moon and the sparkling Misses Star prefer the evening service," spoke up Perdita, whose amusement got the better of her silence.

"Yes, and there is that pale Miss Snow, who so melts under Dr. Wood's warm eloquence; but she cannot be friends with the Violets, who persistenty shun her neighborhood and declare that her very breath is chilly, to say nothing of her manners."

"They are fond of Mr. May, however, and always hanging about him, showing off their blue eyes. Will you come with us Mrs. Slaughton," asked Chandy, smiling at Perdita.

"No," she replied, "I like the cathedral best when Dr. Spring leads the service, and Deacon Greenleaf is usher."

7

"Well! did I ever listen to such nonsense!" exclaimed the dame, who had been impatiently glowering at each speaker in turn. "I should hope Perdita would go to her own meeting."

This kind of talk was new to the Parson's daughter, whose fancy had never been much encouraged; and she did not know how her face lighted up as she followed Chandy's fanciful presentation of names, nor how bright her eyes were. She forgot where she was, and who were her neighbors. She felt as if she were reading a fairy story, or looking at a picture, or hearing music, as she went on following out the train of whimsical conceits; and it was not till the old lady's matter-of-fact interruption recalled to her that the gentleman opposite her was her husband, who did not love her, and also that he was unpleasantly observing her at that very moment, that she drew her brows together in a dark frown, which shadowed her eyes like a swift rising cloud, so quickly did the brightness of her face disappear.

"I shall of course go to the orthodox place of worship, madam. A minister's daughter has been properly trained, I hope, in that, as in all other respects."

"But Dr. Wood's views are so wide! his expressions so liberal! His very atmosphere is worship! Every thought he inspires is of the majesty and glory of our Creator; every strain of the music of that cathedral is pure praise; every response a thanksgiving. Better come with us, Mrs. Slaughton."

The bridegroom made a slight movement of impatience, which Perdita detected and violently resented. "He need not fear that I shall thrust myself into his neighborhood," she thought. "Nothing is farther from my desire or intention."

She rose haughtily from the table, and was going away without an answer, had not Chandy stood up also, and bowed; she remembered then that she must reply to his invitation courteously.

"For a simple girl like me, Mr. Goldsmith," she said with a slight accent of bitterness she could not restrain, "the old

fashioned road which leads under orthodox roofs is the safest ;
but that does not prevent my wishing you a very pleasant
ramble." -.

————◆————

CHAPTER XXII.

"THESE BE MY JEWELS."

CHANDOS kept pretty well to his promise
to say no more to his friend about his
private affairs ; but that did not hinder
his malicious desire to bring the young
wife into his notice, so that he could not
choose but observe her.   He had a good-
natured intention of trying to better matters between them.   He would have liked
to see them on comfortable, friendly terms, if nothing more,
and gave a good many thoughts to the best means of bringing
it about.

Chandos, we know, had chosen for his own having a brunette ;
he admired them, as a rule.   He found Perdita handsome,
even in her constrained situation, where no feature or faculty
was allowed free play ; he was able to surprise her into brilliance both of color and utterance.

Having heard Samuel's side of the case, and understanding
his feelings and intentions towards his bride, he was curious
to learn what motives had induced her to become an unwooed
wife, and the more he studied and observed her, the more per-
plexed he got.   It did not look like ambition, for she evidently
cared not at all for the wealth or position she had gained.
It could not be blighted affection or pique—she was so fresh,
so *naïve,* and had led such an isolated life.   It was not with any

hope of winning the love she had a right to, for she was persistently careless and indifferent to the man. It could not have been slavish fear or habitual obedience, for she had shown in a thousand ways already that she had spirit and power and temper enough to resist where resistance seemed worth while.

Chandy had some half-formed intentions to engage Bertha's countenance and assistance for the young creature, so inexperienced and in such danger of making shipwreck of her happiness. He reflected proudly what a valuable friend his steady, sensible wife was able to be. But he had signally failed, thus far, in his approaches to that subject. A proposal for Bertha to visit the postulant was coldly received by Mr. Slaughton, and an invitation to fetch his wife to Roaring River was distinctly and decidedly declined.

"Mrs. Slaughton, stay a moment," said Chandy one evening, as they rose from the supper-table, it being Perdita's habit to withdraw from their company as soon as the evening meal was finished. "Stay, I want to show you my family; I brought them down on purpose."

"Certainly," replied she, looking at her husband in a perturbed way, seeing that he had stepped indifferently backward to give her full egress to the library.

"Let us all admire, won't you?" asked the old lady, pattering after them. "I'm *desperate* fond of looking at pictures; so is Samuel."

"Oh, with pleasure, madam. There is no vanity so utterly vain as your true parental vanity."

Mr. Goldsmith had meanwhile placed a chair for Perdita, and seated himself by her side. He drew from his pocket a handsome book of Russia leather, which had his name in gilt letters on the cover, and opening it, displayed his wife's face; good, true, pleasant as the Bertha we knew in her innocent girlhood, and on either side of her a child—the girl fair and winsome as Chandy's baby self had been, and the boy with great eyes and firm mouth, as masterful as Uncle Otho.

While Perdita was bending her head over them, thinking what a pleasant home that wife should have, with this husband, who carried about with him her picture that he might employ his leisure in contemplating her charms, and who spoke so often and so proudly of her, quoting her opinions, recalling her remarks, interlarding so habitually his talk with " Bertha said " —" Bertha thinks "—"Bertha scolded "—" Bertha was pleased," insomuch that it was plain that the wife was queen in her household, and in some sense a law unto her careless, handsome spouse, who chose her and married her because he wanted her for a friend and companion. While she pondered so deeply and so bitterly that she forgot she ought to say something, the dame fitted on her glasses and came and peered over her shoulder, and exclaimed :

" Beautiful boy indeed ! as handsome as a cherub ! Oh, my son ! " she tiptoed over, and whispered in that gentleman's ear, who had seated himself apart, and did not look amiable. " Oh, my dear son ! Sammy will be just as bright, and as smart, and as pretty as that child ; and I shouldn't wonder if he was a deal finer. There's a great many good-looking folks amongst your father's kin ; and if I do say it myself, that shouldn't, my relations were mostly reckoned personable, and I had a good color myself when I was young. Your father used to call me his little ' Rosey Posey ' for a great while after I got married ; and oh, my dear Samuel, my earnest prayer is that the Lord will mercifully keep back my last summons till I've felt the joy of holding dear precious baby Sammy in my arms—the beautiful little darling ! "

Chandos was speaking to Perdita.

" My wife gave me this book last Christmas. Thoughtful of her, was it not ? Oh, yes, it 'was a gentle business and becoming the action of good women ; her pretty playing did outsell the gift and yet enriched it too.' How do you like her looks ? she is of the sort who wear well ; gets nicer every day. I heard once of a fellow, who, being engaged to a girl, refused to marry her because, after a careful study of her picture, he made up his mind that the original was sure to become an ugly old woman. Now, on the contrary, I have from the first been in the habit of assuring Bertha that she would make a lovely elderly lady; and do you know, in my innocence I never once surmised that I was teazing her, till she finally burst out at me: 'Chandos, I really do wish you would leave off gazing at me and saying, "Oh, well, Bertha, you will be a handsome *old* woman," as if I was a perfect fright now, and your lot needed the alleviation of hope to make me bearable.' I assure you I abandoned from that very moment that sanguine outlook into my future, and entirely changed my base of compliments. Samuel, don't you think Mrs. Slaughton has much the same type of beauty as my Bertha?"

Mr. Slaughton, who was at that instant withdrawing from his mother's most obtrusive and inopportune prophecy, rose and left the room quite abruptly while Perdita unconsciously lent her ears to his expected reply; and she drew back with hasty pride, feeling justly offended with his unnecessary rudeness.

" He declared so peremptorily his will that our lives shall be so managed that outsiders shall be able to pick no flaws in our conduct towards each other, and look how he is all the while violating the very spirit of our compact! What if I am the opposite of all he admires, he might learn to cloak his aversion before folks. If he goes on in this manner, I shall most certainly and decidedly hate and abhor him, and that will be inconvenient. I had much rather regard him as a harmless person, in whose house I keep my Betty and earn our daily bread."

CHAPTER XXIII.

"IF YOU WISH FOR PEACE, PREPARE FOR WAR."

ATURDAY morning the artists came across Perdita in the hall. She had a broom in her hand, and a little sweeping-cap of crimson cambric on her head, into which she had tucked her black braids, and her short scanty dress of dark gingham showed her low-cut shoes tied with red ribbons, and her crimson stockings. And Chandy stopped to look at her, and chat a little before setting out on their day's work.

"Armed with the besom of destruction, I see," remarked he easily. "Well, there is plenty of rubbish and nonsense in the world which needs clearing off by good, innocent women like you, Mrs. Slaughton. I wish you success."

"I wage no war with other people's follies; this is only the new broom which sweeps clean. Your grace finds me here part of a good housewife; the last day of the week is a busy one among thriving Christians."

"I am sorry to hear you say that so positively, because I was about to beg you to come out sketching. I really wish you would. I can't get any good of Sam nowadays, he bothers so to come home before we have fairly got our canvas up."

Mr. Slaughton was furious, especially as Perdita received the outrageous statement as if she felt it a most natural declaration of a perfectly patent and accepted truth.

"Impossible, Mr. Goldsmith, there is to be jelly-cake for supper, and Malborough pudding for Sunday; and I dare not risk my reputation by neglecting them. I shall be glad to look at your sketches, though. I think I might be rather fond of good pictures."

"Sam! I say, Sam," called out Chandos, as if struck with a sudden inspiration. "Let's you and I make each a picture of your wife in this costume, for the Toptown exhibition. We could call it the 'The Young Housekeeper,' or 'A Weapon of Defence,' or——"

"I am afraid Mistress Bertha might object," interrupted Sam dryly, just glancing at the two over his shoulder, from the place of waiting he had taken outside on the piazza, within ear-shot of the colloquy.

"Oh, I see, you don't relish any intrusion on a privilege exclusively your own. Well, I can't blame you, with so ador-able a subject. I won't press the point. I know how it is my-self. There are chords in the human breast, Mr. Guppy," Chandos pumped up the "Guppy" from his throat in such a droll way that Perdita could not help smiling, though she turned about to conceal her face as she did so, and enmeshed her broom in a cobweb which Hannah had neglected. She felt provoked with him for his impudence, and angry with her husband. "You remind me," said she, pulling her trophy off her besom, "of a photographer who was ordered by his sitter to make her handsome. 'Madam!' said he, after a scanning glance, 'I decline the job.' Unless you are willing to get dreadfully dusted, Mr. Goldsmith, I advise you to stay not on the order of your going, but go at once, because I intend to raise a cloud of witnesses to my thriftiness. See, they are coming now," pointing to the shining motes dancing in the sunbeams." So saying she walked away and began to ply her broom with speed and vigor.

Chandos, finding no further chance for chatting, lazily saunter-ed out and joined his brother artist, whose impatience was visible.

"Look here, my friend!" began the host pointedly, as soon as they were outside the gate, "you and I'll have to quarrel, if you don't mind. I can't stand everything."

"What can you mean?" exclaimed Chandy, stopping and confronting him with the innocence of an astonished lamb.

"I call it ungenerous, after my free-hearted confidence in you, to go on like this, trying all in your power to make me uncomfortable and ridiculous. I shall not put up with it much longer."

"You and I quarrel, Sam, 'who have sat on one cushion, both warbling of one song! both in one key! we who grew together like to a double cherry; seeming parted, but yet a union in partition—two lovely berries moulded on one stem——"

"Pshaw! Chandos, don't be a fool," retorted Sam, grinning against his will. "I don't feel in a merry mood myself."

"You are mistaken in my motives, Samuel. I am doing my best to show you that you have it in your power to be extremely comfortable, not to say happy."

"Allow me to be the fittest judge of my position," interrupted Sam, getting very red. "I will trouble you to keep your advice to yourself till it is asked for. I've known duels fought with less provocation than you've given me. Yes, and death-wounds given. By Jove! you presume on my friendship. You have no delicacy. Your conduct to the young woman in yonder is unbecoming, to say nothing of the continual rasp, rasp, you keep up at me."

"Don't let's quarrel, Sam; I'm going away Monday. You cannot surely be such a churl as to object to my making myself agreeable to my hostess. I cannot afford to be considered a bear by a handsome woman; whatever reputation you are willing to make with her, I don't wish to fare like poor Tray, because I happen to be in surly company. If *you* delight to bark and bite, 'tis not *my* nature to; God hath not made *me* so."

"Chandy, you are incorrigible," replied his friend, smoothing out the deep frown from his forehead and bursting into a laugh. "Forgive me, old fellow. I wish to gracious you had stayed away at this peculiar epoch in my destiny; but as fate sent you here, I know it is impossible for you to refrain from extracting all the

7*

amusement out of me the case calls for ; and I won't ask you to
be easy either, for somebody ought to get a measure of enjoyment
out of the queer fix.   I should laugh if it was any other fool in
my place.   Heigho ! when I look at you I can scarcely believe
so many years have passed since the old Rosenbloom days.
You must have been a happy fellow to keep so absolutely your
youthful jollity.   As for me, I feel as if I was a hundred."

"Samuel, my dear old chum," Chandy turned about and
looked in his friend's eyes, his clear, handsome face lighted by
real affection and honest feeling, "it is not so long ago; we
are hardly in our prime yet.   You've got as good a chance for
a rich, full life, as a man ever had ; and I believe you'll find it
out too.   I did not mean to be unpleasant.   You cannot deny
that I've put your lovely model into lights and shadows you
never could have managed—nor would have tried, perhaps.
There are rich traits there, Sammy ; strong points, interesting
studies of variety in expression, in play and feature, unconscious
graces mental and bodily, well worth your artist attention,
deserving your friendship as a friend, your ardent love as a man.
Paint her picture, Sammy, and make her talk while you are
doing it."

"You are best fitted for that, Chandos, for 'tis truly true of
you, what was said of Lawrence, 'The blandishments of your
pencil are only equalled by those of your tongue.'"

"I've merely supposed the case in her hearing, as it ought
to be in her life.   Such a beauty, so ripe and real, should have a
true worshipper in her nearest, who should be her dearest."

"You are forgetting, Chandos, the truth we were drilled into
under our master ; 'the perception of the beautiful is a psycho-
logical operation, by which perfections are perceived in an object external to us, approaching to the ideal form which has
already existed in the mind.   It is the *mind* alone that is beautiful, and in perceiving beauty we only contemplate the shadow
of our own affections.'   This girl does not in any way resemble
my ideal ; *ergo*, I am not able to perceive any perfections in

her. I find about her no shadow of my affections; therefore I will not paint her face, nor bring myself into needless contact in any manner with what I find wanting in graces and charms."

"Oh, well, let's drop the subject, then. I must insist, if we go on, that there is munificent reward for your study in your young wife; but I refrain. I hate that ugly line you've got between your eyebrows. It gives me warning of lowering weather as surely as the rainbow, which the sailors dread to see spanning the heavens at evening, portends a tempest.

CHAPTER XXIV.

THE PICNIC IN THE WOOD.

HE friends did but little talking over their morning's work, which grew in graceful lines and fitting colors under their fingers with rapid, practised touches; and both were busy among their thoughts. When noontime came, they sat down in the cool shade to enjoy their lunch with hungry appetites, and to compare progress.

"As usual, Sam," said Chandos, "your trees are your strong point; such light, feathery foliage as you are able to work in! By Jove! I don't see how you do it. Look now! Though you give us but a peep at a time of the limpid azure overhead, through the dense masses of leafiness; such brilliant clusters, too, that if their originals were not glowing up above there, I should say your tinting was impossible. Yet you are free from opacity or heaviness. I could walk up that steep footpath and scramble over the patched fence into yonder forest,

if I could manage to push through those armed briar-bushes ; ·
and I know that the sunshine would fall warm on my head,
were it not for the rustling canopy of leaves which screens
me from its ardent touch.   Sam, you've studied nature to a
purpose."

"Praise from Sir Hubert Stanley," laughed the artist, who
was much more interested in the sandwich he was munching
than in his friend's partial admiration.   "Let's pack our traps
and go down the hill towards the west.   You can find that
wonderful effect of golden haze you wanted to study with the
afternoon shadows."

"After a while, Sam.   Let's smoke the pipe of peace first.
I've earned my daily bread already to-day.   We won't push
the curse too far, which is a blessing in disguise, taken
moderately."

It was three o'clock when they reached the brook by the
roadside, singing to itself in the solitude ; and as they paused
to listen, they heard a clear voice trolling out "Jerusalem the
golden," occasionally helped by tenor and bass—rather light
and youthful, 'tis true, but very fresh and not inharmonious ;
and sending a look under the low branches into a cleared space
beyond, they discovered a party so busy among themselves as
to be entirely oblivious of their neighborhood.

"Whom have we here?" whispered Chandos; "they look
like Bohemian gypsies, but they sound like a Methodist camp-
meeting.   Those wood-notes are a little wild, but by no means
wooden.   Bless us and save us, Samuel! that sweet singer of
Israel is Mrs. Slaughton."

"Of course it is," answered Sam dryly ; "and surrounded
by all the well-bent twigs of the Hethwaite tree."

"And there's the puppy Sam at her feet, in silent and devout admiration, as every Sam ought to be—a most discerning
animal, that dog."

Seated by a blaze, kindled in a rude fireplace of stones,
Teddy Hethwaite was bending his face over some frogs' legs

which he was busily skinning, and which he plunged into a pail of water as fast as finished.

Dolly was standing in a shallow pool, into which she made frantic dashes after the nimble jumpers, whenever the long stick she pointed at them, like a magician's wand, induced them to come within her reach.

Malcolm fed the blaze from a pile of twigs he had amassed for the purpose, and Perdita, the jubilant singer, was perched on a log, swiftly dressing with her scissors some small trout, which were evidently the captives of her own angling, for a slender rod leaned with its line against the tree-trunk behind her.

Little Bettine had her lap full of beech-nuts, and she eagerly devoured them, while the chattering of some angry gray squirrels over her head showed whose hoard had been sequestered for the child's pleasure.

"There, Samuel! if our genius was able to put that sylvan scene faithfully onto canvas, our fame would be immortal."

"They seem to be having an outrageously good time," said Sam in a vexed tone.

"That is a fact beyond demonstration, and I think there is such an overplus of enjoyment, that they can afford to spare us some ; let's join them," and added Chandy to himself, " kind fortune has surely led us to this spot ! here's an opportunity for him to get acquainted with his wife. One can make more progress at one picnic than in many weeks of ordinary life."

Meantime he was busily pushing his way through the rotting, tumble-down rails. (Parson Hethwaite's fences were a cause of much profanity among the unregenerate of his neighborhood.)

"No, thank you," returned Mr. Slaughton, drawing back. " I don't care to meddle with their joys. I'll go home."

" I actually believe you are afraid of that woman. Sam, your avoidance of her amounts to cowardice. It appears that her beautiful black eyes are as baleful as basilisks to you."

" Pooh, Chandy ! what flumadiddle ! Come on, then, if you

are determined to intrude uninvited on a select family party,
where *I* by no means feel secure of a welcome.   You shan't have
it to say I deserted you in your extremity.   It is the duty of a
host to endeavor to be complaisant to the most exacting
of his guests."

Little Betty was the first to espy them.   "Oh, Perdita,"
whispered she fearfully, " there's a man down there."

"What of it, child?   We are on our own ground; tisn't
father, is it?"

"No, it is Mr. Slaughton!" cried Dolly, springing nimbly
out of the water, " and here I am bare-legged!   What did Billy
want to hang my stockings on that tree for?   I can never reach
them.   Oh, my! what shall I do?"

" Hallo! you gypsy band! what are you about here?" called
out Chandos.

" Catching frogs!" replied Malcolm, who was very concise
and not over-hospitable in his greeting.

"Catching cold, I am afraid, Mrs. Slaughton," retorted
Chandy, leaping over some scattered logs; "of a truth, you
will get coughs and what not on this damp ground."

" Oh, no," answered Perdita, coolly continuing her occupation.   " I never allow myself any improprieties of that kind."

"May we come into your camp and get our fortunes told?"

" That is as Dolly says.   This is her frolic.   As to the fortunes, if you make them yourselves, you can tell them better
than anybody."

" Sam is so satisfied with the present, he don't care to peer
into the future."

Perdita threw a swift glance into his laughing eyes as he
spoke, and was vexed at herself for doing it; because she
somehow could not help including in it the gentleman who
stood near, and whose face looked anything but satisfied; and
she gave her head an impatient little toss, as she observed that
it was the dog who munched fish-heads, who was pleased with
his passing moment, according to Mr. Goldsmith.

"Cakes and pies all finished?" asked the saucy fellow, seating himself on the other end of the log.

"Yes, sir. This is my half-holiday out."

"And she comes to spend it with *us /* We were afraid she wouldn't," cried Billy triumphantly.

"It *was* a sacrifice," said Perdita, with scornful emphasis. "But you see, I had strength of purpose to tear myself for a brief period from the matchless delights up yonder, that I might mingle in your simple pleasures."

"Are you going to cook those frogs' legs and trout?" asked Chandos insinuatingly.

"Yes, she just is; and she's the bully brick to do it too. She used to get up at five o'clock, and fry our fish, and we used to eat them all up before father got out of bed; we haven't anybody to make good times for us now. I think you might have married some other girl, and left us our Perdita," and Billy glowered quite savagely and vindictively at Mr. Slaughton, who nearly looked sheepish under the concentrated fire of the resentful eyes they all turned upon him.

"Don't prate, Billy," said the angler, snipping and snipping with her sharp scissors, and seeming engrossed with her occupation; and she turned out the dressed fish so rapidly and deftly that Chandos was filled with admiration.

"How swiftly you do that! it is really wonderful."

"When one has only a half-holiday to one's self, it is necessary not to waste time; the sun goes down so very early."

"Yes, and then she'll have to go off up yonder again. And who's going to help me learn that old Sunday-school lesson, I should like to know?" and again Billy frowned at the silent gentleman, whom he evidently considered a thief and a robber who had stolen away his sister. "I don't know a thing about the nasty plagues. I wish *I* had a staff that could do things—I'd fix out some folks I know of."

"Mind your fire, Billy," said Perdita.

"You will please observe," whispered Chandos behind his

hand as soon as she got out of ear-shot, hunting for the salt, which seemed to have been overlooked, "it is a clear case. These young folks wanted what you have got. Trust them for knowing the true value of the friend you took from them. Many have done virtuously, but she excelleth them all, don't you see?"

"Don't prate!" returned Sam, borrowing Perdita's reproof, and removing from his friend's neighborhood.

"I am so fond of frogs' legs," called out Chandy in persuasive accents to Dolly, who was still hiding her feet under her petticoats; "mayn't I have some of yours?"

"I suppose so," answered she pouting, "if Perdita likes it."

"Do you like it, Mrs. Slaughton? Oh, say yes."

Chandy was so bent on stopping, that he ignored the scant welcome of the young ones, who plainly considered them intruders, and wished them farther; and he was confident of being able to make them change opinions on his desirableness before they parted.

"I have not the least objection, of course, if you can find it worth your while," replied Perdita quietly; "but you will have to wait a long time before you get anything to eat. We did not come early ourselves."

"Couldn't I help you? to be useful is my wish. I had that for a copy when I was a little shaver, and I never felt so much like putting it into practice as right here, in this most charming epoch of my existence."

"Can you skin frogs?"

"I flatter myself that I can. I was familiar with their anatomy as a lad, and that sort of lore is apt to stick by a fellow when the ' Lamentations of Isaiah ' slip clean out of his memory. So I am not afraid to boast my ability."

"Then you might help Teddy."

Now, if there was one class of humanity more than another with whom Chandy was able to be at home, it was with boys and girls. He always seemed for the time as young as they; he did not oblige himself to descend to their level, but just sailed along with them as naturally and easily as if he had counted no twenties among his years, and had given his entire time and attention up to this precise moment to just such skylarking and pranks as they most delighted in.

He took out his jack-knife and set to work, and while his hands were busy, he talked to the shy lad (who was bending his head close down, and peeping through half-shut eyes at the delicate joints he was severing) with so much youthful fun, that he not only made him smile and grow bright, but Malcolm pricked up his ears as the horse smelleth the battle afar off and cries aha! and speedily drew nearer to listen and enjoy also.

Mr. Slaughton did not at all relish his position as an outsider, of whom nobody seemed to make much account. *He* was accustomed to be good friends with young people and children, and he approached Dolly, and asked her how she liked camping out in the woods.

But Dolly hadn't on any stockings or shoes; therefore she was ashamed, and she wanted him to go out of sight, so that she could get up and put them on. And she was, besides, dreadfully afraid of the well-dressed gentleman who looked not in the least like the Batts or the Pratts of whom she saw most in her everyday life; and she blushed and stammered, and said "Yes, sir," or "No, sir," and had a great mind to put her finger in her mouth and cry.

The boys and girls Sam affected were able to look him in the face and answer back; therefore he presently withdrew from this poor child, giving her up for a red-cheeked romp without brains, and left them all, after a vindictive glance at Mr. Chandy, who at that precise instant was laughing in concert with his listeners, and seemed entirely to have forgotten his presence.

After a while Billy came along looking pleased and content, as if Chandy's good nature had made him merry.

"See my flies, what Perdita made me," said he, showing a couple of hooks skilfully hidden under bright feathers.

"Don't chatter, Billy," advised the sister, rising from her completed task and walking towards the brook. "You mustn't think fine gentlemen, who spend money on their angling, will be interested in your little traps."

She did not look at the fine gentleman as she passed him, but moved swiftly on about her business ; and though Sam felt hit, he could not tell what particular folly she was flinging at, and experienced a kind of general all-overishness of shortcomings and incapacity. Her air and manner undervalued him to that extent; it seemed to say : "My foot is on my native heath ; and though I promised to be housekeeper and teacher in your house, I'am free and independent here, and I'd as soon you knew it as not."

As she passed Dolly, she threw her her stockings. "Put them on quickly," she whispered, "and don't look so put out. You have consented to their stay, though I don't see what they want to for. So now you must make the best of it. Fortunately, they can't spoil another Saturday for us. Hurry now, and see if the potatoes are roasted."

Billy took himself and his hooks away from Sam's neighborhood after his explicit shutting up, and being cut off from companionship, that gentleman had no better occupation than watching the mistress of the feast, who moved hither and thither, brushing the turf with light steps, arranging the sylvan meal.

She pulled an old saucepan from a hollow tree where it had been covered with dead leaves, and set it on the fire with slices of pork, which I grieve to say had been borrowed without leave from the family barrel by the young rascal, Billy. His mother, who came upon him in the midst of his appropriation business, did not order him to put it back ; on the contrary, she whispered hurriedly, "Make haste, Billy ; your father might come —run now ;" and she gave him a piece of the *Religious Herald* to wrap it in, and smoothed her face as demurely when the divine approached as if she had not just aided and abetted a piece of work which would have earned her a sure reprimand, and her son a whipping, if it had been discovered.

" Poor dears ! they would never have a good time if I was as severe and close as he'd like to have me.   And Perdita 'll be there to-day, too."

Dolly meanwhile had washed and dried half a dozen great clam-shells, which served for plates, and had been also stowed in the chestnut stump ; and some rude knives and forks, hammered from iron hoops and cut with Malcolm's jack-knife.

" Oho ! this is your pantry ! " exclaimed Chandos, who watched all the proceedings with boyish interest.   " You dwell here on the edge of the forest, like fringe on a petticoat.

> " ' Who doth ambition shun,
> And loves to live i' the sun,
> Seeking the food he eats,
> And pleased with what he gets,
> Come hither, come hither, come hither ! ' "

" *You* will be pleased when you eat one of Perdita's frogs' legs," said Billy ; " I tell you they are bully ! "

" Did you call me ? " asked Teddy, who had caught only the refrain of Chandy's rhyme, and came hurrying up, thinking he was wanted.

" Oh, no ; I merely sent out a general invitation to the right-minded to leave off delving for filthy lucre and running after vanity, and do as we do."

" I hope nobody more will come," grumbled Dolly, discontentedly.

" No danger, Dolly ; that sort of folks are not plenty enough to be troublesome," said Perdita, turning the hissing fishes in the pan.

" You are robbers as well as gypsies, it appears," observed Chandos, pointing to Betty's beech-nuts ; " the squirrels are angry with you."

" Feeble folk like squirrels and women must learn to endure without grumbling what they are not able to prevent," answered Perdita.

Mr. Slaughton hovered about near enough to hear and see all, and out of patience as he was with his friend, was forced to yield to the contagion of his high spirits, and laugh occasionally; and he was besides much amused and interested in the family traits and developments of the Hethwaites, who, beyond the paternal ken, showed capacity for pranks and drollery; he had already spent some attention on the tiny child, frail and fair, who so demurely shelled the small brown things, so satiny and so little that they seemed just made for her.

Her skin was clear-hued and transparent, and though she was not much bigger than a Christmas lady doll, she was beautifully shaped and finished in all her minute proportions.

When Mr. Slaughton reminded himself that this child was the impelling motive which had so strangely pushed his wife into his house, where she meant of her own choice to dwell a stranger and an alien to him, its master, and her lawful lord, he examined her with extreme interest.

Pretty soon she looked up in his face. Her white teeth met on a nut at the same instant, and crushed the shell; and she returned the smile he unconsciously gave her, while she examined him and decided upon his manhood, from some secret standpoint of her own.

"Will you let me shell those for you with my knife?" asked he; " I can get them out whole, and faster than you can."

She hesitated an instant; looked about her for Perdita, and then reached out her small fist, and placed its contents in his palm.

When the young wife perceived this commerce of eyes and hands, she looked black and frowning at the pair. A jealous fear possessed her lest her darling, for whom she had risked so much, might be tempted or lured into opening her precious heart to admit another love besides hers; she could not bear

the possibility of sharing this only treasure of her life with anybody—especially the man who despised and disliked her, and
who desired to show himself coldly superior and indifferent to
her. She could not rest easy until she had sundered the child
from the companionship of this unpleasant person. Both the
mite and he seemed well pleased with the new acquaintance ;
they smiled and chatted, while Sam's busy knife was swiftly
piling up a little heap of white meats in the lap of the small
creature, whose nimble fingers made constant journeys to her
wee rosy mouth without impoverishing her horde·; and all the
murmuring talk and dainty thanks she gave the diligent laborer
were gall and wormwood to the watchful guardian.

"Come here, Bettine," said she presently, "look what a gorgeous caterpillar. He's yellow and red, with little trees of
plumage on his back."

"But I shall lose all my beech-nuts, if I get up."

"Drop them, then. You have eaten already too many.
They will make you sick."

"Let me put them in my pocket, please."

"No, no—throw them away, and I will open more by-and-
by."

Bettine looked wistfully up at her "cracksman"—such a
queer old glance, deprecating his displeasure, and pitying him
that his good offices were so made light of.

"I'll keep them for you," whispered he, smiling, who easily
guessed the cause of Perdita's evident disturbance ; and as he
scooped up the nuts into his hands, and Bettine sprang up with
a little shake and toss, like a bird ready to fly, he admired her
light, flitting motion, which was like treading on air.

"Ugly thing !" she exclaimed in her bright voice, a thread
of music pellucid and soft, as she fearfully shrank away from
the crawling worm, who had urgent business of his own, and
was getting about it as fast as his sixteen legs could help him.
"Let's kill him."

The savage and remorseless advice was in as absurd contrast to the sweet small notes in which it was uttered, as was her retreating terror from any murderous intention.

"Oh, no, Betty. You know God made him. He wants him to live ; he belongs to God ; you must not hurt him."

"No, I won't, then. Betty don't kill God's things ; she lets God's things alone. Did God make all these flies too."

She pointed to a myriad of darting gnats who sported in the sunshine.

" Every one ; every fly in the whole world."

" Oh, yes, I know ; and he lets me have some of his flies down to my house, don't he ? "

Perdita laughed merrily, and the sound was echoed softly behind her. Turning quickly, she saw Mr. Slaughton, who had gathered the beech-nuts into his handkerchief and followed Betty ; and she found on his face the first really genial, friendly look it had ever assumed in her neighborhood, and she let her eyes dwell one instant upon him, while a strange emotion surged through her heart. "What if she really belonged to this man, as she did lawfully ; could she find happiness in the owner-ship ? " It was but a passing thought, which she banished with swift, strong will.

"Perdita," whispered Betty, "I like Mr. Slaughton. May I go back no him now ? "

"Yes, come, baby," said the gentleman, holding out his hands. "There is no reason why we shall not be good friends."

Perdita surrendered her unwillingly, and she tried to hide the jealous pang she felt. " You may stop just while I finish the cooking," said she ; and though she busied her hands with work, she turned her eyes constantly and uneasily to the two who played with the dog, and her disquiet was not lessened by a remark which might have been either malicious or reas-suring.

" I offered no bribe, held out no inducements. The child takes to me because she cannot help it, and I receive her because I am able to understand innocence, because I like children."

He did not speak to his wife, did not look at her; but a gleam of mischievous triumph shone from his eyes, and the uproarious antics of the frisking dog seemed immediately to absorb all the attention of the new allies; so that, after a few natural and habitual turnings towards her on the part of the child, both appeared to forget Perdita's neighborhood.

The meal was ready at last, and the young wife hastened to claim her charge and place her near herself; and the whole party sat down around the cloth spread on the grass, while the appetizing viands served on the clean white shells sent out a most savory odor.

The sketchers brought excellent inclinations to the cheer, as well as the givers of the feast; and Chandos was so convivial and chatty that Teddy was in raptures with his talk, hanging on his words, and getting as close to him as possible, that he might admire the play of his handsome features. Such a magnificent fellow as he appeared to the home-bred lad, with his beauty, his culture, and his well-made, easy-fitting garments.

"Sir John Chandos," thought he aloud, after his near-sighted vision had been some time busy, keenly and inquisitively, with the artist's face and figure.

"How do you find me compare with your ideal of the brave knight?" asked Chandy good-naturedly.

"I don't know—I did not mean," stammered Teddy in secret confusion.

"I must explain, said Perdita, with sedate composure. "The adventures of that mirror of chivalry have been full of interest for Teddy and me, and I expect he feels the same sort of incredulous surprise I felt when I found his namesake walking among us."

"I hope I have not disgraced the name," returned Chandos rather proudly. "My father was fond of the old chap, and he gave me a book one Christmas in which he had copied out the whole career of the warrior-gentleman, and enriched it with illustrations colored with infinite skill. Chris and I got down the dear old Froissart, after we were grown, and found the passages marked by his hand. I feel rather sure that the spirit of Sir John has helped me through hard places sometimes. I fully believe he and my father often compare notes on my progress; and I fervently hope they will not get so high among the spheres as ever to lose sight of me while I am a militant individual, warring against the lusts of the flesh. Ah, Sam! My father was a wonderful man!"

"He was, indeed, Chandy; there are few such."

"Did he make one of John de Clermont and Chandos when they met, with the same device on their armor?" asked Teddy, who had been eagerly listening.

"You've got me there," replied Chandy, laughing; "that is an exploit I wot not of. What was it?'

"I can't tell stories. Perdita can; she is the greatest girl for learning things by heart! Say it, won't you, Perdita?"

"What for?" inquired she coolly.

"Because I want you to."

"Yes, indeed, and to please me," echoed Chandy.

"'Me' includes only Teddy, thank you," replied Perdita, smiling.

"And me," spoke up Malcolm.

"And me," added Billy.

"And me," put in Dolly.

"No, no; all me," piped up Betty.

Perdita glanced at Mr. Slaughton, whose eyes were fixed on her. "Don't prate, children," chided she shortly.

"That means, keep silence while I recite, I trust," remarked Chandos, drumming on his empty clam-shell. "Silence, all!"

The little matter is not worth so many words," said the young wife. Her face looked dark and displeased. The expression was perhaps a reflection from her husband's; at any rate, his saying rose suddenly to her memory—" A brow of Egypt."

She began in an uninterested voice, which soon grew mellow and pleasant as she saw how Teddy was listening and following her narrative.

" It chanced on that day that Sir John Chandos had rode out near one of the wings of the French army, and Lord John de Clermont, one of the King's marshals, had done the same to view the English. As each knight was returning to his quarters, they met. They both had the same device upon the surcoats they wore over their clothes. It was a Virgin Mary embroidered on a field, *azure,* or, encompassed with the rays of the sun, *argent.* On seeing this, Lord Clermont said, ' Chandos ! how long is it since you have taken upon you to wear my arms ? '

" ' It is you have mine,' replied Chandos, ' for it is as much mine as yours.'

" ' I deny that,' said the Lord of Clermont, 'and were it not for the truce between us, I would soon show you you have no right to wear it.'

" ' Ha !' answered Sir John Chandos. 'You will find me to-morrow on the field, ready prepared to defend and to prove by force of arms that it is as much mine as yours.'

" The Lord of Clermont replied, ' These are the boastings of you English, who can invent nothing new, but take for your own whatever you see handsome belonging to others.'

" With that they parted, without more words, and each returned to his own army."

" Did they fight ? " interrupted Billy, with a lad's interest in a scrimmage. " Who beat ? "

" No, they did not fight in duello ; but Lord John was wounded the next day in the battle, and he could neither get up again nor procure his ransom. Some say this treatment was owing to his altercation the preceding morning with Chandos."

8

" You do not believe, however, that the knight had any hand in it?" asked Mr. Goldsmith, as quickly as if it had been a personal imputation on his honor.

" No, I do not. Even making all allowances for the rude and rough doings of those times, it seems to me Sir John was not the man to countenance such dastardly revenge."

" And you are right. No brave man—and he was brave— would murder a helpless enemy. Say, Sam, with your leave, I'll make a study of those two disputing over their device, and present it to Mrs. Slaughton. May I?"

" That is as pleases the lady," replied Mr. Slaughton.

" Mr. Goldsmith, permit me to speak for myself. I should like it very much," said Perdita, while her eyes flashed.

" Did Sir John Chandos ever get married?" asked Dolly, who was still viewing the picture her sister had conjured for her, and who also kept in mind her mother's good wishes in her behalf, " I hope it may be your turn some time."

" Of course, Miss Dolly. I, his sole representative, am able to answer that question. All wise, good young people get married."

" Yes, they marry in haste to repent at leisure," said Perdita angrily. She was provoked beyond bearing by the studied indifference of her husband's manner.

Malcolm, who was as hungry as a tiger, had heaped his plate, or shell, so high with fishes that Dolly was troubled for her share.

" You must not take so many," said she, pulling his sleeve; " let Perdita help you."

The lad blushed red to have the eyes of all so suddenly turned on him; but he answered, " No, the gods help those who help themselves," and he watched an opportunity to pay the girl back, which he soon found. " Dolly!" he called out in a loud voice, " I wish you would shut your lips when you eat. Don't you know it says in the Bible, ' the sound of the grinding is low?'"

" ' A fool also is full of words '—isn't he, Mr. Goldsmith?"

"Why do you appeal to me, Miss Dolly? I hope you don't mean to number me among the babblers?"

"The babbling rhyme for fool is school, and that is where Dolly often wears the dunce cap," retorted Malcolm.

"Oh, dear! to-morrow will be Sunday," exclaimed Dolly, turning her back on the grinning lad, who was treating her to a ferocious *moue*. "I hate Sunday! Don't you, Mr. Goldsmith? You have to keep so still, and read pious books. Mother always puts away everything Saturday night but the Bible and Fox's Book of Martyrs."

"*I* won't do so, when I'm a man. *I'll* be as wicked as fun. I'll crack nuts, and spin my top, and make 'lasses candy, and eat lickerish, and have two pieces of mince pie, and I won't learn a bit of catechism," said Billy.

"Do you really think it is wrong to have good times on Sunday, Mr. Slaughton?" asked Malcolm of his neighbor, towards whom the good supper had amazingly ameliorated him.

"I believe in keeping the Sabbath," answered Sam. "I am of Johnson's opinion: 'One may walk of a Sunday, but not throw stones at birds; relaxation, but not amusement.'"

Perdita grew to be almost sorry for her last speech, and to find the gentleman nearly bearable, as she glanced bright-eyed at Teddy, much pleased to see how he was slowly taking in the humor of the quotation, rubbing his hands and squinting through half-shut lids at the quoter.

"Look here, Billy," said Chandos, taking up a little red-cheeked apple, which had made part of the dessert; "Did you ever see a cannon-ball that killed an emperor? No? Then look here, can you do this boy-trick?"

He turned his hand backwards and quickly jerked the fruit up in the air, expecting to catch it through the crook of his elbow in front when it came down; but his youthful skill so far deserted him that it flew across the table and narrowly missed Perdita's temple.

"Excuse me, but I believe that is the apple of your eye, Mrs. Slaughton," said he.

"No, sir; I have not room in my eye for two apples, and I consider your contribution *de trop.*"

"I understand; your eye is filled already. Yes, Sam *is* a proper fellow to take the eye of a woman," replied Chandos, pretending to approve his friend with a discerning scrutiny of his traits. "I think his smiling becomes him better than any man in Phrygia."

"Pshaw! Chandos," said Mr. Slaughton, with disgusted emphasis; "for a fellow who is forever gleaning from a rich author, you do manage to bring away the most astonishing number of inappropriate, nonsensical nothings!"

"Is that your candid verdict! Come, then, you shall shine awhile, you shall sing to us of Chiabidos:

> "'Songs of love and songs of longing,
> That our feast may be more joyous;
> That the time may pass more gayly,
> And our friends be more contented.'

Now then, Sam, sail in; we are all pleased attention."

Chandos adjusted his face and attitude to elaborate expectancy, and all the others following his lead, seemed figuratively to open their mouths for the words of wisdom about to fall.

"Gammon! don't be a boy."

Perdita heard the growling tones and observed the displeased face of her bridegroom, and remarked quietly:

"I like boys better than men, because in boys you are able to see grand possibilities, while in men you are obliged to · observe their deficiencies."

"Don't, Mrs. Slaughton. You will discourage Sam so much that he will be able to put no fire into his Chiabidos," remarked Chandy.

"Humph!" ejaculated the artist, with contemptuous mirth.

"Don't be over-modest, Sam, I beg. Pray begin. You

remember the beautiful address to Laughing Water; let us have it."

"I couldn't think of trespassing on your especial forte."

"Oh, very well. I am quite willing to be Chiabidos; and you can't object to my putting Mrs. Slaughton in the Indian maid's place while I speak the speech, of course."

> " 'Oh, thou wild flower of the forest !
> Oh, thou wild bird of the prairie !
> Thou with eyes so soft and fawn like,
> If thou only lookest at me I am happy
> As the lilies of the valley
> When they feel the dew upon them ! ' "

Chandos sang the words to a pretty air enough, and in such a sweet and melodious voice that all ears were pleased to listen.

"I am sorry," said he when he finished, "that you would not raise the tune of our little ditty, Sam, because you excel me as the lark does the tree-toad; and I know you admire 'Hiawatha.' "

Mr. Slaughton seemed unreasonably rasped and aggravated at the audacious eyes Chandy had made at his wife during his rôle, and replied quite shortly :

"On the contrary. I think Andrew Fairservice's words amazing apt to describe it : ripperty, tipperty, poetry nonsense."

"Sam has quite a staccato style of delivering his opinions, has he not?" remarked Chandos, turning to Perdita. "I hope you don't agree with him?"

"I have no idea on the subject. I have never read the book. What you have just given us certainly has a pretty jingle."

"May I inquire what sort of poetry do you admire?"

"I like the Iliad, and the Lady of the Lake, and the Ancient Mariner, and Lamia, and——"

"And Patient Griselda," put in Chandy mischievously, while

she hesitated an instant, as she happened to observe that her husband's eyes were scanning her with what seemed to her supercilious attention.

"No," she exclaimed positively; "I think Griselda was a fool, an impossible fool!"

"Hillo! what ails Teddy?" shouted Malcolm, hurrying after his brother, who had risen swiftly and scurried from the group with a hand to his cheek, running to the brook, where he stooped over the water, laving in its coolness.

"I expect he *et* too much fish, and has got a headache to pay him for being a greedy-pig," said Billy, who was still busy among the remains of the feast. "Father says it's a sin to be greedy."

"Father is a sinner; he owns up to it every morning. He tells the Lord he is the chiefest of sinners, and I believe him," remarked Dolly. "What is it, Mat? what's the matter?"

"He got kicked by a bee," answered Malcolm, returning out of breath and throwing himself upon the moss.

"Then he must not lurk where the bee sucks," said Chandy laughing.

"Pooh! a bee can't hurt much," spoke up Billy. "I *fit* a whole nest of yellow-jackets t'other day, myself."

"And did the yellow-jackets fit you, Billy boy, roving Billy?"

While the big boy was chaffing the small one, Mr. Slaughton's ear was attracted by Bettine, whose low, thrilling voice pronounced her sister's name.

So true and loving was the tone—so sweet, like the prayer of innocence, that he listened in unconscious eagerness for his young wife's reply.

"What, darling?"

The instant the unaccustomed utterance passed her lips, Perdita felt a sort of shiver, it was so new, so strange to her. No terms of endearment were ever used at the parsonage; no pet names. Mrs. Hethwaite had once been severely scolded in the hearing of her children for having inadvertently called one of them a "sweet angel."

"Beings born into a fallen world, of depraved and sinful stock, who are certain to be damned unless God elects their salvation—who are prone to evil as the sparks are to fly up-wards, are very far from being angels, Mrs. Hethwaite; and I trust you will repeat no more such idle words, of which you must give account at the day of judgment. Let your commu-nication be yea, yea, and nay, nay, hereafter," said the Parson.

Violet Wemple had not been able *then* to forget all the courting *pleasantries* her wooer had talked to her; and the look she gave him in reply to his pretty husband-speech irritated him.

"What are you thinking? out with it," he demanded with authority.

"I remember the time you told me you saw Heaven in my eyes," said she plaintively.

A very unclerical word came from between the good man's shut teeth, as he left her; and certainly *he* was no angel for a couple of days afterwards.

The sudden impulse Perdita felt to give voice to her great and strong love for Bettine seemed born of her freedom, and the child fastened swimming eyes on her after a troubled glance of mute inquiry at her new friend, who she felt must wonder how it had come to pass that Perdita said such things.

"Am I your darling?" asked she softly.

"Yes, you always were, you always shall be."

"Have you any more darlings but me, Perdita? am I all?"

"Yes, all, unless it might be Sam," she added, caressing the dog, who crouched and whined at her feet, as if he felt left out and neglected.

Chandos winked at his friend, who frowned dreadfully, and was evidently in dread that he would take the opportunity to teaze.

" And will you call me darling every day? I like darling better than Bettine. Say it some more, Perdita."

" But you wished to ask me a question, did you not——" She hesitated an instant, then added the endearing word for which the child was eagerly waiting ; and as she did so her eyes were full of love as fresh as was the new epithet to her lips, and a flood of sweet content glowed over the wee thing, beaming in her glances and dimpling her face with smiles.

" Tell me, Perdita, did I ever know Aunt Prudence ? " she whispered.

" No, darling, she died before you were born ! "

" But did I *never* know her ? " she persisted, fixing her gaze on the blue sky.

" No, Betty, how could you ? "

" Why, if she went up before I came down, we must have been there together ; and I should think she would have seen me, because she loved you ! "

" Do you remember any tales they told you up there ? "

" I cannot tell. I think so many things. I don't know who told me. I don't believe I got them all here ; we have no music, no flowers, no pretty-pretty people, such as I dream of when I sleep in your arms."

" Hush, Betty ! " exclaimed Perdita, suddenly recollecting herself, and looking at her husband ; " you must not tell all you think, except when we are alone together. See, the sun is almost down ; it is time to go home."

" Yes, Perdita," pleaded the child ; " and won't you come too. I want you so bad ! Dolly pulls my hair. Father says, ' Betty, be still ! ' Oh, Perdita, do come home ! "

It required some self-command to unclasp quietly the arms of her pet, which were suddenly thrown around her neck, and to put away from her cheek the tender little face she loved so well to feel pressing hers ; but with those curious eyes studying her, she forced herself to composure.

" Now, Betty, don't begin to cry. Come hither, till I tell you."

When they were away from the others, she knelt upon the ground and placed the mite before her.

"Listen, Betty. You must be patient just a little while, and I promise to fetch you away. You shall live where I live, and you shall never leave me any more—never, never! But mind, don't speak about it where father can hear you, or he won't let you come. Now, can you be good and quiet till I am ready?"

"I'll try," answered poor Betty, with an old look of resigned sorrow; "but don't be long, it is so dreary."

"I won't, darling. I'll come soon. Now we will all hurry and put away the things, and go, or father may find out where we are and spoil our meeting next Saturday."

"But you'll come a little way with me, won't you?"

"Of course I shall. I mean to carry my darling in my arms, away down the hill to the old apple-tree."

The artists lingered about till the party broke up; but any expectation they might have encouraged of walking home with the mistress of the feast were now signally disappointed, for she bade them good evening in the most careless way, making it patent that she had neither thoughts nor inclinations in their direction, and walked briskly off among her brothers, with Betty's golden hair floating on her shoulder, and Betty's heart beating close to her own so strong and loving.

Mr. Slaughton had not said much during the merry-making, but he had gotten some food for reflection, and a number of mind-pictures which often presented themselves to his memory. He might have named them every one: "Perdita dressing fish," "Perdita at the pool;" "Perdita worshipping her sister," and so on. Quite amazing pictures they were, too: vivid in color, pleasing for grace and expression, really startling in character.

As for Perdita, the sibilant song of the grasshopper never sounded in her ears without recalling to her this first afternoon under the old oaks, with her stranger-husband.

8*

CHAPTER XXV.

"WITH ROSES AND LILIES AND DAFFADOWNDILLIES."

R. SLAUGHTON, I wish to consult you," said the young housekeeper on the following Monday morning, as she turned from the piazza, where the family had taken leave of Chandos Goldsmith.

"Certainly," he replied politely, bowing and holding open the library door for her entrance. It might have been because she had treasured every one of the unpleasant things he had said, that she felt rising resentment at what appeared to her a scarcely controlled feeling of bored endurance in him.

"I suppose old Hannah has been equal to all the work of the house," she began without any introduction ; "but as it appears you are likely to be subject to incursions of the Goths and Vandals (excuse the phrase ; Teddy is forever lugging it into his talk), I meant to say ; visits from your friends, like this one just ended, it will be necessary, for the credit and respectability of your housekeeping, to get more servants, to be retained while you may remain here."

The gentleman, who had been mentally wondering what was to be the theme of the conversation, watched her face while she spoke. It was composed and business-like, apparently attending only to the subject in hand.

"You will oblige me by arranging their number and quality to suit yourself, and let me thank you for doing it," he said, as soon as she paused, and his face flushed hotly. "I assure you I have been much mortified by their lack."

"Indeed ! I hope there has been no apparent hitch in the housekeeping. I have done my best ; but, as I am not blessed with several pairs of hands, I dare say some slips were visible —in fact, I know there must have been, and that is why I mention this affair to you, a little after the fashion of shutting the stable door behind the stolen steed. But I suppose Mr. Goldsmith is not your only acquaintance, and I desire to acquit myself as well as possible next time."

"I have friends with whom I occasionally foregather; but if I had none, it does not appear seemly to my eyes that the mistress of the house should cook breakfasts, however admirable they may turn out, even as worthy of the table as your much bepraised fish-cakes."

"Indeed!" replied Perdita in real or pretended amazement, "my father thinks otherwise; and I know that I got a character as cook before your mother made up her mind to take me. I understand then, do I, that you see the plain necessity I have brought to your notice, and acquiesce in the new help."

"I beg that you will fill every department," said Mr. Slaughton quickly.

"Of course I shall, since you sanction it. I learn that the Vance children are expected; and then I shall, without loss of time, proceed to assume the second office you engaged me for. The new help will then be indispensable. The arrangement need last, however, only till you leave the country; because after that the house will be closed to guests, I dare say, and the expenses curtailed."

The husband was startled by so plain a hint that his absence was counted on as a certainty, and puzzled to know what she meant by it, as he had made no announcement of his going. While he was thinking about this, and the extremely unpleasant attitude his mother had pushed him into, she spoke again:

"There is another point I desire to mention." She raised her head and brought her dark eyebrows together in a slight frown. "No house can have two mistresses, any more than a man can serve two masters. Either Mrs. Slaughton, your mother, must be authority here, or *I* must take control. If it is I, I will not tolerate any interference, either with expenditures or arrangements. I keep accurate accounts, and I shall offer to you every month my book of disbursements, for examination and sanction."

"Poor mother!" thought the husband, as he observed the positiveness and determination of the proud young creature before him. "Did I not warn her, and isn't she coming right into the thick of the fusses I prophesied?"

"I understood from my mother, in a conversation she vouchsafed me previous to a certain event——"

"No wonder you hesitate; the event had so slight an interest for you as to be scarcely worth naming or mentioning; you have already informed me it assumed not the least importance in your mind. Pray go on. I am all attention."

"Your attention would certainly be most flattering, if I had sought this conversation; but as I wait on your convenience——"

"Your mother, you were about to say, conversed with you——"

"Yes, she did," answered he almost in a fume; "she said she ardently desired to put upon you the entire management of the household."

"I am glad to know that; and have I your permission to take it?" she added pointedly.

"You have supreme and unlimited power to do just what you please."

She curled her lip slightly as she noticed his evasion.

"He dodges the issue. He is afraid to take sides. He is afraid of a couple of women—afraid of me, for instance."

"Thank you! My road is plain now," said she, dropping her eyes to veil the twinkle of amusement she felt was lighting them at their queer positions and his disturbed face.

"And easy also, I trust," he replied.

"I do not covet ease. I should not know what to do with it if it came to me, especially here. I only know a life full of work."

"Teaching obstreperous young ones, I should think, would be a daily penance for wicked sinners. You will soon grow weary of it and leave it off."

"I shall *not* leave it off, if I do get weary ; because it is the daily price and payment for my Bettine."

She made her answer in candid simplicity, and true earnest, and Mr. Slaughton looked at her and spoke more pleasantly than he would have thought it possible he could ever look at and speak to the girl he did not admire.

"Now, if you have quite finished your business with me to your liking, I must beg a single moment of your time. I desire to consult *you*."

She bowed, and drawing herself together, to be ready for whatever might be coming (and she of course expected nothing agreeable), she waited with her steady glance fixed on his face.

"Permit me to ask your presence in the dining-room." He stepped on before her, with an easy saunter, as if neither his time nor hers were of value to anybody except themselves. The parsonage folks did not walk that way. They went as if driven by stress of work and must make haste to coin all their minutes into something to keep body and soul together. She had noticed the same careless lavishness in Mr. Goldsmith. He was never in a hurry. She rather liked it, and the thought passed through her mind, that the right to loiter, and rest, and take leisure, must be pleasant. But she did not propose to herself any such license. She even noticed a slight movement of the gentleman's shoulders, which nearly amounted to a hitch as he stepped, and that she scarcely could hear his footfalls on the thick carpet. The parsonage carpets were thin, and the Parson made the place resound with his clumping tread. Mr. Slaughton's mode of progression seemed a proper and suitable one, he being an independent man, able to make his own fashions and follow his own likings ; and it was not by any means ungraceful either ; and when he reached back to his pocket and pulled out a fine white handkerchief, from which she caught a faint perfume, that also seemed suitable. The Parson's bandannas would have been out of place for this gentleman ; and they were never redolent of spring violets. You see, everything about her was as new to Perdita as if she had stepped into another world. So it is not to be wondered at that she observed and treasured the merest trifles.

"Here, now," said he as they entered within the door, "you perceive this room is a wretchedly cramped place ; quite too narrow for even a small family. It will scarcely hold the thanksgiving turkey and chicken-pie, to say nothing of their consumers. I hate of all things being crushed at table or bumped by servants ; you must have noticed the inconveniences of the nook. Now, I've been thinking that if we were to inclose the immense piazza, which rears the whole west end of the house, we might gain an admirable, light, roomy hall, just suited to our purpose. What is your opinion ? "

" I should think it an excellent idea, but hardly worth your while to spend so much money, and take such a deal of trouble for your brief stay in the country."

" I am not aware of having announced any intention of departure," replied he in a displeased tone, "although you seem to have taken up the idea as a fixed fact. The wish is father to the thought, most probably. You will oblige me by no further reference to it. It looks to me as if you were counting on my absence and dating from it."

"I beg your pardon most humbly, I'm sure. I had no idea you were tetchy on the subject. I happened to overhear you proclaim quite positively such a plan in a conversation with Mr. Goldsmith. Unless I am mistaken, you not only said you would go soon, but mentioned also the object and terminus of your journey—killing tigers in Timbuctoo ; and of course I looked at the departure as a certainty. My lips are hereafter sealed. The idea of your motions being of consequence to anybody but yourself, and especially to me, is simply monstrous."

"No doubt that is your view of the matter. Why should they interest.or influence you, who are so independent of all people and things?" replied Mr. Slaughton, who was much piqued at her indifference, and also somewhat disconcerted, as he recalled his very free talk with his friend, and wondered how much she had heard of it.

"On the contrary, I am so very dependent that I am about to remind you of a promise. Sam, you scamp, leave my hand alone."

"I beg pardon!" exclaimed the gentleman, starting back. "Ah! I see it is the puppy who annoys you with familiarities."

"Yes, sir, only the dog."

After her explanation was uttered, it sounded so very absurd and so suggestive, that she could not help laughing a little.

"Don't you think Scamp would be a good name for the creature, so leaving off the other and avoiding all chance of confusion?"

"But is not that an unseemly sequence, or definition of the one I gave him first? and besides, your touching epitaph must lose all its point and rhyme."

"Not of necessity; it might be revamped thus, for instance :

> "Here lies a poor scamp,
> Who found a dam damp."

"Very good, indeed! but, if you please, I shall retain the name I gave him at his baptism. I had your permission, you remember. I have heard that it brings ill luck to change. And now that Mr. Goldsmith has gone, I don't see the need, either. There is nobody about the place who will make mistakes. I notice your mother always calls her son 'Sammy,' when she wishes to be fond."

She made the word so flat and silly in her pronunciation that Mr. Slaughton changed the subject.

"You mentioned a promise of mine, I think."

"I did, and I hope you are still in the mind to keep it."

"You may be sure of that, whatever it was," replied the gen-tleman quite eagerly, considering how distasteful to him was the speaker.

"Thank you. I want my sister Bettine to come here when the Vance children arrive."

"The little fairy of the wood? I shall be most happy to welcome such a beautiful child. I must make Uncle Sam her especial playfellow."

Mr. Slaughton's warmth was something malicious, I fear, be-cause he had observed quite plainly how jealous was her fond-ness for the mite.

"You are most kind, sir; and I promise you she shall be no charge to you except her bit and sup."

"You wish to insult me, it appears," replied he, flushing deep; "and I have done nothing to deserve it—to-day, at any rate."

"Quite true. I have to thank you for your patience. I might have put it more pleasantly. Pray excuse the seeming implication, and believe *you* were not in my thoughts. I must explain exactly what it was, that you may not think worse of me than I merit. Your mother has made it plain that she will not take kindly to Betty's presence here. Indeed, I am glad I am already used to economy, or I might be worried and discouraged by the constant harping on its necessity. I cer-tainly do not intend to waste your substance."

Her voice trembled, and he thought there were tears in her eyes, and saw that the recollections of some passages there had been between the old lady and herself aroused resentful feel-ings; she gave him no time to speak before she concluded:

"I don't say this as an appeal to you. I want no inter-ference of yours. I stated my expectations in the very start of our conference, and I absolve you from all responsibility. I shall manage as well as I can."

Her face looked so downcast, as she finished, that he nearly felt sorry for her. He knew his mother's propensity for nagging, and he felt that she had been exercising it on this stranger.

"Betty will be most welcome, for her sweet little self; and I truly hope she will help out your life, which I know must be irksome and heavy, and is about to become more so. I feel it so strongly that I would surely lighten it if I knew how."

His words were so unexpected, and so earnestly kind, that they brought a quick, vivid flush of surprise to her face, and her eyes were kindled with strange light as she answered him.

"You have lightened it, Mr. Slaughton. Your reception of my request is amazingly noble. I truly hope my sister will like you, *a little*—but she is mine, all mine."

Saying this, she folded her arms above her breast, as if she guarded a treasure.

"But I hope you will not forbid me the pleasure of a little romp with her occasionally ; and while we are rather friendly, I must tell you I do not relish the position you gave me Saturday. I never in my life before appeared in the character of ogre. I do not find the *rôle* suits me."

"I believe I do not quite understand."

"Why, just this : young people generally do not shrink away and get dumb at sight of me."

"And pray who does ? " asked she, smiling a little.

"Your sisters and brothers ; and I don't like it."

"The children of the father-in-law whom the devil gave you to pay off his grudge," was the first thought which came to Perdita. She did not utter it, however. "They are reasonably fond of *me*, and I dare say what you set down to dislike was only awe of such a fine gentleman."

"You can sneer, it appears, as smartly as a fine lady ! I am sorry to see it. I had a dim idea that we might be friends."

"Friends, Mr. Slaughton, must meet on equal ground, and I cannot forget your declaration that this arrangement of my life assumed not the slightest importance in your mind."

"A most uncalled-for and unnecessary remark of mine," said the gentleman, striding pettishly about the room.

"You made it, however, and you also told me, very plainly, that you could not love me. Not that I desire any affection of yours," she added quickly. "I merely recall your words to show how inconsistent you are. Children are swift observers ; they can point a rapid moral and draw acute conclusions. Any carelessness or rudeness to their Perdita is likely to be resented by my brothers and sisters, and you haven't been such a wonder of affability as to deserve their gratitude."

"I might have been more agreeable, perhaps," answered Mr. Slaughton. He did not in the least care to analyze his state of mind. He saw a fresh, candid young girl before him, who had come and said, "I wish to consult you," and who had looked spirited, vexed, astonished, pleased, grateful—nearly humble—and decidedly provoking, during the few minutes just passed, and he found her interesting in each phase she had shown him of her character, notwithstanding her black brows, her intense eyes ; and in spite of all that was said and done, he really wanted to be easy and agreeable. I don't know at which precise point of time he had discerned such a desire among his wishes, but he certainly felt it now. He had got to sit opposite to her every day, and he found it was not so dreadful as he had at first considered it ; and he called after her as she turned to go, although her parting speech was not conciliatory.

"I am not able to give an opinion on your capacity for being agreeable, as I have never seen you try your powers." That was what she said, and she gave her head a little toss as she said it, and stepped off without looking at him.

"Stay one moment. I'll try not to be churlish now, at any rate, while you give me your opinion on the new dining-room."

"With all my heart, sir. I am quite at your service."

"Then please step out on the piazza, where we can get the true bearings of the case. Now, for instance, if we were to

put glass doors in the centre, and a conservatory beyond, opening into it, and steps leading down——"

"Oh, a conservatory!" exclaimed Perdita. "I never saw
one in my life. I have read about them in novels; it should be
beautiful; but that is not economy."

"I hate that word!" burst out the gentleman. "It has a
mean, sordid, pinched sound, most unpleasant, not to say rasp-
ing. Pray drop it! It is not the business of life to study how
little we can spend, but how much enjoyment can be got out of
our money."

"That sounds pleasant," replied Perdita, shaking her head;
"but it is in such direct opposition to all my teaching at home,
and here also, that I am afraid it is heresy."

"It is safe for you to forget all previous lessons and commence a new chapter. *I* am authority on that topic in this
house," replied Mr. Slaughton, with such haughty decision as
made his face quite commanding.

"I am convinced. Pray go on." Perdita liked so much the
power and will she recognized in him that she listened and
looked at him with a good degree of complacency. She almost
felt as if he might get to be a requiting study.

"About fifty feet wide, I should say, with roses climbing up
the pillars; cape jessamines in tubs, camellias, and orange
trees in the centre on a raised bed; and mounting to the roof,
and along the sides, all sorts of sweet flowering things," explained Mr. Slaughton, waving his hand about enthusiastically, inspired by her flushed and eager attention. "I've been thinking you might like a house full of blooming plants, since I
noticed you hanging over the tea-rose in the window yonder."

"Teddy bought me that with some money he earned chop-
ping wood for Mr. Easy. I had its first blossom too. Oh,
yes, I love it dearly."

She stopped short. A sudden memory flashed over her of
the time and place when and where she had worn the flower,
and she felt so much afraid that the husband before her might

suppose she was cherishing some recollections of the *bridegroom* among her secret treasures, that she looked quite cross and scornful.

" Of course," said Mr. Slaughton, drawing back in a hurt way, " I don't suppose any roses *I* could gather here could give you the same sort of pleasure as that does."

" Certainly not," she replied hurriedly. " Teddy denied himself to buy it, and I think of that. Gifts from those we love, which have cost them some striving, are always precious."

" I am too old to chop wood, I am afraid, and unfortunately I am not able to make any sacrifices to build a green-house. So the poor, prosaic flowers will have to waste their sweetness in a very hum-drum way ; in fact, I ought perhaps to hesitate before I add to your cares the trouble of culling them."

" You like nosegays on your table," replied she, appearing to consider, although she could not help seeing how piqued and annoyed as he was. She was glad she had been able to explain about Teddy's rose, so that he must see *he* had no share in her liking for the gift.

" Yes, if that is the way you choose to put it. They are a necessity to me ; their presence is inspiration, their perfume an elixir."

| " I shall not mind the trouble in the least, and I truly thank you," she added with pleasant frankness which ignored the sneer in his answer. " You will not lack a posy for every meal. You might have been disagreeable about Betty, and you were not ; you might have omitted to furnish me this enchanting occupation, and you have not omitted it, for I must confess that a prospect of hours among lovely blooming flowers enchants me. You are exceeding kind and pleasant, and I am willing to be grateful."

Mr. Slaughton smiled at her significant phrase, which clearly defined her state of mind towards him.

" I hope you are also willing to come to the library after tea, and look at some plans," he asked in a glad tone. " I shall set the men at work to break ground immediately, and it will go hard if we are not able to deck our Christmas with flowers."

"I will come right gladly. I like drawing plans, of all things. I have always dreamed of houses I would build."

Perdita thought so many new thoughts that morning, that she was obliged to remind herself quite firmly who and what she was, and who was the man she had left, and also that Sabrina Bradshaw was the only woman in the world worth loving.

Mr. Slaughton took a long walk, and he took Perdita with him in his mind; and though the dog, who had, contrary to his custom, volunteered to accompany him, was very troublesome in his jumpings and obstreperous gambols, he received no rebuke. Yet he must have been a reminder of the mistress who had adopted him, as she had looked down by the margin of the pool when she had refused any gift from a man she did not like, and had finally accepted the puppy to save his life. He also recalled every word she had just uttered, and had a precise and living picture of her, from her coal-black hair to her crimson stockings and trim shoes tied with red ribbons; and he looked forward to the evening's consultation with interest, when he should find himself in her company, with opportunity to look at and listen to her again.

CHAPTER XXVI.

THE DOG SAM HAS AN ESCAPE.

 BOX had just arrived by express for Mrs. Slaughton. Mr. Slaughton brought it up himself from the village. Perdita chanced to be on the piazza when he appeared, selecting some wax-berries and rose-tips with which she had a fancy to fill a vase for her room. This seemed fortunate, as it saved the gentleman from a dilemma. He had never yet addressed her by her new name; and he shrank also from the familiarity of calling her by the one her christening gave her; and as he never spoke of her except in reply to the remarks of others, he had thus far avoided the necessity of speaking words which refused to form themselves on his lips.

"Mrs. Slaughton," Chandos had said, when he left her the morning of his departure, "I am going to send you those flowers we talked of. It is rather late for planting, but they will do well if got in immediately, and I know you have not forgotten all the learning on the subject I was at such pains to show off. We will have parroquettes gay as a butterfly's wing. Nonpareils as red—as red as your shoe-ribbons. Heaven save me! I came near saying stockings—and how dreadfully improper that would have been. And I will add some bulbs whose creamy flower-cups nod and bend over the pool to admire their beauty, when they get the chance, like that vain fellow Narcissus (vanity in a man is abominable; I thank heaven I am not as other men); and some annunciation lilies, such as the angel bears in his hand (Sam can tell you lots of things about those old pictures); and some of the blue Iris which the goddess brought with her when she descended from the rainbow, and hosts of others; and when I come next summer (I know you are going to invite me), we'll have the retired leisure which in trim gardens takes its pleasure, and I'll help you weed."

Perdita was delighted with the gift. Nobody had ever given her anything before, except a pattern of home-made flannel at one of the parsonage donations, or a hank of stocking-yarn, which she had to knit for "the boys"—and she hated knitting.

A box by express, sent on purpose to give her pleasure; not even the Mrs. Slaughton which stared at her on the cover, and which looked so new and strange, could destroy her satisfaction.

She was so eager and so bright, while her husband made good his civil offer to draw the nails and open the case, that he more than half wished he had been the author instead of the messenger of the gratification; that is, he did not entirely relish being obliged to witness such enjoyment of so small a treat offered by an outsider, and recalled to his memory how, on the occasion of his proposed lavishness in the matter of the conservatory, which would be a whole houseful of blooms, beside which these poor dozen or so were not fit to be mentioned, she had been careful to make him distinctly understand that it was *his property* of which he spoke, and she felt nothing more than a steward's right in it. She had said, *you* shall not lack a posy for *your* table. But she had on the whole been rather nice during that colloquy, and he had decidedly enjoyed the chat over the plans in the evening.

"You seem quite excited about your tulips," said he with some scorn as he drew them from their bedding of moss. "I have seen ladies make less ado over costly gems."

" I did not know I was making an ado, sir."

" No, of course, not an *ado*. The word was ill-chosen. I meant only to say how refreshing it is to meet a woman from whom a trifle like this can draw out so much ecstasy. You looked as you look now, I dare say, when you got the precious tea-rose."

"My appearance or feelings in any part of my life cannot have the slightest importance to you. So I wonder at your making them the theme of remark," replied Perdita, drawing back haughtily.

"Let us change the subject at once, and talk of something which has vital and present interest to one of us at least. Where will you plant these bulbs?"

"As they must go into your ground, it is proper for you to appoint the spot. I hope you will allow them a sunny one."

"I am at your service now, if you choose to come out and select such as suits you."

"Please lose no time, then, for Mr. Goldsmith told me it was already almost too late."

"Won't you let me put them in for you. I will engage to do it by plummet and line, the depth of the trowel, as all good florists order."

"If you are inclined to undertake such hard work," said Perdita in surprise.

"Why should I not, pray?"

"I thought you detested exertion. Mr. Goldsmith said you were——"

"Well, what? I pause to learn what I am.

> "I am as I am, and so will I be ;
> But how that I am, none knoweth trulie.
> Be it ill, be it well, be I bond, be I free,
> I am as I am, and so will I be !"

"Since you are so fixed and firm, it can do you no harm to tell you your friend's opinion. He called you lazy." Perdita waited in malicious silence for the effect she expected from the word which had been such a stigma and reproach at the parsonage ; but he laughed easily as at a good joke.

"Lazy, said Chandos, did he? Well, so I am, unless I see good cause and reason for activity. Nevertheless, I can dig and delve with the best of them. There is no time like the present when one has a labor to accomplish; therefore, come to the garden, Maud."

"Jocular and merry with the brow of Egypt, are you?" said Perdita, looking after him as he stepped away to fetch the necessary implements for their task. "Not but the banter and jest become you, too. I wonder if gentlemen are wont to be so amiable towards their housekeeper or governess?" Pretty soon he joined her, bringing a hoe and spade; and he was whistling, actually whistling.

"We still lack a narrow board for measure," said the amateur florist, when they had fixed on a sunny bed for their digging. "I dare not trust my eye in so important a piece of work. I desire to shine in my new occupation. I intend to point a moral for Slowgo. I shall set him a pattern."

While he was gone to the workshop in search of what he needed, Perdita heard a vociferous barking and yelping, which seemed to suggest that the setter Sam was in mischief or in trouble, or perhaps both.

From the hour of his arrival at the mansion, he had been the drollest, sauciest wag of a dog that ever wagged a handsome tail. He had at once adopted the family, and showed each member such attention as seemed to him their due. He frolicked and did tricks for his mistress; he took care of the master's slippers, and he put them where he liked best to have them, in odd corners, under the piazza, or up-garret. He set at and worried the old lady, and he purloined and hid Hannah's possessions, till he got to know right well the look and feel of her broomstick.

Away over in the clothes-yard he had found the dame, and was engaged in a paw-to-paw encounter with her, and now he was sitting on her barege cape-bonnet, and gnawing the reeds, which snapped between his sharp teeth like nuts to crack, as indeed they seemed to be to him. He had come on her in a corner made by two grape-trellises, and he kept her there, worrying her and shaking her skirts whenever she attempted to

9

pass him ; and every time she reached out to reclaim her head-gear he would make a dash at her and threaten her ankles. The scolding voice in which she hallooed at him seemed but to amuse and encourage him, and he replied as well as he was able with very well accented and expressive barks.

"You hateful brute !" said she, "quit *chawing* up my calash ! I wish you was skinned alive, I do !"

" Bow-wow-r-r-r-r-ow—bow-wow," he retorted.

" Once in a while she managed to drop a blow on his nose, which he took in excellent spirit, as part of the pleasant little game they were playing. He gave his head a shake, lopping his ears and sneezing, and then looking at her sidewise with a roguish leer in his bright eyes which seemed to say, "Come, now ! be sharp ! what will you do next ? "

He had no reason to like the dame. She was his enemy from the first. She chased him out of the house ; she grudged him even the barest bones, and his mistress was obliged herself to attend to his meals to insure his peaceful devourance of them ; and having treed his prey, so to speak, there is no know-ing how long he would have kept her there, had not Hannah come to make a third in the engagement, bringing her broom with her.

" You fetch out the tea-kettle, and give the nasty pest a good scald ; maybe that'll drive him off for good."

" That will I, mistress," replied Hannah, with ready alacrity.

Perdita could not hear the order, but she felt suspicious of some ill-usage for her favorite, and still more when she saw the old lady come out on the piazza after a brief stay in the kitchen, with a plate of bones which she threw down to him, such remarkable generosity looked alarming. And then, with the careless cruelty women will use towards troublesome animals and vermin, Hannah appeared, bearing the steaming kettle in her two hands, and the poor puppy, busy with their treat, was about to suffer a cruel torture.

Perdita sprang forward with flying steps, keeping her eyes

fixed on them ; but before she had passed over half the distance she stopped short. Mr. Slaughton was among them. He had seized the kettle when a single drop had not yet been shed, and she heard his voice loud and angry.

" Good heavens, mother, what ferocious angels you women are able to be ! the men who would in cold blood boil the hide off a dog are not plenty this side the Feejee Islands."

" He's a nasty, scratching, messy torment, Samuel. I want to drive him off the place ; he's no business here, any way. I can't bear him."

" You will have to bear him, mother ; he belongs to the lady of the house."

" No, he don't, either. I'm the lady of the house myself."

"Oh, I beg your pardon, you are old Mrs. Slaughton," replied her son with a malicious smile.

" I don't feel in the mood for jesting, and I wish you would give back that tea-kettle before the water all gets cold."

" You may put away the utensil, Hannah ; the puppy has taken care of himself. There he goes, bounding along, as merry as if you admired him. Mother, if you cannot be generous, try at least to be just."

" Hoity toity ; I don't understand this kind of talk."

" Won't you please make an effort to comprehend, then ? " added the gentleman, after the servant had gone. " You have introduced into this household a young girl who has *rights*— her rights *must* be respected."

" I hope you don't mean to encourage Perdita in fetching all sorts of pets about the place."

" The dog *I* gave her ; she did not ask it of me. She seems fond of him ; let her get what comfort out of his friendship she is able. Hannah," he added, as the servant approached with a panful of apple-parings she designed for the pigs, "you must not molest or ill-treat the dog ; and if I know that you drive him away, I shall be displeased."

" I don't owe the creature no grudge, I'm sure," grumbled

Hannah. " He may sit hisself down and bide till he's gray, for all I care."

Mr. Slaughton found Perdita where he had left her. She was seated on the turf assorting the bulbs, and she helped him plant them out. She chatted and smiled quite pleasantly, and her bright face and brisk, pliant motions made the task a real pleasure.

" He can be both just and generous, *when he sees best.*" This was her conclusion. She felt grateful, and did not mind letting him know that she did, and they both looked good-humored, and actually loitered a couple of minutes after the last row was placed and the bed raked smoothly, and he lifted his hat with a very friendly bow when he left her at the door.

" I trust our morning's work will give you a host of flowers next spring."

" If they do thrive I shall be obliged to thank you for them."

" And a thankful frame of mind is not one which you desire much to cultivate."

" It is certainly not habitual to me. Thus far I have never found great cause or occasion."

" Perhaps the future will be more propitious."

" Perhaps."

Mr. Slaughton walked off very fast. " Paying compliments, are you, sir ? " he said to himself, " as glib and sweet-voiced as Chandos. Come, don't be a fool, if you please. First you know, the girl will be getting fond of you."

CHAPTER XXVII.

PERDITA CARRIES A POINT WITH THE PARSON.

ELL, mother," exclaimed Perdita, as she stepped into the keeping-room of the old parsonage. "I've come to take the bull by the horns, that is, I'm going to speak to father about Betty."

"Oh dear! must you do it to-day?" replied Mrs. Hethwaite uneasily. "Hadn't you better put it off a little longer?"

"No; the Vances are coming, and I must settle it now."

"Oh, how the blood does rush to my head! I feel so bad. I'm afraid he will say no. Do be careful! try to look obedient."

"You are nervous, mother. I don't see how he can refuse. He must see it is a great good for his child; he will be relieved of her keep, and I can do plenty of things he is not able to compass, even if he had the will."

"If you so much as hint that, Perdita, you will lose her. I really believe he would choose to have us all starve before we took help from an outsider. It would need more crosses than he has ever had yet to crush out his pride."

"I wish his pride ran to working for you, mother. I should think a good deal more of it."

"Couldn't you manage so as to have it seem somehow as if you didn't care much about it, and felt it a pity to take her away from home, such religious privileges, and his teachings."

"No, mother, I can't; and you don't want me to lie, either."

"Of course, not *lie;* but Saint Paul says we must be all things to all men, if thereby we may gain some."

"Which means, according to your rendering, let us cajole and hoodwink so as to carry our point. No, thank you, mother. I begin to think I might cajole father, bear as he is; but I won't."

Mrs. Hethwaite looked at her daughter in a startled way, and without answering she stooped again to the ironing which had busied her hands when she was interrupted.

"Mother! where's Dolly, that she is not helping you?" asked Perdita, observing how weary and worn she looked.

"I can't get much out of Dolly; she's too flighty; she's as fond of play as a child; no whipping could ever beat it out of her, I do believe."

"You sit down and rest, mother; I am going to finish that basketful."

"Oh, no; I can't let you slave in two houses. I didn't put up with what I have, in getting you loose, to fetch you into this drudgery when you are free."

"But, mother, I love to work for you?"

"Do you? now, I want to know. It is queer how kinder natural that sounds; my children don't talk to me like that; but I used to say such things to my mother, and she used to kiss me. Oh, deary me! what a queer thing life is! I had such a good mother."

"Oh, mother! dear, precious mother!" As Perdita poured out these rapid words, she hugged the unresisting lady in her arms, and covered her poor faded face with eager kisses. So sudden and violent was the impulse which had burst all bonds of habit and education, and so warm and hearty was the glowing girl, that the mother quite broke down, and made no attempt to check the sobs as she lay in the arms of her child, whose bright eyes were wet with tears. The old lady was the first to speak, and as she did so she struggled to free herself from the embrace which held her fast.

"Your father might come, Perdita. There! isn't that him?"

Such a condensed history of her wedded experiences needs no comment.

Perdita thought so, and with a parting squeeze, she wheeled around. Taking a hot iron from the stove, she began to work as fast as she could.

Parson Hethwaite came in presently, and seeing his daughter, he bowed quite ceremoniously, calling her "Mrs. Slaughton," as he had taken pains to do ever since her marriage.

Although Perdita felt the change in his manner, and was willing to profit by the new state of mind, she did not find that she experienced any access of affection for him. On the contrary, she could not subdue a rising of resentment and displeasure. "He worships the Mammon of unrighteousness, for all his religion; and feels more respect for the owners in possession, than the inheritors of all things who look for their portion in the heaven he preaches."

"You observe, I fall naturally into my old place, father," said she. "I should not be a mite surprised if you were to box my ears, or send me to bed without any supper."

"That sort of discipline ceased with your second decade, Mrs. Slaughton, which also installed you mistress of a fine mansion."

"You make so little of the husband, which was a part of the bargain, that you astonish me, since I know how much you have always made of the one my mother took, when she left off being Violet Wemple."

Being warned by a deprecatory gesture from the poor wife, she remembered how much she needed to be pleasant and conciliatory; and before the Parson had time to look all the astonishment he felt, she proceeded rapidly:

"I've come on business this morning, father; Mr. Slaughton has promised Bettine a home with me, and I stepped over to mention the matter to you. The plan is so good for all parties, that I know it needs no discussion; you will be relieved of expense about her, and she will receive an education with the

Vance children, whom *I* am to teach. In fact, I give the lessons to them on the condition that she shares them, so I feel that I owe the Slaughtons nothing, as the salary of a governess, which I save them, would be double—yes, more than double what Bettine's living will cost."

While she went on volubly, explaining and dilating, the wife's anxious face was a study—it mirrored so many emotions: fear, lest her husband might refuse, being predominant; and perhaps it was lucky his attention *did not* happen to be drawn to her fidgeting and grimaces, or his contrariness might have been aroused.

"Mrs. Slaughton, I must say you are developing the excellent sense and sound judgment I had the right to expect from the careful and judicious training I have bestowed upon you. I consider it my duty to fall in with the leadings of Providence, which seem quite plain in the child's behalf, so far as to consent to her present removal from the paternal roof; reserving, of course, the right to decide whether or no the atmosphere of your house is good for her. And should I detect in her vainglorying or lightness unbecoming the offspring of a Christian minister, I shall assert my authority as beseems me best."

"Yes, you'd bring her to your paternal endearments and your daily codfish," said Perdita, looking after the Parson as he ascended to his study. "Let me once get her safe away, and I'll manage. You may count on me, mother; Bettine has had her last whipping."

"I don't scarcely dare to hope so. She has such scared turns when her pa takes hold of her. I feel afraid sometimes she won't get her breath again; she's just as limpsy as a rag. She had one yesterday."

"Did he whip her yesterday?"

"No, he only shook her a little; but she dropped down white as a sheet, and he was almost frightened himself, I guess, for he didn't say a word against my holding her on my lap;

and generally, you know, he won't let me touch the children when he has them in hand."

"I wish I could carry her off to-day; but things are not ready up there, and I must wait. Poor little Bettine."

"I feel thankful to you, Perdita, and I don't believe he'll touch her again right away."

"There, mother! all the ironing is done. Now, is there anything else I can do for you?"

"No, child. I feel real bright and strong, I've got so many good things to think of, and they all come of you."

"That's nice; if you go on feeling so, I can be bright and strong too, and I'm coming again to-morrow.

———

CHAPTER XXVIII.

PEINE FORTE ET DURE.

PERDITA hurried on after her last hug of her darling sister, who came in time for a few squeezes; and her thoughts were so busy that she felt all aglow. And who shall say which of her musings rose most readily, as they turned towards the man whose name she bore.

"Only a housekeeper and governess;" that was what she said half aloud as she passed in through the great gate which opened into the wide space fronting the horse-barn. Before her stretched the roadway, which swept around the rear of the terrace and from which she could see the broad meadows and mowing-land, dotted here and there with rocks too massive and deep-seated even for blasting. It was a pretty view, and

9*

she paused an instant to admire it, when her attention was very
unpleasantly arrested by a sight which aroused all the indignation, anger, and disgust which instantly kindles in an impulsive
woman at the display of brutal cruelty.

Slowgo had harnessed the little mare Lightfoot to a new hay-
rake which Mr. Slaughton had purchased a day or two before,
and behind the machine was gathered a heap of autumn leaves
it had collected.

The dainty little mare was what is called stakey or balky;
and she stood with her pretty head turned on one side, champ-
ing the bit and showing the whites of her eyes. The only consciousness she evinced of the blows she was getting from the
pitchfork the farmer beat her with, was a slight quiver and
gathering together of her slender legs.

Slowgo was in a dreadful state of exasperation ; his face was
inflamed, and he gnashed his teeth like a boar at bay, and
poured out strange oaths. He was a forbidding fellow at best,
and just now he looked as men do look when the wild savage
brute gets uppermost, as tigers look when they scent blood, or
hyenas when they seize their prey. His big neck was covered
with black hair, as were his muscular arms, and his skin was
tanned to leather by constant exposure. He was able to toss
about the bowlders on the point of his crowbar, and boasted
that he had felled an ox by one blow of his fist. Altogether, such
a man as you would hesitate to intrust with tender, frail things ;
and his eyes seemed to be filling with blood, they were so red
and staring ; and his voice was no more human speech, but
brutish growls and bellowings.

Suddenly Lightfoot reared high in air and threw herself on her
side, a mute expression of despair. The farmer drew back his
pitchfork and plunged it into her haunches, and spouting blood
followed the stab.

Perdita felt beside herself, and uttering a wild scream, was
about to rush at the madman, whether to disarm him by seizing
his weapon, or by entreaties, she did not pause to consider,

when a swift step came along beside her, and a voice begged her to stop where she was.

"Don't go down there ; you'll get hurt. I'll settle this."

Mr. Slaughton walked close to his man, and took the pitch-fork from his clutches ; he took it forcibly, and he gripped it fast.

"What are you about, Slowgo ? "

The tones in which he asked the question were scarcely louder than the soft half-drawl which was habitual ; and as he struck the prongs of the fork in the ground, and leaned on the handle, you would not have detected any signs of rage, except perhaps the slight drawing back of his upper lip, which showed his teeth through his fair mustache, and a gleaming flash in his eyes. Perdita, who was watching him, noticed also that his hands clasping the staff were bloodless.

"I'm breaking the mare, sir."

"Do you know I have the greatest mind in this world to break your head, you infernal, cruel savage ? Unhitch her, and take her to her stall directly."

"I've lived with many gentlemen, and I was never called such names as those, sir."

"Then you never got your due, which is quite likely."

"And I've the reputation of being the best trainer in the country."

"I don't train my horses in that way. When I want my mare butchered, I'll send for the offal-man ; have that cut you've given her well washed with arnica. If any harm comes to her from your brute's temper, it will be the worse for you."

"I haven't harmed her. She'll never be good for nothing, nohow."

"Not for your driving, Slowgo. It needs a man who is able to manage himself to manage her. Did you ever hear of a certain rule called the law of kindness ? "

"I like a good whip myself, sir. If that mare was mine I'd just lace her down to it. I'd break her, or I'd break her neck —a d—d cantankerous devil."

"Don't swear, Slowgo. That won't suit me; and now that I am on the topic, I'll tell you what is the matter. You thought I did not know, I dare say, that the first time you hitched her up to haul the boards for the shed, you put on load enough for a pair; and you beat and abused her, and you made a balker of the best colt that ever was foaled."

"Who told you that yarn, sir?"

"Never mind who, Slowgo. It is enough for you to know that I have a witness who will swear to the fact, and you may think yourself lucky if you don't have to pay me for the spoiling of an expensive horse whom I prize highly."

"She staked, and I thrashed her. You can't make any more out of it. Anybody would have done the same thing. Lots of folks would have treated her worse nor I did. I'd sell the blasted creature, if I was you. The street-cars would be the best place for her—they'd soon take the tricks out of her."

"I haven't a doubt but you would sell her, Slowgo. *I* would put my pistol to her ear and shoot her dead, before I'd hand her over to be tortured."

"Oh, well, Mr. Slaughton, you can afford to do as you please; but when a poor man buys a mare he must get his money out of her. I've seen fires built under 'em, and hooks put into their jaws, I have."

"And you rather enjoyed it; there are several points you must amend, Slowgo, if you want to keep your place on my land. You must lash the oxen less, and leave off kicking the cows. It is a bad sign when dumb animals are afraid of a farmer; and I notice that even the cat drops his tail and sneaks off as soon as he catches sight of you. I will have everything about me kindly treated, mind, now; I never speak twice about the same fault."

"All right, sir. I didn't suppose you minded them sort of trifles. I never lived with a gentleman before that found any such fault."

"I'll train the mare hereafter, Slowgo."

"Very well, sir."

Mr. Slaughton turned on his heel after his man had led off Lightfoot, and Perdita, who had been entirely interested in the talk, was still lingering and attentive when her husband walked up to her.

"I hope he will not ill-treat her any more," said she. "I felt as if I could stick him with needles when I saw how wicked and cruel he was."

"A feminine punishment which might be tolerably annoying if properly persisted in, I should think," replied Mr. Slaughton, smiling. "I don't intend he shall have the chance to train the mare again. I shall have Stephen groom her, and I'll try my hand at driving her. Like most balky horses, she is nervous and high-strung, easily flurried and bewildered. When I touched her pulse I could hardly count its beats. The fault which procures this sort of animal so much hard usage generally arises from confused ideas. He gets too much excited to know what is required of him, and every lash makes him worse. I never come across a poor victim getting pounded and kicked but I long to shoot him and end his misery. There is not one man in a hundred who has enough of good sense and coolness to dominate a balker, and I really think if I could start a society for the prevention of cruelty, I'd have a man on purpose to kill balky horses, and a fund for buying them up."

"Can't they be cured by kindness and patience?"

"Not so as to become reliable servants; they will take freaks. The memories of former wrongs or sufferings seem to come over them at particular places and times, and they are deaf to everything. Horses are a good deal like Indians; they bide their time. I heard of one who seized his groom by the shoulder, after a long course of horrible, savage abuse, and tore him to shreds."

"I wish Lightfoot had known enough to defend herself."

"It seems to me there is a spice of revenge in your composition. I don't believe you would tamely bear harshness."

"I have borne it all my life, and I never even remonstrated."

"It was a sickening sight for you to see—this brutality of Slowgo's, and I am sorry you witnessed it," said Mr. Slaughton, observing how her face clouded over.

"You mean that I ought to have gone away, instead of stopping to watch him? That it was indelicate, or improper?"

"I mean precisely what I say; pray don't try to interpret my plain English. I assure you it is so clear that he who runs may read."

"I must run, without tarrying to try. The morning has been flying while I have stayed, and there is to be a tipsy parson for dinner."

Leaving the gentleman in a maze of perplexity as to which of the neighboring clergy it might be whom she so stigmatized, she stepped off in a great hurry to attend to her preparations.

CHAPTER XXIX.

PERDITA DEMANDS HER WAGES.

R. SLAUGHTON, I must speak with you. Breakfast is not ready, and I will not hinder you long," said Perdita, overtaking the house-master in his hall, on the way to the dining-room.

He was beginning to enjoy these consultations. He generally found something relishing and sharp among the utterances of the young housekeeper, who jingled her keys conspicuously as she accosted him. Certainly he could not accuse her of placing herself in his way, unless she had a call to do so, and he had never once surprised in her a wish to make herself attractive to him. On the contrary, her manner always said positively and distinctly how utterly impossible she found it that there could ever be any tender exchanges or love passages between them.

She had a couple of account-books in her hand, which she opened and extended to him as soon as they were inside the door.

"My first month of service having expired, I wish you to look over the bills, and let me know if they are satisfactory."

"My mother and you, surely——" began he, backing off.

"I understood, sir, that your mother selected the person to fill the vacant place, and that you agreed to pay the bills, like a man. I prefer to bring my reports to the head of the establishment. I do not think highly of dealing with women in money matters."

Mr. Slaughton took the books which were thrust out towards him, with marked unwillingness. As she stood before him, with her feet firmly planted and her eyes full of will, there did not seem to be any way to refuse.

Her statements were concise, to the point, and most undeniable; but he could have beaten himself for being dragged into this dilemma, which each day presented fresh absurdities, ever-renewed awkwardnesses, among which the knowledge he had gained that the quick-witted girl was all the while passing judgment on his behavior, was extremely provoking.

He ran his eyes down the columns of figures—very nice, lady-like figures they were too—the fives especially pretty; and the eights, instead of resembling bloated spiders, as they are apt to do with female rendering, were dapper and neat.

"Well, sir!" said Perdita, who was impatiently watching his dallying scrutiny of her work, "no errors, I hope?"

"No, oh, no! far from it indeed; all as admirable as possible."

" What is the matter, then, that you hesitate so long ? something must be wrong ; do pray tell me what it is ? "

" Since you press me and insist, I should say you've rather a large bill for soap," he stammered, closing and returning the little book with eager politeness ; and he laughed inside at the ridiculous statement he had brought forth in a set, decorous voice, feeling it imperative to say something which should show that he had conned her statement, and trying hard to look the steady householder ; and he wondered what Chandos would think of his predicament, and thanked his stars that he was safe at Roaring River.

" I weighed the article myself and gave it out each week," said Perdita, bending her brows over the book. " I have always used old-fashioned steelyards before ; and perhaps I do not correctly adjust the scales you have here. I shall be more particular."

" Oh, I merely threw out the remark," returned he airily. " I have not the least idea whether it ought to take one pound or a hundred for the month's consumption. Don't be governed by me, I beg ! "

" But I shall be governed by you implicitly ; of course, you ought to understand your own business ; how else can I know if I suit you ? "

" I will give you a written character, if you say so. This is to certify that Perdita Heth——, ahem ! that you are capable, faithful, and honest."

" I do not need such a help at present, sir, though there might come a time, perhaps," she replied, with a half smile. " The next topic is wages. I find on inquiry that housekeepers receive from four to ten dollars a week. As I do not wish to rate myself with the cheapest, nor yet to be exorbitant, I shall put my services in the happy mean, and say eight dollars."

" By Jove ! you remind me most unpleasantly of a thing I ought to have seen to. I supposed my mother—I really— this is confoundedly ridiculous ; quite a scene for a painter ;

might be called "Debit and Credit." I am much to blame. Be so kind as to draw on me for any sum you wish; I am ashamed to have forced you to this step, the most inhospitable and abominable way to treat a stranger. Here are a few bills; I implore you to take them; I ought to be shot."

While he had gone blundering on, getting redder and redder, he had pulled open the private drawer of his secretary and hauled hurriedly out a roll of money, which he offered his wife without looking at her.

Perdita kept silence, watching him in an offended, annoyed way. If she felt amusement, or found in the interview anything ludicrous, she did not let it appear in her face, which seemed intent on the business she had stated.

"Please explain what you mean, sir, by all this!" said she, stepping backward out of his reach. "Is it so unusual for a housekeeper to present an account and expect her wages? I must remind you that this is my first place. I do not understand the manner used by such people. Perhaps there are forms; I should have written a humble note, maybe, and handed it on a salver. You must be so kind as to overlook and excuse my inexperience. In the meantime, as I have broached the subject, I will not withdraw without finishing, and I feel no shame in getting what I have honestly earned. Four times eight is thirty-two dollars. I have the receipt all made out; so it is easily settled."

"This is nefarious! it is abominable!" exclaimed Mr. Slaughton, excitedly throwing down the money. "You insult me wantonly! I will not bear it!"

Perdita watched him writhe, without an emotion of pity. "Who insulted me wantonly?" she thought. "Who took the trouble to forewarn me that he could not love me, and did not mean to try, leaving me only the housekeeper's place in his house?"

"Your conduct is so extremely strange, that I begin to perceive you have some reason for deferring this settlement. I wonder if you assume this pleasant little manner with all the people who come to collect their dues of you. A light bursts in on me. You have intended smaller wages than I have named. I shall stand fast. It is well said, those who make little of themselves are sure to be made naught of by others. Permit me."

She picked up the discarded bills, and proceeded deliberately to count them ; wetting her fingers, and going half a dozen times over the roll, whispering the additions to herself, as if the task was almost too much for her powers of calculation.

" If I have done it right, there is eighty dollars here, sir. I trust you will allow me to take out what belongs to me— thirty-two dollars ; and I shall be glad to go, because I have a plum pudding to make, and the coffee is on the table."

As he did not open his lips, she carefully placed the remainder of the bills in the desk, as if fully aware of their value.

" Oh, well, I know you are counted an honorable man, and it does not become me to be over-particular about the receipt. But here it is, and I leave it in your care. I shall also make a minute of the sum at the bottom of the page. Will you please come directly to breakfast while it is hot ? It makes such a difference in the taste of things if they are eaten cold, and I feel *so* anxious that you should be well served. It is only justice to myself. I do not disdain the proper desire to excel in the sphere of life to which the leadings of Providence have called me."

Mr. Slaughton followed her without a word. She seated herself at the head of his table, and presently offered him a cup of coffee, clear as amber, and of most delicate fragrance. She offered it with a respectful pains-taking bow ; as he took it, he touched her fingers. They were cool and soft, most pleasant to the sense, and the agreeable contact moved him to look at her hand as she withdrew it ; the glance followed up the plump round arm to the shoulder, whose smooth tip was defined by her prim gown. She had laid aside the cape or vandyke which

was the habitual finish of a country girl's dress in those days—
in places remote from fashion's changes, while she was busy
with her duties.

Perdita's neck was a little long. Teddy was accustomed to
tell her it was a good neck for a hanging, and to recite the pitiful speech of poor Anne Boleyn; "The headsman will not have
much trouble to cut off my head, because I have such a little
neck." Yes, it was long, Mr. Slaughton noticed that. It did
not seem too long either, with all that mass of raven hair floating over it, caressing her cheek, hardly restrained by its snood
of crimson ribbon ; and she certainly carried in her face an expression of goodness ; whatever emotion was paramount, goodness was there also. And when she raised her great black
eyes, dazzlingly brilliant, he took a second look into them in
spite of his amazed, incensed state of mind.

Dame Slaughton had a habit of beginning to talk at table,
looking at the person she addressed, while she extended her
hand indiscriminately over the edibles, some one of which she
vaguely desired. A sudden spirit of mischief inspired Perdita,
to make haste and lift each dish, and place it beneath the working fingers ; and as they failed to pounce and accept, she removed and substituted another, shaking her head as she did so,
and saying, "No, it is not that," as if it had been a game ; the
old lady all the while oblivious of the proceeding.

Mr. Slaughton, while politely attentive to his mother's remarks—they being addressed to him—saw also what his wife
was doing, and enjoyed the fun in spite of himself, and thought
that Perdita's arch smile was certainly bewitching, and the low,
bubbling laugh with which she disposed of the last plate was
without dispute musical.

Presently the dame, on housekeeping cares intent, found a
good deal to say about a chestful of sheets in the attic, which
wanted turning.

For the benefit of such of my readers as are too young to
have been victims of this abominable thrift which was practised

in families who made and used their own linen, I will explain that "turning" means ripping the whole length and joining again the outside edges, which makes an overhand seam quite interminable, as contemplated by a child's eyes. Ah! what weary work it was, to be sure. And how we used to measure, and sigh, as the sun went down on the flowers and birds, and the gay world outside, and we poor wretches were held to our "stint."

Perdita thanked the dame for her information, and replied, as naturally as possible, that she should certainly try to get them finished before the Vances arrived, that she might be free for her school duties.

"Mr. Slaughton," said she, when this topic had been fully aired and disposed of, "have I your permission to put up autumn leaves in your library?"

"What! stick them onto the wall?" inquired the dame, pricking up her ears. "It'll tear the plastering all to bits, won't it?"

"Not at all, ma'am. I shall use fine cambric needles. They will not injure the hard finish in the least; no one can detect their marks."

"Oh, dear! waste good needles! ten cents a paper! it will take a great many, won't it—and a deal of time? Rather foolish, isn't it?"

"Is this also your opinion, sir?" asked Perdita, looking full at the gentleman, and determined to make him declare himself on one side or the other.

"I admire the bright-tinted leaves very much, and if you desire to weary yourself with their arrangement, I see no objection."

While Samuel was speaking he was roiled inside at the mean spirit his mother showed; and trying to feel it the girl's fault, since it had never rasped him so before her coming, his voice and face were as ungracious as his words.

"Not even the cost of the needles, nor the waste of the time which might be spent in turning old sheets?"

She felt that her answer was provoking, but no more so than his was uncomplaisant; and she was never quite able to forget for long how much she had to resent, and she justified all her flippancies, feeling that he deserved them, and millions more.

"Well, well, my dear, we will talk the matter over by-and-by," said the dame, wishing to postpone and temporize; "plenty of time to decide about it."

It seemed as if she began to be afraid of the daughter she had been so anxious to get. She had not a breath of unkindness to complain of; no idleness or unthrift; in fact, nothing except the very wishes she had put forward in her talks with her son. She had obtained a person to lift care and responsibility off her shoulders, but she had not expected so much to miss the accustomed burden; and she did not calculate on the new incumbent's taking so easily the head place, and keeping it so steadily, always advancing, never retreating nor losing ground.

Everything went smoothly enough as long as she kept her fingers out of the domestic pie—and that was so difficult to do. Even then there were no hard words, scarcely any black looks; but a steady bearing on, a quiet carrying of the point.

She was forced to admit that the housekeeping was admirable, the order perfection. But the old lady was self-dethroned; no longer mistress of the mansion to which she came a bride and had ruled to her liking ever since; and to make matters worse, the new servants told her quite curtly that "Miss Perdita was boss, and they weren't going to have two bosses; what *she* ordered they was going to do, and nothing else."

CHAPTER XXX.

THE AUTUMN LEAVES AND THE FIRE-DOGS.

 SHOULD like to be carried over to Mrs. Brandigee's, this morning, Samuel. I haven't seen them for a month," remarked the dame, a couple of days after the settlement of the wages question.

" Certainly, mother. I'll drive Lightfoot over. I want to look at an Ayreshire bull Brandigee has imported. I think of buying him. Slowgo has let the stock depreciate fearfully on this farm. I must give immediate attention to it."

" Well, Sammy, we'll go by ten o'clock, and come back before sunset. I don't like being out too late these cool evenings."

Mr. Slaughton glanced across at his vis-à-vis, wondering if his mother meant to include her in the arrangement. She was also looking at him ; she was thinking what a deal of interest he showed in farming, for a man who was so soon to depart for Timbuctoo ; and here a question presented itself with considerable pertinacity : " Do I wish him to go, or stay ? " She pushed away her coffee-cup with hasty gesture, and tried also to put the theme and its object from her consideration, as being entirely outside her legitimate province.

The house-master was soon enlightened as to his mother's intentions.

" I suppose you will be likely to commence on the sheets to-day, Perdita, as there will be no fuss about dinner. A capital time for you to eat bread and milk ; I reckon milk is healthy once in a while, especially for young folks."

Each day, these constantly recurring remarks were getting

more and more distasteful to Mr. Slaughton, and he flushed up under this one, as if he had been insulted. Not so Perdita, she was as cool and indifferent as he was hot and disturbed.

"Milk makes bone; bread makes muscle. I am likely to need both, and fortunately I am well used to the diet. I shall not work at the linen to-day. I have something in hand which I intend to accomplish.

"I suppose you don't want to tell what it is; you seem to hate to answer questions as bad as a lawyer."

"I don't wish to speak prematurely. As you will have a long ride, I dare say a hot supper may be acceptable on your return. So, if you will please state the hour, I shall have one ready."

Evidently there was not a thought of neglect in her mind. She did not count herself in their arrangements, and she looked glad to have the house free of their presence. Mr. Slaughton had no right to feel offended at this; but he did, and he said with some acrimony, after his mother had left the table;

"I see you are delighted to be rid of me."

"Rid of you? what an unpleasant way to put it! I *am* rather satisfied to know that the litter I mean to make will disturb no one, so that results, not means, will be apparent."

"A state secret from me also, I suppose"

"Really, Mr. Slaughton, you make my projected occupation so absurd that I shall hardly feel like carrying out the plan. I intend to go this morning to finish my collection of leaves; it is so late that I shall have to wax them, but they will answer very well; fortunately there are still plenty of white ferns down in the hickory wood, and Dolly and Malcolm have been for weeks pressing dogwood and sumach; I rather forestalled your permission, you see, in setting them at it."

"Of course you will take Slowgo, and one of the horses. You can't think of walking all that distance."

It was the first time he had shown the slightest interest in her movements, or made a suggestion to her.

" Thank you, sir," she replied proudly ; " I am accustomed to use my feet, and I don't intend to get out of practice. More-over, I don't feel in any humor for a tête-à-tête drive with your farmer."

The gentleman felt dreadfully snubbed, and wished he had held his tongue. As he left her, she watched him with gleam-ing light in her black eyes.

" Slowgo indeed ! no, sir ! I am not fallen so far yet as to accept the escort of the man, where the master does not think it worth his while to offer his company. Not one of your horses shall ever carry me an inch till I am properly invited, as becomes the house-mistress."

You see, Perdita had her little inconsistencies as well as other women, although she kept them tolerably to herself.

She worked all day, and much to her satisfaction. The sort of labor was so new to her ; the fact of being able to take time for decorating and beautifying without fear of reproofs and hard words, was so pleasant, that she forgot everything in the glow and ardor of her progress, and as night drew on the library was transformed into a woodland bower, where all the trees were represented by their best and ripest foliage. Over each picture was massed a group of resplendent maples, redder than blood, yellower than gold ; they filled all the space between the suspending cords with wondrous color.

The whole chimney above the low mantel was covered with maiden's hair and vines of the trailing woodbine, which drapes old walls with their autumn splendor ; so that the picture of Master Samuel in petticoats, which hung in the midst, with ringlets as stiff as pine shavings, framing his *smile*, a dreadfully wooden kitten tucked under an arm as plump and flesh-like as a pump-handle, and a whip in his hand which twisted and twirled like a garter-snake, seemed the centre of a fairy grotto.

All along the cornice drooped branches of the bitter-sweet she had gathered by the old mill the day she had saved the dog

Sam, who deliberately chewed up one of the best specimens, before she·got ready to place it, and was well chased and slapped for his industry, and stood with his ears lopped and head cocked on¯one side, wagging his tail a couple of minutes afterwards, meditating a dash at the clusters she was cunningly twining around an invisible wire, which, when suspended, seemed springing from their high place of their own wild will.

The old-fashioned mirror had a mass of yellow fern above it, and all the vases were filled with gorgeousness, scarlet, crimson, and gold, everywhere : the perfected summer work of wood and dell.

"The old woman has got a pair of dogs up-garret, mum," said Hannah, who was on her knees before the hearth, scrubbing and cleaning.

"A pair of dogs !" exclaimed Perdita, from her lofty perch on the top of the step-ladder. "Who put them there ? how long have they been there ?"

"I don't know who put 'em there, mum ; they's been up yonder since afore I came here. They're tied up in the corner, with flanning on their heads and legs."

"Dogs tied up-garret ! how revolting ! positively, it sounds like Uncle Tom's Cabin."

"And sure 'tis the safest place for 'em, mum ; they're out of the way, and the flanning smothers 'em entirely."

As Perdita paused in her work to listen to this strange tale, Hannah looked up at her, and scratched her nose with her sooty finger. "Fire-dogs," said she, "for the chimbley."

"Fire-dogs !" echoed Perdita apprehensively, "what do you mean ?"

"Those are things what you pile the wood onto, mum, to make a fire. Lord bless you, mum ! I can't make it no plainer," said Hannah impatiently ; "I'll run and fetch 'em down, if you say so. I could brighten 'em up with rotten-stone and ile in half a jiffy, and they'd make a bonny finish to your

10

work of an evening, lighting up all your pretty leaves and things."

"Oh ! you mean andirons," said Perdita, with cleared countenance. "An excellent idea ! Pray fetch them at once ; run quickly. I dote on a wood fire, where I can see the blaze ruddy and red, and the castles and towns, and the caves and grottoes in the coals, all shining like gold; it is amazingly pleasant."

It took a good deal of what Hannah called "elbow-grease" to restore the dogs to their pristine lustre, much dimmed and tarnished by their long imprisonment ; but they rewarded her outlay at last, and she contemplated them with reasonable pride when she placed them on the clean hearth, massive solid brass, that you could see your face in, and the smooth maple sticks she piled on them soon sent forth a cheerful glow, which nestled and hid among the wall-beauties, like household fairies.

The young worker was putting the last touches to the lace curtains, upon which she fastened butterflies and ferns, when the Slaughtons returned. There was a strong smell of wax and varnish, mingled with paste and vinegar, which the dame sniffed apprehensively, as she peered into the room around her son's arm, who stood in the doorway.

"Superb ! glorious !" exclaimed he, "who would have believed that only autumn leaves which fall around us, ripened, finished, got through with, and dropped to decay and forgetfulness, could so adorn and beautify this dreary place ? Positively, I have always been in the habit of considering it sombre and uninviting. And a fire on the hearth ; that looks like old times, mother. I was not so big as I am now the last time that fire was lighted."

Mr. Slaughton's face expressed so much surprise and pleasure, that Perdita quite flushed and glowed to find her work so well appreciated. Not so the old dame.

"A fire in the fire-place is a dreadful dirty thing, Sammy.

The ashes and cinders all flying about so, and the smoke settling into the curtains and pictures."

Mr. Slaughton glanced uneasily at the girl, whose countenance was not in the least disturbed by the remarks she had
expected and made up her mind to beforehand, and would
have been rather disappointed not to get. She surveyed
serenely her results, and experienced the satisfaction a woman
always feels who finds an admirer of adornments planned by
her taste and executed by her fingers.

"I think it *is* rather magnificent," said she. "If I could
only have managed some lambrequins, I should have been
quite content, with a small fernery for the east window."

"What were those first things you spoke of?" asked he
eagerly. "I should like to procure them if procurable."

"Only boards to be hung on the top of the windows, cut
into nice shapes, so that I could cover them with massed
leaves. I feel sure the effect would be fine."

"That is easily done; I am a good sawist myself. If you
will give me the patterns, I will try what I can produce."

"I don't wish to trouble you. Teddy has the patterns, and
only waits your permission to complete them."

"Pray let Teddy do them, then," said he curtly, turning on
his heel.

"Yes, sir, thank you, I will; and I will hand you the bills."
The status was of the gentleman's arranging, but he did not
like it. He had helped her plant her tulips, and felt rather
moved to exert himself a little further, under her guidance.

It seemed as if she was a bit sorry for her short putting aside
of his offer, for she said as he was going:

"I hope you have brought home an appetite. There is a
nice-smelling stew on the stove. I put in curry and wine, and
everything Soyer orders. I expect it will be good. Then
there are fried sweetbreads, and baked potatoes, cold potted
pigeons, a broiled partridge, and a couple of birds he called
woodcock, that I bought of a fellow I found shooting them

in your wood; and we have also puffovers, and honey, and a Washington cake."

"Too much! too much! entirely too much, Perdita; wicked wasteful extravagance!" exclaimed the dame hurriedly.

"No, no, mother; I like variety, and I can do ample justice to all the good things in this most admirable bill of fare. Shooting woodcock, was he?"

"Yes, among the alders; he says he sells them."

"I think I'll get out with my gun, and try my luck."

"I should think it might be safer than killing tigers 'in Timbuctoo!'"

Perdita wished she had not made the silly speech as soon as it was uttered; and she hurried to arrange the supper on the table, and hoped that in the bustle of getting seated and served it might have been lost. It was not, however, for as they left the dining-room Mr. Slaughton turned and said to her:

"Safety in any particular position depends on many contingencies."

CHAPTER XXXI.

"A CHILD IN A HOUSE IS A WELL-SPRING OF JOY."

 HE family carryall stopped at the door, and out bundled the three children.

Cicely Vance, the eldest, a slim-shouldered, thin-limbed girl, with a good deal of flaxen hair hanging down her back, steel-blue eyes set deep under beetling brows, a heavy animal under-jaw, and teeth which were much discolored for lack of care, and edgewise in her mouth, a low forehead, thick, flat nose, with round, clumsily finished nostrils. Yet despite all these defects she was so admirably colored that the first glance filled the beholder with marvellous admiration. Rarely were seen such brilliant cheeks and lips ; the best damask rose at its richest was no match for them ; the softest, creamiest wax was not so soft and creamy white as her skin.

Her straw hat, trimmed with black velvet ribbons, was crushed out of all shape ; her dress was minus a couple of buttons, her frills and cuffs soiled and rumpled, her stockings had holes in them, her shoes were rusty and trodden over at the heel, and her gloves and handkerchief missing ; but her rose-colored sash was tied in a smart bow at the back, and she had knots and ends at her throat, dingy and frayed. It was quite evident through all her careless untidiness that she was devoted to finery and ambitious of making a show.

This child was thirteen years old. She was a stranger to the younger ones, having been placed by her roving, dissolute father in a convent, and kept there, out of his way, as long as he lived, so that she had grown up thus far an alien every way, her head filled with notions which could scarcely be dignified as ideas, which were likely to be troublesome in her new home, and her habits were not such as upright women like to encounter.

Bertram, the next, was a hearty, roystering boy, full of noise and dash and frolic, who always wanted what he wanted "dreadfully," and felt as if he couldn't live another minute unless he got it, and was careful to let his needs be known, though speaking did not seem to relieve him ; headstrong, self-willed, knowing no law but his own desires. The world during his ten years of life had been an arena for his exploits and experiments. The strength of most articles with which he came in contact was tested ; and a general topsy-turvyness was apt to result from his stay in any habitation.

Little Pandora got out last, as waggish an imp of mischief as ever teazed a housekeeper. Handsome, dimpled, fat, and cunning ; caring for no person alive except her brother, whom she admired and followed, and imitated as far as her shorter legs and smaller powers allowed her. She was turned of seven.

You may be sure that the governess-to-be looked curiously at her future charges, as they came racing and screaming up the steps. She had heard frightful accounts of their insubordination and waywardness.

. "Well, children! here you are!" exclaimed the dame, "and a frowsy, mussy set, to be sure; all dirt and dust. But that can't be helped, I suppose. Come and kiss your Aunt Perdita, who is going to take care of you, and tell her you mean to be good children."

" No, I shan't do it; I don't want to; I ain't a going to; I won't," screamed Bertram, reeling off the words so glibly as to prove them frequently on his lips. "Jim Duncan says it is the badest boys that's the best fellows; the good ones is pokey. I hate pokey squirts; I like jolly bad chaps."

"So der I," chimed in Pandora; "I'm going to do everything Bert does, I'm going to be worser nor he is."

"*I* shall be good, Aunt Perdita," said Cicely, sidling up to the lady. "They're so noisy and vulgar I can't bear them. It isn't ladylike to make a noise, is it. I love you, Auntie; may I have a piece of cake?"

Perdita instinctively withdrew from the embrace of this girl, whose voice broke in an unpleasant way, and whose laugh was like the crackling of thorns under a pot for music; whose tiny, beautiful hands were clammy and cold; though as she did so she observed her resplendence of color, and the deep dimples in each pink cheek. She felt ashamed of her repugnance, and reached down in an instant and received the proffered caress, and said "Thank you" for the protest of affection; but she seized with a good hug the small Pandora. This time her attentions were not made much of, for the child struggled to be set free, after a quick pressure of the little arms around the new aunt's neck, and a rub of her cheek against the one as ripe and found as her own.

" Put me down, quick ! I want to see the girl behind you ; who is she ?"

Betty, who was clinging affrighted to her sister's skirts, had that morning arrived in her new home. She looked as if she might have come from fairy-land, she was so tiny and beautiful, and delicate. She had on the first fruits of Perdita's wages, a soft white merino, embroidered with floss silk, daintiest of dainty slippers, and she peeped out through curls of pale gold, as an elf-child might have looked at a mortal—a glance of wonder, curiosity, and dread.

" This is my Betty. She has come to live and play with you, and I hope you will be dear friends. Kiss her, Betty darling ; see, she holds out her arms to take you in."

While the mite endured dutifully the hearty squeeze Pandora was ready and willing to give her, the dame exclaimed, in a mighty flurry :

" What ! what ! what is this you say ? That child live here ? A monstrous idea ! Of course you can't be in earnest : as if three children are not enough ; to talk of taking in another. Nonsense ! stuff and nonsense !"

" I do not *talk* of it, ma'am ; I have done it. Mr. Slaughton consented to my request before I had been in his house an hour, and has since confirmed his excellent benevolence in the most decided manner," replied Perdita, maliciously stabbing the dame in a tender place. " It is all settled ; her box is here, her clothes are hanging in my closet, and this is her home as long as it is mine."

" And I not consulted ! This is a pretty kettle of fish ; why didn't you ask my consent ?"

" I carried my business to the house-master, to whom I conceived it to belong ; I do not recognize any other authority. You must have seen enough of the Hethwaite family to know how we were trained in that particular ; I act up to my lights."

" I won't have a little, troublesome, white-faced brat here. I didn't bargain for the whole family. I'll speak to my son"

"Do so by all means, ma'am. I assure you there is no doubt whatever on the subject. Betty will stay with me."

"Go it, Aunt Perdita! I'll bet on you! Give her goss, granny; it's fun to see women fight. Jim Duncan says he likes it."

"Don't cry, Betty; nobody shall hurt you," said Perdita, lifting the mite to her old place in her sheltering arms.

"Will *she* whip me?" whispered the child, as she clung trembling to her sister's neck. "Can you make her let me be."

"Yes, yes, darling. You shall have good times. Everybody will be kind to my Betty." Singularly enough, "everybody" was at that instant represented in the young wife's mind by a tall, fair man, who hated trouble, but who had thrice during her short acquaintance with him interfered in behalf of helpless and dependent creatures who were in danger of suffering from the strong or cruel; and she remembered with a little thrill of pleasure how he had said, "I will have all things about me kindly treated."

"Come, children," said she briskly, "let us go up, and see the school-room and the nursery."

"Who is going to be nursed?" shouted Bertram. "I ain't going to! She is," pointing to Betty; "she is the baby to rock in the cradle.

> " 'She is little Polly Flinders,
>   A sitting in the cinders,
>   A warming her cunning little toes;
>   And her mother came and caught her,
>   And whipped her little daughter
>   For spoiling her nice new clothes.' "

As he chanted the rhyme, jumping up and down before Betty, shaking the skirt of the white dress, she curled in her feet and shrank as far away from him as she could, burying her face in her sister's neck.

"That's a 'fraid little mouse, that is!" observed Pandora.

" She is not a stout girl like you, but she will soon get used to your fun," answered Perdita, leading the way into the north wing. "See ! here is Cicely's chamber, with the pretty white curtains ; this is Bertram's ; and here Pandora will sleep—all close together. You can play that Cicely is the mother, and you are her children."

" I shan't ! She's been a-trying to make us mind all the way out here. Mothers are no good to boys, anyhow."

" Indeed ! You sprang armed from Jove's forehead, like Minerva, I suppose."

" Who did ? Who sprang ? How did he spring ? "

" That is one of my nice long stories, which I keep to tell evenings, when my scholars have learned very good lessons. I don't give away my stories, they have to be earned."

" But I shall do no lessons," said Pandora, with a positive little head-shake. " I shall run and race in the fields. I hate lessons ; so does Bert."

" I mean to go fishing. I'll catch some gray squirrels to tame, and I'll make them turn a wheel. I'll give one to Betty and one to Pandora."

" And one to me, brother Bertram," said Cicely.

" Call me Bert, as Pan does. I'm not an old priest with a gown on. I'm a boy. I'm going to play horse, and I'll let Bet and Pan be my team, and I'll drive 'em and lick 'em like fury."

" *I* shall study, *Aunty ;* it's unladylike to play and be bois-terous, isn't it ? " said Cicely. " May I dress for dinner ? I have a pink poplin in my trunk, and a turquoise blue sash. Can I put them on ? and will you tie a butterfly bow and curl my hair ? "

" She's all the while talking about her *close*," said Bertram. " She's told me of that dress fifty times to-day. She's no good."

" You wear quite a smart jacket yourself," remarked Perdita, smiling, " and the brass buttons are as bright as gold. You

10*

have been down in the mud with it, though, as appears from this great spot on the back."

"That wasn't my fault, Aunt Perdita ; it was the old umbrella. The wind blew hard, and just took me into a puddle before I knew it. I didn't want to spoil my coat a bit; it was made of the end of the tail of papa's great-coat, and *she* laughed."

"I didn't laugh, did I? *I'm* some good, ain't I?" said Pandora, creeping up to him ; "you like me, don't you?"

"You're well enough, but you cry when you get knocked over. I thought they'd have boys here ; haven't you got any boys, Aunt Perdita?"

"I've got a small brother, named Billy."

Before she proceeded a step farther, Bertram pinned his new relative till she told him how high, how strong, and how much of a racer was the prospective friend.

"We shall not go into school till next Monday," said she at last ; "so you will have ample time to do up your extra romping, and get settled to things ; but when we once begin, it will be dead earnest."

"You don't expect me to mind you, do you?" inquired Bertram, after a close study of her face.

"I shall mind you, my boy; all the minding you can take," replied Perdita, smiling.

"How jolly ! Jim Duncan says the women ought to mind the men."

"I agree with Jim ; but first, let's define mind. I understand by it, to watch, to attend, to take care of; that is my part of the minding."

"Oh, oh ! I don't believe Jim meant that."

"If Jim means to obey, that minding will be on your side, because you must obey me. I am old enough and wise enough to guide a boy like you, don't you think so? There ! you need not swell up like a hop-toad and try to look rebellious. Wait till you sample my minding, it is half and half, you see ; some for you, and some for me. If you don't like the partnership, you come and tell me in a month. That's fair, I am sure."

" I like your looks, Aunt Perdita ; I wouldn't mind a *humbly* woman, anyhow."

" Nor I ; I won't get *no* lesson, just as true as I live and breathe," said Pandora.

" We'll see about that when the time comes. Now I'll show you our school-room.

" Can't I help you, aunty ? " asked Cicely. " Let me carry your pencil, or your thimble. I love to be useful, and I'm *so* affecshunut, you can't think ! will you give me a dime to buy some candy ? "

" And then you can just pay me the dime you owe me ; you said you'd pay me to-morrow."

" But this isn't to-morrow, this is to-day ; to-morrow never comes."

Cicely burst out laughing at her brother's disturbed face. Such a dissonant noise as she made. It caused Perdita to turn quickly and look at her. There she stood, rosy-hued and brilliant ; but what an expression in her eyes, and what discolored teeth showed between her carniel lips !

" Isn't that true, aunty ? I've got the best of him, haven't I ; Sister Loyola told me so ; she said I was her little rose-bud, and must come back and be a nun like her. But I'd rather be yours, aunty. The nuns are always in black and have no bows nor flowers, and their bonnets are ugly. I shall have beautiful things when I grow up, and a lover to write me notes, like Miss May did in the convent. I'll tell you a good joke I had on old Sister Josephine ; it will make you laugh. She was so cheated, I thought I should die. I used to pretend to adore her ; I used to kiss her black gown and everything, you know, and she thought I loved her so much. But I didn't ; she was horrid, and she had a glass eye. I've seen her take it out and put it in. And she made me go up and sit by her at table. She thought that was a great honor ; but I didn't like it. There wasn't any fun up there, and I thought I'd manage to get away from her; and she used to send me for the hot water to wash the cups, and I spilt it all over her. I expected she'd be mad and order me down, but she only said I was awkward, and must be careful. But I upset my milk, and pushed over the things, till she was glad to get rid of me; and she said, 'My dear, you must not think I don't love you, but you will have to go back among the others,' and don't you believe she heard me laughing over the fun I had made of her, and she was so put out that she never gave me another good mark that term. Wasn't she a crazy old sister, to think I could be fond of her?"

"I shall be on my guard, Cicely, if you profess affection for me. I shall not believe you."

"Oh, now, auntie! You are pretty! You are sweet! I do love you! may I have some ginger cakes?"

CHAPTER XXXII.

A WILD DAY AT BLITHEBECK.

 HE young housekeeper left the children up-stairs, while she descended to the kitchen to give some directions for the dessert; and taking down the recipe-book, she sat with it on her knee, busily watching the frothing egg rise under Hannah's beater, and thinking about the curious complications every day of her new life was bringing her, when she was so startled as to spring hurriedly to her feet, by an abominable bellowing down the speak-

ing-tube at her very ears, like the roaring of wild buffaloes on a prairie.

"That's them children, mum," remarked Hannah, disgustedly; "they puts their mouths' to that round thing there, and it seems as if they'd split their throats. But they don't, oh, no ; they only make other folks deaf. Lord bless you, mum ! there ain't no livin' with them children, they are such a pair of torments. I thought I should jest go daft last summer. I didn't need to pay my money to go to no caravan to see wild animals while they stayed here. Miss Cicely, she seems a nice little lady."

Perdita had never observed the contrivance in the wall before, especially as the other end of it was in Dame Slaughton's room, which she had scarcely entered ; and she examined it with some curiosity, and her first impulse was to treat the rogues to a return blast, but she caught the servant's eye, and restrained herself in time.

"They will soon tire of that amusement, and after all, it does not hurt anybody ; " said she philosophically, returning to her puddings.

Hannah looked her over in surprise, evidently expecting a tempest of anger. "Law, now, how queer !" was the mental comment of the critic below-stairs ; "there's temper enough under them eyes, I'll be bound ; but children don't seem to be the ones to stir it up.

Quiet was destined to be of short duration ; for not an hour had passed, when a sound of mighty rushing water overhead brought Perdita in haste to the stair-foot, and lo ! a swelling flood was pouring down ; a swift torrent, turbid and angry, like a cataract "on a bust."

Bertram and Pandora had turned the stop-cock of the tub in the bath-room at the head of the flight, and the floods were descending at a rate which threatened speedily to empty the tank.

Perdita ran up, regardless of wet feet, and found a smooth sheet flowing over the whole mouth of the tub. Closing the faucet, she soon stopped it and then discovered the immediate cause of the accident. They had been sailing a cigar-box boat and the handkerchief they had used for a flag had so sucked into the overflow as to effectually cork it. When the little pickles had finished their game and hunted out another, their lake went on quietly filling and filling, till at last it reached a result.

Hastily calling for brooms and mops, and working hard herself as well as keeping the maids up to it, the mischief was in due time stopped; but the carpets had to be lifted, being completely soaked.

It was truly a trying day. Before night they had broken a couple of valuable vases, dashed to pieces a cheval glass, which they tried to make turn around like a wind-mill, annihilated a rocking-chair, by all climbing into it and upsetting for a railroad accident, led by Bertram, who was engineer and whistled " down brakes " too late, and got a fearful bump, which had to be dressed with arnica and brown paper. They unhooked the pendulum of the hall clock, that they might play prisoner in a dungeon, in the dark cupboard where it was accustomed to swing, and nearly frightened little Betty out of her senses, by making her their victim. They hopped and jumped and hooted, and so persecuted Taffy's kittens, that the distracted mother took them in her mouth and travelled to parts unknown. They kept the dog Sam yelping and barking like mad. He evidently thought the world was forgotten, and all things returning to chaos.

I feel almost ashamed to say that Perdita was so well amused by their wild antics, which had all the free, wilful mischief of rampant childhood, and was a phase of existence she had only known as an irrepressible outburst occasionally, which called for severe punishments in her own youth, that instead of getting angry, she enjoyed the hubbub, and she laughed the more as Dame Slaughton raged and stormed, and threatened to bundle them all off instantly.

In fact, the old lady came to an issue with her grandson long before sundown. She got so exasperated that she tried to shake him ; but the sturdy urchin was so firmly planted on his stout legs that she was not able noticeably to disturb his equilibrium. His feelings, however, were outraged, and when she took off her hands he eyed her an instant, swelling and puffing, and then he strided to the door, which he flung open.

" Grandmother, I'll let in the bears onto you. Come, bears ! and tear her all to bits ! "

When the prophet called down fire from Heaven upon the idol altar, he did not look more resolutely expectant.

Poor little Bettine spent the day in an ecstasy of fright. No timid lamb set among ravening wolves could have been more dismayed ; she peeped through door-cracks, or hid shivering in closets, starting and trembling with every fresh uproar, till finally Perdita took her to the safe asylum of her own room, and even there she fluttered and turned pale as she whispered :

" What are they doing now ? "

Mr. Slaughton did not return home till supper-time, and he came in just as they were all ready to sit down at table.

Bertram and Pandora flew at him with noisy welcome, which he good-naturedly returned ; and Cicely spread her butterfly bows, shook out her skirts, and elevated her shoulders, arranging her wrists into a kangaroo flop, such as she had admired in some of the parlor boarders at her convent. Having made the most of her pink poplin and blue sash, she wriggled up deliciously.

" How do you do, Uncle Samuel ? " said she. " Here's your little rose-bud Cicely. I want to kiss you. Sister Loyola says my mouth is as sweet as a flower, but I must not kiss the men. I don't care what she says ; she can't give me any more lives to learn. If you was a father, I'd have you for my confessor. The girls all went to Father Xavier, he was so handsome ; but he was not so handsome as you, Uncle Samuel. You would scold those children if you knew how they had been behaving to-day. I have been a nice little lady ; haven't I, grandma? Can I go riding with you to-morrow?"

Mr. Slaughton looked at the girl a moment before he answered her. There was little in his words, as they met Perdita's ear ; but his face said a good deal. "There don't seem to be much Slaughton here, mother. The Vance blood has the best of it;" and releasing himself from the rather close *empressé* clasp of his niece's arms, he turned and lifted Betty to the level of his lips, looking in her eyes as he did so.

"Are you not a little my darling, also?" whispered he.

"Just a tiny bit, Mr. Slaughton, if Perdita can spare any of me."

"No ; not Mr. Slaughton. Uncle Sam ; that's my name."

"But Perdita told me I must say Mr. Slaughton," replied she timidly, her voice about as loud as a callow wren's.

"After supper, you ask her if I am not your Uncle Sam."

"That will I, right gladly," answered the mite. I like to have you for my uncle as well as those. Cicely says you are not uncle to me ; only to her."

"Cicely ; oh, that is her style, is it? Will you ask what I told you?"

"Won't you please do it? She'll mind you."

"What makes you think so? I never found it out."

"I heard her tell their grandma that you was the one to mind."

Perdita had stood restlessly waiting till he should release her sister, who seemed in as little haste to go as was he to have her; and Dame Slaughton, not much pleased either, remarked tartly :

"There! there, Samuel ; don't make a fool of that child, pray don't! You'll have trouble enough, Perdita, if you don't teach her to be modest. I don't think any great of girls who run up and hug strange men. She looks to me as if she needed a tight rein."

The mite flew to her sister, covered with confusion and

blushes. Though hardly old enough to take in the full value of
the dame's remark, she understood right well its tone of reproof and the unfriendly frown which accompanied it.

"Sit here, Bettine," said Perdita quietly. "This is where
you belong, close by me. That's right, tuck up your curls
while I tie your pinafore; I expect all you little people are
hungry enough to want a great deal of supper, after such a
busy day as you have made."

Mr. Slaughton was disturbed, and fearful that his intimacy
with the child he had taken such a fancy for might be nipped in
the bud. I cannot suppose it possible that he had any other
motive for his caresses than real liking. Of course not; how
could he? He did not say anything, because he did not know
what to say; and he tried to follow his *vis-à-vis'* course, who
appeared to ignore the taunt altogether. He wondered if she
was as indifferent as she seemed. He had already found out
that she kept many of her thoughts and feelings hidden from
everybody.

Cicely Vance, having expended her blandishments on
"Aunty" without marked results, now transferred her attentions
to grandma, and was "so affecshunut" to her.

Bertram chose for himself a place by his uncle, as man of
the house, watching his every motion, and evidently building a
code of table etiquette on his model, which he carried to the
length of making a wisp of his napkin and carefully rubbing his
plump mouth right and left, cleansing an imaginary mustache.

Mr. Slaughton listened in wonder to the familiar chit-chat his
wife was keeping up with the children, laughing at their smartness, joining their nonsense, making herself one of them.

"Childish among children," he thought again, as he had
thought at the picnic in the wood; and truly she looked not
much but a child in her simplicity, with her flowing hair and
scanty dress.

A very indistinct idea flitted into his mind, how a society
robe, elaborate and rich, with jewels, and coiffure *à la mode,*

would become her, and a half wish to see her so arrayed, and a vision of a gentleman—as it might be, Mr. Slaughton—with her on his arm, entering a drawing-room, presented itself before his imagination. But it was quickly obscured and spoiled by the shut-out feeling awakened by the liveliness she promoted, and seemed quite able and willing to enjoy, in spite of him. When most genial, she never chatted with him, nor seemed to think such converse possible or desirable. The best approach to confidence he had found was their consultation over the building plan, and afterwards when they planted the bulbs ; and even then she kept herself aloof, as a housekeeper should.

It seems difficult to say why her pleasant prattle and pretty ways, so unconscious of him, should annoy him, absorbed in her charge, amused with them. Yes, no doubt of that ; one look at her animated face proved it, and her smile was certainly arch, her countenance expressive, sweet, candid, full of feeling. Her great black eyes, just as they rested this instant on his, were kind, loving, sparkling, brilliant ; but the glance was not meant for him, it was just carried over to his face, by chance, from a look at Bettine, as a brimming cup overflows.

Mr. Slaughton felt a desire to make some table-talk with her —quite a new desire. Attending always to his duties, he had been polite and silent, and quitted the board as soon as possible, since Chandy left them. Perhaps it was the dame's presence which restrained him. Once or twice it had seemed to Perdita that her suspicious observance was a check and trammel on his freedom of speech and action.

He had a latent dread of seeming inconsistent, changeable, and could not forget how very positively he had declared lasting and sublime indifference to the girl of her choice.

"*Le sang reste toujours jeune.*" Our friend Samuel was only thirty years old, after all, and a beautiful, attractive woman under his roof, continually in juxtaposition with him, and in the queer relations growing out of their attitude towards each other, could not be otherwise than an object of intense interest—

could not help kindling his feelings, even although he had deeply loved Sabrina Bradshaw ten years ago. Ten years is an age for a man to remain faithful to a lost love. How many times in a century does such a marvel find place ?

On the very rare occasions when he had addressed a remark to his wife and she had pleasantly replied, the old lady had cut in with some tart observation, putting an end to further talk, and her son found her as owly as did Slowgo.

She was in a particularly testy humor this evening, which was not to be wondered at, considering the day she had passed, and she nodded ill-naturedly to a whispered communication of Cicely Vance's.

· " Grandma, hasn't auntie got shocking table manners ? She holds her fork in her fist. This is the way, isn't it ? "

The affected little minx spread all her fingers, and straightened the little one till it quite took leave of the others. It was such an absurd caricature of the lady boarders, and she was such a palpable bundle of pretensions, that her uncle burst out laughing. With all her trifling levity, she was sensitive to ridicule, and she blushed a beautiful crimson, while her eyes glistened under her bent brows with such lurking malice that her child-face looked malignant, in spite of its superb coloring.

Dame Slaughton told her not to mind, and said it was a shame for grown folks to make game of children, and while she talked she looked at Perdita, who had not opened her mouth, and she heaped Cicely's plate with seed-cake and prunes, and did not offer Betty any. Fortunately, the mite's taste was not trained to sweets, so that she did not miss them and was quite content with her cup of milk and white bread.

" Look, Betty, what my grandma gives me. She don't give you any, do you, grandma ? "

" That sounds spiteful, Miss Cicely. You must be careful how you develope such traits, if you want to be friends with me," said Mr. Slaughton, severely. "Rose-buds should distil no venom among their sweet juices."

"Why, Uncle Samuel, I don't know what you mean!" exclaimed Cicely.

"Now I have a riddle for you to guess," said Perdita, evidently wishing to change the topic. Netticoat, netticoat, with a white petticoat and red nose; the longer she stands, the shorter she grows. While all the piping voices were going at once with guesses, Dame Slaughton eyed her new daughter. She was every day more and more convinced that she was not the patient, yielding creature she had been led to expect by Mrs. Hethwaite, and she felt as if deceived and imposed upon—nearly defrauded, as if her neighbor had gotten the girl the place on false representations. This was the more disagreeable and hard to bear, as she had no recourse in complaining to her son.

On the occasion of the increased help she had tried that safety-valve to her surcharged feelings, and he had blandly assured her that the affair was of her own choosing, and she must try to put up with any little disappointments she might meet, as well as she could; and further, as to the matter in hand, he quite agreed with the new incumbent, and hoped he should never again be mortified by too few servants, as he had been during the late visit of his friend. Thus plainly demonstrating, not only that she could hope for no sympathy from him, but that he was likely at any moment to go over to the other faction.

CHAPTER XXXIII.

WHAT PERDITA SAW IN THE STUDIO.

 ERDITA opened the school-room door and looked out. She missed the little rogue Pandora, and was wondering what could have become of her.

While attending to Cicely's lessons (which never progressed without a good deal of personal supervision, the geography being supplanted by a story-book or rag-baby as soon as her back was turned), the child had slipped in to beg for a drink of water—that never-failing want of restless scholars, and had danced off, and had not danced back again.

As she listened, she heard pounding and racket in the upper regions, and, stepping to the attic stairs, she distinctly caught her own name, muffled and shut out, as if the voice was shut in behind walls.

"Aunt Pud-e-e-e-e-e-ter !" Yes, that was Pandora, and she ran swiftly to the second landing.

"Aunt Pud-e-e-e-e-ter !" It was inside the studio, and was getting hopeless and pitiful, and ended with a wail and a sniffle.

She tried the door, it was fastened ; she knocked and called, "Pandora, Pandora ! hush ! what are you in there for ? "

" Oh, let me out, Aunt Perdita, I won't never do so no more ! "

" Who locked you in ? "

" I turned the key round a little bit, and now it won't go back. Oh dear ! Aunt Puditer, can't you open it ? Shall I have to stay in here till I am starved to death, and never see nobody no more ? Won't Uncle Samuel break the old door down with his ax and let me out ? and there's mice in here; ooh—ooh !"

"Be quiet, Pandora; little brown mice won't hurt you. Keep still now, till I see what I can do."

She looked about her. There was a key in the door of the cedar room opposite. She pulled it out and tried it, talking all the while to the captive in a cheerful voice.

"Now, Pandora, can't you pull out your key? I can't do any good till you do. Try hard."

A jarring and poking followed, and then a successful "There !" which proved the feat accomplished ; and Perdita opened the door and found Pandora with terrified face, and daubed from head to foot with her uncle's colors, the tints of which she had been trying, and there is not a hue known to painters which was not represented somewhere on her face, hands, or pinafore apron.

"Oh, you naughty little mischief, what have you been at ?"

"I tried to make a picture, Aunt Pudeter, but it wouldn't make so good as I wanted."

As soon as the terror was off, the waggish elf was as confident and saucy as ever. "Look ! this is my house, and this is my chimney ; and here I am, in my front door."

Perdita glanced fearfully about, dreading the havoc the sprite might have effected among precious things which seemed strewn on every side, and she looked with curiosity too.

A studio had been a mythical region to her. While her eyes were occupied with antiques, vases, goblets, broken columns, half-finished heads, casts of arms and feet, suits of armor suspended from the wall, as if their owners had been sentenced to be hanged and had dried away and been forgotten ; studies and helps which the artist had collected during his foreign life, Pandora pulled her impatiently by the skirt.

"Come clear in, Aunt Pudeter, and see the beautiful woman."

"No, indeed ; you have no business here. I don't know what your uncle won't do to you."

"Uncle Sam won't hurt *me*," retorted Mischief confidently. "I've been in here before with him, and grandma showed me all the pictures her own self. Look, Aunt Perdita ! just look ! Grandma says it is a Bible girl that was very good to her folks."

The young wife put aside the feeling that the *Master* should be the one to exhibit to her the treasures of his sanctum, which was strong in her. Youth and feminine curiousness had the best of all restraining impulses, and impelled her to peep in at the "den" the two friends had spoken of together, and where her husband passed so many of his hours in a seclusion he had never invited her to share. She took a couple of steps forward, and as she did so her eyes followed the pointing finger the child extended.

Turning about as she crossed the threshold, she stood motionless, filled with strange agitations.

The Ruth had been carried to the east end of the long room, which took in the whole length of the mansion, and beneath it hung the young girl bearing a pitcher in her hands.

Its position had been changed at Chandy's suggestion, for the western light which flooded it, and brought it out like life.

A pure, adorable face ; a wonderfully symmetrical head covered with masses of dead gold hair ; a proudly-poised head.

This was—it must be—the only woman Mr. Slaughton had ever seen worth loving ; was it the pride which had kept them asunder ?

While she gazed, her husband's words came vividly to her memory. "This black-browed woman resembles my ideal as much as darkness resembles light. It was true. Absolute contrast indeed.

She did not know how long she stood gazing at the pictures, so many tumultuous emotions crowded her mind ; and there was born within her a new passion—*jealousy*.

She had got each feature, every tint, by heart. The whole conception was hers to minutest perfection, even to the faint blue vein which threaded the fair forehead ; and the bunch of purple violets on the white breast, which seemed to her excited sense to rise and fall with the pure breath which came through the parted lips ; and the eyes, so spirituelle, so full of feeling, *so liquid*, so fathomless, seemed to pour their ineffable splendor into her deepest soul, irradiating her secret thoughts.

Perdita could not leave that room precisely the same woman who entered it. She had seen her husband's first and only love ; she had found her such an adorable beauty as a man could not fail to worship. With the new-born jealousy sprang also a grain of pity for the poor fellow who had lost this wondrous treasure. He had gained a new interest in her mind ; he became a subject for her fancy's picturing, and in the days which followed she looked at him often. She followed him in imagination through the life he must have lived at Sabrina Bradshaw's side when those lustrous glances dwelt kindly on him, those humid sweet lips smiled replies to his talk, that lovely hand touched his.

She let herself dream out a romance with those two for actors, and she almost wished she was enough the friend of the man whose name she bore to ask him why he had lost his love.

Mr. Slaughton, coming and going in her neighborhood, scarcely felt any change in her. Once or twice, when he was moved to look at her, a pitying gentleness, which melted in her black eyes and attuned her voice to softness, set his pulse beating quickly. It was a fleeting, evanescent, intangible charm, which was scarcely materialized to consciousness, subtle and delicate.

It brought them into no better harmony, however. She held quietly her way, ordering his house into completeness. She kept sedulously the daily school, was positive with the children, ceremoniously civil to the dame, and she dwelt almost as much apart from her husband as if she inhabited another star.

There might have been some magnetic current between them too. He thought of her, remembered her words, and was moved to exert himself for her pleasure, because he brought one evening a handsome carved fernery, and placed it in the window she had indicated as the desired spot for such a thing; it was filled with begonias, callas, trailing arbutus, ivies, and foliage plants; and it was indeed the finishing ornament of the library. He waited all day for her to see and approve, and at evening he was impatient.

> "Come to your pleached bower,
> Where honeysuckles, ripened by the sun,
> Forbid the sun to enter—like favorites
> Made proud by princes, that advance their pride
> Against the power that bred it.

"That is to say, will it please you to come into the library and see what a busybody has been about there."

Most unluckily her thoughts had been all the morning dwelling upon Ruth in the studio—his first and only love; and so he got none of the pleasure for his pains he had counted on.

"It is rarely beautiful," said she, "and well filled. I shall see that it thrives as it ought. You may count on all the satisfaction you expected from it, sir."

He left her, chafing at her unsympathetic manner; and as he went briskly off, she watched his going.

"Had it been Sabrina," she thought, bitterly, "how graceful she would have been; how gracious he."

The more the poor child mused on the gorgeous womanhood her husband's pencil had emblazoned on his canvas, and which must be after all but a faint shadowing of the real person, the more she let her eyes see and her mind admit the worth of the man who had lost it—the more bitterly she felt her own deficiencies and demerits, and the cruelty of the fate which had bound her to a husband whose taste rejected her, finding her displeasing and insufficient as he did. Had she not his own

11

words, very plain and explicit, to make her certain of the fact ? The worrying sting of the wretched truth wounded her most when he made any effort to be complaisant.

" He pities the girl with the brow of Egypt ; he wishes to be civil to his housekeeper."

Courage was not born of her knowledge. She had been allowed so little time for deliberation ; had been so pushed, so hurried ; she was such a child in experience, in familiarity with strange people ; and then, besides, the intense mortification she had felt when the affair of the letter written to warn her not to marry in haste reached her, grew and grew each day with her brooding over it ; so that, even when she found in herself any emotion of gratitude or friendliness for its author, she smothered it as improper and unbecoming her woman's dignity.

Parson Hethwaite had been her type of manhood ; his wife the type of wives. In a larger sphere theirs was the life she had seen in prospect in her new home ; and she had brought to it all the earnestness of her nature, fully believing she should need it. That though bearing this yoke, she might still retain such measure of freedom as steady resistance could insure her ; and thus far, through all her unrest and perplexities, she had never for a moment lost sight of the ultimate object to be gained when she let herself be passively wived—some ability and space to aid those she had left at the parsonage.

The person, the mind, the tastes, the culture of the *man*, which had not entered into her account up to the day when she stood on his threshold, waiting a bidding to enter his house, were becoming of paramount importance, even in her divided isolated life near him, now that her mind had awakened to new impressions.

Chandy Goldsmith's visit had showed her novel sort of gentlemen, and Mr. Slaughton suffered not a whit in comparison with him. Everything around her had been closely studied ; much only partially understood, because she examined from her own standpoint, having no previous experiences or information to go on ; and to all her insights, all her conclusions up to this last day when had been revealed to her the wonderful beauty she discovered in the studio, she had found no reasonable expectation of any change in the line of life she had at first marked out for herself—housekeeper and governess.

But though there might be little alteration in her demeanor, or prospects, there certainly were springing within her new impulses—faint, scarcely discernible. hardly felt, not really recognized or acknowledged by herself—just germs of something possible.

CHAPTER XXXIV.

"IN PIPING TIMES OF PEACE."

AME SLAUGHTON was on a visit to the Brandigees. She was hugely enjoying herself in talking over her daughter-in-law with her old friend, who " Oh'd " and " Ah'd ! " and said, " I want to know," and " Do tell," and gave in exchange sundry confidences concerning Mrs. Richard Pritchard, who had been early left a widow, and lived with her children, with her husband's family.

Mr. Slaughton was in Toptown, making arrangements for the hanging of a couple of pictures in the Exhibition rooms, preparatory to the autumn opening.

He worked constantly at his art ; he drove away at the farming till Slowgo found him almost as " owly " as his mother. He was no idle man, as his many finished landscapes fully proved. Though Chandy called him lazy, he painted to sell, and he did sell for large prices. He was as indefatigable in his profession as his father had been in bridge-building, and he made it pay in good hard money.

The nation's festival was at hand, the presidential proclamation of thanksgiving for the twenty-seventh of November had been read from all the pulpits in our wide land.

Mr. Slaughton felt a new interest in the approaching day He was experiencing a sort of pleasurable curiosity to ascertain how his girl-wife would carry herself at the head of his table, which he meant to fill with her family and his own.

Timbuctoo was far in the dim distance, and home interests were becoming paramount.

When Mr. Slaughton put himself in the train he also deposited in the baggage-room sundry packages : 1tem—one keg of white grapes, one drum of figs ; one box of Dehesia raisins, one of selected oranges, wrapped in tissue-paper, also a basket of French confections, snapping mottoes, etc.

Mr. Slaughton felt eminently pleased with his purchases, and he smiled as he drew from his pocket a book of parlor games ; and he perused it attentively to the end, and noted particular pages with his pencil, and after he had finished he began to think.

Thanksgiving seemed to him a good time for a prosperous progress towards an amicable understanding with a dark-eyed girl he knew of. Indeed, I believe his interest in the festival centered right there ; no other motive would have been sufficiently powerful to move him to such trouble and pains as he was taking. But with his cogitations was mixed a certain sheepishness born of the new rôle he was playing, and diffidence of success. He was afraid that he had not yet learned to woo his wife so agreeably as to induce her to forgive her first day of wedlock.

He returned twenty-four hours sooner than he expected ; he hurried his business that he might do so, and he was obliged to walk up from the depot in consequence.

As he set foot within his gate, he paused a moment to listen to music.

It came from the library, which was so cheerily illumined that long, slant sheets of light lay on the ground beneath its windows. Miss McLeod's reel, played in such sprightly time as dancers like, swiftly-flitting figures, and merry childish voices, hinted at a frolic.

He stepped upon the piazza and looked in ; he saw a pretty scene, like a Rembrandt interior, vivid and glowing.

Bathed in the warm brightness of the autumn splendor on the walls, and the fire-shine in the chimney, which ruddily blazed, were grouped the children, laughing and gleeful. Even little Bettine was flying about like a fairy by moonlight.

The study table had been pushed into a corner, and on it was perched Perdita, whose small ankles in their red hose were quite visible, as she swung her feet to and fro in time to the soft, penetrating strains she was drawing from a yellow German flute at her lips, and she was so wholly absorbed by her occupation that she did not observe her husband, who stood some seconds framed in the doorway, a presentation of no despicable manhood.

His artistic tastes were gratified with the pleasing picture. His wife's oval face, delicate-featured, clear and pale, shaded by jetty brows and coal-black hair, seemed to him exquisitely lovely, and in her uplifted eyes he found a tender pensiveness they never showed when conscious of his neighborhood. He liked her better, thus off the defence she seemed always to maintain in his presence. She looked sweeter, more careless and unrestrained than he had ever seen her, and as he stood gazing at her he wished he knew how to behave so as to be able to get her companionship at its best and richest.

Her long, slender neck, soft and smooth as satin, was encircled by a crimson ribbon, from which depended a carved heart of apple tree wood, which Teddy had this evening brought to her, and he fell to thinking how a certain case of uncut rubies he had in his cabinet would become it, with their blaze and resplendent radiance. Not that he had any fixed intention of offering them to her; it was merely a suggestion of his fancy, for a study he might make, if she wore them.

Cicely was everywhere, colored like a damask rose, giving orders in her cracked voice, pushing the others into their places, and frisking down the middle, while she bowed and nodded to the head couple; she said, " Now I am in my elements," and she really was enjoying the frolic and forgetting her airs and borrowed graces as much as was possible for such a surface-child to do.

The young folks from the parsonage were all on the floor except Teddy, who had taken refuge in a corner and was bending over a book he had found in the case, and which absorbed all his faculties.

Pandora was the first to catch sight of her uncle, and she sprang forward and seized both his hands.

" Oh, Uncle Sam! I am so glad you've come; now I shall have you for my partner; Cicely says I am too clumsy."

The flautist slid down from her perch, and dropped the instrument to her side, as she stood with her head up, provoked and surprised, but also somewhat shamefaced, despite her proud attitude.

" Good evening, Orchestra," said Mr. Slaughton, advancing and bowing low; "pray don't stop for me. It is said to be difficult to arrive pat between too early and too late; but I feel for once I have hit the very nick of time.'"

" You said you would not be home till to-morrow; at least, your mother told me so."

" If I had known that you hold revels in my absence, I would have come anyhow; and I thank the luck which has pushed me into the middle of them. Oh! yes, I should have come, even if I had foreseen the sorry welcome I am getting. This room is such a gay scene as the old house has not shown for many a day, if ever. It fills me with wonder."

"I took the opportunity of your and your mother's absence to give the children an evening of pleasure," stammered Perdita, feeling almost guilty under his scrutiny.

"We had to earn it first, though, I tell you!" shouted Bertram, coming up and leaning fearlessly against his aunt. She's a woner, she is; she wouldn't give in till we suited her. I had ten pages of British Chronicles; Cicely got every line of the "Pied Piper of Hamelin."

"I did the map of Africer in my gografer, capes, promintories, and all," said Pandora.

"I wish you would not wait till I am out of the house for your frolics," said Mr. Slaughton reproachfully. "I am fond of them. You will persist in treating me like a household ogre."

"I put it in your absence on purpose to save you annoyance. I understood you disapproved of clatter and chatter."

"Grandma said that; I heard her," spoke up Pandora, "She says she won't have the Hethwaite young ones always coming here, eating dinner and supper."

The gentleman looked quickly at his wife, and saw by her face that the little mischief spoke truth.

"I hope—I really—trust—I feel much annoyed," he began.

"If you wish to let me know that you are troubled by the very plain Saxon I get, you are wasting unexpected sensibility. I intend to take my own part; it is a necessity of my bargain. There is the good I esteem sufficient to outweigh anything," glancing at her sister. "She is rosy and happy; that contents me."

It seemed to Mr. Slaughton that her voice sounded a little dispirited as she went on; that might be because her tasks looked so terrific to him.

"I mean to discharge my whole duty to the Vances, as I consider best. I felt the lack of all pastimes in my childhood. They shall not; and as I know of no truer, more honest children than my brothers and sisters, I shall invite them to share their sports.

"I hope so, indeed; I am glad to hear you say so. It is a capital plan. I heartily approve your idea, and trust you will carry it out to the full," replied the gentleman eagerly, as if glad to be helped out of a disagreeable dilemma; and he reached down and picked up little Betty, who had come noiselessly and slipped her fingers into his.

"Ah, fair Titania! wilt kill me a red-hipped humblebee on the top of a thistle, and bring me the honey-bag; or shall we go seek some dew-drops here, and hang a pearl in every cowslip's ear?"

"No, no, Uncle Sam, put me down, please. I want to talk to Bertram; I was glad for you to come home."

As she flitted off backwards with airy motion, her light hair dancing and her small lips smiling at them, Perdita sent after her a glance freighted with unutterable love.

"If she grows up in full blossom of her winsome budding, there will be scores of broken hearts," said Mr. Slaughton.

"Heaven grant her grace to win and keep one," replied Perdita.

"Can it be that she has other lives beside her sister's, in her mind," thought the gentleman, studying her eloquent face.

Cicely had meanwhile gone and thrown both arms around "auntie," while she looked up "so affecshunut," and over at her uncle, intending him to observe her sweet ways.

"Betty! Betty!" she called out, when Perdita placed a caressing hand on her as she made it a duty to do if the motherless child offered her any demonstrations of fondness. "Betty, look at me; I'm in your place! Don't you wish you was me?"

Perdita let the girl go, giving her a little push; she could never find anything real in her; all her actions seemed prompted by unworthy motives—they were either put forth to further a secret scheme for pleasure or gain, or to tantalize and worry somebody else.

Mr. Slaughton soon followed his wife to the window, whither she went after Cicely's outing. He wished to bespeak her interest in his Thanksgiving dinner ; and he was encouraged to the attempt by a friendly smile her face wore while her attention was fixed on Betty and Bertram, who were exchanging confidences ; and he also paused to hear what they were saying.

" Look, how pretty those clouds are !   I should like to be an angel and fly up among them.   Shouldn't you ? " asked the mite.

" Could we fly if we was angels, do you suppose ? " inquired the boy, shaking his shoulders as if he felt pinions starting beneath them.

" Oh, yes, we could, just as easy as butterflies ; mother says we shall have beautiful white wings, as white as those clouds by the moon, when we die."

" Have we all got to be angels, boys and all ? "

" Yes ; it is lovely to be an angel ; we shall want to be it awfully."

" What ! all covered with feathers ? "

Betty considered a little, this point being not fully revealed in her teachings ; but as the context seemed to imply it, she replied quite confidently at length :

" Yes, feathers ; beautiful, soft white feathers."

" Legs and all ? "

Here was another poser, but she did not hesitate, and asserted promptly and decidedly, " Yes, legs and all."

Bertram made a wry face, and passed his hands up and down his short, plump limbs.

" I should not like being an angel at all ! good enough for you girls ; but how am I to get on my pantaloons without rumpling my feathers ? "

The two listeners smiled at each other ; but by common consent they refrained from breaking in on the conference, and left the small teacher to get out of her predicament as she best could.

" You have a novel accomplishment for a lady," said Mr. Slaughton, keeping by Perdita's side, and looking at the flute she still carried in her hand.

11*

"I suppose so. I did not choose it; but as I had nothing else to play except a jew's-harp, and the whistles Teddy used to make me, I picked it up for the sake of getting something capable of sweet sounds."

"It looks very old, and is wonderfully sweet and mellow."

"My father played it at college. No one would believe it; but I know he was fond of music before he got to be a minister."

"We are told that Minerva played the flute, and thought well of her skill, till one day, when she happened to catch a glimpse of herself in a pond over whose margin she leaned; then she threw her instrument into its depths in disgust at the faces she made, so disfiguring to her lovely mouth," said he, rather pointedly, studying the red lips, ripe as a cherry, which seemed to him positively beautiful; they were not the same hue at all as Sabrina Bradshaw's, either—as different as a rose pink from the brilliant glow of a pomegranate. "Perhaps you never look in your mirror while discoursing sweet melody."

"I don't. I don't think I have thought to do so," answered Perdita bitterly; "my mirror and I are no good friends. If I was a blue-eyed maid like Minerva or other people, I might love to admire myself because I should know I had charms; but as it is, I don't mind.

She left him and went and sat down in a corner, and looked so beclouded that he wished he had not started the topic. He more than guessed her thoughts, although he did not know how she had filled her imagination with his youth and his first love. He was not much astonished, because he had as yet few pleasant replies to such speeches as he felt moved to make, bearing on jovialities, and as he followed her with his eyes he nearly made up his mind there was not, nor could be, for him anything better than commonplaces, as safe ground for their daily life—the very condition of affairs he had wished to make certain at the first, and here he was studying ways and means to overset all his arrangements, so nicely established and fixed.

Betty having ended her angelic teachings, got the great Bible, almost as big as herself, and laid it on her sister's knee, settling herself to a satisfied study of the old pictures.

"What does this one mean, Perdita?" asked she.

"That is Jesus, who is riding into Jerusalem on an ass's colt; although he made the world, and everything in it, he is riding on that mean little animal."

Betty looked silently at the figures a good while, and then she spoke, her words expressing the culmination of her child's conception of the strange event.

"Good morning, Mr. Jesus! is that the best horse you've got?"

"That sounds impious," said Perdita half to herself, "but I believe, if Christ had met a little girl like my Bettine that day, and she had said so to him, he would have smiled at her, and patted her pretty, innocent head."

"That is a natural inference from the teachings and conduct of our great teacher," replied Mr. Slaughton, who had for some reason again become her neighbor. "I fully agree with you."

"There is no love in my father's creed," remarked she thoughtfully.

"Nor in your father's daughter's either," said Samuel significantly. "If I could only find peace on earth and good will towards one man, I wouldn't generalize much further."

It was a strange speech for him to make; and he uttered it in swift words and a strong voice, as if he had not meant to say such a thing till the very instant when it passed his lips. She seemed astonished, both with the outing and the flash and flush of the speaker. She rose immediately; any reply she could have made would have sounded unfriendly. She was utterly untrained in polite platitudes, knowing no use of language except to explain ideas or thoughts.

"Put up the Bible, Betty. Excuse me, sir, if I attend to the children; it will soon be time for them to end their frolic."

"Will you lend me your flute?" asked the gentleman,

determined to be agreeable. " I used to play it years ago to Chandy's guitar, when we went to serenade the girls. I shall be glad to accompany your piano. I did that sometimes also, in those days.

" Yes! with Sabrina Bradshaw!" thought Perdita. What wonder that she drew back and answered coldly—so coldly that it was positively disheartening to the man who was trying his best to find a place of approach to a better understanding with her.

" That is impossible! quite absurd, in fact. Joys which you've tasted may sometimes return ; but I am unable to help you recall any such pleasant memories of your vanished delights. I never studied the piano. I think I mentioned to you that this flute is my only instrument."

" Mr. Slaughton desired to impute her reply to simple vex ation at her lack of skill in the young-ladyish accomplishment; and made haste to say :

" Oh, pardon me ! you did tell me so. I am not sorry you never undertook the piano, because here, in this old house, you will be sure to find great amusement and occupation in lessons. I shall immediately send up a Steinway for the chil- dren ; and will you oblige me by learning of their master? I will take care to select one apt to teach."

" No, sir. I am too old for that and many other things. It is too late ; I have no time."

" And yet you find time to read Italian and Spanish every day."

" How do you know that ! "

" I told him," exclaimed Pandora, who had left the children and was listening open-mouthed to their talk.

" You are not angry with the child, I hope," said he, trying to interpret the signs of unrest in her darkened face.

" Of course not, why should I be ? Pandora is a box of mischief, and what she has in her must manifest itself. The Italian I indulge in is quite harmless, being only such scraps as

I have been able to glean by myself; and the time I give it is all my own; being out of housekeeper's and governess's hours."

"How very unkind it is of you continually to place me before your eyes in so mean a light, as if you were a paid hireling!"

"So I am. Do I not get my wage in dirty bank-notes every month?" retorted Perdita, secretly amused by his evident disrelish of her very plain statement.

"It shall be gold next time. You can't hinder my giving you 'gold! gold! gold! bright and yellow, hard and cold!'"

"I shall not try; it may be true what your witty author teaches, 'People with naught are naughty.' I never had a gold piece in my life. I hope you will."

"And you must send the piano, Uncle Sam," said Pandora. "I shall teach Aunt Pudeter all I learn. She says I do teach her things all the while."

"You teach my sister!" called out Malcolm. "I guess not."

"Oh, yes, I learn the grace of patience," replied Perdita, smiling, "and she gives me fair chance to become perfect."

"Oh, aunty!" exclaimed Cicely, who had been nursing her resentment at the rebuff she had received, "oh, aunty, what a funny color your arm is!"

She matched her own milk-white member beside the smooth, round wrist which rested on the table.

"Grandma says you must be part Creole. Ugly, black things Creoles are—aren't they, Uncle Sam?"

"My sister is not an ugly thing!" screamed Malcolm. "You are ugly yourself!"

"Bless the boy!" said Mr. Slaughton, patting the lad's head. "It would be as safe to attack a young elephant protected by its dam (and even tigers are afraid to do that), as to speak lightly of your sister in your presence."

"It is good that somebody stands up for her in this house," replied Malcolm, much provoked, and twisting his head from under his uncle's hand. "That Cicely there says she hates her."

" I never said *any* such thing, so now," replied Cicely, coloring to the roots of her hair, while her blue eyes seemed to retreat into their great sockets, from which caverns they flamed like blue steel. " I *love* aunty. I wrote a pretty little letter yesterday to Sister Josephine, and told her how kind my dear Aunt Perdita was to me. I think you are real mean to say such a thing, Malcolm Hethwaite ! I'll pay you off for it, see if I don't !"

" It is true all the same," maintained the lad. " I don't care if you do look as if you'd like to tear my eyes out. I'll leave it to Bert if he didn't hear you."

" Bertram, come here ! " said Mr. Slaughton. The perpendicular line between his eyes was very deep, and his voice was exceeding clear and incisive.

The lad approached fearlessly and seized his uncle's hand.

" Well, here I am ! as little Sammy said to old Eli. What did you call me for ? "

" Bertram ! oh, say, Bertram ! did I tell you I hated aunty ? " spoke up Cicely in a hurry, trying to catch his eye and give him a head-shake of warning and entreaty not to betray her.

" Yes, you did ! after she gave you twenty words to learn, when you tore the lesson-leaf out of your gografy."

" Oh, what a horrid lie ! I never in my life ! "

" Mr. Slaughton, permit me," said Perdita. The gentleman looked so angry and disgusted as to appear quite ferocious, and she felt really afraid for the girl. " Permit me ; this comes clearly within my province as governess. Malcolm, you are much to blame for repeating Cicely's foolish words ; a tattler is a reptile. I am afraid you did not learn all those long Proverb chapters to much purpose. I don't like this bluster at all ; you need not fight any bugbears for me. As for you, Cicely, your liking or disliking will not in the least alter my course. The lessons *must* be learned. When you go upstairs to-night you may add this lie to your list. Saturday we will count them up, and see if you have made any headway against your favorite

venial sin this week. Dismiss the subject now, and let us finish the evening with pleasure, as we began it. You are entitled to all the amusement you can get out of the frolic, because
it is the promised reward you had in mind when you did your
excellent lessons this morning."

While her status and sentence were in abeyance, Cicely wept.
Her tears fell from her long flaxen lashes upon her cheeks, like
rain-drops upon rose-buds—such profuse grief, such glowing
penitence !

"Perhaps Mr. Slaughton will take you for his partner, while
i play another reel."

"I will play if I may ; I shall be glad to give you a chance to
dance," replied he, much astonished at the adjustment of the
affair, but entirely disinclined towards the partner offered him.

"Impossible ! I never danced a step in my life ! You
surely forget that I am a minister's daughter. I really hope
you will at last arrive at an end of the list of my deficiencies,"
she added in a vexed tone ; "so many open to you hourly that
I fear I may after a while be thought incompetent to the place.
Luckily, there was no mention made in my engagement of
piano or dancing."

"When you vacate your present place, I trust it will be
because you feel called to accept something you like better."

While Perdita was looking at him, trying to get the value of
his ambiguous speech, she caught a beam from his eyes which
filled her with curious agitations.

He had picked up Bettine as he ended, and turned away
among the children, who quickly ranged into lines, all eager
for the dance.

"Thus," thought she, "might he have looked at Sabrina
Bradshaw while he painted the Ruth ; such a tone his voice
might have had as they chatted together, kind, persuasive,
exceedingly pleasant."

"If you please, Orchestra," he called out presently, "we are
ready."

He nodded across to her and smiled. Tall, symmetrical, every inch a man, his figure showed to much advantage in his easy-fitting suit of dark blue; and from her corner she caught the flash of diamonds he wore, which, sumptuous as they were, seemed a fit finish for his attire. His cheeks were dyed "like a peach in the sun," his blue eyes were bright and friendly, although the lids dropped a little at the corners, as his habit of half closing them at his work occasionally asserted itself; his full lips showed through his light brown mustache as red and fresh as a girl's; a choicely gentleman to be lover to a maid, a right noble husband for a wife to be proud of; and it is a truth, she heard him tell it: he has found Sabrina Bradshaw the only woman in the world worth wooing.

This being the bitter ending of her scrutiny, her flute answered not so well as usual to her will, and she had to summon all her pride to her aid to keep back some foolish tears.

Cicely's pupils had learned the reel; and they danced with young enjoyment; and while Mr. Slaughton dos-a-dos'd and whirled with his elfin partner, his thoughts and eyes were much occupied with the flutist. Her cheeks were no longer pale, nor her face tender; she had retreated from him into the remote distance in which her life near him held her so far apart; the trembling of her small brown fingers was too slight to attract his notice, and the breath which might have exhaled in sighs, being poured into the old yellow flute, its fragrance was distilled there into sweet music.

Visibly she devoted her energies to her task—the payment of a just debt she owed her pupils for their perfect lessons.

The girl Cicely gamboled and skipped like a brainless animal. As soon as the danger of disgrace and punishment was lifted, she was light-headed as a shuttlecock, and her never-ceasing laugh and chatter were bestowed on Malcolm, he being the tallest lad in the room. In no manner mortified or out of sorts with herself by the exposure he had made of her lies and treachery, she did not half feel the boyish disdain and disgust he took no pains to conceal, nor understand its source; while he only wondered how she could have "*the cheek*" to look at him, "let alone chippering and frisking like an old red squirrel. If one of *us* had been found out in such a piece of flam-bam gammon, we would have dropped through the floor, so we would!"

Malcolm's sisters were true, genuine girls, to whom *lies* were not *venial* sins.

After the reel was finished, Mr. Slaughton brought Bettine over to her sister, and remained in her neighborhood while the dancers fanned themselves and discussed the finished pleasure. Cicely's eyes had retreated into their caverns, and she darted evil glances at Malcolm, having at last gotten such a repulse from him as she could not help feeling. She had long since found out that he considered it manly to despise tenderness and affection (especially towards females) which sought expression in caresses, and it would be strange if he did not look down on women and girls as his inferiors, if he at all followed his father's example. Poor Mrs. Hethwaite felt troubled by the manishness of the budding lad, which occasionally sent her back sharp, saucy answers for her mild reproofs; and showed too plainly how little he thought of the pious truisms she felt it her duty to deal out once in a while, when, the head of the house being absent, the fun got too fast and furious even for her patient endurance; and she complained about him to Perdita, and said she was afraid he was going to turn out bad. That was when he spent a whole afternoon in burlesqueing the Parson's behavior on examination day, although he did his part so well that she laughed till tears ran down her face, and felt dreadfully ashamed and penitent as soon as she could.

Perdita made light of her fears, and told her mother such a good, honest fellow as Malcolm must be treated with forbearance; and she added, "I can wait till he trims himself into the right shape. I know Malcolm will be a gentleman."

Whatever could have made the young wife blush so, as she

spoke ? and how happened it that her thoughts travelled unbidden to the breakfast-table, when she had that morning sat opposite to a fair-haired man and handed him his coffee.

Now, Cicely Vance was always winding her arms around people and embracing them "so affecshunut;" especially such as happened to own something she wished to possess. Cicely's manners towards boys were not pleasant, she frisked and giggled so much, and was so vivacious apropos to nothing; and when she learned by experimenting, that Malcolm did not like kisses, she was always saying "Come, let's go and kiss Mat;" and she got some rude pushes and several hard slaps in her attempts to carry out her proposal. When she snivelled over them, Perdita told her "if she played with boys, she must take boys' play." Still undaunted she made a confidence to Dolly.

"I mean to have Malcolm for my sweetheart; he shall write me notes and give me things, as Mr. Leighton did Miss Easygo in our convent."

"Your sweetheart," laughed Dolly. "Well! he will be a queer one; he don't think much of girls."

Teddy, during the reel, had been pouring over a book he had taken from the shelf, and after it was over he felt moved to read aloud, not choosing any special auditor, but merely that he might treat his own ears to a passage which had forcibly struck him.

"There is not a single domestic animal which in some country has not drooping ears; the drooping is owing to the disuse of the muscles of the ears, the animals not being much alarmed."

All voices were hushed as soon as Teddy began. His contributions were eagerly welcomed, and the children grouped around him to listen. Cicely seemed to find the occasion she longed for; and she took hold of Malcolm's auricles, which were, to say truth, somewhat bent forward from the constant pressure of his cap, and of a size to denote generosity.

"I say, Mat, what an easy life your grandpas must have led to give you such flappets as these."

Mr. Slaughton looked at Perdita, who also looked at him. This interchange of glances seemed quite involuntary, and they both smiled with the same thought, which the young wife uttered aloud :

"Oh, yes, indeed ; she has weapons offensive and defensive."

When the fête was over, the parsonage folks gone, and the Vances on their way upstairs, Mr. Slaughton said eagerly to Perdita, who was the last of the group, and laden with all the odds and ends the others had left :

"I beg you will do me a favor."

"A favor ! that sounds odd. Perhaps I shall not dare undertake anything so much out of my line ; *duties* are what I am accustomed to hear about and do. I shall be glad to have you name the favor, though."

She speered at him over her shoulder. She could scarcely be expected to turn and face him with all those books and things on her arm. She looked alert and suspicious, entirely on her guard.

"Will you let me carry that trash up-stairs for you ? "

"Certainly not. Whatever you desire to have well done, do yourself ; and I do not want the trash, as you call it, scattered all over the floor. If that is the favor——"

"But it isn't. My natural politeness dictated the offer of help. I dare say I *should* have spilled some of the bundles."

"I think it more than probable, so unaccustomed to such chivalric service."

"I can be useful, as I will prove, if you will not disdain my assistance. It will give me pleasure, too."

"You remind me of Cicely, your niece. 'Auntie,' said she, "may I carry your thimble, or your scissors ; I do want to help you *so* much ? "

As she unconsciously reproduced in perfection the child's voice and "so affecshunut" manner, Mr. Slaughton writhed in disgust.

" I will never offer you my aid again," said he pettishly.

" And how about the favor ? Please don't be long, or my arms will be tired and I shall drop these books."

" I want you to sit no more evenings in the school-room, but come down to this bower, which you have shaded."

" But the school-room is the proper place for the governess —among her charges ; my labor is not ended till the children are in bed."

" Get them off at seven, then, for I will have you here."

" You *will /* I understood it was a *favor* you asked."

" I have thought better of it. I demand my right."

" Am I to conclude that you issue an order for my appearance ? "

" Yes ; I *order* you to come ! "

" Oh, very well, sir. I am trained dutifully to obey orders What time does your honor appoint for my attendance ? "

" Sharp seven—that is, directly after tea, you shall come armed and equipped with work-basket, knitting, crocheting, or whatever woman's occupation you give your evenings to."

" I mostly read of evenings."

" Very well ; we will have books. Your frolic was a marked success. I congratulate you. By the way, you must bid me good-morning as well as good-night. I am going to Toptown on the early train."

" At six o'clock ? "

" Yes. Pray don't disturb the house for me. I shall get a cup of coffee at the depot."

" Indeed, sir, that is not my rendering of my housekeeper's part. I could not feel satisfied with myself the whole day, if I, out of laziness, permitted the house-master to depart fasting on a journey. Will it please you to be down by half-past five ? "

Mr. Slaughton whistled a good deal in a very soft, absent way, while he was undressing ; but his old couplet found no place among the airs he was rendering, and the eyes he was thinking of certainly were not Sabrina's.

CHAPTER XXXV.

PERDITA READS LONGFELLOW.

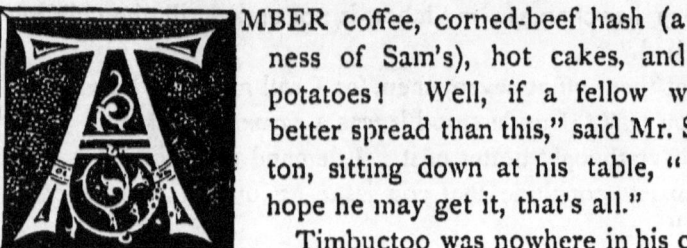

MBER coffee, corned-beef hash (a weakness of Sam's), hot cakes, and wafer potatoes! Well, if a fellow wants a better spread than this," said Mr. Slaughton, sitting down at his table, " I only hope he may get it, that's all."

Timbuctoo was nowhere in his calculations while he discussed the meal with healthy appetite; the tigers in their native jungles were not in the least prospective danger. His thoughts seemed running a good deal on music, and he asked little Betty, who sat close to her sister, watching him out of her elfin eyes, if she would not like to have a harp, and a guitar, and a lute, and a dulcimer, when she grew up; and if she would sing hymns and psalms and spiritual songs, and chant among the pious maïdens; and he quoted Longfellow:

> " He goes on Sunday to the church,
>   And sits among his boys;
>   He hears the parson pray and preach;
>   He hears his daughter's voice
>   Singing in the village choir,
>   And it makes his heart rejoice."

He did not say much to Perdita, although he glanced often at her with a pleased, satisfied face; and when he took leave of her, bidding her good-morning at the door, he held her hand one instant longer than was necessary, and he looked at her ripe lips, before he picked up Bettine for a good-by kiss.

Perdita was getting used to these greetings and adieux, these

morning salutations and evening "pleasant dreams," which
had seemed such strange fashions and unnecessary compliments
at first.   Chandy had been so profuse of them, and so graceful
and kind ; he had given her so many bows and pretty speeches,
and Mr. Slaughton never omitted polite forms, even when most
indifferent and chilly.   Perdita liked it ; she wished she had
been brought up where such observances were the commonplaces of life.   The morning and evening kisses which the son
gave his old mother looked seemly.   As she witnessed them
sometimes, she wondered how Teddy or Malcolm would look
kissing their mother ; how she should feel kissing her father.
It had not once occurred to her that Mr. Slaughton could
dream of touching even her cheek, easy and natural as the
caress seemed to come from him to the dame, or Bettine, or
Pandora ; that was an outside impossibility—not cognizable—
to her, at least.

The atmosphere of friendliness the traveller left behind him
seemed to envelop the slender young housekeeper after he
was gone, and she found herself repeating the stanza he had
recited ; and she went and got down the book and read the
whole story, and then she went on to " The Wreck of the
Hesperus," and "The Luck of Edenhall," and she had a
thoroughly good time with the poems till she came to " Annie
of Tharaw.

> " Annie of Tharaw, my true love of old,
> She is my life, and my goods and my gold.
> Annie of Tharaw, my light and my sun,
> The threads of our two lives are woven in one."

She turned to the fly-leaf and found on it " Samuel Slaughton."   She shut the volume and laid it back among its com-
peers.   There were pencil-marks drawn around the lines, and
so often had the verses been read that the leaves parted there
of themselves, and Annie of Tharaw must be a living woman to
the person who loved to con her praises ; therefore, Annie of

Tharaw should read Sabrina Bradshaw. She turned from the room with a pettishness quite unusual to her. It seemed hard to be every hour reminded of that "only one;" to find in every step of her new path traces of the idolatry which had been—nay, was still hers.

Perdita sat among the children that day with a very still face. Two or three times she caught herself speaking impatiently. Cicely Vance fretted and disgusted her, Pandora exhausted her endurance, and Bertram's *numerousness* provoked her almost beyond bearing. She was glad when the lessons were over and she could get out in the fresh air, and taking Betty with her, she tried to race and jump and skip into good temper. The dog Sam gazed at her with his wistful look while she sat on a great rock deeply thinking. Even he was able to find a lack in her face; and when she put her hand on his head and smiled, he leaped up with a joyful bark and whine which besought her to be merry.

It was dark night when Mr. Slaughton returned, and she heard the noise and fracas of men and horses in the yard and pretty soon six stout fellows came slowly up the steps with a parlor grand Steinway among them, under whose weight they staggered, strong as they were.

They set it up in the drawing-room, and the tuner who accompanied them, bringing his instruments in a box, went to work on the strings, which he tortured and fretted as long as he thought good, and then he sat down and played a grand sonata with great finish and style. A day or two afterwards a master appeared, and the young ones set to work in such real earnest that the poor piano was vexed and tormented into squalls and wailing all hours of the day by one or another of them.

CHAPTER XXXVI.

"COMMEND A WIFE, BUT REMAIN A BACHELOR."

NE morning, not long after the beginning of the musical era in the Slaughton family, the house-master happened to be passing through the hall, when he heard the sound of the piano, and he opened the drawing-room door and looked in to see who was so industriously practising. To his great surprise and delight, it proved to be Perdita. She had given him no opportunity to speak to her on the subject since the evening of the fête in the library, and he felt afraid she did not intend to avail herself of his offer; and as he was conscious of having blundered so dreadfully on that occasion, he hesitated to disturb the fair understanding he had established in the matter of the evenings, which were anything but disagreeable thus far. The work-basket had been brought down, a little talking had been done, and some loud reading. He had recited "Cumnor Hall," and got in return Mrs. Piozzi's "Three Warnings," smiling secretly at the odd selection. There had been a few words said, also, which he could not comprehend. While he was sitting with his hand to his head, thinking what short poem he could recite next, Perdita offered him a suggestion.

"Why not 'Annie of Tharaw,' since you like it so much?"

Her scornful air and aggressive look were patent. Was it that she despised the verses and his taste? It was true he had a liking for the pretty trifle; but how had she found it out?"

He did not render it, nor anything else, that evening, confining himself to a copy of Beattie's "Minstrel" he fetched without invitation from the shelves.

In general, however, he counted the sittings a gain; and there was enough in every one of them to keep him thinking through the days, and to cause him to look forward to his easy-chair in the cosy room, with its hearth-fire and student lamp, and a sight of the dark, slender young creature who came in such a proud, shy way, and sat quietly down in the place he offered her with scrupulous politeness. Sometimes she sewed on and on without looking up at him; and as the light streamed over her bent head, over her small hands, and glistened sharply on the bright needle she plied so swiftly, he had opportunities in plenty to study her face and figure in repose or at least, in stillness. He knew the length of her eyelashes and their shadowy curling, and the arch of her brows, and all the lines of cheek and lips and chin; and that when she did look up at him she would give him glances of wondrous radiance; and that if she *should* smile, her sweet, rosy mouth would be arch and winsome, and "her large black eyes, so blackly fringed," have witchery in them sudden and delightful.

Mr. Slaughton all this while was standing by the door of his drawing-room, and before he had been there a second he discovered that the student was weeping bitterly; while her fingers were busy among the keys, tears coursed in torrents down her cheeks, dropping unheeded, while she counted in a broken voice interrupted with sobs, "One, two, three; one, two, three."

"I never can do it; never!" she exclaimed, dropping her hands helplessly into her lap. It is useless. I am too old, too dull. I have no talent, no taste. I'm a poor nobody!"

Now, why couldn't the gentleman have gone quietly away, and left her to battle it out with herself? If he had, she would have presently wiped her eyes, and possibly her nose, and set at work again as resolute as ever. A woman would have had tact enough to know that words, either of pity or railery, were not in place. This man felt moved to teaze and essay a jest. Curious creatures these men are, to be sure!

12

" Excuse me," said Mr. Slaughton advancing, "but I never saw a piano go by water before ; is it an improvement ? "

The girl sprang up blazing with anger. " How dare you spy on my actions ? Let me pass."

" Spy ! me a spy ! Take back that unwholesome word, I pray you," he replied, striving to smile, but managing only the points of his lips, while his face turned white as death. " I happened to look in. I wish now that I had looked out."

" You hunt out my defects ; you ask questions to bring them into notice. Can I dance ? can I play? when you know I cannot do either. You just do it on purpose, so that you can curl your scornful lips and look contemptuous. You are glad to find me lacking where others excel. I have seen it a thousand times ; I have felt it as keenly as you could desire. Not that it is of the least consequence what you think of me outside of my engagement."

Mr. Slaughton listened to this violent and contradictory statement in amazed silence, and he did not make an effort to stay her ; did not so much as lift a hand, when she burst into a fresh passion of tears, and dashed past him, flying up the stairs, and banging the door with resounding clamor, as she hid herself in her own room.

He stroked his long beard a good while in a very brown study, after he mounted to his studio—a knight of most rueful countenance. He failed to find himself guilty of the accusations his wife had hurled at him ; and severe and provoking as they were, and violent and unjust as she had been, he dwelt more on the vivid beauty of her passion than its wickedness ; on the grace and abandon of her hasty flight rather than her furious scorn in going ; and he palliated her conduct with many excuses.

" Such an impulsive creature !   So proud ! so hardly tried ! What wonder that she lost patience ? and how clumsy of me to intrude my folly so inopportunely ! " and then he went on thinking of her again, wishing vain wishes ; he felt them vainer than ever and more hopeless.

When they met at dinner, he made haste to place her chair, and he studied eagerly her face, although he did not speak to her. Not but he would gladly have said something pleasant, only he did not know how. He seemed dimly to guess that the key to the whole might be deep and bitter mortification that he should have surprised her trying secretly and trying vainly to acquire an accomplishment in which others excelled.

She was composed and quiet. She answered the dame's remarks respectfully, she conversed a little with the children, and she poured the usual fondness into Betty's eyes; but she seemed either unconscious of or indifferent to his neighborhood.

CHAPTER XXXVII.

"AFTER THE HARVEST, GOLDEN SHEAVES."

IGHT had drawn her sable curtains round, and the house-master was still in his library.

Outwardly, he appeared quite easy and comfortable, with his cigar in his fingers, and his head reposing on the soft cushions of his easy-chair—in fact, he had arranged himself into a picture of luxious *dolce far niente;* but the seeming was not real, for inwardly he was experiencing sundry misgivings and much trepidation of spirit.

He had chosen a position fronting the door, and was waiting to ascertain whether or no Perdita would present herself according to her new habit. He had not to wait long, for at the accustomed time she came and stood on the threshold.

"Shall I come in, sir? Or do you choose to be alone?"

Her long, slender neck bent in a graceful curve as she looked down at her hands, holding her work-basket, and a brilliant crimson went creeping and creeping up in her face till it was all aglow; lips, cheeks, and forehead—even her pretty ears, were dyed celestial rosy red."

"Come in, I beg of you! wherefore not?" cried he, springing to his feet with a hasty earnestness, and bow of welcome.

"I did not know. I have been hesitating, but as I recieved no counter order, I took it for granted that the one already issued still held its force, and so I am here. I have behaved very badly; I cannot even yet understand how I could so far forget my housekeeper's station as to fly in the face of my employer with such abominable violence. I could bite my tongue out for presuming to utter such rude nonsense in your hearing. I beg you to forget it; I shall endeavor to keep proper bounds in future."

As he remained silent, not liking—I might almost say not *daring* to speak some words which rose to his lips, and trying to choose such as might suit her mood, she added:

"I dare say I have overrated the importance of my folly to you. Very likely you have already let it pass from your mind as of no consequence, but even in that case, I consider it due to myself to speak my apology in your hearing."

"Pray be seated, I ought to have known better than to make absurd jokes, interrupting your work and disturbing you; I'm very sorry, I'm sure."

She accepted the chair he was holding for her near the table; and she watched his fingers which eagerly adjusted the lamp to her convenience.

"Sorry! not at all. You have a right to say what you please, of course."

"Rights are difficult to adjust between you and me," said

he in a hurried voice; " and apologies are breath wasted, since
it is not possible that they can commence at a proper beginning.
Pray let them cease where they may end—that is, just here.
What book shall we have to-night ? "

She looked with a glance of clear, thoughtful inquiry in his
face while he was speaking. When he ceased, she dropped
her eyes upon her work.

" I shall listen with attention to whatever it pleases you to
select," she replied, and began putting rapid stitches into a
bunch of flossy roses and buds which grew in graceful stems
beneath her skillful fingers.

Mr. Slaughton felt exceedingly awkward and embarrassed.
He hunted for smooth topics of easy-flowing talk, and found
none. On previous occasions they had offered in plenty ; and
though never garrulous or playful, as he often saw her among
the children, Perdita had conversed pleasantly. But this
evening she was so reserved, so proud in her sensitive humility,
and dropped so quickly with monosyllables such themes as he
started, that they fell flat and insipid.

Finally, in sheer desperation, he launched into his projected
Thanksgiving festivities, to which she listened with curious attention. Her first impulse was to refuse utterly to show herself
to her father at the head of the table, where it had pleased
him to place her without asking if it would please her, not
caring at all whether she wept or smiled, was happy or
wretched.

The Parson had never taken a meal in the mansion house,
or invited either his daughter or the Slaughtons to partake of
any hospitalities. Of that she thought no wonder, knowing
well the pride and poverty which jostled and disputed in the
old home, and she secretly smiled as she remembered the fish-
cakes and johnny-cakes and pop-robins and poor-man's puddings, and tried to fancy Mr. Slaughton tasting the dainties
she had fed on in those days so distant now.

Her second resolve was to fall in with the suggestion offered her, which might open a road for the furtherance of her desires concerning her brothers. The friends and influence of her husband were a part of the price she had in mind when she let herself be disposed of; and would it not be sheer folly to throw any obstacles in the path of a better acquaintance between him and her father?

A certain elation, also, crept in among her other reflections, that she had it in her power to show her severe parent what good times were to be had outside his rule and authority, and to make him see and understand that she, Perdita, could and would devise and carry them out and mingle in them—she, who had never been allowed any amusements, would have sports and games after the Thanksgiving dinner. A vision of a *reel* presented itself, and she enjoyed prospectively the horror and amazement such a vain and sinful proceeding would call out all over the Parson, as rise the quills upon the fretful porcupine.

While Mr. Slaughton talked she went farther, and planned a new cap for her mother, on which she meant to plait a nice frill and tie some knots of ribbon. Only a bit of a cap—a mere head-dress, in fact, quiet and simple—because it would be a shame to cover or hide the gray hair, fine as silk, which had been matched to a raven's wing when she was pretty Violet Wemple, and had a young minister for a lover. And she hoped that Dame Slaughton would be agreeable, and that her mother would hold her own with her, and not let herself be quenched and sat upon. And there was Dolly. Dolly had a new gown; the chicken-money and rag-money had bought it. Dolly would look fresh and pretty; but Dolly was quite apt to tip over tumblers and spill things at table. Oh, dear! what if she should spoil the Thanksgiving cloth with one of her *gaucheries?* Billy had an awful appetite; he didn't seem to know when he had eaten enough of turkey or mince-pie. What if Mr. Slaughton should think him a pig or a glutton? She remembered fortunately that the house-master was a healthy eater himself; he had been a boy; he might make allowances.

She had time to pass her whole family in review, looking at them through Slaughton eyes, before her husband asked her to come out and inspect the stores he had brought from Toptown and hidden in the barn.

She volunteered to carry the invitations, because, now that she had really entertained the notion of the feast, the prospect of having her mother to dine off sumptuous fare, with plenty and to spare—a meal which had cost her no labor, and which she would not have to count the expense of, nor clear away afterwards, began to be pleasing.

The excellent Parson might turn stubborn and sour at sight of the good clothes and general prosperous handsomeness of her husband, and "bow-wow" a surly refusal to his pleasant words ; therefore Perdita arranged to go herself, and she gave considerable thought to her errand and its probable results, as she walked briskly down the hill to the old homestead.

CHAPTER XXXVIII.

"BETTY IS A LADY, AND WEARS A GOLD RING."

PPORTUNITY served her to lay open her business to her mother and the others before the lord and law-giver came down stairs, and she felt quite pitiful to notice how eagerly the poor woman snatched at the promised pleasure, and how anxiously she watched her husband's face while his daughter talked to him, trying to divine his mood. Would he bark and bite, or only softly growl ? And when he began to work his horny hands, and scowl, and

make his habitual grimaces, and, opening his mouth with the impulse which always impelled him to say " No," to any project or proposal, began to *bark*, "I don't think it will be conducive," the poor old wife's face fell drearily, and she wiped her watery eyes on the corner of her apron.

Dolly burst into tears ; the invitation had elated her so much, and the sudden dash of disappointment was so very overwhelming, she could not help it.

" What is that girl crying for?" demanded the father in his biggest voice.

"She's afraid she can't go," answered Mrs. Hethwaite, supplicatingly. "Poor child ! she has so little pleasure."

" Pleasure ! who does have pleasure? I bade adieu to all that years ago ! If she is so carnal-minded as to be all agog over a turkey, and so silly as to blubber, she had better stay at home ; and she will if I see any more of her tantrums. Shut up directly, or I'll give you something to cry for ! "

Dolly choked in her sobs, and instantly looked rigid and stony. The parsonage young folks had been early taught to keep tears out of sight, it being a part of the paternal discipline to forbid their gush, and to whip them till they stopped crying, when enduring the chastising earned by their youthful slips.

I sometimes wonder if parents ever realize what refined cruelty they practice when they hurt their children, and forbid them the natural expression of suffering ! Even a dog has a right to howl when he is beaten. I don't believe any of us will ever forget the great lump of agony in the poor throat when the sobs and cries, which would have been such a relief, were forcibly stifled.

" Don't put yourself out any to come, father," said Perdita, "It is not my idea, you know. *I* should never have thought of asking you if Mr. Slaughton had not desired me ; in fact, I quite dread going through such a dinner. I shall have to work very hard ; and as I never had any chance to learn how to be festive or convivial, I dare say I shall make a wretched mess of it."

"I see no good reason why you should not be fully equal to your place, Mrs. Slaughton. I live in an old house and I wear poor garments—such is the will of the Lord; but I have brought up my children properly. You will do well to remember, in the station to which it has pleased God to call you, that your father is a gentleman."

"Yes, sir ; and that my mother is a lady, which seems to me of vastly more consequence. My Aunt Prudence has often told me that Violet Wemple was very pretty and much admired. It must be so, or you would not have selected her."

Perdita laid her hand softly on her mother, and as the worn and weary woman felt the electric thrill of the light touch, she straightened her bent shoulders, and her faded eyes seemed to gather blackness as she lifted them to her daughter's face, and her hollow cheeks were dyed with crimson, so that the likeness between the fresh young beauty and the old wife was almost painfully clear and strong.

The Parson felt it, as well as the antagonism to him which his daughter took no pains to hide, with a sort of wonder. It was only one instant; before he had time to wither his wife with a glance he was accustomed to use for that purpose, she had stooped again to her habitual patient endurance, and he scarcely heard her murmur : "So vain and sinful; so vain and sinful."

"Your Aunt Prudence might better have been saying her prayers ; but, being a woman, she must act out what was in her, I suppose. It is vain to expect 'grapes of thorns, or figs of thistles.' You may present my thanks to Mr. Slaughton ; I intend to be present at the dinner. Your mother will probably accompany me ; as to the others, their going or staying will depend entirely upon their behavior during the intermediate time."

As he scowled ominously on Dolly, she immediately made haste to fetch the broom and dig out the corners of the room

12*

with immense alacrity and dispatch, baring her plump arms to the shoulder and stirring up the furniture and dust as if her highest happiness was "*housework.*"

Mrs. Hethwaite followed her daughter to the door, and thanked her as cringingly as if she had been a deacon's wife bringing them a donation.

When her husband had clumped up-stairs, which he did after his very pleasant acceptance of the invitation, she whispered : "You shouldn't have talked so, Perdita ; as like as not he will go himself and make us stay at home."

"He will not dare to show himself without you !"

"Dare ! he'd lock us all up on bread and water if he took it into his head ; he dare do what he likes to us."

"He'll come, mother, and he'll fetch you, never fear. I wish I could bring my share of the grand dinner down here and eat it with you—only us two and Betty. Look at Dolly !"

Mrs. Hethwaite turned where Perdita pointed. The broom was lying idle against the chair, and the girl was twisting her hair before the little old mirror.

"Yes. I reckoned her industrious fit wouldn't last long after *he* was out of sight. She won't ever be so good a worker as you was, Perdita."

"She'll steady by-and-by, mother. I should have been happier if I had followed my likings as much as she does. I shall come down to-morrow and make you a pretty cap, and show you the neatest way to wear it. And mother, how many eggs do you put in your gingerbread ? I mean to whip up a card, and put it right before father on the table. He always told us it was the only sweet-cake fit to eat. He shall see how I treasure his precepts."

"I am glad you can laugh, Perdita. I'm glad you can afford to. I can't. But you had best be careful, or he'll get mad, and as likely as not he'll forbid you his house."

· "No danger of that. I am a rich man's wife ! I am an heir in possession, you know."

CHAPTER XXXIX.

MISS MEDDLESOME AND HER GRANDMOTHER.

HEN Dame Slaughton was consulted about the dinner, she said she'd have over the Brandigees, who must stop all night; and she gave minute and particular directions as to the old couple's room, and took Hannah up-stairs to sweep the two designed for Mrs. Richard Pritchard and her children, and thereby brought out some growling from that faithful servant, who said she "didn't want to be bossed by t' auld woman."

After some pondering, Mr. Slaughton went to Perdita, and proposed that she should give the little people a table to themselves in the small supper-room, with an independent turkey and chicken-pie, and that Malcolm should carve, and Cicely preside. She looked at him in astonishment. It was such a novel suggestion! so very strange and startling that it hardly seemed proper.

"I never heard of such a thing!" said she breathlessly.

"What can we do with the children, then? Our table will never hold us all."

"Make them wait, I suppose; that is the only way I know, to dispose of small vessels of wrath, when there isn't room among the large ones."

"That would be cruel," laughed Mr. Slaughton. "I am afraid they wouldn't give many thanks during the ordeal. No. Let us put them by themselves; it will be so droll to see them manage."

"It will be a pretty sight. I wonder what father will think when he sees it, and hears their noise."

The new dining-hall was all complete, and a very handsome and commodious place it was. Perdita especially admired its wainscoting of oak and tulip-wood, and the panels of fish and game, and the "three landscapes with cattle," which Mr. Slaughton brought out from some packing-cases where they had lain *perdu* for years, and she was much amused to see the dame gloat over her solid silver, while she was setting it up in state on the massive sideboard.

"I've always kept it locked away," said she. "I hadn't any good place to show it off, and it does kinder worry me when it's around ; some pesky thief might get in and steal it. I declare ! how harnsum it does look ! I don't suppose you ever saw any real silver before, did you, Perdita ?"

"Excepting my grandmother's porringer and my grand-father's shoe-buckles, I am afraid I never did, ma'am."

"Well, this is all solid, and it'll all go to Samuel and his heirs. I should think it would make you feel sort o' grand to think you have married into a family that has so many nice things."

"Auntie's folks are pretty poor, I expect. I feel sorry for poor folks that don't have any beautiful silver tea-pots, and sugar-bowls and milk-cups, like us ; don't you, grandma ? You are real rich, ain't you ? May I have some seed-cake ?" said Cicely Vance, who was everywhere, meddling with everything, listening, and making comments on all she heard.

"Is not Miss Vance neglecting some lessons, in order that she may confer on us her very charming presence ?" inquired Mr. Slaughton with a wry face.

"No, she is not, Samuel," spoke up the dame tartly ; "she wants to see us fix ; don't *you* go finding fault with her, I beg ! She has a hard time enough without that. Here, Cicely ! here's a handful of raisins for you, you poor motherless child."

It was not long before the dame discovered the motherless

child amusing her leisure with rubbing her fingers all over the solid silver ; and lapping it with her tongue, insomuch that its fine burnish was streaked and blurred ; then her petting was changed to fretting, and she gave the motherless child a smart cuff and a push.

"Go along with you, Miss Meddlesome, and leave things alone."

Cicely stuck out her lips, and jerked her shoulders into a corner close by the table, and the raisins, which she pilfered by fistfuls, and munched slyly.

The old lady came around after a while and stood opposite to her, folding carefully the tissue-paper in which her treasures had been wrapped, and placing them in a drawer for future use, and she noticed some strange motions of her granddaughter's mouth, caused by the haste she was making to dispose of its contents and look unconcerned, not to say hungry.

"Cicely ! don't gnaw your lips that way ; it makes you perfectly *hegious*," she called out in a scolding voice.

"I don't think young girls can look hegious ; I never saw one that was. I saw an old woman once that was perfectly hegious ! "

Her blue eyes resting on her grandmother, unwittingly pointed her meaning to one of the present company, who glowered threateningly.

"You did, did you ? Well, you'll see a girl that'll stop upstairs Thanksgiving day, if she don't look out."

"Oh, I didn't mean you, grandmother ; I meant Sister Josephine ; she was a sight to behold."

"You are crafty to locate your example of ugliness as far off as your convent," remarked Mr. Slaughton, eyeing his niece with great disfavor.

The dame did a great deal of fussing and fretting during the preparations, and frequently mislaid her temper and rated the children ; but she did not much disturb her busy daughter-in-law, who entered into the mysteries with such zest and abandonment, and had so much to discuss with the house-master, that she almost forgot to be distant and respectful.

It was such a wonderful thing to assist at a feast like those she and Teddy used to dream of, with plenty on the board, and pleasant faces around it, when he should be Professor in his college, and she kept his house ; and Mr. Slaughton's ideas so far outstripped her conceptions of practicability, that she was filled with surprise and pleasure.

She flitted hither and thither ; she swept and dusted ; she baked cakes and pies, and whipped up eggs and dabbled in sweets and spices, and her face bloomed like a fresh rose, she was so warm over the baking and the jellies, and she made not a single failure ; each was perfection in its kind. Thrice fortunate cook ! would that we all might be as lucky and successful.

CHAPTER XL.

"LET US EAT, DRINK, AND BE MERRY."

> " And Jane Maria and Ann Sophia,
>   And all the children livin' ;
> And Hezekiah, and Jerymiah,
>   Shall come to our Thanksgivin' !"

HE Brandegees arrived first—a nice elderly couple, who prided themselves on their good blood, and had always behaved well enough to warrant their claim.

Mrs. Richard Pritchard, a pretty young widow, commonly called Dickey among her friends, brought her two little girls, who were very lively and spirited, and soon on frolicking terms with the Vances, and needed a good deal of chiding to keep their boisterousness in bearable bounds.

The Parson appeared in a suit of rusty black and a wide white neckcloth, well-polished high-lows, and with manners stiff and ungracious, ready to dispute in his bow-wow way with anybody, and fore-inclined to be displeased with everything in this rich man's house.

His faded old wife was in a faded old dress, *so* rusty and worn that even the neat muslin cap failed to smarten her much.

She sat down, a gathered little heap, on the edge of her chair, with her feet as close together as she could possibly put them, and her hands in her lap under her handkerchief, an un-conscious effort to hide their clumsiness (Violet Wemple's hands had been very soft and fine and pretty). She was an apology from her head to her toes, agreeing with all that was said, and constantly nodding and repeating her "Yes indeed; quite right," and "Dear me! you don't say so!" till her daugh-ter felt nervous, and wished she would contradict somebody, if only to show she was able to hold an opinion.

"Red-cheeked Dolly was fresh in the new suit which the chicken-money had purchased, and the boys looked like gentle-men, although their clothes were homespun and home-made. So thought Perdita, viewing them from the Brandegees' genteel standpoint.

A little ludicrous circumstance, which developed immediately after the Parson's arrival, stirred him to captiousness, and knotted deeper the discontented wrinkles in his face.

Clothes-presses were small, and the hooks in them scarce, at the parsonage; and as the cold weather drew the family into narrower limits, or winter quarters, avoiding as much as possi-ble the deadly chill of the never-heated rooms, all wearing apparel was huddled into the least space and most accessible proximities. That was the reason why Mrs. Hethwaite, on re-turning from church, had pinned her best bonnet upon the tail of her husband's Sunday coat.

The Parson's feeling concerning that sable garment was like the woodman's for his lost axe, when he cried, "Ah me ! where shall I get another ? " and he always took it off, and hung it up the minute he entered his house.

When Thanksgiving day dawned, he gave out at the breakfast-table that he would have no dilatoriness, and if his family were not ready at a certain time which it pleased him to fix, he should proceed without them.

Of course it was the easiest thing in the world for him to be punctual, as Malcolm brushed his shoes, and he had nobody to look out for but his own high-mightiness, while the others had chores, and dishes, and other hindrances to bother them, not to mention the extra care needed to make themselves fit for the great festival. Mrs. Hethwaite especially was anxious and nervous, and when the clock struck she had got only as far as her stockings.

"Very well," said the Parson, " I tarry for no laggards ! and if you don't catch up with me before I get there, you will hear of it when I reach home this evening ! "

If he had been pleasant and agreeable, somebody might have seen the unusual and unnecessary appendage swinging in his rear as he clumped off, and his wife might have been saved the dreadful flurry which caused her to forget where she had bestowed her velvet scoop.

As the young people became clamorous, and besought her to get started, she finally was obliged to don her old hood, and they were all blown and panting when they neared the mansion house, whose door had already shut behind their autocrat, who was shaking hands pompously with the company and keeping a look-out for the delinquents, nearly deciding that they should hear from him then and there.

Suddenly a gush and torrent of mirth sounded behind him. The children gathered there had held their hands over their mouths, till it was of no use—the laugh had to burst out. And when he wheeled about to confront them with a frown, the elders discovered his decoration, and heartily joined the glee, which was contagious beyond resistance, the Parson getting redder and redder, till Dickey Pritchard unpinned the trophy and displayed it before his astonished eyes. And as he gazed at it he muttered some strange sounding words, which might have been familiar to him in his reckless youth.

It took a good deal of blandishment on Mrs. Dickey's part to induce him to converse with her; but she persevered, and she prevailed, insomuch that his family slid and sidled into the room almost unnoticed by him, he being in the very conflux of a description of a Choctaw war-dance, with gestures and explanations; and it was not till he happened to fix his wife with a look supposed to be hurled at a fighting Indian, that he remembered to scowl wrathfully at her.

The Hethwaites had not been an hour in the house before Mr. Slaughton discovered that Perdita had cause for annoyance and alarm on the subject which lay nearest her heart.

Bettine came down in the new merino, with its flossy roses and pinks, a nice sash, dainty little slippers, and her soft hair in light curls; and as he reached out his arms for her, he said, smiling to her sister :

"See how like she is to Aslauga the fair daughter of Sigurd, when she appeared to her knight in the flowing veil of her golden locks, as if a golden rosy-tinted summer's cloud was passing over the deep blue sky. Say! beauteous Aslauga, wilt thou give me a kiss in thy loveliness and brightness?"

And the child smiled a glad and happy smile as she threw her white arms around his neck, hugging him close, while she pressed his cheek with hers, so smooth and round.

This is what the Parson saw and heard, as his youngest born came thus, and was thus welcomed. He looked so hard and glum that he seemed about to snort with contempt, and he presently took an opportunity to hold forth upon "stupid nonsense," foolish vanities, and vain woman, gew-gaws, tinsel and fripperies, and he covered all Bettine's motions with such

savage disapproval that Perdita suspected he might be capable
of tearing the new dress off her pet with his own hands, and
"committing it to the flames," that having been his favorite
disposition of many trifles she had dared to treasure and value
when under his paternal rule and direction.

Not so the child's mother. She could not take her eyes off
her lovely baby, and she seized on her and wept over her some
secret tears, for pure, fond yearning and tender admiration,
mingled with wonder that such a fine, graceful, delicate thing
should have been cradled in her poor arms, and drawn its rich
life from hers, so thin and worthless.

She still gazed after her, when the mite had slipped away
into a corner, full of content, where she nursed a waxen doll,
handsomely dressed—the first one a Hethwaite had ever owned.
It had come in a box from Toptown that very morning, with
four others, Mr. Slaughton's gifts to the little folks ; and as he
did nothing by halves, of course Mrs. Dickey's young ones
were sharers of his bounty.

Mrs. Hethwaite was afraid of her husband ; but try as hard
as she might, she could not keep her joy and pride in Bettine
out of her face. Perhaps the sight of it, as well as the bliss in
the corner, made him angry ; he seemed watching an opportunity to pounce on and put an end to it.

Not that he put it that way to himself; in *his* mind he read,
" I will make them feel my wholesome authority."

" Bring that thing to me, Bettine ! " said he in a loud voice,
reaching out his huge hand, and gripping and ungripping his
horny fingers.

She started up in affright, and crept timidly and most unwillingly towards him. All conversation was instantly suspended
in the room ; and if he had thought worth his while to glance
among the people, he might have found some very decided
opinions of him and his conduct mirrored in the different faces.

" The best thing to do with this absurd caricature of a silly
female, is to put it on the fire." As he spoke, he seized the

doll which Betty was clasping close to her beating heart. As
he pulled it from her, she screamed and reached after it in piteous sorrow.

Perhaps the good divine had not meant to destroy the
plaything ; perhaps he intended only to terrify and chasten his
tender offspring. But he happened to throw a look at Mr.
Slaughton, which also hit old Mrs. Brandegee in passing, and he
got in return such very pointed opinions, that he felt nettled by
them ; and his pendulous lip went down at the corners, and he
hurled the doll among the glowing coals with an unregenerate
gesture.

" Next time, learn not to raise your arms in rebellion against
me, your father ! " said he, taking hold of Betty with his powerful grip, and hauling her between his knees, where he shook
her violently.

The poor little creature cast a hopeless and beseeching
glance at her sister, who sat silent, with gaze fixed on the carpet. The deep frown between her eyes and her mounting
color showed how she was inwardly chafing and fretting over
her powerlessness to shield the treasure who was in danger of
being ordered back to the dreary home from which she had
snatched her at such cost, and she used all her power over
her emotions to hold herself steady and quiet enough not to
spring on the man whom she was inwardly calling a tyrant and
a monster, and pour out all the pent-up injuries of years in such
a torrent of reproaches and truths as must have made them
strangers forever.

Suddenly the sobs and cries ceased, and the child fell back
pale and motionless.

" Oh dear ! oh dear ! She's lost her breath ; she often
does when she's hurt or frightened," whispered Mrs. Hethwaite, fidgeting and hovering around the limp body she dared
not touch without permission.

Mr. Slaughton rose and took it in his arms. He spoke not
a word. What was there to be said ? It could never have

been shame which made the Parson give her up ; his idea of his right in his family was so absolute that such a feeling could not possibly have affected him. As he loosed his hold of her he glowered on the company, and called out in a loud voice :

" Stupid nonsense ! "

Perdita followed her husband silently up the stairs ; her face was colorless, and her eyes glowed like stars. She pushed open the door of her room, and made a sign for him to lay his burden on the bed ; the motion was imperious and looked disdainful, not to say disparaging and contemptuous. But Mr. Slaughton did not appropriate to himself any of the scorn or disapprobation, and stood quietly waiting to find out how he could help her, as she went swiftly and eagerly about the necessary remedies.

When Betty opened her eyes, she seemed doubtful and dis- turbed. There were two faces bending over her ; one of them she had never seen in that place before, and the first words she uttered were these :

" Uncle Sam, this is Perdita's room. You must not come in here."

" You'll do, Betty," replied he with a light laugh, as he turned on his heel ; " make haste now and come down to dinner ; you must not monopolize my housekeeper."

Poor Mrs. Hethwaite dared not follow her children, even with her eyes, and she tried to be conciliating and apologize for the occurrence.

" Betty always was a timorous child, afraid of her shadow," etc.

" Woman ! hold your peace ! " roared the Parson. " I believe a good sound whipping would soon cure her of that trick she's got, and all this fuss over her won't help her any."

" That's just my notion, Mr. Hethwaite," chimed in Dame Slaughton, with sharp emphasis. " Perdita spoils that child dreadfully. And as to clothes, I tell her I don't know what is

going to be good enough for her to wear when she is grown up,
if she puts it all on now."

"Is that your opinion, madam? I have been much displeased with what I have observed myself. I shall take early
and stringent measures to counteract——"

"Nonsense, Parson Hethwaite!" cried Mrs. Richard Pritchard, who saw with woman's sharpness the meaning and drift
of the whole proceeding, and already knew something of Perdita's passion for her sister. "Nonsense; she has no more
nor finer clothes than any child needs. Look at my Susie!
That is a gros grain sash; the embroidery on her dress is
hand-work, worth a dollar a yard; her saque came from
Warner's and cost me thirty-five! It is silk velvet wrought
with floss. Now, I happen to know that Betty's things are all
the products of Mrs. Slaughton's industry and taste, and you
must admit that the result is perfection. The child is as lovely
as an angel, and her clothes suit her. Coarse, common things
on her would be an outrage, which any person of good
sense and proper feeling *must* resent. No, my dear sir, you
might as well think to teach a rose how to blossom, as a young
woman to dress a baby. Your fashions, Mrs. Slaughton, are
old-time fashions; your ideas, Mr. Hethwaite, are out of date.
Let the two alone. Ask Father Brandegee; he'll say I am right,
won't he, mother?"

Mrs. Dicky carried it by her audacity. The old man patted
fondly the head she laid on his shoulder, and said:

"Yes, darter, I dare say. I'm too wise to meddle with
such women's affairs."

Then she went over and drew a chair close to the divine,
and begged him to tell her something about a new science she
had just heard of called "Ouranography;" and she listened
with her knowing *widow*-eyes on his face, drinking in his talk,
so that he dropped Betty and her minor interests in the delight
of a handsome auditor, who listened so willingly that the
cockles of his old heart were quite warmed and stirred with

pleasure. Whenever he remembered Mrs. Dickey afterwards, he thought of her as a most charming and highly cultured woman, though she had not uttered a dozen words during the colloquy, and Betty's return to the circle was not greeted by any of the high looks and hard words he had mentally prepared for her.

Mrs. Hethwaite took the first opportunity to creep up to the shrewd widow and squeeze her hand, and whisper her broken thanks for her good nature.

While Mrs. Dickey returned the poor creature's grasp with a cordial and hearty pressure, she looked at Perdita's erect figure and glowing beauty, and wondered if time, and any husband whatsoever, would ever be able to reduce *her* to such a faded abasement.

Betty's perils were not over, however. The children were all at play at one end of the long drawing-room, while Mrs. Brandigee and her daughter chatted with the other guests around the grate. Susie Pritchard was holding the mite's hand, and talking to her, when Cicely Vance came along with an orange in her fist.

" Look a-here, Betty," said she, " see what a nice orange I've got ! Don't you want it ? "

Betty reached out and took the fruit with a good deal of childish wonder in her eyes at the unwonted kindness, and was busy imbibing its grateful juice, when Dame Slaughton entered from the pantry, where she had been muddling the house-keeper's orders with suggestions of her own.

" Where did you get that orange ? " asked she crossly.

"Cicely gave it to me," answered Betty, who began to tremble.

" I didn't, grandma ! I only showed it to her, and asked her if she ever saw such a little one ; and I was going to put it straight back into the dish, and she snatched it right out of my hand, she did ! so there, now ! "

" Well ! here's a pretty caper ! that child steals and lies

both!" exclaimed the dame triumphantly pursing her mouth
and nodding to her friends. "I'll teach her better than
to meddle, at any rate. There! take that! now see if you
can learn to leave things alone!"

Perdita came in just in time to witness the blow, which stung
her as if she had received it on her own cheek.

Little Betty did not shed a tear; but she looked fearfully
over at her father, who was conversing with his host—such an
old, apprehensive glance, and she glided swiftly up to her
sister.

"Don't say anything, Perdita," she murmured; "she did not
hurt me much. See! my face is not sore a bit. Oh, dear! is
father looking at me? will he whip me? will he take me
home? I *did* not tell a lie; Cicely *did* give it to me."

The instant Cicely uttered her characteristic statement, Susie
Pritchard flew to her mother, and pointing at her, exclaimed,
"Oh, mamma!" in a frightened voice, as if she expected to see
some dreadful punishment overtake such an audacious sinner.

Mrs. Dickey, being one of those mothers whose ears are apt
to be alert when their children are about them, had seen and
heard the whole; and she was so filled with amazement and
admiration of Betty's self-control that she rose and joined Perdita.

"You are a dear, good, brave little darling," said she stooping and kissing the mite. "I don't wonder your sister adores
you—who could help it? Don't mind, Mrs. Slaughton," she
added; "of course it isn't proper for me to meddle; but I
can't help seeing that your road is a little difficult in places. I
know just how it is; I have things to bear myself sometimes,
and I feel it hard to have others thus punish and control *my*
children. I have to bite in to keep my temper, I assure you.
As for that Cicely, she's just like her father! she's a viper!"

Whether Mr. Slaughton heard and saw the fracas did not
appear. If he did, he adopted the part of discretion and kept
his distance. He was more than commonly tender to his small

favorite, and Perdita almost felt as if he was exerting himself to help her over the hard parts. His genial watchfulness might have been only a portion of his host's duty which embellishes and adorns his own house, and spreads general ease and content around his own hospitalities.

The young wife took her place at the table with some trepidation and embarrassed blushes, especially after the trials and vexations which had preceded the dinner. But she reminded herself that she must do honor to the place, for, after all, said she, I am the lady of this mansion in the eyes of these guests, however secluded and unnatural my life may be in private. *He* shall not look at me and find me wanting. Let me show Mr. Slaughton that I am able to dispense his entertainments with the dignity he has a right to expect.

Fortunately, the cooking was excellent ; the chicken-pie rich, melting, juicy, delicious ; everybody praised it, and Dame Slaughton remarked to her neighbor :

" Oh, yes, Mrs. Hethwaite, you needn't be a mite ashamed of Perdita's pastry ; it's every bit as good as mine."

Dickey Pritchard was a great help to the young hostess. She sat at her right hand, and served the gravies and the pickles, and she made so much talk with everybody, and did so much laughing, that she saved her any unnecessary outlay of words.

· The children's table was beautiful, their turkey tender ; and Malcolm carved remarkably well, considering that it was the first fowl whose joints he had ever essayed to find.

Cicely Vance presided at top, with as many airs and graces as if the affair of the orange had not happened. *She* had evidently forgotten all about it, and she stuck out her fingers and giggled, and hinted to Josie Pritchard about Dolly's "shocking table manners," drawing attention to the way she was gnawing a wing-bone ; and she told what poor folks her father and mother were, and how she had only two or three dresses, and how her best hat was made over and dyed, and such other pleasant little items as she could think of ; and she made such fun of her, that the Pritchards left off talking to the stranger, and stared openly at her.

Cicely's friendships always tended to corner-groups and whispering secrets, which left out some companion in the cold, neglected and unhappy.

Cicely gorged herself habitually at table. Like all soulless animals, the pleasure of eating was paramount. The pantry was robbed of its cakes by her clammy white fingers; her pockets were always full of the crumbs of pilfered delicacies. What a future for such a creature, except wallowing in all the lusts of the flesh, all pride of the eye, all gratification of the palate?

So mused her uncle, as he observed his lovely-hued niece slyly slipping aside raisins, nuts, and macaroons, for secret devourance, pilfering from plenty what was never denied to her; choosing to steal and lie rather then live honestly and openly.

All through the day Perdita felt the heavy trouble of which the morning had warned her. The stern, disapproving looks her father darted at her darling every time she came within his notice, and her mother's nervous apologies for every move the child made, filled her with anxieties; and she wished, oh! how she wished she had power to hold the bonnie wee thing safe in her enfolding love—so safe that no tyrant's hand could reach her.

When Betty hung about Mr. Slaughton, she watched him carress her; as she clung fondly to him, a sure way to make the child secure suggested itself to her.

" If he were to adopt her legally, father would have to leave her alone. If he only would ! "

She put aside the idea as impossible, even if her husband were willing, which was not likely; the dame would never consent ; such a move would suppose a sharing of his wealth with the stranger whom she disliked as an interloper ; and she knew quite well that the Parson would refuse such an offer with acrimony ; the jealous spite he had shown so many times

13

already made it sure that he would not only flout the proposal, but abuse its author.

The knowledge which the Thanksgiving festivities thrust on his notice, that another man could give ease and elegance to children of his, while he gave them only poverty and hard lines, was evidently rankling in him like venom. He proved it by his actions and looks, and his flings at "rich people;" and Dame Slaughton's remarks made matters worse, so that Perdita almost expected him to carry off the child that very night, and her soul died within her at the appalling prospect.

So many bad passions were stirring in the heart of the divine, as jealousy, envy, pride, and uncharitableness, that his countenance was more than usually grim and repulsive. His discourtesy did not hinder Mrs. Dickey's amusing herself with him, and his "bow-wows" only made her laugh. She persisted in arguing on the immortality of animals, and assured him that every dog and horse he had owned here would be ready to greet him on the other side of Jordan, and asked him how he liked the prospect. And she quoted Montaigne: "If my cat and I entertain each other with mutual apish tricks, as playing with a garter, who knows but I make my cat more sport than she makes me? Shall I conclude her simple, that has her time to begin and her time to refuse to play, as freely as I myself have?"

The Parson replied pleasantly that Montaigne was a fool, and the rubbish he penned all "stupid nonsense."

"Why, bless us and save us, Mr. Hethwaite!" exclaimed Mrs. Dickey; "you might be one of the six who stood on Mount Ebal, you deal out your decisions so forcibly."

There were not wanting some mirth-provoking incidents during the day, which the young wife enjoyed in spite of her worries and perplexities.

After dinner the children had the dining-hall for a play-room, and their first exploit was to build a den of chairs roofed with the table-spread, into which they inserted little Susie Pritchard, to represent the prophet whom the Babylonish king cast to the

savage beasts. When she was properly crouched in an attitude
of humble prayer, Bertram and Billy sat down in front of her
and began to roar with all their might, while Malcolm leaned
over the top and helped them with his deep, bass voice. Soon
she began to tremble and cry out for assistance, quite pale with
terror.

"Ro-r-r-r-o-o-r ! r-r-r-r-r-o-o-r," screamed Billy ; "have faith
in God, Daniel ! We haven't half done yet. R-r-r-r-o-o-r !
r-r-r-r-o-o-r."

The feigning proved too real for the nerves of the child, and
her mother was obliged to release the captive and nurse her in
her arms, and point out to her that it was only two small boys
who made the terrific rumpus.

"But they roared, they acted like lions. I don't like boys
that act like lions ; I like them to act like boys," replied the
sobbing Daniel.

Josie took quite another view of their exploit, and experienced admiration for their wild prowess.

"Mamma," whispered she, "who prayed for me to come down
from heaven ? "

"I suppose I did, if anybody."

"Then why didn't you pray sooner ; so that I might have
been Malcolm's sweetheart, he is so big and strong."

Sam the setter was full of care and anxiety about Mrs.
Dickey's poodle-dog ; and no sooner did he see the little white
bundle getting caresses and attention, than he showed the most
intense jealousy ; and he took every opportunity to crowd him
off and place himself in front of his mistress, where he went
through all his best tricks, standing on his head, walking on his
hind legs, and begging ; occasionally interrupting his show to
snarl at the interloper, and keeping a watch on him out of the
tail of his eye, in such a funny way, that Perdita laughed merrily, until her father came to look on ; then she lost all her
enjoyment of her dog, and made haste to turn him out before
he should be denounced as " stupid nonsense."

When night shut in, and the curtains were drawn, Mrs. Dickey volunteered to play a reel, and proposed that all should join in it.

" An excellent suggestion," said Mr. Slaughton. " Of course you have no objection, Mr. Hethwaite."

" Objection to what ?"

" Seeing the little folks dance."

" Dance I objection I I'll soon show you. You can do as you please ; but as for me and mine, I shall countenance no such devil's work I Wife, get your bonnet."

" The one you wore up here pinned onto your coat-tail ? " spoke up Cicely Vance. " I'll fetch it ; but it's all smashed to death, as flat as a pancake."

" And yet you used to dance, sir," said Perdita, "when you were young and spry enough."

" Perhaps I might have done so, while I was a bondman of sin, if I had known how, which I rejoice to say I did not ; I am at a loss to conceive who could have put such a silly notion into *your* head."

He glanced at his wife, who looked terrified.

" Nobody told me, sir. I argued that a poet must probably dance ; and I know that you wrote verses in ladies' albums, and poems to your charmers—this one, for instance :

> " ' Prythee, sweetheart, be not so sad ;
>   Else shall I think thou lovest me not.
> For she that loves to love is glad,
>   And loving, hath all else forgot.
> If that the Past doth seem unkind,
> I will a better Present find.
> If present things should bring annoy,
> I'll make thy future bright with joy.

> " ' If friends to thee have proved untrue,
>   *I* will be all they should have been ;
> If fortune frown upon thy view,
>   I'll give the smiles thou should'st have seen.

> Thou shalt not want for anything
> That he who loveth thee can bring ;
> And love makes all things to be had.
> Prythee, sweetheart, be not sad !' "

Perfect silence reigned in the room while Perdita recited the lines in a clear, vibrant voice, and Mrs. Hethwaite sat with her head bent at first, and her fingers working restlessly with each other. Soon she stole a glance at her husband, who was scowling angrily on her from under the *guard-house* of his shaggy brows, while his pendulous under lip-drooped like an amiable bull-dog's.

Some old, long forgotten feeling, began to stir within him presently, however ; some buried memory was rekindled, for his face changed and almost softened as she went on.

" I am not the author of those lines, Mrs. Slaughton," he said shortly, when she had finished. "I could not rhyme half so well."

"But you gave them to my mother."

"That may be. I don't propose in my old age to be brought to book for all the follies of my youth," he protested dryly.

"Don't call that folly, Mr. Hethwaite. What would this poor world be without young love and young lovers ? And I am sure the selection is wonderfully beautiful—now, is it not ? " said Mrs. Dickey.

"The poetry is well enough for poetry ; but all poetry is stupid nonsense, as *I* have lived long enough to find out."

"Meanwhile these dear children are losing valuable time. I hope you won't object to their playing a little game called eight hands round ; it is very simple and innocent, as I will soon show you," entreated Mrs. Dickey insinuatingly.

"Calves must frisk, and puppies and kittens must jump, Parson," put in old Mr. Brandegee, with a merry twinkle in his eye. "So must children have their fun. Start your game, darter. I'll warrant you won't put them up to any harm."

They were quickly ranged into places and the music struck up—some old, soft, sweet Scotch tunes, which take all the black piano keys; and Mrs. Dickey showed them how to make the changes, which they did with light steps and merry faces, while Mr. Hethwaite came near beating the time of " Bonnie Doon." That was once a favorite air of his, in the days when he used to pour it out of his yellow flute.

" There, Parson," called out old Mr. Brandegee, when they had finished, "what do you think of eight hands round? Quite a neat little game, isn't it ? "

" I see nothing in it but jumping about."

" But then tisn't wicked, like dancing, you. know," replied the old gentleman, winking at his daughter.

Mr. Slaughton went over to his wife, who was standing in a corner, looking at her father with a troubled countenance.

" Do you always pay your debts with such interest ? " asked he.

" I am afraid the measure I have meted will be measured to me again," said she, sighing. "If he takes little Bettie, I shall be too miserable to live."

" But why should he ? She is healthy here, and he must see that she thrives."

" He threatens it; he worries my mother about the child's danger. He says she needs training ; you had a specimen of ·his tender discipline."

A thought flashed into the gentleman's mind.

" Do you know what Betty told me this morning? ' Uncle Sam, I wish I was your little girl ! ' Can it be that she is afraid of being torn from you ? "

" She has experienced some sharp reproofs, you know, to-day, from different quarters. She looks heavy-eyed and tired. I think I'll try to steal her away and put her to sleep."

" I would. Heigho ! Life isn't a bed of roses for anybody," he added, in a vexed tone. " How would it be if I were to buy your pet legally? Then I might resign my title to her, and you could rest in peace."

Perdita experienced a strange emotion. The idea she would not permit herself to harbor had also dawned on him. It was certainly most remarkable, and exceedingly thoughtful and kind.

" My father would never consent, nor would your mother——"

" But if it could be brought about, would you promise me a boon?"

" What boon?"

" That you and I should be better friends."

CHAPTER XLI.

"JACK AND JILL WENT UP THE HILL."

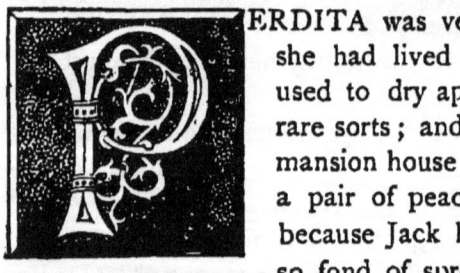ERDITA was very fond of fowls. When she had lived at home, she and Teddy used to dry apples and sell them to buy rare sorts ; and when she came up to the mansion house her brother sent after her a pair of peacocks they had got cheap, because Jack had so fine a tail and was· so fond of spreading it in the highway, that he frightened the horses and caused accidents. So Farmer Batt let them have the pair for three dollars, throwing in the hen as of no worth.

" We might eat the critters," explained the farmer. " They say you wouldn't know 'em from turkey ; but we've got a big lot of poults coming on, and 'tain't no object. I kinder hate to part a faithful couple, if they are nothing but pea-fowl, and I'm glad to do you a good turn, Perdita. Your pa and me, we

used to be cronies together ; many's the night we've crep' out
of the wood-'us winder, to steal off to huskin's, or some such
shindigs.   Your pa used to be chuck full of the old boy when
he was young.   Land ! I can't never forget seein' him go down
into a barrel one time, on account of the head breakin' through,
when we was stealin' grapes.   How the dust did fly ! And
there he stood, a regular jack-in-the-box.   That's when we was
as full of sap as green sugar-maple in March.   Tell your ma
I'm goin' to kill next week, and I'll send her the pluck."

Jack was gorgeously beautiful, carrying as many eyes as Argus,
and he liked everything about his new home except the Houdan
rooster.   With him he had a feud from the beginning, which he
carried on in the most original manner.   He would go behind
his enemy whole hours, stepping as he stepped, keeping him
from business and pleasure, giving him no time to rest, scarcely
allowing himself time to eat, and making the Houdan's life a
burden to him.

Dame Slaughton's thrift was outraged by the habits of the
strangers.   She railed at their gluttony, their horrid voices, and
never lost an opportunity to chase them from the window under
which they delighted to bask in the sunshine, speering about
for such tidbits as their mistress occasionally flung to them.
Neither would she leave them at peace in the barn-yard.   She
said they gobbled what was meant for the hens, which was quite
likely.   And so the poor things took to roaming.

Jill soon came to grief.   Cicely Vance conceived a fancy to
collect feathers ; and finding she could run down the clumsy
bird, and tire her out, so that she would drop panting in her
tracks, she chased her whenever she got a sly chance, and she
had hoarded quite a boxful of her pretty plumes, when one
day the poor thing disappeared entirely.

Although the girl heard Perdita lamenting the loss of her
favorite, she did not tell her that she had fallen on her in the
heat of pursuit, and hurt her to death, and that she had her
bonniest spoils laid away.

After the loss of his dear Jill, Jack wandered up and down lamenting, and calling for her in such a penetrating screech, that the dame grumbled and scolded about him more than ever; and as he was often absent at roosting time, he was a source of much anxiety to his mistress, who liked to count her pets and know that each was properly asleep with head under wing, when the sun went down.

"I wonder what has happened to Jack. I cannot find him anywhere; I have not seen him for two days. I have hunted the meadow and orchard and garden," said Perdita to Hannah one morning, while the poultry were flocking to the kitchen-door for their treat of bread-crumbs.

"And a mighty small loss, *I* should say, if you never see him again," replied the dame. "I hope he has taken his squawks and squalls somewhere else, for my part; a disagreeable glutton, of no use in the world."

"Except to give me pleasure, ma'am," answered Perdita quietly.

"Well! 'pears to me a married woman might entertain herself with her work. That's what I've always had to do. I think more like than not, Stephen Batt has killed the old thing. He threatened to give him a dose of salt a week ago. Slowgo told me he complained that he stole the oats out of his crib."

"Salt!" exclaimed Perdita. "If I thought he hated Jack that much, I should call him a very bad neighbor indeed."

"I don't see what that has to do with the case. Nobody wants a great trampling plague around. I do hate guzzling beasts, always eating when they're not splitting people's ears with their noise. I don't believe in keeping anything on a farm that don't pay—no drones. Now what are you smiling at in that disagreeable way, I should admire to know?"

"I was thinking how Darwin tells us that the barbarians of Terra del Fuego kill and devour their old women in time of famine, as of less value than their dogs, whom they thus preserve alive," replied Perdita disdainfully.

13*

Of course there could be no excuse for the speech, and it was the greatest pity in the world that the girl did not bear all the nagging and badgering she got without letting her temper get the best of her. As she went swiftly out of her mother-in-law's presence into the hall, she ran against Mr. Slaughton, who was laughing softly, in spite of his reverence for parents, at the quick change his mother had received for her tart speeches; and he also scanned admiringly the glowing freshness of the saucy speaker, who made no effort to conceal her passion.

"You hit rather hard, don't you?" said he, as she stopped to get breath and apologize.

"I am already ashamed of my impudence, and I am going back in about three minutes to say so. I must get over my rage first, or I shall make bad worse. The fact is, I am annoyed about my poor pea-fowls; Teddy and I earned them. Jill is dead already, and I shall ask my brother to take home Jack, if he can be found, which is doubtful."

"I shall be sorry to have you do that. I admire the magnificent fellow as much as he does himself, and that is saying a good deal. Hello! here he comes now."

"Oh, I am glad! Jack! Jack! Yes, here he is. I must hasten and fetch some crumbs," said Perdita, stepping swiftly and airily away.

When she returned, she found the farmer talking with her husband.

"Slowgo can tell you what became of Jill," said Mr. Slaughton.

"Yes mum, but I don't want to get the girl into no trouble; she is apt to chase the fowls, and yank out their feathers, and I reckon she kinder hurt the hen; in fact, she tuckered her clean out, and she stubbed her toe, and pitched right onto her, and I spec that's what killed her."

"She told me she did not know anything about her."

"Oh, well, mum, she knows she drapped; and she knows

she twitched out her tail-quills. She didn't stop to see what happened arterwards; mebbe she thought the critter was only stunted, and got up again. I can't say, I'm sure, about that."

The farmer walked off shaking his head and saying, "I can't tell; I can't tell; I only know what I see," till he was out of hearing. Mr. Slaughton waited to observe his wife, and he was quite surprised to see her eyes fill with tears, and a hopeless look drop upon her face.

"I am afraid I cannot reach the good which must be in her. I don't know how. I have tried so hard. If I could only learn where to come at any tenderness. If I could only make her feel sorry or glad about such things as the others feel sorry or glad for."

"I will not have your life troubled with this good-for-naught girl. I will pack her off to boarding-school."

"What! and lose all my hard work? Not yet, if you please. I must not give up yet!" answered she, much comforted by his sympathy. "There surely is a tender place somewhere. If she has a soul, I will find it. I am not so perfect that I can afford to cast off any other child as worthless. I do not love Cicely Vance; I cannot! I do try to find her agreeable, but she repels me. She says she loves me. I know better. There is a secret, sure prompting within us which lets us know without mistake when we are loved."

"Are you certain of that?" Mr. Slaughton put his question in a hasty way, and seemed eager for her answer.

"About Cicely?" Her mind was full of the child; she was not thinking in the least of him. "Yes, I believe I am right. I wish I could make her behave! If I keep on trying, I trust I shall. Now I must go and say 'I am sorry,' and that does not come easy."

"Grandma, dear grandma," said Cicely, as soon as Perdita had left the kitchen, "Oh, I'm so affecshunut; *you'll* let me stay and see Hannah cook, won't you? Aunty says servants are not fit company for me. Hannah won't hurt me, will she, grandma? you think everything of Hannah, don't you?"

"Hurt you! Of course she won't. Pretty teaching that is, I should say. Don't meddle with the dough," added the dame, walking off.

"You'll give me a seed-cake, won't you, Hannah? and bake me a little man? I think you are ever so nice."

"As the mistress pleases. I'm puttin' in me time, anyway," answered the woman curtly. "If I'm pisen, I'd best leave; and I think I'll be tellin' Miss Perdita so."

"Oh, no, don't. She didn't say exactly that; don't tell."

"What did she say, and what didn't she, then? Speak now, will 'ee?"

"She said the parlor was the place for me, if I was a lady."

"Very well! then go to the parlor, and don't be blatherin'."

"You're a real cross old thing! I hate you!" retorted Cicely, upsetting all the cake-pans and tossing the wiping-towels out of the window, as she kicked up her heels in an uncouth hop, and departed, munching the sweets she had filched—the raisins and citron and sugar.

"My judge! what a cow-caper!" ejaculated the tormented cook; "if I ever come across such a kelpie! My dish-clouts in the mud, and my patty-pans rollin' hither and yon, the thief of the world."

When the kelpie reached the parlor she found her grandmother setting up some rare fans in the corner, and that reminded her to ask a question.

"Grandma, will salt kill peacocks?"

"Yes, if you can get them to eat it."

"I should think that would be hard work."

"It can be done; hand me that feather."

"How, grandma?"

"Mix it with their meal; they'll swallow it if they get hungry enough. I've a couple of minds to give that squalling wretch a dose. There he goes with his 'squehaw,' enough to scare the owls. And serve Miss Impudence right, too. Old woman indeed!"'

"Dear me! this lesson is so hard. I can never learn it," groaned Cicely, making a piteous face.

"You needn't, then! Go play! she is entirely too severe. I don't approve her course with you. Girls are crammed with too many ologies nowadays, when they ought to be learning to sew and knit. Here you can't do a plain overhand seam."

"But I must learn my lesson, grandma, or I'll have fifty words more, added to these twenty. That's the way she does us. We have to get five words out of the dictionary for every little thing. I wish I was back to my convent; there I only had to study the saints and the prayers; they always let us off from the lessons."

"You poor, abused child! Put your book right away this instant. I won't have your back crooked over that stuff you can't understand, when you ought to be playing tag out-doors. Does your head ache?"

"Yes, grandma, awfully! I feel real sick."

"Sick! Stick out your tongue! You must have a dose of elixir. Now, go and get me the bottle and I'll give it to you right away."

"Oh, no, grandma, I'm better now; I guess it was looking at the letters made me dizzy. I'll lie down on the sofa, may I, and rest a little while?"

"Yes, lie down, and you can have the medicine when you go to bed. There! Keep this wet cloth over your eyes."

As soon as the Dame was fairly out of sight, Cicely recovered her health suddenly enough to make a first-class miracle for her convent, and got up and whisked over to the window. She saw her uncle and aunt and Jack outside, and her blue eyes retreated into their caverns with a thought which came to her; and after they were gone their several ways, and the coast was clear, she slipped softly to the pantry and emptied the salt-box into her hand and ran with nimble legs to the barn-yard. The fowls scattered from her approach in all directions, and the doves beat their wings with a whirr as they ascended to the eaves. There they looked at her sideways out of their pretty pink eyes, and cooed in safety.

She found the feed dish, into which she threw the salt, stirring it round with the meal, and wetting it from the horse-bucket ; and though she was quite alone, and out of sight and ear-shot of the house, she looked constantly and stealthily about her, while she waited for Jack.

Presently he came, spreading his feathers to the sunshine.

" Jack, Jack," she called softly, " come here."

He stepped with slow stateliness towards the dish, which she set on the ground where he could see it, dropping his plumes and managing his tail as a fine lady does her train.

Jack had been vagabondizing, and he had brought home an appetite which was still keen and sharp, and he greedily devoured the mess, not pausing till the basin was quite empty, and even its sides were cleaned.

Cicely sat crouched in a heap on the ground, and although the wind was keen and penetrating, and she shivered with cold, she waited and watched. The bird went about as usual, hunting for grains, and selecting such as looked tempting. Cicely lost faith in the virtue of salt. She supposed he would have dropped instantly dead. After a while she heard Slowgo coming down the drive-way ; then she got up quickly and hurried out of sight. All day she thought of what she had done, and seemed to see her victim writhing in torture ; and she trembled to think what might be the consequences, if he did die and she was found out. She tried to brave it down, with her ready, " I don't care. Grandma said she'd a great mind to give him a dose ;" and she threw up her heels with a kick and a caper as she repeated a rhyme she had picked up some-where, and which was often on her lips :

> " Whipping don't last long ;
> Scolding don't hurt none ;
> Kill me she dassent."

"I don't believe Uncle Sam will mind. She isn't a true aunty. She's only a governess, anyhow. I heard her tell him so, and he didn't contradict her. They didn't know I was listening. I always used to listen in the convent. Sister Josephine told me to ; I heard lots of things."

Half a dozen times that day she stole down to look about the barn-yard ; and at last, towards evening, she stumbled on Jack right in her path, dead ! His feet were drawn up and his claws twisted, his handsome feathers draggled and dirty, and his bright eyes glazed. She felt wild and excited ; cold chills crept over her as she stooped to draw out some of the the pale brown feathers from his under wing, which she especially coveted ; and while she did so, she experienced the same sort of desperate terror and fury which maddens a murderer who rifles the clothes of his victim in search of the spoil which incited him to the deed. If Cicely Vance had grown up an abandoned creature, bloody with crimes, she could only have intensified her sensations of that evening. The limp hand of a dead man, dropping from her grasp, would have sent the blood knocking with the same thud at her heart as she felt now, when Jack fell back on the ground, a dead thing whose life she had stopped. Cicely had learned how it feels to kill with a soul full of murderous purpose.

When they all assembled at the table, the dame was quite alarmed by the pallid face of her granddaughter, and regretted that she had not given her the Elixir Pro.

" Why, Cicely, child ! what *is* the matter with you ? are you worse—are you faint ? How strange your eyes *do* look ! as if you had seen a ghost ! "

Perdita, whose attention was drawn to the girl by these exclamations, said to herself, "What piece of cruelty has she been at now ! She wears a visage she might have bought from a feast of the ghouls. I wonder is it another crooked pin through Taffy's tail ? or has she strangled one of the kittens ? "

The next morning, before she was dressed, she heard Bertram

screaming under her window. As she did not open it, the enterprising youngster began to pelt the panes with pebbles. She threw up the sash, and looked down. She had a cup of water in her hand, and she was smiling archly, her face full of merry mischief, and as fresh as a rose.

"Take care," said she, "how you disturb my slumbers. I think I shall sprinkle you."

"You will sprinkle Uncle Sam as well, then," answered the lad. "See what we've got."

Putting out farther her head, she saw that early gentleman, and made haste to set down the cup and inquire what was wanting.

"I've found Jack; he's dead—dead as a door-nail, Slowgo says." He was holding the bird by a leg. "Poor, handsome Jack!" said Mr. Slaughton whimsically, "his last squehaw is squehawed; his glory is departed."

Perdita's eyes flashed. "Both killed, are they? It is to be hoped somebody feels better."

"My! How hard his crop is!" exclaimed Bertram, who was kneeling on the ground beside the *corpse.*

"Hard, is it? then it has eaten something that was not good for it. Wait one moment, Bertram, till I come down."

She ran swiftly to the barn, bringing back the feed-dish in her hand. "There!" said she, showing it to Mr. Slaughton, "just put your finger on that and taste it! Well, what is it?"

"Salt," replied the gentleman, spitting out the result of his trial, "salt, plain enough."

"Now, the question is, which of the two did it?"

It came to Mr. Slaughton's lips to ask "Which two?" But he thought better of it; and Perdita, after instructing Bertram to carry the poor fellow away and beg of Stephen to bury him; walked into the house.

When they were seated at the breakfast-table, Bertram began to talk about Jack, his head being full of the subject—wondering and guessing ; telling how he looked, and how heavy he was, and where he found him.

"Do you know who killed Jack, Cicely?" asked Perdita.

"Well, I do declare! what will you put on that child next?" spoke up the dame tartly. "Why don't you ask her who killed the old ram they found down in the hollow the other day?"

Perdita kept her eyes fixed on Cicely during this speech. The resplendent color had mounted in her face till she glowed like a rosy sunset.

"I asked you a question ; did you hear it?" She said again, "Do you know who killed Jack?"

"No, aunty, of course I don't; how could I know? I haven't seen him for ever so long."

"You did not feed him salt, then?"

"Salt!" put in the dame; "what about salt?"

"Only this; you taught your grandchild, who sits there beside you, that salt would kill fowls. There has been salt in the feed-dish, and my peacock is dead."

"Why don't you ask if I killed the beast myself."

"Quod facet per allium facet per se," replied Perdita. "I have heard of tell-tale blushes. What do you think of those for a sample?" pointing to Cicely.

After enduring the scrutiny of the table an instant longer, the girl burst into tears. "I didn't do it. I don't know anything about him," she sobbed, with her face in her hands.

"You had better finish your oat-meal, Cicely," suggested Perdita quietly; "you will be hungry before long."

Not another word was said on the subject during breakfast. The dame treated Cicely as a suffering innocent, and looked very glum and grim at her daughter-in-law, who chatted with the children and listened to them with much of her accustomed sympathizing attention.

Mr. Slaughton followed her into the library. "What will you do with that horrible child?" asked he with intense disgust; "that young Vance?"

" I will try to make her sorry for what she has done," she replied.

" I shall go to Toptown to-morrow and order half a dozen pairs of pea-fowl, and I will add as many gold and silver pheasants, if you will take them in place of Jack and Jill, so ' foully murdered.' "

" Thank you, not for me. My pets thrive ill here. I don't want any more ; " she left him and walked half the length of the hall, then turned and retraced her steps.

" It was kind of you to think of that ; I am not ungrateful." Her voice was constrained, and she hardly looked at him as she spoke, and she did not seem to expect any reply, as she stayed not to hear what he might say.

He smoked out his cigar and pondered over the events of the morning, and his young wife's carriage and demeanor from the instant when she thrust her pretty head from her window, and he so narrowly escaped a sprinkling ; and on his mother's very evident partiality for Cicely ; and debated in his mind whether or no he ought to interfere, and almost felt as if he had and would. But each whiff of his cigar puffed away the shadowy resolutions which had been trying to get strength out of his purpose to materialize into action, when suddenly he heard Perdita's voice in the new conservatory calling " Sam."

Although he understood perfectly well that it was the dog she was speaking to, he thought best to appear.

Cicely Vance, with a watering-pot in her hand, was busily helping " Aunty," so " affecshunut," and showing no remorse, no shame, nothing but unclouded self-satisfaction.

" Oh ! " remarked Mr. Slaughton in a low voice, " so this is your method of awakening contrition, is it ?   Well, how does it succeed ? "

" As you see ; careless, noisy, light-headed ; when pushed into a corner from whence there was no escape, she confessed that she killed Jack. I asked her why, and she replied as usual, 'I dunno,' and her manner said, 'I don't care.' When I threatened her with punishment, the loss of her holiday, and an afternoon alone in the school-room, locked up, she fell on her knees and begged in such abject abasement of mind and body that I hated to look at her. When she felt in no more danger, she wiped her eyes, and asked me for a new bracelet, or "bangles," as she called them, with bells. Look at her! *do* you suppose she has a soul? I feel as if she must be something uncanny, a water-ugly, a changeling. She makes me chilly."

While they were talking there came a dreadful crash up-stairs, mingled with terrific screams. They rushed to the scene of tumult, which proved to be the nursery.

This room had been furnished with the old-fashioned things which were from time to time rejected of the rest of the house. An ancient bureau, with a deep drawer at the top, stood in one corner. On it was an old clock, besides books, baskets, dolls, playthings, and all sorts of heterogeneous articles for use and amusement.

Bertram had induced Pandora, without much coaxing, to seat her plump little self in the half-opened "upper drawer," where she was supposed to represent the old woman living in her shoe, who had so many children she didn't know what to do. But before she had got so far as to whip them all soundly, the whole thing tilted forward, like Mrs. Gamp's chest of drawers, upsetting the clock, which was not able to come to time, spilling off baskets, dolls, etc., and disturbing materially the housekeeping of the numerous family supposed to be in the various stages of butter and bread and the rest, and scaring the adventurous children half out of their wits.

As soon as Perdita ascertained that nobody was hurt, she laughed merrily, and her enjoyment of the odd scene was rather increased by the appearance of the dame's head in the doorway, and her rueful manner of regarding the confusion.

"Well, young ones," said she in a resigned voice, " if you

leave the walls all standing, and don't tear the hard finish off the cellar, it will be more than I can reasonably expect."

"These outrageous pranks don't seem to spoil your temper," said Mr. Slaughton to his amused wife.

"No; I must confess that I find them entertaining; natural, original, noisy children are always wonderful to me. I never had any such license in my tender years. I can bear anything but deceit and falseness."

CHAPTER XLII.

"WOMAN'S BOOK IS THE WORLD."

 NE bright, sunny morning Mrs. Richard Pritchard and her mother drove over the hills to spend the day. Mrs. Richard was a fearless horsewoman, and she had in hand a span of colts which she had herself trained to harness.

"Are you strong enough to manage those wild creatures without any men to protect you?" asked Perdita, who happened to be the first to welcome the guests.

"Why should anybody protect me from my colts. They know me. They don't like or respect me any the less because I speak to them in a soft voice, and wear petticoats," replied the lively lady, laughing. "They don't pattern after your sex there, exactly, do they, Mr. Slaughton?" she added as she shook hands with the host, who came hastening out to meet his mother's friends.

"*I* like soft voices of all music in the world; and I admire the drapery you are pleased to call petticoats, when such women as you wear it, Dickey, in those simple flowing lines ; and as to your horses, I should not wonder at anything you might do with them, your skill is so patent and so famous."

"Do you mean that as a compliment, or a sneer ?"

"Neither ; I state a fact."

The two old ladies settled to a good long neighborly crooning over their knitting, and Mrs. Dickey pursued a study she had begun at the Thanksgiving feast, of the pair whose position towards each other excited her curiosity. She was very chatty and pleasant, and Perdita watched her and listened to her with exceeding interest as a new species of the genus mulier ; and the ceaseless flow of talk between her and the house-master astonished her. It was the first opportunity she had had of seeing him in the company of another woman, young, pretty, and accomplished, whom he took the trouble to entertain. There had been some talking during the library evenings ; but if she had ever made up any opinion concerning his conversation, she would have thought him decidedly a quiet man, not given to chatter. To-day he paid compliments, talked art, told stories, laughed a good deal ; he even sang some songs to Mrs. Dickey's accompaniment.

Perdita felt rather bewildered, as if she was making a new acquaintance. She began to be afraid of the garrulous gentleman, ill at ease with the lively lady, whom she wondered at and admired ; afraid of her smooth manners, her good looks, her practised smartness.

Mr. Slaughton watched his wife closely ; and when Mrs. Pritchard appealed to her, he listened for her replies. They were never silly ; often laconic ; once or twice, bright and playful ; then he smiled within his mustache, secretly pleased.

When the bouquet-making took her to the dining-room he lost himself in reveries, and paid less attention to Mrs. Pritchard's conversation, which fact the shrewd widow discovered and sniffed at. "I am useful to make talk, but his wife is his inspiration ; she is absent in the flesh, and his spirit follows hers."

Perdita returned soon. It was polite of her to come ; but I doubt if politeness alone would have brought her. I think she felt drawn by curiosity, interest, or some unacknowledged motive. She had hardly entered the doorway when Mr. Slaughton rose with more briskness then he commonly showed, being, as we know, rather slow—rather given to sauntering.

"Come upstairs to the studio, Dickey," said he ; "I want to show you my two pictures. They are the best things of my life. I have been looking them over this morning ; I mean to have them in the Toptown exhibition"

"Your best efforts, are they. Oh, yes, dear Mrs. Slaughton, no new sight to you, these wonderful masterpieces ; but we will try to pick some flaws, point out some weak spots, shall we ? "

Perdita's face had been lighted with smiles ; a dark cloud dropped instantly upon it, her eyes flashed, her lip curled with proud scorn. She withdrew from the caressing fingers with which Mrs. Dickey-sought to draw her towards her—she was never pleased with the touch of stranger hands ; and as she answered the invitation with which her husband seconded the widow, there was a slight tremble of sorrow, of mortification in her voice.

"She resents my being asked first ; she is jealous, silly child," thought Mrs. Pritchard, who had felt the slight repulse she had received.

"Don't you take interest in pictures ? " asked she.

"One may take an interest in them, and not desire to see them."

"I don't understand that; please explain."

"You may set down my speech as idle words, which need no explanation, and do not let me detain you."

Mrs. Pritchard bowed and stepped after the artist, who mounted the stairs.

As they ascended, Perdita pursued them with her eyes and thoughts.

"He will show her the two pictures of his first love ! And

did he for one instant dream that I would go up there and stand beside his beauty, that he might observe the contrast— the brow of Egypt on this side ; on that, his golden-haired Sabrina ! Yes ! the best pictures he ever made in his life, because he put the worship of his life into them—his truest soul —the soul in which I have no share."

When the two descended they found Perdita by the window, with both arms around Bettine, who stood on the window-sill, and leaned her small head on her sister's shoulder.

"I do believe you idolize that child !" exclaimed Mrs. Pritchard.

"She satisfies me, and I am all she needs. I am comfort, helper, companion and friend."

"You cannot be much more to your husband ; I should think he would get jealous of the fondness you lavish on her."

Perdita smiled such a bitter smile, and she held still closer the mite who struggled to be free.

"I want to go to Uncle Sam," she whispered. "See, he is crooking his finger at me. Oh, Perdita, you squeeze me too hard ! you hurt me ! "

After a strange look into the pleading face lifted to hers, she opened her arms, and the little fairy ran to her other friend, who received her gladly, and also showed a measure of triumph at his success.

"You give up your treasure easily, and she seems quite anxious to leave you, considering that you are all she needs. I wonder you did not hold her fast," remarked Mrs. Dickey, with a spice of malice, while she admired the graceful, flitting motion of the child, and the cuddling sweetness with which she settled into the arms of the strong man who held her.

"I do not desire to keep the body when the heart is yonder," replied Perdita.

The dame called Mrs. Pritchard to come and look at her new tidy ; and as she left them, Mr. Slaughton said, half in play, half in earnest :

"Betty, tell your sister you have full room in your heart for two loves."

"That sounds odd from a man who is so constant in his friendships as well as his deeper affections, that he believes in one undying, unchangeable love, outlasting all time," replied Perdita, as she sat down with a fixed, cold countenance, and waited impatiently for her darling to return of her own will to her embrace.

She chafed in secret, and coveted all the bright smiles and cunning caresses Betty gave to the man who seemed able to draw to himself whatever he desired.   Even the dog Sam would sometimes desert her to fawn on *him*.

Then, as she watched him, there came a new sort of satisfaction that the one beautiful woman whom he had wished to win had turned away from him.   It was such an unworthy thought that she could not harbor it long, and she felt ashamed and dropped her eyes, as if he might have read it there, and despised her for it.

Mrs. Richard Pritchard finished her visit without arriving at any definite conclusions as to the status of the married pair. In fact, she was more puzzled than ever.   She found the young wife an interesting study, and she considered her jealous.   Mr. Slaughton, in reviewing her conduct, her refusal to visit his studio in the widow's company, etc., would have been glad to set it down to jealousy, because jealousy includes love ; but he found no sufficient grounds for such an opinion.

CHAPTER XLIII.

"HOW NEAR TO GOOD IS WHAT IS FAIR."

—EMERSON.

EVERAL days had passed, when Malcolm came up to the Mansion House, lugging a basket, upon which he carefully held down the cover.

"What have you got there?" inquired his sister, espying him from her window, and running down the walk to meet him. "Are you in the rag and bottle line?"

"Not much. There's a couple of rabbits in this contrivance," said he, placing his burden on the ground, and setting his foot upon it, while he wiped the sweat from his face. "It's heavy, I tell you! About as good a weight as I want to carry up-hill."

He lifted the lid, that he might indulge her with a peep.

"I bought them of Jack Batt, for my best dog-knife and that pair of stilts father told me to chop up. Look, Perdita! They've got young ones. I never saw any like them; these two are as much the color of our old Maltese cat as if they were her kittens. I saved them for Bettine's birthday. You know you said you meant to remember it this year and give her a present."

"Oh, what a dear boy you are, Malcolm! Yes, we will have anniversaries and festivals, like other folks, now that I've no lawgiver over me to forbid them and call them "tomfoolery" and stupid nonsense. How pretty they are, sticking their heads out of the straw. What great ears! and such soft slate-color—the real subdued mouse. How delighted Betty will be!

14

Stay, though," she added, knitting her brows ; " I don't know as you had best leave them after all ; my pea-fowls are dead. I am afraid they won't fare any better."

" I must leave them, Perdita," replied Malcolm, much disappointed. " Father will have them killed and cooked, if I take them home. Mother said so. She told me to fetch them right away this morning, so as to make sure of Betty's getting them alive."

" Poor mother ! how cruel it would be to force her to roast your rabbits ! I know he would do it, and devour them with relish afterwards. That shall not happen, however. We will take our chance. Betty's pleasure is too pretty a sight to lose ; everybody had best leave them alone. But where shall we put them ? "

" I'll make a hutch. I suppose you can find a box somewhere, and give me some nails and a hammer ? "

" There's one that the china came in. Wait till I wrap up Betty, and we will all go down to the barn together."

There could not have been a happier child in the world, that day, than Bettine Hethwaite. She defied the cold while she watched the young mechanic, and the leather hinges were nailed on to the door of the hutch, and the wooden button screwed to its place, and the straw strewn over the floor, and the rabbits began to jump about and examine their new home, before she could be coaxed away from them, they seemed to her so precious and beautiful.

She brought Mr. Slaughton first of all to behold and admire ; then the children, timidly, but with great pride of possession ; she flitted among them, and piped in their ears her small voice, a little silver thread of music.

Such a rich owner ! her father's " all things " would have been but a superfluous addition to her bliss, the measure of her enjoyment being full to the brim.

" Mine, Pandora ! Mine, Bertram ! Malcolm brought them in a basket ! Mine ! all mine ! the black ones and the white

ones, and the spotted ones and the beautiful blue ones. Oh, I
love the blue ones best of all! I love Malcolm! I love Perdita! I love everybody."

Each morning, for a week, she made them a visit. Once,
when it was too blustering for such a wee tender thing to walk
abroad, Uncle Sam carried her in his strong arms, and he set
up his foot on a saw-horse to make a seat of his knee, that she
might enjoy at her ease; and the two gazed down at the pets,
who ate and listened, and scampered, and then listened some
more; and when they chased each other all around the pen,
and sat up and washed their faces, and old Bunnie got so tame
as to rise on her hind legs and take cabbage from the mite's
hand, it became too wonderful and overwhelming! Her joy
rose to ecstasy.

Uncle Sam was late to breakfast, and his cheeks were red
with running, when he finally did come; and as he lifted Betty
into her chair at her sister's right hand, she said in a soft
whisper:

"Oh, Perdita! I love Uncle Sam, and he loves my rabbits."

The dame sniffled and grumbled, but nobody seemed disturbed by her mutterings. Mr. Slaughton applied himself to
his cutlets with amazing relish, and he winked at Betty over
his coffee-cup; and Betty's little elfin laugh rang out as she
caught the token and returned it with both eyes, and she ate all
her oat-meal and cream, and asked for more.

Bertram had a pair of squirrels which cunning Stephen had
snared, which could turn their wheel so fast that you couldn't
see the wires, and he offered to trade them for the Maltese
pussies; finding no bargain could be struck on that basis, he
threw in a couple of white mice; still she shook her head, and
said, "No, oh, no! I cannot, I cannot give you my pretty
things, which Malcolm gave me."

Cicely Vance went pretty often to gaze at the collection, and
she stole seed-cakes to entice them with; and her eyes retreated into their caverns sometimes, while she watched them and

looked at Betty; but she was "so affecshunut" to the dame, that it seemed as if she had some plan in her blonde head which needed only opportunity and time to climax.

CHAPTER XLIV.

"A ROSE WITH ALL ITS SWEETEST LEAVES YET FOLDED."

R. SLAUGHTON'S emotions had been quite diverse since that 25th of September which was a good day to be married on. He was humble enough now to wish to woo this wife he had so despised and slighted in the parlor of the old parsonage, and meant to win her, if his good angel would but teach him how.

He confessed that much to himself—only to himself, however; but though he covered his feelings under his habitual easy *bonhomie*, they would come to the surface in looks and actions really unmistakable. Even Perdita, settled in her belief, built on what she knew, had felt more than once or twice the magnetism a true friendliness must communicate to its object, and had yielded to its power.

She had been on her guard and reserved, it is true, and he found her so pleasant even thus, that often as the question had trembled on his lips, "When shall our interests be one? When shall this mock marriage be a true marriage?" he had found no pat and proper time to risk it. Even in the few moments when she had been genial and merry in his company, he dared not dash his pleasure in her by words which might alarm or offend her, and so take her out of his orbit and influence.

His home was becoming truly charming. The library, lighted and warm, was a pleasant resort of evenings ; and the slight, dark, lustrous lady who sat by the table was an absorbing study —ever fresh and ever new—and he began to consider himself quite a family man when the children gathered around him with their books and games ; he felt his easy-chair remarkably easy, and he positively enjoyed his cigar better before that cosy wood fire than in his den of a studio.

Since the visit of Mrs. Richard Pritchard, an impassable barrier seemed raised between the pair she took so much pains to study ; so that he could neither engage his wife's attention, enlist her sympathies, or approach her as familiarly as before. She lived more within herself, she talked less, smiled less. It seemed to him she was restless, ill-poised, and he often felt that the unchanging routine of her daily life was irksome. Even Bettine's presence failed to fill her with satisfaction.

The two pictures in the studio were rarely out of her thoughts ; and she scarcely ever looked at her husband or heard his voice without thinking how careless of her, how unnecessarily unkind he had wished to be, when he would have brought her face to face with the " best works of his life."

His declaration that they were so sounded almost coarse to her—it made so little of the ties which bound him, and announced so offensively his disregard for them.

She wondered what had been the conversation of the artist and his guest while they stood before his " best works "—if he had talked about Sabrina Bradshaw—how he loved her ! how he lost her !

She turned the theme over and over and dwelt on it, and was morbid, and bitter, and proud, and sometimes angry, sometimes sad, altogether estranged and unhappy.

It seemed a pity that she had not accepted his invitation that day. It seemed a pity that he could not guess her thoughts now.

It is most fortunate, *generally*, that our best and dearest friends are not able to know what we think of them ; but there are moments when soul-reading would be a blessing, saving unhappiness and averting mistakes.

The young people from the parsonage were at the mansion house occasionally, though their sister did not encourage very frequent visits ; and Mr. Slaughton became much interested in the young fellow Teddy, finding him a retiring, modest scholar, forever poring over a book, and reading aloud in an absent, absorbed way such scraps as happened especially to interest him.

Really, it must be confessed that all which pertained to the black-browed, dark-haired girl, who had seemed to him so unbearable and forbidding, was assuming wonderful interest and importance in his mind, so that he was often able to see objects and aims through her eyes.

The close friendship between this brother and sister had ripened with their separation, and being unpretending and unaggressive, it pleased Mr. Slaughton as a natural outgo of very warm feelings. Sallie Vance had never been to him what Perdita was to Teddy ; she had been his elder tyrant. He remembered her selfish, overbearing, dictatorial. This sister was helpful, sympathetic, sweet-voiced, sweet-faced, in her confidences with the near-sighted youth, who got very close to her indeed while he talked (a right and habit which the husband envied him, but dared not imitate), and he felt much inclined to be one of them ; and on several occasions he put in his oar, when the young man's hopes and wishes were discussed, and an inclination grew within him to try how soon and how well he could fashion the hopes and wishes into prospects and realities.

He had discussed the merits of different colleges and their courses of study, and listened with curious smiles to the glowing pictures Teddy drew of a professor's life, as he imagined it, till he began to ponder and plan how the chair might be attained.

All this commenced long before Mrs. Richard Pritchard's

visit; and although his young wife's silence and reserve shut him off somewhat from Teddy Hethwaite, it did not change materially his feelings and intentions towards him.

After her brother had gone home one evening, Mr. Slaughton detained Perdita as she gathered together her work for departure.

" I've been thinking," said he, " that if I may be allowed, I am able to be of use to Teddy. I have a scholarship due me at Rosenbloom ; I earned it when I was about his age. I should like to offer it to him, with your permission. You need not feel the least obligation," he added hastily, seeing her draw back. "¶It cost me nothing ; it is lying idle, and if he does not take it, it will be wasted."

" In that case," replied Perdita, considering, " I think I ought to accept it. It seems precisely what he wants, and I shall say 'Yes,' and be—grateful, provided father does not say 'No,' and I feel almost sure of setting it in such a light that he will consent."

" If it suits his son, I don't see how he *can* refuse."

" Then I must say you have not observed very closely my father's characteristics, one of which is a measure of bitterness towards men 'condemned to be rich,' as old Isaac Walton says. The very fact that you are able to offer Teddy what he cannot give him may stir up his gall. However, he treats me quite differently now that he can no longer control me ; and I will go down and broach the matter to him. In any event, I trust you will believe me grateful."

" Gratitude is no doubt a virtue ; but I don't see how it can be exercised by you towards me. It is a virtue expected of subordinates and dependants, and excuse me if I find your constant avowance of it a trifle monotonous."

" Oh, you prefer me not to express it."

"Couldn't you express some other emotion for a change ? "

" For example—such as——"

" Love ! " No ! he did not say it ; he did not find himself

able to bring out the word, with her cool, inquiring, irresponsive, collected glance fixed on him.   He seemed to know that she would hurl it back at him with scorn.   He dropped·the subject for one of plain matter-of-fact.

"I hope you did not make a mistake in shying his poetry at him, Thanksgiving Day.   He looked as glum as a grave-stone while you recited it."

"I was an idiot, and I plagued my mother, I am sure I did. That comes of having a temper.   I must repair the blunder as well as I can.   I'll beg him to read me his sermon on our great possessions.   I'll bake him a pound-cake.   I shall go to-morrow morning.   Such woman's wit as I possess I'll use, and I'll get my way, and Teddy shall have his wish ; and Mr. Slaughton, I truly thank you for the interest you take in my brother."

"That sounds nice for you to say, and truly, I should like to accompany you part of the way at least, as I have to look at some rails Slowgo wants me to buy for the low pasture fence. Can I go ? "

He put his hands together and stuck his head on one side.

"Certainly ; wherefore not ? " replied she, smiling.   "The highway is broad enough for two.   Enemies could walk in it."

"That is true ; if it were only a foot-path, I might jostle or crowd you.   I take the hint.   I shall keep at a respectful distance."

CHAPTER XLV.

"HOW SHALL I YOUR TRUE LOVE KNOW?"

ERDITA found the Parson in his study, bending his back over a sermon weighty enough in doctrine and verbiage to break it, if packed on all at once ; but as he had toughened himself to it, like the man who carried the calf till it grew to be an ox, and so did not die under its weight, he kept on his way, though his recapitulation of the text and heads made him groan occasionally. He rose on her entrance, and ceremoniously saluted her.

"I wish you a very good morning, Mrs. Slaughton."

Though habitually satirical on rich men and lawyers, who can hardly enter the kingdom of Heaven, he had been rather more than usually agreeable since the Thanksgiving dinner, and little by little she had lost her fears for Bettine, and the talk between her and her husband had never been renewed. Indeed, as he did not again refer to it, she had reason to suppose he had forgotten it as a mere passing suggestion, born of sympathy and exhausted in words.

She accomplished her errand easily enough. The Parson fell in with the plan without demur or contradiction.

"I believe it is foreordained that Teddy should make a figure in the world, and as Malcolm is large enough for the farm chores, I shall spare him quite well. Luckily, the vacation comes in haying-time, so that he can do the mowing and make the crop."

"I hope it is foreordained that he shall rest from the farm drudgery, which has already made him old and worn," said Perdita, with a disgust, at the selfishness which never thought of

14*

standing in any lot, she could not help showing, and she inly determined to hunt a place which should take Malcolm away from it, also.

" Fortunately, I am able to help his outfit, father," she added, opening her purse and producing her small roll of bills.

" I had rather not," replied the Parson, putting his hands behind his back. " I believe the Lord will finish the good work he has begun ; we can sell the heifer."

" I think you will have to sell her any way. What I offer is not much ; you need not feel delicate. This money is not a gift from the Slaughtons ; it is mine, honestly earned and laid up for Teddy."

" Your own money, Mrs. Slaughton ? " said he doubtfully. " I hope you are not bringing a shame on your husband by making it seem as if he did not provide for you. I trust you haven't been working for other folks. You said *earned*, I think. You will make talk, foment scandal ; it is your duty to avoid that at all cost. You have a position to support—your husband's reputation. I should be much offended if *my* wife were to parade her wants by trying to earn money."

" No doubt," thought Perdita. " You'd rather starve her, and keep her nose at the grindstone, while you sit upstairs scribbling ! " (Don't be shocked, gentle reader ; this girl was only country-bred, you know, and she spoke as she heard.)

" Be easy, father ; I am not disgracing the Slaughtons. You will have to take my statement as I give it. I believe you know I was too well whipped in my tender years for lying, to take up the practice now that the motive is removed."

" Motive for lying—what was it, pray ? "

" Fear, sir. I was afraid of you. I lied to escape the whippings you gave. Fear is what makes children liars, and so the parents are in a good degree responsible for the fault they punish, and which they ascribe to depravity. I don't deny the depravity ; but as that is also an inheritance, the fathers ought to whip themselves quite as faithfully as they do their offspring."

"Since when, Mrs. Slaughton, did you begin to think so boldly and state so freely your convictions?"

Perdita felt the latent sarcasm under his question. Although he was looking almost fearfully at her, he seemed trying to identify her with the girl who used to shrink and turn dumb at sight of him.

"I began to think as soon as I began to feel resentment, and that is so long ago that I cannot recall its beginning. I began to speak as soon as I got the chance. There it is, father; twenty-five dollars. Enough to pay Teddy's travelling expenses, and may the Lord send you a good price for the heifer."

As she left him, the Parson looked after her. "A very smart girl that, a very handsome girl! I am glad she is married, and if her husband does not keep her in order, it is his own fault. The man is the head of the woman : 'Wives obey your husbands.' I have Scripture for it, and I thank God I have been steady to carry it out."

At the foot of the stairs she was waylaid by her mother, who begged her to come into her bed-room a minute, where she shut the door softly and spoke in a whisper.

"Oh dear! my child, I do wish you could manage a little help for us out of your abundance. Your father's best coat is all gone, and he isn't fit to go up any pulpit stairs. If you could bring down one of Mr. Slaughton's, I might alter it, and sponge it over, and press it out—he has such handsome clothes —and I would just lay it on the bed when your father dresses himself, and he wouldn't inquire about where it came from. As for me, I'm a sight to behold! I can't go to meeting much longer looking as I do ; the folks in the poor-house are decenter than I am. *She* must have dresses she don't care about—nice ones, that I could wear. Couldn't you just ask——"

"Don't mother! I'd die first!" exclaimed Perdita, looking angrily at the cringing, thin, pinched creature who could harbor a mean design of pushing *her*, the proudest of the proud, into begging of the people with whom she lived on such strange terms.

"Ministers' folks always expect to have things given them," said poor Mrs. Hethwaite ; "and though your father never will look thankful, I believe he is glad enough to get them. I'm sure it's no disgrace. He is as good as anybody, if he is poor ; and he knows more than the whole of them put together. I can't think which way to turn. He don't get any preaching that pays. The day he filled the South End pulpit they only gave him a dollar ; the hens have stopped laying, and the cow is drying up. I don't have any eggs to sell, and I can't scrimp on the butter any more than I do. And there's the whole of them to feed and keep decent. I wish you wouldn't look so cross at me, Perdita ; I'm sure 'tisn't my fault."

Her troubles and vexations were souring the poor lady's temper, and her voice was sharp and querulous, and she threw herself upon the bed, and dropped her hands in her lap.

" I've a great mind to give up, that's what I have. Oh dear ! I little thought at your age that I should ever feel as I do now. I haven't any pride or courage left."

"Come, mother !" said Perdita, ashamed of her hardness towards such a timorous, broken-down wreck. " Come, cheer up ! I've good news for you, and I've money enough of my own to buy you a dress, and that will be much nicer than wearing any of Mrs. Slaughton's old cast-offs, won't it, now ? As to father's coat, let him take care of himself. Look ! here are ten dollars ! "

She emptied her purse into the trembling hand she took in both hers, patting it softly—"Perdita's first gift to her mother. Now let me tell you." She hastened to unfold the plan afoot for Teddy, and to talk cheerfully ; then she also washed the dishes, and moulded the bread ; after that she sat down and made up a ruffle, from a strip of muslin she brought with her, into beautiful plaits, and she basted it into the neck of the Sunday gown ; and she did a dozen other little things before she walked up the hill.

When her mother kissed her good-by, the poor lady looked

quite rested and refreshed, and she said: "What a comfort you are, my daughter! May God reward you with the love of your husband, and such an abundance of this world's goods that you may be able to keep it. God keep you from poverty, for poverty·kills love."

The unwooed wife carried this wish, which ought to be a real blessing, in her thoughts all the way through that winter walk. "The true love of her husband!" That was impossible; it belonged to Sabrina Bradshaw. Benevolence, natural goodness, an easy disposition, often impelled him to be pleasant to her. He was pleasant even to Cicely Vance; he was kind to the servants; yes, he was kind to his housekeeper.

The companionship of this man was so full of interest and charm, even thus, that she could ill afford to lose it; and since the goodness she was able to have was so bounteous in content, how precious and soul-satisfying should be the true love she had not?

CHAPTER XLIV.

"THE MORE THERE IS OF MINE, THE LESS THERE IS OF YOURS."

ERDITA was not out of sight of the mansion house when Cicely, who had been watching her from the window, turned to the dame, and said in the snivelling voice she found potent with that relative when urging requests.

"Grandma, shan't Betty give me a pair of her rabbits? She's got ever so many; she's just as stingy as ever she can be."

"Rabbits? Where did they come from; what do they eat?"

"Oats; Stephen pours a great lot into their box every day."

"Mercy on us, what waste! We shall drop on the town at this rate. Who did you say fetched the things?"

"Malcolm made them a present for Betty's birthday."

"The land alive! Well, I'll make you a present of half of them for yours; it's a poor rule that won't work two ways."

"Thank you, grandma, I only want one dear little pair; they can't be missed amongst so many, I'm sure."

"You shall have them! If they have got to be kept here, eating our feed—and I suppose they will, if my lady pleases— it's only fair that my daughter's child should share."

"Yes, grandma! How I love you! I'm so affecshunut! She isn't going to stay here for always, is she?"

"Who?"

"Betty Hethwaite; she's only a visitor, is she?"

"Visitor! I should say so! I can't bear her! A little shame-faced thing, always in corners, as if she was going to be whipped, the minute my Lady Sharp-eyes, is out of sight; and the way she pussies round my Samuel is enough to make a cat laugh. Of course she's put up to *that*."

"Yes, grandma; and will you get the rabbits for me this morning, before aunty comes back. She'll say you mustn't, if you wait to ask her; I know she will."

"Ask her! I should admire to see myself doing it."

"Well, come, please, now! I've found a nice peach box that will hold them ever so good. Oh, how I do love my dear grandma! I'm your little rose-bud, ain't I? Aunty isn't my true, sure-enough aunty, is she? I only call her so. She isn't half so good as you. Uncle Samuel don't like her much, does he?"

"Tut, tut, child; that's none of your bread and cheese. You best be careful how you talk."

"Yes, grandma, I am; may I carry your thimble for you, and will you please come down to the barn now? Good, pretty grandma."

The transfer was soon made under these blandishments, and the dame got ready a speech she intended to pour out when the matter came to be discussed, touching hard on some folks' partiality, their hatred of poor innocent Cicely, Sallie's oldest child, and enlarging on the way she was made the scapegoat of some folks' humors; and she had an idea of throwing in hints about the unwelcome presence of an alien, with her troublesome pets, eating folks out of house and home.

She understood well, by this time, that she must choose her opportunity for airing her little pleasantries when her son was not a listener. Although he had never opened his heart to her, she could see what was working in it. Her woman's penetration and motherly jealousy showed her—no need of words; and a deep-settled sense of damage and resentment had long ago distorted all Perdita's looks, words, and actions into injuries. She had had occasions for anger, had the dame; her daughter-in-law was no saint, and when pressed hard, was apt to turn; and she had a sharp and caustic wit which could cut all ways, though to her credit it must be told how she regretted such outbreaks, and how she took care to make her best amends by saying she was sorry.

The dame allowed herself the spiteful pleasure of speaking of the wife she had urged on her son, to the Brandegees, and even to the servants, as "My Lady," "Miss Smartie," or "Fiery-Eyes," and quoted the proverb, "Set a beggar on horseback," etc. She interviewed the domestics, and pitied them for having to work so hard, forgetting what a martinet she had been in her own day; and said it was "too bad," and "*she* should do so different if she could."

Perdita's life was made harder by these little aggravations and troubles; and though she was not always as patient as she ought to have been, she was seldom aggressive—never, in fact; and notwithstanding the dame's sly malice and meddling, the servants were obedient and respectful. They acknowledged her a lady, and among themselves resented her trials, which of course they saw, and said "she was much put upon by the old woman, so she was;" and when her orders were interfered with, they told the dame "*she* was not boss, and that they hired to Miss Perdita, and took orders from her and nobody else at all."

It was with blue eyes deep under their beetling brows and most baleful in expression, that Cicely Vance accosted Betty on her return to the nursery, after she had gained her wish and become possessed of what she coveted.

The mite was contentedly nursing her doll, and keeping a promise she had given her sister to remain in the room till her return. She looked startled when Cicely entered, and threw her apron over her baby as if she was afraid it would be snatched away.

" I've got a pair of your rabbits, Bet ! The prettiest ones ! the Maltese ones ! Grandma gave them to me. She says I may keep them for all of aunty. You've no right to be stingy ; you've no right to anything. You don't belong here. You ain't going to stay here always ; I be. Grandma can't bear you."

" Uncle Sam likes me," faltered the mite.

" You haven't got no Uncle Sam ! He's my uncle, he ain't yours. Hand me that old doll ; let's toss her up and have some fun ! Give her here, or I'll pull your hair all out, I will ! "

Without a word Betty resigned her treasure, and after watching it in Cicely's possession as long as she could bear it, she slipped out of the door, and left the small tyrant to follow her amusement of dragging the doll over the benches, and throwing her about, laughing the while such a grating, soulless cackle, like the filing of a saw or the crackling of thorns under a pot.

CHAPTER XLVII.

"WHAT IS MINE IS THINE, MY PRETTY BETTINE."

ERDITA had returned later than she had intended, finding so much help and cheer needed at home; and she was so busily pondering her morning's work, that she did a thing quite unusual with her—she forgot little Betty, and went straight to her own room without seeking her for a welcoming kiss.

She had let down her long hair and was brushing it, when she heard a soft rustle and stifled sob in the corner.

Betty had come in so still, and she was so preoccupied, that she had not heard the patter of the small feet which commonly awakened an echo in her heart of hearts.

"Ah, my darling!" she said in a soft voice vibrating with fondness. "What! did you grieve for my absence? did you miss me? Crying? don't do that. You must not weep for trifles, you must be brave; I was not gone so long. See, I am here again; don't sob so, dear Betty," she cried, dashing down the brush and springing forward. "Betty! what is the matter?"

She caught the child in her arms, who let her head drop upon her sister's palpitating breast, without a word. So full of grief was she that she could find no voice, and her small frame shook with the sobs she was trying to repress.

"Tell me quickly, who has hurt you?" exclaimed Perdita, giving her a little shake.

"She has got my two Maltese ones," whispered Betty, "my very prettiest, the ones I loved the best of all."

" Who has ? "

" Cicely."

" The little wretch ! Has she dared to meddle with your pets ?
Is there nothing safe from that horrible girl ? "

" She says "—sob—sob—" she says—oh, dear ! how my throat
aches, Perdita ; she says her grandma gave them to her."

Perdita darted to the door with Betty in her arms. She felt
the child's weight no more than a feather ; her black brows
gathered together, her eyes flashed, and her red lips half
opened for the passionate breath which panted through them.

This was the sight which met Mr. Slaughton's gaze at the
stair-head ; he had his soft hat in his two hands, and the crown
was filled with hen's eggs, which he was bringing for a present
to his young wife.

Once, on one of the library evenings, she had said what a
queer thing it would be to see chickens hatched under a woollen
mother. It was after he had been reading an account of some
winter broods, and of the old Egyptian method ; and she
laughed at the notion, looking bright and pretty, and she laid
down her work and gazed into the coals ; and when he asked
her what she saw there, she said she was thinking about some
seabrights she had once, and of a plume she made of their red
feathers for her Sunday hat ; and how Teddy had called her,
" proud bird of the mountain," and how they had done " Loch-
iel " together.

" Father made me burn it up as soon as he saw it, and said,
' When you can afford plumes, let them be ostrich, and till then
leave dung-hill fowls to wear their own finery.' Teddy was very
angry ; but I didn't care much, I had had such a good time
with the spouting."

Mr. Slaughton paid a fabulous price for the eggs he was
bringing up the stairs ; perhaps he hoped to get smiles and
thanks as his reward.

" What has happened ? " he asked in quick alarm ; " is Betty
hurt ? Pray tell me ! What is it, Betty ? "

"'This is too much! I shall not bear *this*," said Perdita, trying to pass him. "My poor child shall not be abused and trampled on, and plundered and reviled, and——"

"Who? what? which? where? when? Stay! stay!" Mr. Slaughton placed his broad shoulders across her path, as she pushed on, scarcely noticing his presence; but as the staircase was only of ordinary width, her attention was of necessity called to the formidable obstacle she had encountered, and she paused because she could not help it.

"Just tell me who has dared to hurt my pet," said he again, and the perpendicular line deepened into a dangerous frown between his eyes.

"Uncle Sam, Cicely has got my rabbits, the blue ones that we liked best," exclaimed Betty, reaching out her hands to him, while tears streamed down her face. Mr. Slaughton reached over the baluster and carefully placed his hat on the floor, and took her out of her sister's clasp with gentle force. The arms, relieved of their burden, dropped aimlessly, and the young wife turned her face to the wall and burst into tears; no summer shower, refreshing and restful, but a storm of anger, and hurrying, vehement agitation, exhaustive to mind and body.

The gentleman stood looking at her, not knowing what to do or say, filled with consternation and trouble. Perdita with dishevelled hair was a wonderful picture—such masses of inky blackness as enclouded her! such a slender girl as she looked in the abandonment of her passion! He could have clasped her little waist in his two hands almost; and, really fond as he was of Bettine, he would rather have held her sister in his embrace than the small fairy. If Perdita must weep, *his breast* was such a safe rest, and his heart beat below it full of sympathy.

He remembered acutely this scene at the stair-head afterwards; he recalled it when their lives were running in such strange channels that it seemed impossible they could ever meet again in an even flow.

Betty dried her tears at the sight of Perdita's emotion, and whispered in Mr. Slaughton's ear :

"Tell her not to mind. Poor Perdita! I don't want her to feel bad. I'd rather Cicely kept them, if she won't cry."

It was not long before Perdita came to herself, and dashing away her passion, she said in a low voice, still tremulous and a little broken.

"You know Malcolm gave her those rabbits, and you know how she doted on them. Now your mother has taken out the pair she thought the most of, and given them to Cicely Vance —a piece of arbitrary oppression and injustice I will not bear! She may treat me as she likes, but I will not see my Betty wronged."

"It is atrocious! abominable! I shall go instantly and insist upon restitution, and I shall speak my mind."

"Pray stay," answered Perdita quickly. "Do not interfere in any way; do not add to my mortification the knowledge that I have procured a quarrel between mother and son. Whatever may have been your motive for the course you have pursued, it has been wise. You have not interested yourself in my situation towards her. You have kept silence when there has been a chance of discussion. And I beg you will not break through your line of conduct. I can manage for myself to-day as well as I have other times. I feel I have been violent, raging. I don't know if I said anything rude—I hope not. If I have, pray overlook and forget it.

She gathered up her tresses, and as she met his eyes, she straightened herself, tall, proud, defiant.

"What do I care if he does hate black hair?" she thought. Then, remembering what a stormy fury she must have looked, she tried to feel angry and indifferent. "A housekeeper and governess has a right to wear such looks as suit her, so she attends to her duties." "But," she added aloud, "right is right, and Betty is mine; I must look out for her."

"And mine too," added Mr. Slaughton. She recalled his

look and tone afterwards, and felt how blind she must have been not to understand him.

"Uncle Sam," said the mite in her sweet, clear voice, "let Cicely keep the rabbits. I don't want them any more; I could not have good times with them. I should always remember how Perdita cried, and how troubled you looked. I don't want Cicely's grandma to be angry with my Perdita. Only tell me, good Uncle Sam, am I truly your little Betty—truly—not make believe?"

"You belong to your sister, and as much to me as she will permit."

"Have I a right to stay here, in your house? This *is* your house, isn't it?"

"Why yes, I suppose it is; and what is mine is thine, my pretty Bettine—house, land, dolly, playthings, and all. This is your home."

"I am so glad. I did want a part of their grandma, but Cicely said I shouldn't have any. They may keep her now. I have got a true Uncle Sam. She says she can't bear me. You don't think I am stingy, do you? You won't let them starve my rabbits, will you?"

"She is getting some life-lessons, you perceive," said Perdita, "and she has taught me one. Pray do not say anything about this. Betty and I can afford to lose her pets, if we can learn to keep our tempers."

The storm was all cleared off her face, which was bright, smiling, and friendly. The gentleman breathed a sigh of relief —matters had so arranged themselves that no interference was necessary. I don't suppose he could help feeling glad that he was excused from coming to the fore. No man likes to fall out with his mother. All men love peace at home, and Mr. Slaughton certainly did not the less admire his young wife because she refused to set him at odds with the dame, who was likely to say quite a number of very disagreeable things; and a family broil must interrupt and destroy the flavor of all the quiet pleasures he was getting fond of. Little Betty came in for a share of his satisfaction ; she had behaved well. Children who " give up" are admired by most men ; they save so much trouble. Right *ought* to prevail ; but if it won't, and the injured parties are peaceable under wrong, they are to be commended—they have " good dispositions."

As for the old lady, she braced herself in vain for a battle which failed to come off. Her exploits were not commented on, the transfer of Betty's property being taken as matter of course.

------◆------

CHAPTER XLVIII.

" UNDER THE TUB THE SLIPPER GOES."

HE Vances had not been long under the care of the new governess before she discovered that the one ruling passion of the eldest was finery, and also that her ideas of meum and tuum were obscure. Lying was a venial sin ; so she had been taught in her convent by precept and example. It could be atoned for by a slight penance, and no harm done. Therefore, Cicely not only paid no heed to the truth, but it really seemed as if she lied for exciting amusement, as children run swiftly over a narrow plank, in constant danger of a plunge into the brook below, counting their escapes.

Perdita made another unpleasant discovery. No bureau, no press, no box or basket was safe from her meddling fingers ; and after she had caught her pilfering from everybody's belongings,

she concluded that she must either keep everything in the
house locked, or allow the girl to grow up a confirmed thief.

She puzzled much over this trouble, and could not account
for it on the score of blood, because the other two, full of
mischief and wild as deer, were true and honest. Pandora,
especially, was frank and brave to a fault.

Remembering what Mr. Slaughton had said to his mother,
the day the children had arrived, she concluded that Cicely
had inherited all the Vance proclivities, or that she was spoiled
by her education, viz.: "The end justifies the means"—eaves-
dropping, fibs, and the like being permitted as necessary and
excusable under certain circumstances.

Cicely had a pair of clumsy boots, whose ugliness was a
sore trial to her. She, like many fine ladies, preferred wetting
her feet to protecting them in such stout shoes as would make
them look large. When the journals are spreading the important fact that a certain woman of fashion wears ones, the size
of the female foot assumes an importance which takes pre-
cedence of virtues.

Cicely neglected no opportunity of dodging the hated boots
and getting on the slippers or kid ones which belonged to
holiday attire. She could not have gotten much comfort out
of their wearing, either, because she was obliged to go crouching about to keep them out of sight, and was always obliged
to remove them as soon as discovered. The dame scolded,
and boxed her ears, and the child shed many tears and did an
immense deal of pouting.

One Saturday afternoon in January, a walk down to the
village, including prunes and figs at the store, was the reward
of good lessons. All were delighted, especially as the young
Hethwaites were to be of the party.

The weather was fine and clear, and the roads smooth;
no snow had fallen, and everything was frozen.

Cicely Vance came down rather late; she was dressed in
her best, and had on her feet a pair of red morocco ties, which

she tried to conceal by keeping behind the others till they should be under way, in which case she felt almost sure of being allowed to go. Amusements fairly earned by good lessons were always permitted by the governess, irrespective of conduct.

Cicely meant to walk with Malcolm, and converse as the young ladies did in her convent. She felt that if she could only get a real love-letter from a boy, she should be happy. As love-letters and secret meetings had been much talked of among the girls who were her patterns, that was only natural.

As Perdita looked over her charges with particular care before starting, she discovered the red shoes, which no crouching could hide.

"Why, Cicely! You must not go out of the house in those things. You will get your death-cold, besides looking like a circus-rider. The idea of a thick woollen cloak and low crimson ties with rosettes! Well, child, I really hope I shall live to see what you will wear when you get into things of your own choosing. Run upstairs and button on your heavy shoes, do?"

"I can't find them, aunty, I've hunted everywhere."

"Can't find them! when you had them on only two hours ago! Don't tell that nonsense. Run, I say—directly. You keep us waiting."

"But they are not there, aunty. I looked in the closet, and under the bed, and all around; somebody must have taken them away. I believe the dog has carried them off."

"Don't try to make him accountable for your doings. You know very well that you have put them out of sight."

"I haven't. I guess I know what I do," answered the girl, dropping her under-lip and going slowly and unwillingly upstairs.

Pretty soon she returned. "I cannot find them; so there, now!"

Perdita ran up herself, and turned everything over about the room and clothes-press; they were nowhere to be seen.

"Cicely," said she, when she came down, "I think you have hidden your shoes because you did not want to wear them. I don't believe it is Scamp's mischief."

"Well it is not mine, then, aunty, just as true as I live and breathe; I hope to drop down dead, if it is."

As the girl reeled off the phrase so common among chi'dren, her eyes deepened and her color paled for an instant; sh·was recalling the history of Ananias and Sapphira, which she had been made to commit about a week before, as a gentle reminder of the possible consequence of an aberration from truth in which she had indulged.

Mr. Slaughton was standing by the fire, watching the antics of the children, wondering discontentedly why Perdita would go off with them, when she might stop at home, where he could see her; and of course he heard the whole conversation.

"Have you perfect faith in her word?" asked he in a low voice, while Cicely was upstairs.

It was a sure indication of his change of feeling towards his wife, that he could never refrain from meddling in her affairs, asking questions and offering suggestions; quite different was this appearance of interest from the high and mighty indifference he paraded on the wedding-day.

"Oh, yes," replied Perdita in the same tone. "I have faith that she will utter a falsehood every time she opens her mouth."

"I wonder you don't get musical, and *strike* the *liar*."

"What! such a harp of a thousand strings—not one of which I can control? I've done my best to bring the instrument up to concert pitch, but as yet I have hit upon no method of tuning which will produce anything except jarring discords."

Bertram was the last to come in. "Oho, Cis!" exclaimed he. "So you *have* got on your red shoes, after all."

15

"After all what?" asked Perdita. "Do you know anything about her others?"

"I know she hates to wear them. You know that too."

"But can you tell me where they may be found? Cicely says they are lost."

"Does she? Well, you need not look at me, Aunt Perdita. I'm not going to tell on her. I only thought I'd plague her a little. She burnt up my top this morning."

"But, Bertram, if you know——"

"Now, Aunt Perdita, you hate tell-tales; you said you did."

Perdita was too near childhood herself to push the lad into betraying his sister; so she let the matter drop, trusting to her own sharpness to ferret out the truth.

"You will have to wear your kid boots for aught I see," said she to Cicely. "It is a pity, because you will probably cut them on the frozen road. I shall not forbid your holiday. You have earned it; though I believe you are acting dishonestly."

"How, aunty?" inquired Cicely, meeting Perdita's eyes with an unfaltering look. "I really don't know how you can say so! You will find out that Scamp is to blame, not I; what for should I go to wet my feet?"

"I don't see why you can't send somebody with those children," said Mr. Slaughton decidedly. "I have nothing whatever to do, and it would be so nice and still in the library, with all that noise out of the house."

"Suppose you were to come along, and get an appetite for the pressed chicken we are to have for supper."

"Take a walk with these nine small children! No, thank you, I don't care about appearing in public as John Rogers. If you will cut the duty trip, I will escort you to the mill, or the summit, or anywhere you say."

"Impossible, sir! Desert my post, and leave my charges to run wild? Impossible!"

"You are always chatting and laughing with these romping

things. I wonder if I shouldn't fare better if I were to rid the house of the whole brood? then perhaps you would attend to other people."

"Please wish me a pleasant afternoon before I go," she replied as she tripped down the steps.

She had a remarkably pleasant walk; she felt in cheerful mood—quite buoyant, in fact; it might have been the bracing air. Of course the last words of the man she had left behind had nothing to do with her light heart, nor the picture she had of him in her mind standing in the door and looking after her.

Oh, yes, Perdita enjoyed that walk, notwithstanding her trouble about Cicely, and the puzzle she was. Although confident that she had cheated and lied for a beginning of this party of pleasure, she found her as gleeful and unconscious as a young animal. Her spirits rose as soon as she felt herself safe, and she giggled, and was "so affecshunut" to aunty, and boisterous with the others. The exercise and keen, frosty breeze made a breathing carnation of her, a resplendent creature surpassing all brilliant flowers in coloring.

"Can it be," reflected the governess, "that there are human bodies possessing all senses, all powers of volition and choice, but which are not inhabited by human souls? having no conscience, no love of right, no hatred of wrong; incapable of sorrow for sin, of remorse; not able to be glad and strong by inward goodness; ruled by fear, as a dog is by a whip; never impelled by love, or benevolence, or generosity, or magnanimity; merely up-standing animals, gifted with speech—as inconsequent and unguidable as singing mice."

She listened to the stream of prattle which Cicely poured out incessantly, and to her empty, frivolous, discordant laughter; observed the skippings and antics which were the overflow of abundant vigor, the sportfulness of a kitten, or a little pig, which kicks up its heels and cries "que que."

And yet the girl had the most wonderful memory, ready and retentive, which enabled her to commit whole pages with a single reading. She was fond of playing with dolls, and would imagine and rehearse scenes full of horrors—murders, dungeons, penances, confessions, and tricks, so replete with strange imaginations that it made the listener's blood creep sometimes.

She would dress the dolls from anybody's store she could get at, and she would use anybody's dolls without leave. After her game was ended she generally flitted off, never replacing what she had taken ; seeming to have no dread of consequences —no care to conceal her depredations.

Thus far Perdita had failed to find the key to Cicely's being —she had not discovered any chain of affinity by which to attach her, had never kindled any glow of rapture for duties well done, or repentance for faults. The other children were little sinners, but they felt desirous to be good and merit approval ; they expressed and acted contrition. Cicely never manifested either. Fear she showed of such abject sort as to be revolting ; her dread of punishment was strong ; tears were plenty, promises abundant ; and the instant the pressure was lifted, the danger averted, the kiss of peace obtained, she was all giggles, roses, and dimples, " so affecshunut," and then instantly followed some request, evidently taking the soft, tender mood of her aunt as the proper time to obtain some coveted gaud, some of the goodies of which she was greedily fond.

"Aunty, will you buy me a new hair ribbon ? Aunty, may I have some seed-cakes? Will you give me a dime to buy *liquish ?*"

Perdita had met a rock of stumbling which she found it impossible to surmount or get around; and the notion she had entertained that all children who were kindly and carefully reared must be true and honest, seemed to prove entirely untenable. She began to think a good deal of blood, after all, and to agree with Mr. Slaughton that the Vance inheritance was to blame, and her father's old saying, " Blood will tell," had a meaning and force she more and more understood.

Cicely managed to start off with Malcolm, following her intention to get him for her sweetheart.

"Why don't you come up on purpose to see *me*?" asked she tenderly.

"Can't! I'm busy," replied the lad, striding on with such busy steps that he quite outstripped her.

"You don't seem to make much headway with Malcolm," laughed Dolly. "I don't believe he will turn out just the kind of beau you want; he's as short as pie-crust, isn't he?"

Cicely had two exclamations which served her for all occasions: "I dunno," and "I don't care." The latter did duty this time, and she pranced off as free from mortification, trouble, responsibility, or guilt, as are the lambs who kick up their innocent heels in the pasture.

Perdita saw all this; she pondered it; but she enjoyed her walk. Cicely Vance could not spoil her pleasure that day.

CHAPTER XLIX.

STRATUM SUPER STRATUM.

T was several days afterwards that Perdita found a hiatus of leisure among her duties, and she determined to set about the sheets which the dame desired to have turned.

The key was the same with which she had let Pandora out of the studio, and as she mounted the stairs, she was thinking about the pictures the little mischief had helped her to a sight of, and of Mrs. Richard Pritchard's visit, and of how her husband had behaved to her then and since; so that she had entered the store-room and begun to turn over the sheets before she recollected that she had not used her key, having found the door ajar ; and as she was wondering how it could have happened, she neared the bottom of the chest, and with the last bundle pulled something out upon the floor—Cicely's shoes !

Leaving all, she ran swiftly down to the school-room, and, taking the girl by the arm, without saying a word, she led her out into the hall.

Being a physical coward by nature, and having been taught in her convent to bend to force, Cicely did not attempt to break away ; but she followed with a disturbed, affrighted face and unwilling steps, till they reached the attic stairs. There all her roses left her cheeks, and the sudden consciousness which leaped into her eyes showed that she understood the why and where of her journey. Then she resisted the firm grip which held her with all her might.

" Let me loose, aunty.   I don't want to go up there."

" It is no question of what you want, but of what I will and you shall," replied Perdita, pouring the steady rays of her black eyes straight into the retreating blue ones.   " Come on ! "

The strength and purpose in the captor conquered, and the girl let herself be dragged to the store-room, such a dazzling, fair culprit as was never seen there before.

" Now, tell me," said Perdita, pointing to the shoes, " why did you put them there ? "

Cicely threw around her such a despairing gaze as might be cast by the sinners who cry out for the rocks and mountains to fall on them and hide their guilt.   Overtaken by justice, she dropped on her knees (another habit of her convent life), and clasped her hands.

" I didn't like to wear them, aunty, they are so big.   I won't never do so again ; forgive me this time."

" Do you know what it says in the Bible about liars ? " asked the young judge sternly.

" Not in particular, aunty," she replied, turning pale.

" Come to my room instantly and find out."

No time was lost between the sentence and its execution, and in another-minute Cicely was seated in a chair with a Testament in her hands.

" Now read aloud the verses ! " commanded the judge.

Cicely began the sentence in Revelations which appoints the society and state of all liars, and before she finished, rich crimson flooded her face again, mounting and mounting in her creamy cheeks ; and there was such a strange, baleful glitter in her eyes as she lifted them, that Perdita positively shuddered. She tried to fathom the emotion beneath this resplendent brilliance. Was it fear ? was it remorse ? Or could it be revenge ?

" Do you like the company of that sort of people, Cicely ? " asked she.

" No, aunty. Oh, I am so sorry ! I'll wear the shoes to meeting next Sunday for a penance," cried the girl, dropping her face into her beautifully-formed, clammy hands, weeping bitterly, and convulsed with sobs. " Only forgive me ! "

" You go on the road you are treading now, and you'll land among them, no matter how you shoe your feet, just as sure as the Bible is true."

The abject abasement of the sinner was so complete, her tears so copious, her sighs so profound, her promises so profuse, that Perdita felt hope kindle within her. " At last I have touched a tender spot ! " she thought ; " I have found a human soul ! " And a vision of better things dawned on her.

It was with real womanly sympathy that she took the penitent to her arms, and wiped away her tears, comforting her with good words which flowed warm and glowing from her upright heart. It was akin to the joy of the angels over one sinner who repenteth.

When she put her softly away, with gentle elder-sister touch, and stooped to pick up the sheets, the girl asked a question.

Every trace of grief had disappeared, except the gorgeous coloring, and the melting softness which moistened her eyes, and she tossed off the long flaxen curls which floated over her head, and this was what she said :

"Aunty, will you buy me a new scarf for my white poplin?"

Perdita stopped in the doorway and looked back at her.

"Yes! wherefore not? Butterflies should be gaudy; bask and flutter to-day, for to-morrow you die."

CHAPTER L.

BEAUTY AND THE BEAST.

"THERE'S a man down-stairs that wants to see you, sir," said Hannah, putting her head into the half open door of the studio. "Sharp, he says his name is."

"Ah, yes, my horse-dealing friend," replied Mr. Slaughton; "say I will be with him directly."

"I heerd you wanted a hoss, Square," said Sharp, when the artist appeared. "I've got the likeliest lot of Western horses I ever had. I'll sell 'em cheap, dog cheap! It'll be some time afore there's much fodder, and I don't want to keep 'em on nohow. I've made up my mind to sell right off, and I'll give you a first-rate bargain. I fetched up a pair of roaders for you to look at ; bright bay, no white about 'em nowheres ; warranted sound and kind. I don't never take no stock in white-footed horses. You know the old saying, Square :

"'One white foot, try him ; two white feet, fly him ;
Three white feet, look about him ; four white feet, do without him ;
Four white feet and one white nose,
Take off his hide and give him to the crows.

I think there's a good deal in it, sure as you're born. There, now! that team ain't fixed up a mite; I don't jockey, Square. I ain't one of them fellars that'll whale a hoss in the stable, to make him look lively when he's fetched out. I don't feed 'em no drugs. You see 'em jest as they be; no better, no wuss. I hain't speeded 'em no great, neither; but I know they'll pull in a load of hay about as square as any team you can start. You jest put your silver fixins onto 'em and hitch 'em to your kerridge, and you'll find they'll look about X, that's my opinion."

Mr. Slaughton took an instant liking to the pair; they were handsome creatures, well-built, bright-eyed, good steppers, full of spirit, and obedient to the voice; they were not a perfect match. Every horse lover knows how nearly impossible it is to get a *perfect* match. If size and color suit, there is sure to be a difference in speed, or temper, or something.

I know a man who paid a hundred dollars to get four ears exactly the same size in his carriage pair, and I consider his money well spent. When a person has got to sit behind a span of horses every day, he soon knows every inch of them, and a blemish gets to be unbearable. Besides, good horses are such kind, reliable friends, and one does not like to feel imperfections in one's darlings. I am a full believer in the immortality of animals. It seems to me heaven would scarcely be paradise without fleet, gay horses; how are children to be content without faithful dogs? and the houses not made with hands should have purring cats to make their comfort complete.

Meantime, Mr. Slaughton had struck a bargain, and was become owner of the roaders. He considered his investment as an experiment, from which he hoped for a good result.

Thus far, Perdita had steadily refused to accept a place in the family carriage, and preferred walking to church as well as everywhere else.

Her reason was a childish one, but it was sufficient to make her persist in a resolution she had taken.

15*

Before she had been long at the mansion-house the dame ordered out the vehicle to carry her to the village ; and as she was putting on her wraps, she said to her daughter-in-law :

"Mebbe you'd like to go along, you haven't ever been used to many rides ; I expect it will be quite a treat to you."

Samuel Slaughton, who was to drive, stood by the table and heard the remark, and to Perdita's mind he appeared to coincide in his mother's opinions. It seems too paltry a thing to be treasured up for resentment—perhaps it was the truth of the statement which made it rankle so ; but nothing would have induced her to accept a place after that, and to make it worse, Mr. Slaughton once offered her Slowgo's escort, when she wanted to collect leaves.

It had seemed quite right and proper for him at that epoch, but he would be ashamed to repeat his proposition now.

The time had come when he wanted his girl-wife's company ; he wanted it all to himself, and he meant to have an establishment fit to offer her. He anticipated some trouble before she would consent to sit by his side of her own will ; and he looked for a good deal of exhilarating interest in process of the negotiations ; but he hoped for a favorable result. And while he patted the handsome beasts as they were led off, he was thinking of Perdita ; how she would look, what she might say ; what bright sparkle, what smart quips and biting speeches he should hear, when he brought her to look at his turnout, and begged her to take the first place in the elegant new carriage, which no other woman had ever occupied, nor ever should occupy, if she accepted. If—aye, there came a point to think of, a theme to study.

After the money was paid, Mr. Slaughton, who had been examining the animal the trader had ridden over (a coal-black, with a tail which swept the ground), asked him what he wanted for his saddle-horse.

"Oh, Square ! I don't dast to sell that critter ; to tell you the unvarnished truth, I couldn't warrant him. He ain't noth-

ing but a colt, and as wild as the devil ; if anybody should git
hurt by him I should feel to blame. I ain't afeard of him myself, 'cause I know his tricks ; he'll buck, he'll kick, he'll run,
he'll shy.; there ain't much a hoss can do but what he's up to ;
but he kinder knows me, and we git along fustrate."

"Full of accomplishments !" replied Mr. Slaughton, laughing ; "but I've got a kicking mule in the stable that I'll warrant every time. How will you trade ? "

"Oh, a swap ? Well, I don't know ; let's see your mule."

"Don't get too near his heels !" exclaimed Mr. Slaughton
when Loppy was led out ; "he never gives much warning."

"I'll resk him, though they do say a mule 'll wait ten years
for a chance to kill a man, and drap him at last. Good-sized
fellar, ain't he ? "

"He would be a very valuable animal if he could be broken
of his vile trick. *I'm* rather out of conceit of him."

"Law ! Square, it's their make-up ; they will express their
feelin's with their heels, jest as sure as a minister makes jesters
with his hands ; you must take both sorts as they be. I had a
neighbor that used to heave a billet of wood at hissen every
time he brayed ; that didn't do, and so he tied a block to his
tail, but jest as soon as he took it off, away he went again as
musical as ever ; tain't no use to go agin natur. Wall, if you'll
say a hundred to boot, you may hev the colt, as you seem to
hev took a notion to him. I ain't noways particular."

"A hundred dollars ! Oh, no ; I couldn't afford to make such
a loss. I paid five, but I'll give you fifty."

"Wa'll, it's a trade, Square ; you acted like a gentleman
about the roaders, and I ain't goin' to be mean. I want a
good, strong mule to break up my faller piece, and I'll put this
customer into it. I hate to part with the colt, too ; him and me
we've had some nip and tuck times. I should feel queer to
back a hoss that hadn't got no spice into him ; he'll make a
likely one, if he gits well broke ; he's kind, for all his obstrop-
olousness. The neighbors give him an awful name, and he does

hate the women ; he'll peel his teeth jest the minute he sits eyes on a petticoat ; he acts as if he wanted to stomp on 'em. I tell you so as you'll be on your guard ; 'tain't safe to let any of your women folks go nigh him."

" Forewarned, forearmed ; that's fair, Sharp. Here's your money."

"Thank you. Sharp's my name ; but that don't make no difference, Square. I've heard tell a good deal about your Ayreshire bull ; they say he's a real beauty. I wish you'd let me take a look at him, I think a heap of good stock."

Like all gentlemen who spend money on cattle, Mr. Slaughton felt immensely pleased with the reputation of his Ayreshire ; and he led the way to the paddock, leaving the mule hitched, all ready for a transfer of the colt's saddle to his back when they should return.

Perdita had been watching them from her window, had observed the purchase of the span ; and while her husband stepped about here and there, she had looked at him with complaisance, which almost amounted to admiration. His business among the steeds reminded her of the praises he had bestowed upon Sabrina Bradshaw in the never-to-be-forgotten talk beneath her window; and a sudden desire seized her to ascertain whether there was but one woman in the world worthy of such lavish commendations.

" If I were once on that creature's back, I could ride as fast as he could run, I suppose," said she aloud ; " I'll try it."

The spring was flitting into May, and the day was warm and sunny enough to make the crocus flaunt and the grass grow green in sheltered spots, and the soft south wind kissed her cheeks and coaxed her forth. She leaned on the window-sill, idly dreaming, wishing she could enjoy such pleasure as ladies had who owned prancing jennets and went hawking, when a whinney from the colt fixed her thoughts on him. He looked quiet enough, with his head down ; she had not heard the fearful character which had been given him by his master, and it

appeared the easiest thing in the world to spring on his back
and gallop away—just a little turn to make sure she was able
to do it, while she had an opportunity.

She hurriedly descended the stairs, and running down the
walk she stepped upon the block, close to the animal's head.
Seeing her arrive so suddenly, he pricked up his ears and eyed
her keenly, then laid them flat, drew back his lips, and began
to snort, pulling with all his might at the tie-rein. As it was
buckled about his neck and fastened in a strong knot, he gave
up trying to get away, and reared on his hind legs as if he would
like to trample on her.

She walked quietly past him, keeping out of his reach, singing softly to herself, while she gathered some tender grass,
which she offered him, going close to his head, and taking him
firmly by the bit.

He showed her the whites of his eyes, and tried the strength
of her grip. Finding it steady, he ceased pulling, and treated
her to a few more snorts, a couple of jumps, and then stopped
to see how she liked him.

She smiled, and extended to him the grass she held in her
fist.

"Come, try it, there's a dear fellow! it's very good, it's sweet,
it's fresh, I plucked it for you ; the dew is scarcely off it ; come,
come, let's be good friends. Give me just one little ride on
your back, you handsome thing, do !"

Whether it was her soft voice, caressing and musical, her
fearlessness, her beauty, her resolute eyes, her magnetic touch,
or the temptation of the green blades she offered, or all together,
the colt changed his mind gradually, darting back a good many
times, just as he seemed settled to amicable relations. Finally
he opened his lips and took in the appetizing morsel, and very
gently too, as if not wishing to hurt the little hand which held it.

While he ate, she patted his neck, crooning praises of his
symmetry and strength, as if she were weaving a charm. He
fidgeted when she removed her touch, and nervously watched

her motions while she stooped again, gathering a fresh supply
of temptation ; but he put both his small ears forward in pleased
expectancy, and could hardly wait till she came again, and this
time he took eagerly the treat, just seizing it; and then Perdita
made a basket of her apron and filled it, seeking under the
walls and in all sheltered places for the best ; and she stood
with one arm around his neck while he ate, and her face close
to his sleek head, as if rounding her spell.

She almost forgot to be afraid, and he had no longer any
dread of her. Then she undid his halter, and sprang upon his
back. It was a liberty he had not anticipated, and he curveted
and backed and pranced sideways. The rider trembled
slightly ; he was not a very high horse, but she felt as lifted in
the air. She looked resolute and determined as she gathered
the reins in a firm grasp, and pressed her knee close to his
side. She knew she must cling for dear life now, or be dashed
to the ground. Instinct taught her the sure seat—supple,
swaying to the animal's motions, watchful, wary, as if they were
of her own volition. The praise her husband had bestowed on
Sabrina Bradshaw, the beautiful rider, inspired her ; and she
meant to ascertain whether she was not able to be Perdita, the
beautiful rider.

The kicking mule Loppy had observed the rise and progress
of the acquaintance with bitter envy. The doctrine so full
of contentment to pious souls, "Some vessels to honor, and
some to dishonor, according to the pleasure of the potter," did
not console him. *He* wanted fresh grass ; *he* liked petting ;
and as the new friends dashed past him, he tossed up his heels,
and gave out a terrific heehaw, which sent the colt flying, and
startled his rider, sending the hot blood leaping through her
veins like a battle-cry of freedom.

When Mr. Slaughton and the trader returned from their survey
of the Ayreshire, which had extended to an examination of the
Southdowns and black pigs, they were astonished to find only
Loppy at the hitching-post, flapping his long ears, and rumi-

nating on the unkind partiality of fate, which had doomed him to hardship. "Oh, wherefore am I Loppy?" was the sad refrain of his plaint.

"Your accomplished colt has the trick of slipping his halter in addition to his other excellencies. Well, you made up such a catalogue, that I can't blame your leaving it out," said Mr. Slaughton, laughing.

"My God!" exclaimed the trader, under his breath. He had been looking down the road, shading his face with his hand, and had not heard a word the gentleman said. "My God! she's a dead woman, whoever she is; no female can ever do it and live! Heaven have mercy on her soul; for she's going to be dashed to atoms! There! there she goes! she's off! no, she ain't! well, I vum!"

Mr. Slaughton wheeled swiftly and gazed in the direction of Sharp's pointing finger, and the sight he saw curdled the blood in his veins.

Perdita on the colt, who reared high in the air; so high that only a little pull on the reins must make him fall backwards. How could she help pulling? How could he help falling?

She leaned so close to his neck that her long hair mingled with his jetty mane; and tapping his shoulder a couple of times with an apple-branch she carried, she recovered her seat easily as soon as his feet touched the ground. The two men scarcely breathed while their eager gaze followed her, swaying to his sudden springs, bending to his mad leaps, almost crouching with bowed head and curbed chin; so intent, so alert, so watchful, that the beast felt her his conqueror, he owned it, and submitted to her rule. They saw her strike him several smart cuts as he wheeled and backed, hating to give up, and putting himself through all the motions he knew to be rid of her; and they heard her voice, clear, vibrating, musical, no tremor in it, no fear, not even shrillness, but full of will and power.

The gentleman and the trader were both ardent horse lovers, and they exchanged glances.

"By Jove !" said Sam, under his breath, "she's training the beast, actually training him ; and he knows it."

"That's so, Square, just as sure as you're born. Well, I vum'! Carry me out any bury me decent. I'm as limp as a rag."

Before many minutes the young rider came cantering lightly down the road, and drew rein at the landing-stone, where Loppy was the first to signal their arrival, giving out a jubilant "heehaw."

Mr. Slaughton's eyes were full of tears as he looked at the slender girl, who had dared such peril and had come out of it safely, whose bosom heaved with the full inhalations of her panting breath, whose black eyes sparkled, whose cheeks and lips glowed crimson red, whose long tresses mantled her like Godiva's.

"Perdita !" said he reproachfully. It was the very first time he had ever called her by that name, and a thrill went through her at the unexpected, unfamiliar salutation, and its tone of alarmed tenderness ; but she motioned him aside when he put out his arms to help her dismount, and sprang unaided to the ground, keeping her hold of the colt, who turned his head sniffing her garments, putting his nose on her hand and looking at her, while his sides were covered with white foam and his inflated nostrils showed their ruby lining.

"Some more grass, Beauty ? Indeed, you shall have it, for it is fairly earned."

Mr. Slaughton kept his eyes on her while she pulled the tender green and tucked it between the colt's lips.

"Well, ma'am," said Mr. Sharp, "there isn't a female woman breathin' this here minnit that had a better chance of going to glory than you've took this last hour ! Why, ma'am, I'd no more a let you mount that critter than I'd a stuck my arm into an oven full of kindling wood, all a fire for the Saturday's baking ! If I hadn't a seen it with my two eyes I wouldn't a believed it ! If any man had a told me, I'd a said, 'No sir-ee ; it's a lie, sir ; it can't be done, sir !' That's what

I'd a said, and I'd a stuck to it. Why, all the folks are afeard
of that colt. I never get onto him myself but I know I've a
fustrate chance to break my neck and make Susan Sharp a
widow; and to think that a slip of a girl, a pretty, young, slim
thing like you, should a fit with him and beat him? I vum, its
tremendous, its amazin'! Just see him, Square! See his nose
to them pinted fingers. If I hadn't just swapped him off for
your kicking mule, I'd a gin him to her right out—I would, by
hokey."

Mr. Slaughton's eyes and thoughts were so intent on his wife
that he scarcely heard the dealer's talk. She was worth
looking at; more richly colored than a Castilian maid, impos-
ing as a queen, clean-limbed as a bayadere, full of womanly
graces; and he had found out that beneath her fresh simplicity
there was pride, power, vivid sensibilities, and perfect truth, and
he was thinking "What if I had lost her? What if her rich, pure
life had been dashed out in this fiery race, and only a cold
corpse left, only mourning and sorrow for hope?" A hard pain
gripped his heart, and his voice trembled when he addressed
her.

"You ran a terrible risk, Perdita."

How pleasant the name sounded on his lips! She had been
in the habit of railing at her father for giving it to her. "Why
must he dub me 'Lost Soul,'" she used to say, "before he finds
out that I am non-elect." Perdita! Never had the word been
syllabled so agreeably in her ears; and she veiled her eyes
beneath their long lashes as she listened to his reproaches.

"How thoughtless! how rash! What wicked daring! And
on that saddle, too; how ever did you keep your seat?"

"I don't know how I did it myself," said she, parting her lips
in an arch smile. "I suppose because I wanted to live. I did
not wish to be brought back here in spoonfuls; but he did get
me off once. I know he laughed in his sleeve, that is, not in his
sleeve at all, because he has not got any; but he was pleased,
and while I lay on the ground he frisked all around me, kick-

ing up his heels in the most abandoned manner ; *that* did not
last long, because I got up as fast as I could.   It seemed every
fling he made he must hit me ; he could have trampled on me
so easily if he had wished."

"How dared you mount him again ?   Who helped you ?"

"I helped myself, sir ; I am not afraid of him, at least, not
much ; and I could not think of giving in to a colt.   I have
heard that my mother's people used to carry the motto, ' Vou-
loir c'est pouvoir,' and besides, I had other motives which would
have made me try again, I think, if I had broken my arm."

A wilful pride and a sort of dainty bravado kindled her face,
which made him smile.

"But how did you catch him ?"

"I caught him with guile and grass," said Perdita, raising
her eyes to his, and laughing lightly ; "and I found this stick
before I mounted.   I did not show it to him ; he was much
surprised when he knew I had it, I assure you."

"But he won't bear the whip !" said Sharp.   "I never think
of striking him !   He tears things all to bits."

"He had to bear it, and you see he does not hate me, do
you, Beauty ?"

"Have you had a vast deal of experience with horses ?"
asked Mr. Slaughton, trying to understand how it could be.

"I never mounted a steed before in my life."

"Jehosophat !" ejaculated the dealer, walking around her,
as if she had been a statue of Courage set up for admiration.
"Well, ma'am !   durned if you ain't the best nateral equestreen
I ever seen.   I'll bet a hundred agin my kickin' mule there
ain't your equal in seven counties !"

"Thank you !" replied Perdita, retreating loftily from his
scrutiny, "you compliment me ; I'll give you this stick with
my blessing, Mr. Slaughton," she added.   "Beauty will obey it
like a magician's wand."

"Well, Square, good day !" said the dealer, who possessed
the sharp penetration such men are often gifted with, and felt

that he was no longer wanted. "Good morning; I wish you prime luck with the roaders. If they get obstropolous, you'd better let her break 'em in for you—haw! haw!"

As he mounted Loppy and trotted down the hill, he felt well pleased with his morning's work, and the startling romance he had gathered for his evening rest at the "Jolly Brothers."

"But Perdita, stay!" called out Mr. Slaughton, looking perturbed and anxious, as if he was uncertain of her, not knowing what feat she might attempt next. "Stay; tell me how you came to venture on such a mad exploit."

"I wished to ascertain for myself whether there was but one woman in the world who could manage a horse, whether all the skill and dash, and fine handling was centered in one only. I think I am very fond of horses, Chandy."

He started as he recognized his own eloquence, and it came back to him from this girl's lips with such mockery as was very confusing and unpleasant.

"You have conquered this animal, Perdita, and you have named him Beauty," said he, almost bashfully. "I wish you would accept him for your own. If you refuse, no one shall ever ride him; he shall be an exempt till he dies."

"Thank you, I can't hold property! You forget that I am a minor; but I will exercise him for you."

"But you won't go running off alone, though. You will permit me to ride with you and take care of you," said Sam, hesitating and blushing like a school-boy.

She looked so distant, so reserved; she remembered so well all the disparaging things he had said of her; that he never asked for her society, or tried to approach her nearly; that his heart did not misgive him, feeling that it was of no use; she would never forget and forgive so as to be friendly and confidential.

Had he been less influenced by these thoughts, less diffident, less modest in his estimate of his ability to please—had he gone on chiding as he had begun, showing himself masterful and determined, she might have yielded to his power and kept back a reply which sharply wounded him.

"Thank you, Mr. Slaughton, you couldn't undertake to teach *me*! You do not wish to play Petruchio to such an Ethiop Kate. I have not forgotten how positively you declined the rôle ; you detest black-browed women ; I do not resemble your ideal more than darkness resembles light. Your very words! at least, you must admit that I have an excellent memory."

She left him and walked up to the house ; but though the opportune moment had arrived when she could send back his sayings with double scorn, the time she had dreamed of and wished for, and she had seized it, she felt ill at ease.

Now that the retort was uttered, and its effect was as over-whelming as ever she could have wished in her bitterest mood, she took no pleasure whatever in recalling it, or the attitude and face of the gentleman she had forced to listen to a speech which all the provocation she had received failed to excuse or palliate.

His dignity and hurt silence made her seem the aggressor, and rude beyond apology.

He had allowed her to leave him without expostulations or entreaties ; he was offended, and she had wilfully and foolishly lost her chance of being his friend ; the pleasant evenings must be interrupted, for of course he would never look complacently at her any more, nor chat, or read, or play to her. No more art talk, no more romance of travel ; she had not felt how really pleasant a pleasure it was, till now that it was a pleasure lost.

She turned to look at him when she reached the door. He stood where she had left him, tapping his boot with the apple-twig she had confided to him.

She wished to go back and say she was sorry, but before she gathered the requisite courage, he leaped upon Beauty and galloped away.

He did not come to dinner ; an errand took him to Toptown.

He had a new carriage to order, and he was so particular in his directions, that he was detained till the last train.

She had the library fire kindled as usual ; she obeyed the order still in force to sit there, but she sat alone. When he came in from the stables he went directly to his room ; and it was with a very sober face that she gathered up her work and shut herself into her own solitude.

CHAPTER LI.

"ONLY HOUSEKEEPER AND GOVERNESS."

HE artist spent much time in his studio, during the days that followed, with its door locked. The landau was not yet sent home, and the new "roaders" had never been harnessed. He said little at table, and came no more to the library. He neglected all opportunities he might have found to make his peace with his wife, to whom he was uniformly polite, but not demonstrative.

She could not have been out of his thoughts for all that. He was trying to paint her picture, with only indifferent success. His remembrance of her face was so diverse, he had seen so many expressions mirrored there, that he failed to bring upon his canvas any single one which satisfied him.

"Only housekeeper and governess," said Perdita to herself ; but she no longer said it with the old pride and positiveness ; what had been a defiance was now a lament.

CHAPTER LII.

"LET NO MAN MOCK ME, FOR I WILL KISS HER."

N a little old brown house, at the foot of the hill, across the brook, lived a family who were in no very good repute amongst the neighbors.

Of the father they said, "his fingers are sticky," and the mother was idle and slatternly; there were stories afloat that missing garments from clothes-lines had been traced to their possession, reclaimed by the strong hand, and the woman threatened with the law if she made any more trouble.

Built against a side hill, the house had two stories in front, and but one in the rear; the door of the upper chamber opening on the ground, which had been in some far-off time leveled into a small yard and planted with old-fashioned flowers.

A few peonies, Johnny-jump-ups, and hollyhocks still bloomed in the ragged, neglected beds, which looked forlorn enough to be the graves of the former owners.

Into the upper room strangers rarely got admittance, and people said it concealed the booty of the marauding expeditions of the Teazles, gathered in their nightly prowlings.

In the fall they bagged the nuts off the hickory trees on the neighboring farms, and the young Batts and the Pratts had to be alert to save any for themselves; so of course the young Batts and Pratts had no good words for the Teazles.

When there was squalling in the hen-coops, people felt pretty sure that Plato Teazle was the fox, and he had more than once been peppered with shot, and mangled in traps.

In fact, if Mr. Teazle had put half the hard labor and industry into any honest calling, which he expended on being a rogue, he might have been a rich man and set traps for rogues himself.

Fortunately, there were but two Teazle children, a boy and a girl, the lad a couple of years older than Cicely Vance, and the girl about her age. The boy was a living confutation of the doctrine of blood, for a more right-meaning, pure-hearted child than this timid, yielding, gentle Randy Teazle, could not have blessed any Christian household.

To the credit of his parents be it said, they never tried to make a thief of him, and seemed afraid or unwilling of laying bare their wickedness to his innocent soul.

The girl Sal was a most degenerate plant of a strange vine as bold, cunning, treacherous, and tricky, as her brother was single-minded and harmless.

She was also what in country parlance is known as a "tomboy," full of health and vigor, fond of climbing, leaping, jumping the rope, and an adept in all out of door sports and games, even to walking on stilts, an accomplishment in which she delighted. No height appalled her, and she would mount in the air on her wooden legs and race over the ground like an ostrich.

With the facile readiness her Bohemian training had taught her, Cicely made their acquaintance during her rambles, and she liked their companionship, because they looked up to her as the little lady from the big house, and submitted easily to her whims and exactions. She especially affected Sal for her nimbleness and agility, qualities of body which were her own to a remarkable degree.

It was not difficult to coax Dolly Hethwaite to play with the Teazles. Poor Dolly! who had only recently been allowed any girl-friends, and who had conceived a violent liking for Cicely Vance.

Cicely had seen many people, Cicely had actually lived in a convent—a thing which seemed almost too strange and wonderful to be true ; and although she soon found that Cicely had a malicious tongue that cut all ways, and though she was made to suffer when it was used to whisper secrets in Sal's ears, which made the whisperer and the listener look at her and laugh, and walk away arm in arm, leaving her alone, she was too glad of companionship to hold anger, even when they connived and plotted to bring her into trouble, as they often did, that they might "have some fun."

One day they were all coming up the road, when Sal discovered a stray cow, with a halter around her neck which dragged after her while she nibbled the short grass at the roadside. Quick as thought the tomboy pranced up and seized the rope, making a captive of the animal.

"Hillo! this is somebody's cow. Now I'll drive her to the pound and get a dollar."

"Yes," said Cicely, flourishing a stick she carried, "we've found her, so we'll pound her ; and that's a good rhyme."

"She seems real gentle, doesn't she ?" remarked Dolly.

"Gentle ! I should say so ! You might ride her as easy as nothing ; come, hop up and try."

"Dolly is afraid ! Dolly dassent !" cried Sal dancing about and making aggravating faces.

"How do you know I dare not ?" said Dolly, the sad romp, who was desperately fond of sport, especially when it smacked of adventure. "I'm not going to be taunted about a cow ! Hold her still ! I'll jump on her back."

Leading the beast to a stump, they all got around her, and up sprang Dolly, laughing till tears ran down her cheeks, to find that the patient creature minded her not at all, but just went on cropping the herbage, stepping as she fed.

"Isn't she fast ? How long do you suppose we shall be going to Jericho ? That's a sum for you, Sal ! Given a road and a cow, what rule do you use to calculate her speed ?" said Dolly.

"You'll soon find out," spoke up Cicely, winking at the others while she clapped her hands and tossed up her hat. Sal following her lead, gave Bossie two or three smart cuts with the rope's end.

Away they went like mad, among the blackberry bushes, and though the rider stuck on pretty well, she finally got tossed head over heels into the briers; and having freed herself from her unkind acquaintances, the cow galloped off in the graceful haste peculiar, it is said, to cows and women.

Miss Vance did not altogether escape either, and her hilarity received a sudden check, for as Dame Milk Pitcher started, she ducked her head, and struck out with her heels, and knocked Cicely backwards, where a cruel rock wounded the fair flesh of her shoulder, and set her screeching out such sharp discords, that Sal ran home, and poor Randy turned quite white, and shook in his ragged shoes.

He helped her up, however, and fetched some water in his hat from the spring across the road, and begged and implored her not to cry.

"Maybe Dolly's killed," whispered he, pointing to the bushes; "she don't make no noise."

A feeling mixed of curiosity and terror soon stilled Cicely, and she seized Randy's dirty hand, and held it hard, while they stepped on tiptoe towards the clump of alders and briers, and peeped in.

"There's her apron," said Cicely, "and there's her face. Yes, I expect she's dead; get down on your knees and touch her; dead folks are cold."

Randy tremblingly obeyed, creeping through the brush and reaching out a quivering finger to the cheek of their playmate, scarcely touching it and jumping back in nervous hurry.

"No, she's warm; Dolly, are you dead?"

Perhaps the human magnetism of the sudden contact aroused her, for she struggled up and began to cry.

"Come, Dolly, here's a good place to get out," pleaded Randy, holding apart the bushes, though the vines wounded

16

him sorely. "Do come! don't be dead! you ain't hurt much, are you?"

"No, I guess not," said she, struggling free from the briers, and shaking herself. "I wonder what it was that happened to me. Everything got black, and went round and round, and then I must have gone to sleep, for I forgot you and the cow and all. Well! I am a nice fright! look at my frock! what a whipping I shall get if father finds this out, and serves me right too; but I do hate to be dared."

"Couldn't your sister fix you up?" asked Randy, who shuddered at the idea of his friend being whipped. "She's real kind to you, I think. Do try to have her."

"What's the matter? what are you so scared about?" replied Dolly recklessly. "I guess you know how it feels to get whipped, don't you?"

"I should rather bear it myself than to have you," said the lad, in a firm, low voice. "I would if I could."

"You really look as if you would!" exclaimed Dolly, full of surprise. "Well, I shouldn't have supposed it possible. I always took you for a coward!"

"Did you? maybe I be. I'm afraid to steal and lie, and I'm afraid to plague folks, if that's what you mean; but if you wanted me to hurt myself for you, I'd do it quick."

"How odd!" said Dolly, looking him over in surprise. "Well, I never! If you'd keep your face and hands clean, what a good-looking boy you'd be, Randy."

"I will keep them clean," answered the lad blushing deep, "as clean as you keep yours. Shall you like me if I do?"

"Yes, I shall so. You are just as good-natured as you can be. I'll lend you my Robinson Crusoe."

"What is that?"

"Don't you know? A beautiful story of a man who got shipwrecked on a desert island, and lived in a hut——"

"I wish you would tell it to me, Dolly," said Randy with dejected face. "I don't know how to read."

" Good gracious ! why don't you go to school and learn ? "

" I hain't got no decent clothes ! "

" Oh, well, don't whimper; if you were a girl, I'd lend you some of mine, that is, if I had any to spare, which I haven't. I wonder if Perdita couldn't do something about it; I'll ask her right away."

" Oh, dear me, how my shoulder aches ! " complained Cicely. " You don't seem to think of me at all, Randy, and I knew you before she did."

" I am very sorry you are hurt, Cicely," said Randy, " very sorry."

" You don't look sorry a bit," replied Cicely, pouting. " I don't care whether you are or not ; you are nobody but Plato Teazle's boy, anyhow, and everybody says he's a thief."

" Cicely, aren't you ashamed of yourself ? Now you've hurt his feelings," exclaimed Dolly gazing after the lad, who ran away as fast as he could without once looking back.

" Who cares about *his* feelings ? " said Cicely crossly. " He needn't make such a fuss over you, then, when I'm in dreadful pain myself."

Cicely's shoulder had to be dressed with half a dozen strips of court-plaster, like a black star on her rosy skin ; and as her grandmother applied them she said :

" I am afraid you have spoiled your best dimple, child. Your neck is shaped just like your mother's ; she had dimples in both shoulders."

" Oh, aunty, do you think I have spoiled mine ? " asked Cicely anxiously.

" No."

" Will this hurt prove serious ? " inquired Mr. Slaughton, who met his wife with her hands full of salves and bandages.

" Not lasting, for her flesh heals as nimbly as that of evil spirits, whose bodies, being cut, do with marvellous celerity come together again," said Perdita with a certain impatience of tone and manner, which made the questioner smile.

" Plato tells us that the air is as full of spirits as of snow-flakes in a January storm, but he does not give them any of their graceful shapes, all spiritual bodies being, according to those ancients, round like the sun and moon. We, however, must believe them able to assume forms at pleasure, many appearing as beautiful women."

" Oh, yes ; and as blue-eyed children, and bulls, and bears, and hyenas, and men who laugh and scoff at all things," replied she briskly, as she stepped away.

"Henceforth, my wooing mind shall be expressed in certain 'yeas' and honest Kersey 'noes,'" said Mr. Slaughton, looking after her. "Ah, Chandy ! If I could but find the way to woo my Perdita as Florizel wooed his. 'Were I crowned the most imperial monarch of earth and heaven and all ; were I the fairest youth that ever made eye swerve ; had force and knowledge more than was ever man's, I would not prize them without her love, for her employ them all, command them or commend them to her service, or to their own perdition.' Your Billy Shakes, my boy, was cunning in lore of women's hearts, but he never saw my Perdita, who belongs only to herself and not at all to me, 'for she was as tender as infancy and grace.' Heigho !"

CHAPTER LIII.

CICELY, THE LITTLE ROSE-BUD.

HE young governess had no idea of teaching caste to her charges, but Dolly's mishap opened her eyes to the necessity of keeping them away from the Teazles; and she exacted a promise of her to leave them entirely alone, and having obtained it, she felt no further uneasiness on the subject.

She did not get it without a protest. "Sal is real funny and smart, Perdita; I don't believe she is so very bad. And as for that Randy, he wouldn't hurt a fly, and he isn't a coward either. I'll promise if you want me to, but I do have such fun playing with them, and I've got to lend Rand a book; I told him I would; though, come to think, he can't read. I wish he could read, Perdita; he can't go to school because he has no decent clothes."

"That seems a pity; I must think about it. I should be glad to help him since he has shown such a kind disposition towards you."

"Do, Perdita; he says he will keep his face clean."

"And cleanliness is next to godliness," replied Perdita smiling. "Truly there is a hope for the boy."

"There is, if *you* conclude to look out for him."

The prohibition acted as an incentive upon Cicely Vance; the acquaintance with the Teazles immediately assumed all the interest of an intrigue; and she set her wits at work to elude and evade, and cheat, and play truant, and plan secret meetings. And she got up a sentimental fondness for the harmless lad, in imitation of a love affair carried on in the convent by one of the lady boarders, which had been most admired among the pupils, who looked on the lady boarder as a great heroine, especially when she was sentenced to bread and water, after being caught tossing a billet from her window.

Cicely longed to achieve such a distinction. She transferred to Randy the attentions Malcolm had flouted at ; she told him she expected to be put into a dungeon and was willing to be a prisoner for his sake, and invented heart-rending tales of the treatment she received at home ; she bit her arm, and showed him the marks of teeth in her flesh ; she pulled out as many hairs as she could bear the pain of, and told him she had been dragged about by her curls.

As the lad listened with lack-lustre countenance to her statements, and offered no remarks, it is impossible to say whether he believed them. Sal being an outrageous liar, perhaps he thought it a vice common to her sex.

When she had arrived at the end of her inventions, he said, in a plaintive voice :

"I wish you would tell Dolly, when you see her, that my face is as clean as hers, and so are my hands."

Perdita overheard Cicely confiding to Pandora and Betty that Randy Teazle was her beau, and that she meant to run off with him some day and get married.

"I'm going to write letters to Rand every day, and he'll send some back. I shall have them enclosed to Dolly, so we shall escape discovery and avoid suspicion."

That was the exact phrase the lady boarder had used, and Cicely liked it so much that she repeated it a dozen times.

As her new occupation took the inconvenient form of pilfering everything she could lay hands on for " dear Randy," it cost Perdita some watchfulness. The lad was not to blame, however, for he rejected her goodies, and rather than see them wasted, Miss Vance shared them with Sal, and "had fun" devouring them.

On her birthday Mrs. Slaughton gave her grand-daughter an album, containing the photographs of her brother and sister. It had handsome gold clasps, and " Cicely Vance " was engraved on the cover.   At this stage of the girl's flirtation, she remembered that an album would be a nice gift to offer to her " beau," so she bestowed it, with a set speech learned out of the " Children of the Abbey," half of which the lad did not understand ; and she showed with much pride the fly-leaf on which she had inscribed the following rhymes :

> " He was a child and I was a child,
>   In a wild place by a river ;
>   And we loved with a love that was more than *love*,
>   Randy and I together.
> " (Signed)   Your Little Rosebud,   CICELY."

" Do you want to give me this book ? " asked the lad.

" Yes, of course.   I bought it on purpose for you."

" What for ? "

" Because you are my beau, you know, and folks always make presents to their beaux."

" There's one thing I should like to have."

" What is it, dear Randy?   Only name it, and it shall be yours."

" I should like to own Dolly's picture.   I think she's as pretty as a pink."

" You shan't have my handsome album, and you shan't be my beau, so there now !" exclaimed Cicely, flouncing off in great rage.   "I hate you, Randy Teazle !"

When she reached home she confided to Pandora that she and Randy had had a quarrel, and she was going to plague him a while before she made up.   " That is the way folks always do," she added ; " it wouldn't be any fun to have a beau if you didn't quarrel with him."

Of course Perdita observed many of Cicely's goings-on, and after some pains to see and notice the lad, she found a glimmer of hope beneath the troublesome evil. She reasoned on this wise : there seems but one chance of salvation for this child. Love may new create her, and endow the irresponsible animal with a human soul ; and as the boy Randy was so harmless and gentle and well-disposed, and, moreover, as he was so good-looking, with his clean face, she began to work in her mind a scheme for legitimatizing Cicely's fondness for him, and turning it to account ; and the more she thought of it, the more disposed she became to propose it to Mr. Slaughton for approval.

She meant to separate Randy as much as possible from his sister Sal and his home influences, and bring him into her school, giving him lessons with her pupils, so fostering whatever good there might be in him and keeping the friendship under her own eye and sanction. She had already reached the point of clothes, when she was disturbed by an event which checked the current of her intentions.

The dame was spending a week with the Brandegees, and Mr. Slaughton was in Toptown, when Cicely came to her on Saturday with her " so affecshunut " manner.

"Aunty, may I go down and see Dolly a little while this afternoon ; she has promised to show me her patch-work."

Perdita felt glad to be asked in a straightforward way, and pleased that the girl did not steal off as she was apt to do ; and she readily consented.

"Don't stay to tea, Cicely," she added, knowing right well how scant welcome there was for unbidden guests at the parsonage, especially children.

Cicely flew upstairs, and presently returned.

"May I wear my baby-blue sash, aunty ? "

"What ! with that dark dress ? Certainly not ! Don't you know such a delicate tint with that common delaine would be horrible taste ? Put on a clean white apron."

Cicely went stamping off with her under-lip down, and Perdita, when she heard her sobbing on the stairs, was almost sorry she had not permitted her to make a figure of herself, since she so much desired it.

In about fifteen minutes she came gayly down, trilling a lay, and wearing such an unmeaning smile that Perdita's suspicions were instantly awake.

"Stop a minute, Cicely," said she, " let me look at you?"

"Oh, don't hinder me, aunty," replied the girl sideling out of the door. " I'm in a hurry."

" But have you got your sash in your pocket, Cicely?"

" No, ma'am," replied the rose-bud, readily turning the receptacle inside out. " There! you see! only my handkerchief. I wouldn't do such a thing, when you told me not to wear it, aunty."

"Are you quite sure you haven't it anywhere about you?"

" Quite sure, aunty. I left it upstairs; I'll run and fetch it, and show it to you," remarked Cicely, moving off with suspicious celerity, as she observed her aunty's keen eyes fixed on the waist of her dress.

"What, then, is this bunch in your bosom?" asked Perdita, approaching a protuberance with her finger; "this, right here? Come, pull it forth and let's see; if it is a swelling, it is dangerous and will have to be lanced."

"Oh! I forgot, I believe I did put it there, after all."

Perdita gazed at her in hopeless amazement; only an animal without conscience; a delicately colored animal much frightened; a tear-shedding animal, ready to pour out floods of sorrow, and repeat the same fault as soon as her back was turned.

"Give me the finery!" said she. " I believe it will one day cost you your soul, if you have any."

"But can't I go to Dolly's, aunty?"

" Yes go, and frisk and kick up your heels; get such enjoyment out of life as you are capable of," said Perdita, turning her back on the culprit. She felt sad and dispirited all the afternoon, as if all her labor had been for naught, and everything was vanity and vexation of spirit.

16*

Night dropped upon the world, but Cicely Vance did not make her appearance.

Malcolm came up to spend the evening, and his sister asked him why he did not bring Cicely along with him.

" I have not seen Cicely," was his surprised answer.

" But she was with Dolly ; you might have seen her, if you had chosen."

"She was not ; Dolly and I have been assorting garden seeds together."

" 'Then she must have run off to the Teazles again," said Perdita in a vexed tone ; "that child will worry my life out."

Mr. Slaughton came in just in time to hear the exclamation ; and though he had not spoken much to his wife since the purchase of Beauty, he stopped to look at her, and inquire what was the matter ; she seemed disturbed and distressed beyond endurance.

The gentleman was a close observer of his young wife's troubles ; but after his offer to send away Cicely, he had not interfered. It was not possible for him to be blind to his mother's partiality for the rose-bud, and its unhappy effects.

In fact, as the girl's character developed under his notice, he felt afraid to send her away, lest she might make shipwreck of her womanhood before she knew its value ; and the more he watched Perdita's right-minded pursuit of her duty in her difficult place, the sorrier he felt that this young girl, only a child herself, should have been thrust into such a complication, through his easiness, from which it seemed impossible to extricate her, and he more and more wished that he had had the sense to woo his wife before he married her.

Stephen, the messenger dispatched to the old house, returned in a rasped state of mind, caused by the treatment he had received there. Cicely was habitually both familiar and insolent with servants.

" Yes, ma'am ! She's there fast enough, and she means to stop there all night. She told me to tell you, ma'am, as how she's not a going to come back up here till she gets ready, and you may help yourself."

Mr. Slaughton kept silence. He was curious to ascertain what course Perdita would take under this provocation. Would she give up to the girl, let her make her threat good, and calmly pass it by when she chose to return?

He was not left long in doubt; for after an instant's gaze in the man's face, she said, " Very well, Stephen, you may go." Then she rose and stepped quickly and firmly up the stairs. Pretty soon he heard her coming down, and she passed the door without looking in. She had on her cloak and hood.

He hurried after her. "Where are you going, Perdita?" he asked with kind solicitude of voice and manner.

" To the Teazles to fetch home Cicely Vance," replied she concisely.

" May I accompany you?"

" If you feel inclined; indeed, as this is certainly as much your business as mine, I think you had better."

It was a rapid walk they took; and not finding his young wife in a conversational humor, her husband smiled in silence at her long steps and rapid progress.

When they arrived, they heard a sound of "revelry by night," and Cicely's cracked voice above all, screaming and laughing. They knocked and got no answer; they tried the door, it was fastened; but Sal Teazle lifted the window just enough to hold parley.

"Cicely is going to stay all night with me! Father and mother are gone, and I'm lonesome."

"Tell her I want her," said Perdita.

" Open the door, please, Cicely; it is your aunt, and she will be so angry; do go with her," pleaded Randy.

" I shall not do any such thing. She won't whip me, and her scolding don't hurt any. I'm in and she's out; let her order till she is tired of it. I won't stir a single step. So there, now!"

"But your uncle will come and there will be trouble. I do wish you would go."

"I shan't, then! Uncle Sam is gone; and so is grandma. I'm glad I can plague the hateful old aunty that wouldn't let me wear my blue sash; maybe I won't ever go back any more."

Before the girl had finished her speech, Perdita turned and laid a hand on Mr. Slaughton's arm. Such a firm grasp as showed that the motion was involuntary, but which set his pulse throbbing; she had never touched him willingly since the day when she placed her fingers in his at the old parsonage.

"Are you strong enough," asked she in a low, intense voice, "to break in this door? If you are not able to do it alone, I will add my strength; the idea of being braved by a child! It is not good for her to leave her here. If it were, I would not suffer it. She *shall* come forth, she shall go with me."

Mr. Slaughton smiled in the midst of his anxieties.

"As she gets stubborn, you become firm, I perceive; and you are right. I don't need any help, I think."

He set his broad shoulder to the door, and it yielded in spite of bolt and lock.

"There!" said he. "How do you like me in my new rôle of house-breaker. Now then, enter."

When Cicely espied her uncle she stopped in the middle of a triumphant joy-dance she had been executing over their supposed victory, and turned as pale as death. She retreated to the farthest corner of the room, an impersonation of cowardice.

Sal stood one moment full of astonishment, bold-eyed and impudent.

"You'll get took up for banging our door down, so you will; and you'll go——"

She did not finish her sentence, for by the time she had got thus far, Mr. Slaughton had advanced and laid his hand on Cicely, who screamed like a maniac.

Sal made a spring for the ground outside, and went and hid among the bushes, where she could hear and see what became of her so late jubilant companion.

Cicely never in her life forgot the feel of those strong fingers; nor the mortal terror which shivered all through her when she found herself a prisoner. It was a good thing to happen to her, though; it restrained her a long while from overt disobedience, and the lecture she got afterwards was so formidable that she was dreadfully afraid of offending Uncle Sam again, and as her cunning taught her that the surest way to please him was to be obedient and sweet to her young governess, she adopted a new line of conduct, which was so transparent as to be amusing, and which was permitted to progress as long as it kept her on her good behavior.

She was "so affecshunut" to aunty, again, and she imitated some fashions she had learned in her convent among the sisters; she made a flourish of kneeling down to kiss the ground which Perdita's foot had pressed; she picked up her skirt and held it to her lips; she ate piously the roses she gave her, and even swallowed the cherry-stones she left from dessert. She watched eagerly all occasions to serve or wait on her. She struck attitudes, and folded her hands, as the sisters used to do before their patron saints; all which harmless performances were not interfered with, though they caused some mirth among the witnesses, and an occasional shudder of disgust in their object.

"I remember what you told me about Sister Josephine. I am afraid you are not more sincere now than you were when you cheated that poor harmless old woman and thought it good fun."

"But oh, aunty! I *do* love you. You are so pretty. She was wrinkled and ugly and horrid! I shall never do anything to displease you again. Never! never! never!"

Each "never" was punctuated by a sounding kiss as loud as

Judas', and Perdita had some trouble to disengage Cicely's rosy white arms from her neck.

"Aunty," asked she, as a wind-up of her passionate caresses, "aunty, will you give me some new hair ribbons ? "

CHAPTER LIV.

"SO HE RODE AND HE RODE ON HIS MILK-WHITE STEED."

HE commotion and the companionship had a good sequence for the young couple, who came into a better understanding and harmony because of it ; insomuch that without any reference to their late estrangement, the pleasant evenings in the library were resumed, the readings and the talks ; and Perdita observed with a satisfaction she did not try to explain to herself, that her husband always addressed her by her name ; and she found it pleasant and friendly in him to do so ; she liked the sound of it.

"Perdita, come out with me this afternoon on Beauty ? " said he, as he tossed away the end of his post-prandial cigar, " I have to ride over the hills and far away, and I shall be glad of your company."

He said it with the most matter-of-fact manner he was able to assume ; but he concealed under it some trepidation ; he feared to disturb again their concord, covetous as he felt of the pleasure he sought.

The young wife flushed, and gave him such a sweet look, that he felt sure of her compliance, and rejoiced at the prospect

before him. A sudden thought obscured her face, shutting
it down under 'shadow, and the eyes which had spoken a glad
" Yes," now looked a positive "No ;" and while he waited
anxiously for her to speak, he felt disheartened and displeased.
But he misunderstood her trouble, which was that she had no
habit, and being obliged to refuse, she did it so ungraciously,
and with such haughty coldness, that he left her without asking
her reasons or entreating her to change her mind.

"The old story," thought he ; "the most manly thing I can
do is to stick to my studio, and leave her alone ; and I'll do it,
by Jove ! I wonder what she thinks I am made of ?"

Mr. Slaughton did not bang the door, but he shut it tight,
dragged himself into his painting jacket, and began to flourish
his brush furiously. His manner said, " I don't care a flip. I
won't care ;" but in his secret heart he did care, and was very
sorry indeed.

The next Saturday she knocked at his door. A light, delicate little touch it was too ; but thunder might have startled
him less, and he sprang up in a mighty hurry to admit her.
There she stood, sure enough ! in a blue habit which fitted
exactly her slender shape ; a round cap, banded with Jack's
many-tinted feathers, and looking very meek and shame-faced.

" Will you come out with me this afternoon for a canter,"
said she. " I have to ride over the hills, and I should be glad of
your company."

She looked in his face, awaiting his answer, and he could not
help smiling at her half humble, half proud demeanor.

" On one condition," he replied shortly.

" And what is that ?"

" You shall tell me truly why you refused me."

" Because I had no habit. I can gallop about by myself in a
short skirt ; but I did not dare to offend your critical taste by
any such *absurdities*."

" Is that the real and only reason ?" asked he earnestly.

" Yes ; and a good, respectable and sufficient reason it is.

If you had not gone off in such a hurry, I could have told you then. I've worked very hard since, and I have made this (spreading her arms and looking down at herself), and I am come the very first hour after it was finished to beg you to forget my rudeness and get a gallop." -

"I am afraid *I* might have seemed a little rude. I really——"

"Yes, you did. I felt that you were not polite ; but I am too well reared to expect politeness from men. So you see I set down your behavior to sex, and don't count it."

Mr. Slaughton was only thirty years old, after all, and his mighty resolutions vanished like mist before the sun ; he reached out and seized both Perdita's hands.

"How long must this state of things last between us two ? " asked he in a quick way. "When will you make up your mind to be kind and friendly, so that I shall not dwell on the edge of a volcano, which may break out any moment and ruin my happiness ? "

"When I can forget how I came to this house, and your reception of me," replied she, drawing back. "A man does not look for much happiness from his housekeeper. You had better leave all unpleasant topics alone, Mr. Slaughton. It is the only way for two people to be comfortable who have so many uncanny things to remember. The past is not dead, but vital and full of bitterness. I don't see how it can ever be forgotten."

Her words were not what he wished to hear, but her face was aglow with blushes, and her voice was tender. He had a good deal to say, and would have said it, *probably*, had not the dame suddenly appeared at the stair-head.

He dropped his wife's hands, and looked as guilty as a bashful lover stealing his first kiss.

"Well ; I never ! What sort of masquerading is this ! " said she, snipping smartly the shears she carried in her hand. "You look as if you was fixed up to ride the monkey's pony in the caravan."

"I am inviting Mr. Slaughton to come out for a canter," replied Perdita, frowning.

"Oh, I want to know! Well, fashions *have* changed since my time, I do believe! When I was young, the ladies waited till the gentlemen invited them; but *we* had something else to do besides gallivanting about, dressed like girls in a May fair, fit to be hooted at by the boys; now anything and everything is proper."

"I am sure my habit is neither absurd nor ridiculous," retorted Perdita, getting red. "It is just as quiet and neat as it can be."

"There speaks the dress-*maker*," said Mr. Slaughton, laughing, "and I fully agree with her; it is a most becoming habit, and I intend to don my velvet jacket and buckskins, that I may do it honor. Come, mother, you shall see us off. You are a judge of horsemanship, and you were a good rider, as I know. I remember often seeing you on your bay mare when I was a little shaver, and a fine figure you made."

"That is true, Sammy! I do seem to forget that I was young. I don't mean to; but I do. Oh, yes, I used to catch the old gray in the pasture, when I was only a little trot, and the hateful creature she would start for the stable door the very minute I got cleverly fixed. She knew it was so low she could just scrape me off when she went in; that was her little joke, you understand. She never wanted to hurt me. Well, go and enjoy yourselves before the evil days come and the hours draw nigh when you shall say, 'I have no pleasure in them.' Yes, go, Perdita, and have a good time."

"Thank you, ma'am," answered Perdita, scanning the old lady curiously, wondering what she was wiping her eyes for.

These spasms of kindness, these lulls in her temper, these occasional struggles to be benevolent and indulgent, which were so short-lived, so frequently disturbed by some burst of injustice or impatience, puzzled her. She could not understand the secret bitterness of the mother, jealous of her only son's affection—an experience, which, strange to say, had not entered into the dame's calculation, when she was so eagerly determined to bring him home a wife ; nor the sour, spiteful disfavor which the aged, whose prime is past, whose capacities are weakened, who are laid on the shelf and superseded in their duties, are apt to feel for the young who have yet to tread the life-road, full of the hopes, vigor and spirits *they* have outlived.

There was yet another moving cause for the dame's growing peevishness ; she looked upon herself as doomed, and was waiting for the summons which one more dream of the white horse would bring her. She had formed a habit of watching her symptoms, trying to calculate the natural probabilities in her case. She observed her appetite, complained of bad sleep ; she swallowed all sorts of drugs, wonderful cures of nature's ills were eagerly tested. She began to be fussy about her diet ; sometimes for a whole week she would touch nothing but bread, or rice, or fish ; she fetched all the water she drank from a certain spring. Doctor books became her favorite reading ; she no longer felt her old satisfaction in driving Slowgo ; she muffled herself in shawls, shrouded her head in hoods, and was troubled with draughts. She went about saying : "Also they shall be afraid of that which is high, and fears shall be in the way ; and the almond tree shall flourish and the grasshopper shall be a burden, because man goeth to his long home, and the mourners go about the streets ;" and she marked with her pencil all the lugubrious passages in her Bible, and wept much in secret.

She found so much fault ; showed such a mean, stingy spirit ; she grudged Perdita leisure, pleasure, everything ; she was so spiteful and unjust to Betty, so partial to Cicely, and did so much general nagging, that the young wife had long ago begun to consider her her enemy ; and in the daily life she found a good measure of firmness necessary to avoid being crushed and sat upon ; and yet once in a while there would crop out some vein of unexpected generosity or kind thoughtfulness, which she found it impossible to understand or reconcile.

As the married pair tripped down the stairs, the dame watched them out of sight before she turned to the store-room she had come to inspect.

"Life is short!" she muttered, with a sigh. "I shall soon go; let me leave this world in charity with all; they won't miss me. Under ground I shall soon be forgotten. Well, I hope they will be happy; they're young and well." Then she relapsed into fretting over the unfinished sheets, and nearly drove Hannah out of her senses about a candle-end she found in the soap-grease.

CHAPTER LV.

"TROT, TROT TO MARKET, TO BUY A LOAF OF BREAD."

OT a single day had passed since Perdita had conquered Beauty that she had not visited him in his stall, had not led him out for a little taste of the grass, and petted and caressed him till he just worshipped her. He would thrust his nose into her pocket for sugar, and give her a push if he found none; offer his foot to shake, lay his head on her shoulder, nibble her long braids, pilfer her crimson ribbons, and follow her like a faithful dog.

He was not equally complacent to Stephen, who dubbed him "Divil's Own," and was obliged to have all his senses alert while he groomed him. Although he would "side round" for his mistress as soon as he heard her footstep on the stable floor, he was all over the stall if a stranger offered to enter, and he frequently treated Stephen to a close squeeze before he would allow him to touch his head at the manger. He had a passion for springing out of the door as soon as his bridle was taken off; and once free, the whole force of the place could not catch him, till Perdita called him by name. The instant he caught sight of her he would trot to her side, and let himself be led by the nose, with his head down, as meek as Mary's little lamb.

Poor Beauty often proved the truth of the old saying, "A favorite has no friends," for he sorely tried the patience of Stephen, who pinched his mouth with the bit, and wrenched his head, and otherwise revenged his injuries as he could.

Perdita had chosen her times for riding, when Mr. Slaughton was from home, or busy in his studio. Several strong reasons prompted this choice, which she did not explain to herself; underlying them all was an emulation of Sabrina Bradshaw's perfections.

While dusting the books in the library one day, she came across a treatise on the manége, which she carried to her own room. Then she carefully studied the plates, and conned the instructions, and she learned to manage her horse by rule as well as instinct. She taught herself and him to leap ditches, and she accustomed herself to dismount and get up again, a dozen times in succession, and so infatuated did she become with the pleasure, that she tried all sorts of attitudes and paces, till she was much more expert than any riding master's teachings could have made her.

All this while she had been tacitly looking forward to a time when she should have a companion and critic by her side. "Thus will I sit, so will I carry myself," and so on; but she always ended with, "Not yet, I am too far from perfection."

While she was out on the hills, during this first ride by the side of her husband, chance gave her an opportunity to display her skill and courage, which she had not calculated on.

At the bottom of a long slope she espied a lovely clump of blue anemones, which tempted her to dismount.

"Oh, look! what beauties!" exclaimed she, and before her

escort knew it, she was off, running towards the flowers with her habit gathered in her hand.

As soon as his rider left him, Beauty went up to Mr. Slaughton's horse and bit his ear by way of a challenge to a play. As he got only an ill-natured squeal, he tossed his head, kicked up his heels, and started off on his own account to nibble the bushes.

Mr. Slaughton watched his wife apprehensively, wondering how he should catch her fiery steed, also if she could mount from his hand, really dreading any awkwardness in her which might mar the charm of her delightful companionship, which thus far had filled him with wonder and admiration.

Pretty soon she came up from the dell with her hands full of blossoms, which she was leisurely arranging as she stepped towards him.

"Oh, Beauty! where's Beauty? Do you know, Mr. Slaughton, that your smart horse amuses his idleness with catching your rats? I saw him do it myself. One day I went into his stall, and he did not seem in the least glad to see me, and I found out that he was intently watching something, and in half an instant a big monster ran through his manger, and he seized him in his teeth and shook him, and when he dropped him dead, he looked at me as one would say, 'What do you think of that, ma'am?' Beauty is very cute; come here, Beauty."

"Beauty is enjoying his freedom just now," remarked Mr. Slaughton dryly; "he plays the little game of 'catch who catch can.'"

"He will come to me, however;" she tapped her habit with her whip a couple of times, and called him by his name; the colt trotted up to her, with a little toss of his head, and a shrill whinney, and smelled the flowers in her hand, trying to taste them also.

"No, no, Beauty, they are not for you!" said she, pushing away his nose. "They are for my dinner-vases. Stand still, now, sir, till I get on your back. Don't disturb yourself, I beg," she added, as she saw her husband preparing to dismount.

"Oh, you do not need me," thought Sam. "Very well, let us see how you will manage to make that long jump by yourself."

She led her steed to a flat rock by the road-side, and placing her foot in the stirrup, she sprang lightly to the saddle ; but as she released her hold of the slipper and stooped to place in it her left foot, off darted Beauty before she had touched the reins, or gotten her knee over the horn, and he ran a good quarter of a mile, with her sitting sidewise on his back.

To Mr. Slaughton's frightened eyes she seemed clinging to his side by mere will-power ; but she vaulted to her place, wheeled lightly about, and came trotting down the slope, holding Beauty well in hand, and looking very rosy and animated.

"Is he not a frisky wretch ?" said she, showing her pretty teeth in a bright, fearless smile. "He calls that sort of trick good fun, I suppose."

"But he will throw you off, and hurt you, some day, Perdita."

"He knows he cannot do that, unless he invents a new way. I feel that he does contrive and plan, often, and I am sure he laughs ! Beauty needs but one thing, that is speech. I never thought I could be so happy as to ride and manage such a darling as Beauty. I had no idea a horse could be so knowing and so nice. I always thought a horse was just a thing with legs and strength, and a mouth to hold his bit ; but he feels gay, and sad, and thoughtful, and has whims and wishes, and is wilful and capricious, just as Bettine is ; and I like him in each of his many moods, just as I do her."

"I am glad there is *one* acquisition which interests and suits you in my house," said he significantly.

"He does suit me because I trained him myself. I started his superior ; he never disputed my right to rule ; he never had a mistress before me ; I am the only woman he has ever loved ; he never compares me with any other ; he accepts my friend-

ship gladly, looking neither backward or forward in search of
somebody more worthy or complete. Oh, yes, Beauty suits
me, and I suit him."

While she meant to give the gentleman some subjects for
thought during their ride, she did not wish to have any particular
conversation which might mar his pleasure in it, and she meant
to preserve her anemones as souvenirs. She did not need to
make any exertion to be entertaining, and that she was able to
be so was no longer a question.

"What say you to a little race?" she asked; "here's a good
plain stretch of road, unless you are sure beforehand that you
will be distanced; in that case, I will not challenge you to certain defeat; I'm too generous."

When they reined in their steeds, the horsewoman questioned
her companion's face; and this is what she sought to learn:
"Is there not another woman, named Perdita, who can manage
her horse as well as Sabrina Bradshaw?"

She was so much satisfied with the language of his glances
that her heart stirred with pleasure, and at the landing-stone in
front of the Slaughton mansion, she permitted its owner to lift
her off into his arms—a thing she had never thought to let
happen.

For a full hour after she had disappeared from his sight, Mr.
Slaughton sat dreaming of the pressure of her light, yielding
figure, the sweet waft of her breath he had got, in the one
instant when her lips were so near his own; and the harmonious
glory of her youthful beauty so filled his soul, that though he
smoked in the studio a long long time, face to face with his
golden-haired Ruth, he did not once lift his eyes to her, or give
her a single thought.

CHAPTER LVI.

A ROMANCE IN A CALF-PEN.

HE warm sunshine tempted Perdita abroad. A week of untimely cold and northeast winds had kept her indoors, and though the sheets were not all finished, she meant to go down to the meadows for red columbine, which grew there among the rocks.

The sun shone with fierce beams, but there was a chill in the air as if it blew off some Iceland snow bank, and she wrapped herself in a soft shawl of crimson wool, with which she intended to cushion the moss when she reached the gorge.

She carried a book in her basket, and a knife for digging ferns, and she had a dim idea of remaining abroad the whole morning.

She had much to ponder, and her feelings and sensations were becoming so mixed and unmanageable, that she wanted a large place to reflect in, with only nature for witness and companion.

As she passed through the hall she heard Cicely Vance at the piano, and she frowned to find that she was singing " I want to be an angel," instead of practising her scales ; and she had her hand on the knob, to enter and reprove her for her waste of time, when the dame came along and stopped to listen.

" Don't she sing that hymn sweetly ? " asked she, " the dear girl ! Well, she always was a religious child ! When she was only five years old, I used to ask her who she loved best; and she always said ' God first, and grandma next.' "

Perdita smiled, and concluded to leave the "religious child" to fritter out her lesson-hour, since it pleased the dame to have her ; but the pious mood of the "dear girl" seemed to have become carnal and worldly, for as she left the house she heard her pounding away at "Shoo fly ! don't bodder me," which she screamed at the top of her voice.

Bettine accompanied her sister as far as the barn-yard, that she might count some broods of bantams, and admire their shining white pens, their crimson combs, and their feathery legs, and she chippered no end of talk as she skipped and fluttered about among them.

"Tell me, dear Perdita, why do those old hens over yonder squeak so dreadfully ?   Are they scolding their chickens ?"

"Oh no, they are singing."

"I wish they would sing some tune I know.   Please make them sing Jerusalem the Golden.   I like that."

"But you could not understand their words if they did.   You see, they use Italian ; 'Na, haw, daw,'" answered Perdita, laughing.   She always enjoyed Betty's prattle, and she gave her a little squeeze, as she looked down smilingly upon her. "There now, run in, baby, and nurse your new doll which Uncle Sam bought you, till I come.   Was it not good and kind of him to get you a baby so much larger and finer than the one you lost that Thanksgiving Day ?"

"Yes, indeed.   I love Uncle Sam !   Don't you love Uncle Sam, Perdita ? "

> "'Tis a point I long to know—
> Oft it causes anxious thought :
> Do I love the man or no ?
> Am I his, or am I not ?'"

She laughed as she hummed her parody on the familiar hymn she used to sing in her father's family worship, and she felt a little natural repentance for having dared so to trifle with sacred things.   Betty's thoughts meanwhile had wandered to a new

17

theme, having no connection whatever with anything around them, in the inconsequent and incoherent fashion grown-up meditations are apt to take.

" How much is a canoe worth, Perdita ? " asked she.

" A canoe ! why do you want to know ? "

" Because Pandora read in her little United States History that the folks went down to the bank and took a canoe which some Injuns had put there, and they had a fight and killed each other about it ; and I wondered how many dollars they got, and if the bank was much robbed ; and I was glad it was not Uncle Sam's bank."

" You had better ask him about it, darling," said Perdita, "and I will tell you everything you want to know when I come home.   Run in, now—there's a good child."

" Yes, Perdita.   I wish I could tell you everything *you* want to know," said Bettine, gazing wistfully at her.

" Nobody can do that, dear ; I must find out for myself," replied Perdita, blushing with the clear, penetrating look of the child, which so easily discerned her trouble and unrest.

The consciousness that Mr. Slaughton had assumed a large place in her life, was so often and so obviously thrust upon her notice, that Bettine's suggestions and inquiries were but a following of the thread she desired to unravel, and she felt that she must settle exactly how she ought to treat herself and him.

As she passed through the long orchard she heard a curious noise of bellowing and stamping, mingled with shouts, and as she reached the gap in the wall she stopped suddenly, frightened at what she saw.

The gateway was the bar-place for the field beyond, but was wide open ; all the rails except the bottom one being removed, and piled in a heap close to the wall.

The big Ayreshire was coming full tilt, with his head down, his nostrils flaming red, his blood-shot eyes rolling in rage, and Mr. Slaughton was trying to drive him back with a thick stick, which he flourished threateningly about, while he hallooed and shouted with all his might :

"Whay! whay there! what are you about?"

Why this inquiry should be so constantly addressed to cattle and other beasts is a mystery.   It is generally plain enough to see what they are about.   It seemed to kindle the wrath of the Ayreshire to have it speered at him, and as he out-bellowed the bulls of Bashan, he was evidently concentrating his energies on showing his master what he was about, and that right speedily too.

Mr. Slaughton had already reached the bar-place, facing his enemy, who was just ready to toss and gore him, when, swift as thought, Perdita tore off her shawl, and fixing her eyes on the furious creature, she seized the exact instant which brought him within her reach, and with the skill and dexterity of a matador, she dropped the blind over his head, giving it a little twist as it left her hands, such as a young girl uses who tosses her wrap over her shoulder, and she wiped from her wrist the slaver and foam she received from the bull's lips as they grazed it, and she felt his breath hot and sweet, before she stepped backward out of his reach.

It was entirely unexpected.   Neither the man nor the beast had seen her approach, and it was the very nick of time, too, for at that precise instant Mr. Slaughton fell backward, tripping over the low rail so that his heels flew up, and he must have been at the mercy of his pursuer.

"Make haste and get up!" exclaimed Perdita, as she helped him struggle to his feet.   "Let's run for dear life to the calf-pen."

The advice was too sensible to be neglected, and seizing her hand they darted past the bull, who was bobbing and backing, and giving out muffled roars from under the shawl ; and flying down the orchard, they had hardly time to climb into the enclosure, when the Ayreshire, having torn the blinder to shreds and freed himself from all except the tatters which twisted around his horns like ribbons adorning a prize ox at fair-time, came careering after them, streamers flying in fine style.

It was a square yard built around a great tree, for rearing calves, and it had so strong a fence that the young cattle were safe from the oxen, who sometimes tried to jump in, and the bovine mothers who struggled to get at their offspring.

These soft-eyed young creatures were driven nearly frantic on their long, unsteady legs, with the sudden intrusion upon their privacy, and crowded each other into the smallest corner possible, and panted with terror, while the Ayreshire plunged madly round and round their enclosure, stopping now and then to survey the prisoners and treat them to a ferocious bellow. He smelt at all the boards, tried them with his horns, he dashed his huge shoulders against the posts, and varied the exercises by rearing on his hind legs, tearing up the turf and dirt with his pawing hoofs and pelting them with it, lashing his sides with his tail like an angry lion.

" Rather handsome, isn't he ? and decidedly active," said Perdita from her leaning place against the tree-trunk. " Well worth the two hundred dollars he cost."

" If I had a gun, how quickly I'd shoot him. If I had a club, I'd knock his brains out ! I'd cut his throat with a sickle," said Mr. Slaughton, mopping his face, which was much flushed with his exertions. " I wonder how long we are to be kept here to witness his infernal manœuvres."

" It evidently is a man's first impulse to kill whatever annoys him," remarked Perdita reflectively. " I've heard of bull-fights ; now I am quite able to fancy one. The calves and I are the audience ; you are the heroic matador who will presently dare the creature to battle ; you come (over the fence) ; you see (the red rags) ; you conquer (your valuable Ayreshire).

" Humph ! *I* shall be glad if he ever gets enough of promenading around us, and we can manage to slip out ; what an outlandish noise he keeps up ! I'll have him shot to-morrow, impulse or no impulse."

" He will probably get hungry some time," Perdita continued, secretly amused by his impatience, " or thirsty; let us be thankful that the spring is under the hill, out of sight. Ah ! if you were but the piper who played a tune—'Consider, cow, consider.' "

" You take it coolly," replied Mr. Slaughton, half vexed at her railing.

" Where is the use of taking it otherwise. I am only sorry for these poor frightened calves ; but they will get used to us in time, I dare say. If I could bleat as well as Dolly, I'd try a little brownie conversation ; but I might be profane without knowing it. Foreign tongues are dangerous unless carefully studied. If we ever do get out, I wish to leave a good character behind me."

" I thank you for my life, Perdita ; hadn't it been for your admirable presence of mind, I should have been a mangled thing lying out there, not fit to look at," said he, reaching out his hands thinking to seize hers, which he might have kissed for aught I know.

She withdrew easily beyond his reach, with a low, teazing laugh.

" What, Mr. Slaughton ! A romance in a calf-pen ! pray don't forget that the eyes of these innocent heifers are upon you."

" No ! I won't," replied he, frowning, " you take good care to keep me in mind of proprieties."

" What could have put the wretch in such a tantrum ? " said she, purposely ignoring the bitterness of his last speech. " When I have seen your costly purchase before, he has behaved like a decorous ruminant at peace with himself and all the world."

" I can't imagine, unless it was a bit of foppery of mine. You see, I was striding along, thinking—well, never mind what I was thinking. I don't believe it would interest you to know, or if it did, you would accuse me of impossible nonsense—and feeling warm, I untied and pulled off my neck this red crepe-scarf, which a certain lady admired one evening in the library. Do you remember it ? "

" Perfectly," replied she ; " you were reading ' Othello,' and you said the old Moor never had a handkerchief to compare with yours for beauty, and——"

" Well, what else ? I like to know that you listen to my wisdom ; go on, please."

" You said you wished there was magic in the woof of this one. You would certainly bestow it on somebody."

" And *you* said, affection which needs magic to win and keep it, is not worth having."

" I am glad that you remember my wisdom. Well, what did the bull do then ? "

" Do ! why, the first thing I saw of him, he was rampaging after me, all bellow and horns."

" I wish Beauty could come and see me cooped up here. I believe he would use his heels for my sake," said Perdita, trying to keep up some talk which would not lead to sentiment.

" How you do love and trust that colt !" exclaimed Mr. · Slaughton jealously.

" He loves and trusts me."

" So do I, Perdita."

Her heart beat fast, as she turned aside in haste to avoid his gaze, and he turned so proudly that he said no more.

If she had spoken, she must·have asked a question which, though it had almost trembled on her lips several times of late, she dared not venture to put into words, because her whole life turned on the answer he would give her. She knew he was too thoroughly honest and true to tell her a falsehood, and she shrank from an avowal he might be forced to make.

" Is Sabrina Bradshaw better worth loving than I ? " She understood right well that she had opened her heart to this man, and she must get a whole soul in exchange for hers, or be forever miserable. The impulse which made her peril her life to save his told her so. While she put away his protestations, speaking lightly, she felt that she must further try and know herself and him, before she dared risk the fatal moment which would decide her destiny.

Both were busy with their thoughts, just half a minute and no more, when a great shouting was heard down the road. It was Slowgo and Stephen, who drove the oxen home for their nooning.

Mr. Slaughton climbed the fence, and making a hollow bowl of his two palms, he sent out a shrill whistle, which might be heard half a mile.

"That trick of my boyhood steads me well just now," said he. "Stephen is standing up in the cart to listen. I'll give him another. There! he sees us! Now I'll just shake my red handkerchief. Out of your reach this time, Mr. Bull."

Slowgo and Stephen left their team and ran down the field, full of curiosity to see what might be the matter; and with their great whips and the help of the mastiff Bose, they drove the Ayreshire away, and shut him into his paddock and locked the gate securely behind him. He was not at all subdued, however, and stood looking at them, throwing hooffuls of dirt over his back, and bellowing.

"I feel deep regret that I have not been able to achieve a heroic action, by which to give you freedom; but you know I am a humdrum sort of a fellow anyhow."

"So was Gideon, I suppose; but the walls of Jericho fell when he blew on his ram's horn. I wonder if he made any more racket than you did just now! I am glad our interested attendant is in durance vile, at any price. I could have engaged a thrilling scene full of danger, rife with prowess; but I. must be content to be saved by a whistle. Sam, my precious, why didn't you come and worry the bull?"

"I'll have that dog killed to-morrow!" grumbled Mr. Slaughton; "the idea of wasting such endearments on a puppy."

CHAPTER LVII.

PLEASANT DAYS.

"ICELY certainly has a taste for drawing," remarked Perdita one evening after the children had retired, and she and her husband were left in the library. "Do you think you could muster patience to give her a few lessons?"

"I know a lady who certainly has a talent for it," answered he, "as witness these sketches," producing half a dozen flower-branches from one of the drawers of his private desk. .

"Oh, those awkward scratches!" she tried to take them from his hand. "I wished to copy the pretty things I found in the woods, but I had such miserable success that I gave up in disgust. Pray, where did you unearth them? Let me hide the botches under the 'forestick.'"

"Oh, no! 'Who finds haves,' and I assure you I consider them truly wonderful, to be the work of a person who paints from instinct, without instruction."

"Such praise from such a source," answered she in an incredulous tone, "is immensely flattering."

"I am so much in earnest in my encomium, that I will bother myself with Cicely Vance, on one condition: You shall promise me to come also and get lessons. I will not give them on any other condition."

"How can I hesitate?" she replied, with a surprised face. "I have no confidence whatever in *my* success; but if you desire to see me make a failure, you shall have the opportunity. I never shun any gate of knowledge which opens to me."

"When will you commence?" demanded he, eagerly. "I would have asked you when I first found your sketches, if I had not been a coward. I dreaded a refusal; I will be the most faithful master you ever had."

"It seems we are rather losing sight of the first party to the compact," said Perdita, coolly. "Cicely Vance, who has so many sorts of talent that one would scarcely know in what direction to push her, if she did not stubbornly refuse to develop in any; her touch on the piano is admirable, her ear accurate; there is no limit to the excellence she might attain. But do you know, she just drums out her hour of practice in unmeaning noises, unless I watch her? Her object in life seems to be to learn just as little as possible. Now, if she will only take to drawing. I think I'll tell her she may make a gift to Randy Teazle of the first good picture she finishes."

"Confound Cicely Vance! or at least, I meant to say, shall I expect you to-morrow morning?"

"Certainly! then as well as any other time; but I wish to consult you about Cicely. You know her partiality for Randy Teazle. I have been thinking it might be good for her if I had him come up and study with the children."

"I don't see why, or how; and I am sure you have cares and labors enough already."

"But if Cicely has a true affection for this boy, it may give her a soul. I should like to try the experiment of daily association under sanction."

"Are you in earnest, Perdita? Why should you trouble further about that dreadful child, who has been such a trial and annoyance to you?"

"Because I feel as if I must have made a mistake somewhere, or she would improve under my influence," replied Perdita, earnestly.

"And if love gives souls to animals, what does it give to men to make it worth having?"

"Goodness and strength."

17*

The next morning the artist hardly waited for breakfast to be over before he reminded his young wife of her promise.

" Come up higher, friend," said he, leading the way to the stairs.

" Why not in the library ? " asked Perdita, drawing back and growing pale ; it had not occurred to her that she would be called on to face the golden-haired Ruth in the studio.

" You surely don't mind the steps, such a light-footed climber as you are."

" No, not in the least ; of course I don't," answered she hurriedly, as he stood looking back in astonishment at her troubled face, her crimson cheeks, and agitated demeanor. " Come on, Cicely."

As she entered the door she glanced quickly in the direction of the Sabrina—the enforced companion of her dreams and musings, whose original was the emulation of her life. It was covered under a white drapery, which hid also the girl bearing a pitcher in her hands.

She dropped into the seat which the artist placed for her, and took with trembling fingers the pencil he offered, hardly daring to draw the conclusion which presented itself to her mind. Could she venture to hope that the love he had declared immortal was veiled and obscured in his heart as he had hidden the pictures which he so lately pronounced the best works of his life ? She was full of these thoughts, while Mr. Slaughton placed her bristol-board and explained the first principles of his art. He wanted her to excel, and he was serious and earnest in his instructions, as if she had been a paying pupil, as indeed he hoped to make her in many ways.

Cicely Vance, who was always restless, and whose lawless hands were busy with everything, pulled down a cloth which was thrown over an easel, in a far corner.

" Why, Aunt Perdita I here's you I just as natural as can be," she exclaimed ; " and Betty, too. Oh I how pretty you would be if you didn't look so mad."

Perdita turned her head at this announcement, and beheld the picture of a most beautiful girl, holding a child in her arms, about whom her long raven hair fell in heavy masses; while her proudly-poised head, flashing eyes, and parted unsmiling lips, all spoke passion. It was a richly colored picture, full of spirit and fire.

After a moment's silent survey, she turned to the artist, who stood as blushing and abashed as a school-boy detected in using a pony. " I desired to test my memory," stammered he.

" I hope you are satisfied with your success; if you have not given your work a name, I advise you to call it Tisiphone, the third Fury."

As she returned quietly to her task, he puzzled much to divine whether or no she was displeased with his secret endeavor, and its patent excellence.

When her lesson was ended, he begged her candid opinion of some works which he designed for the Toptown exhibition.

"I hope you will approve," said he, "because I consider them the very best things I have ever done."

She could not refuse, and she steadied herself for a sight of what she dreaded, especially in his company. While she was rebelling against his cruelty in forcing her to look at her rival, and trying to think of some phrase for letting him know that she had already seen his master-pieces, he brought out a couple of landscapes, just finished, and was at infinite trouble to give them a good light.

The old mill, with the wild water leaping over the dam, and in the foreground on the bank a dog crouching at the feet of a slender girl, who held his head in her arms.

The other was a study of autumn coloring of wondrous blending, where the sky was all beauty, and the world was all bliss. But Perdita found not in it the particular charm which riveted her attention to the well-remembered scene where her husband had been both positive and kind. It seemed so long ago, and the events and feelings of that day came vividly back to her and engrossed and centered her thoughts so that she forgot where she was, and seemed again to hear the dash of the fall, and the piteous whine of the dog begging for his life; and she roused with a start when Cicely's sharp voice smote her ear, and looked up to find the artist studying her face.

"It's my turn now, aunty. Uncle Sam is all ready; won't you come and see me make my picture?"

"Certainly," answered Perdita in a flurried way; "and if you do your best, you may give the flowers to Randy Teazle for his birthday."

"Now, aunty! how queer!" exclaimed Cicely blushing and twisting into a dozen shapes. "What makes you think of such a thing? I don't want to give Randy a present. He isn't much; his folks are dreadful poor."

"I am sure you take trouble enough to make us all think you are fond of him; and I believe I shall have him come up to our school-room and study. How would you enjoy that?"

"I dunno!" Cicely, like the man who hesitated to get married because he would no longer have a place to spend his evenings, was secretly thinking that if Randy was made at home up at the house, she shouldn't have any boy to plan secret meetings with. She was quite exhilarated by the idea of presenting the lad with her group of blossoms, however, and worked away rather faithfully. It really seemed as if she was about to develop studiousness and perseverance.

Mr. Slaughton put away his best works, without again asking her opinion of them; but he looked well pleased, and was very chatty and good-humored. Cicely's presence made Perdita feel so easy that she was able to give enthusiastic attention to his teachings; she wished to excel. "I know Sabrina Bradshaw can paint," she said to herself, "and I think I can. I'll find out."

These lessons in the studio were the pleasantest days Perdita Hethwaite had ever found in her short life, and all through the dark times that followed she let her mind rest on them, in wonder at their sweetness and their bitter fruit.

CHAPTER LVIII.

THE PARSON DEMANDS HIS FINE COAT.

 HATE to go to Toptown," said Mr. Slaughton one morning in July, as he stood at the door, waiting for the shore wagon to come around. "I hate to interrupt our studies. I go with anxiety too, for our future; how can I tell but I shall find you distant and frigid, provoking and caustic again, on my return."

"A week cannot effect any marked change in our relations," replied Perdita smiling. "I have not so many friends that I can afford to throw away one with whom I have progressed so far on the good road to friendship."

"Promise me one thing," said he anxiously—so very anxiously that she looked with apprehension in his face, while the quick blood dyed her cheeks with sudden red.

"Anything in reason."

"Be sure and come to the station for me when I return. Let me see your face, first of any, when I step out of the car."

"Willingly," said she with joyful readiness. "What if I were to ride Beauty down?"

"No! I want you to drive the pair. I know you can do it; they are perfectly gentle. I have a fancy for you alone in the new phaeton; you do not feel afraid?"

"No, I think not. I will come, since you ask me to do it, at any rate."

"Would you risk your life for a whim of mine, Perdita? No, I am not selfish enough to permit it. Stephen had better drive down ; he can walk up the hill. I want to make sure of the tête-à-tête with you. I shall have so much to say."

" I have also something to say," she thought, " when I have heard what you mean to tell me."

Life looked so bright that day, that she sang for very joy. She was restless, too. She walked in the garden, after school, and copied some flowers into her album ; she sewed, and played the flute, trying to fill all her hours. That was the first day of absence. The second, she had marked out a task which required all her powers to accomplish.

Early in the morning she mounted Beauty, and rode to the village. There was an important piece of shopping to do ; she meant to purchase a dress—a purple muslin. The assortment at the Birch store was small, and her choice was soon made. A clear white ground with a small leaf in it, which the clerk assured her was " a real spry figger." It was a robe with flouncing and borders. Perdita aspired to a train—the first of her life.

A whole week was consumed in steady stitching, and Friday found her labor completed. There it lay on her bed, pretty, graceful, flowing. She tried it on, and scarcely knew herself in it. The woman her mirror showed her was so stylish and elegant, that she felt half afraid of her, and she hastened to get back into her simple brown gown, and take a good frolic with Betty and Sam, and make sure of her identity. She laid away the fine dress with satisfaction, however, and she anticipated a pleasant triumph when next she put it on. Sunday should be the day ; on Sunday she would wear it to dinner.

The drive from the station was to precede that important event, and she should be—happy. Yes, so happy, that it would be proper to be splendid.

While she was impatiently watching the clock, eager for the moment when she might set off, Malcolm came up to the mansion house with a telegram.

"Business keeps me another week ; will write by next post."

It was a bitter disappointment! seven more days. She retired to her chamber, that none might see her weep. Little Bettine, much troubled, came softly and clasped her neck with her arms, and laid her cheek close to the rich velvet one she loved to caress.

"What is the matter, Perdita? why do you cry?"

"Because I am an idiot; that is all."

She dried her eyes, and forced herself to sport with the children till bed-time. But though she struggled against her depression, she could not conquer it; and when, long after midnight, she slept, it was no refreshing slumber, but only hideous dreams.

While they sat at breakfast the next morning, Parson Hethwaite came up to the mansion house, a thing quite out of the common, for he rarely volunteered to show his lean poverty at this home of ease and plenty.

He brought a letter, which was his errand, and he opened it with some fuss and flurry, and presented it to his daughter to read as soon as they were alone in the library.

"Mrs. Slaughton, I have thought best to confide in you a proposal which has been made to me by my old friend Champlin, regarding my son Malcolm. Champlin was my chum in college, and though our paths diverged early, his leading to prosperity and affluence, it seems he has not forgotten me. He offers my lad a clerkship. He says I was such a good young fellow, he feels sure I should have good sons. Hence we view that the promises are for the elect and their seed after them, as says the Psalmist: 'I have been young, and now I am old; yet I have never seen the children of the righteous forsaken, nor their seed begging bread: for all things are ours.'"

"It seems a plain, straightforward letter," remarked Perdita, who had been perusing the epistle while her father expounded; "which means a good opening for Malcolm."

"Very sensibly put, Mrs. Slaughton. I believe Champlin has a great establishment in Toptown, and he seems to me to hint at something more than a mere clerkship. You observe he mentions advancement. He has no family, has Champlin, preferring to live like St. Paul, therein proving his wisdom——"

"The Catholic priesthood are wise, then, in shirking all the duties and responsibilities which God himself placed upon man ; for this cause has he set them in families——"

"As I was about to observe," interrupted the Parson in a severe tone, "the lad Malcolm is careless and heedless, and much given to frolic and noise. I trust years may sober him ; therefore——"

"You will lose no time in placing my brother," put in Perdita, absorbed in her own deductions, and feeling every moment a lost opportunity till he was gone at once.

"Do not rashly jump at conclusions, Mrs. Slaughton ; there are ifs in the way. You observe Champlin expressly says he will take no steps without a personal interview with the boy."

"It is not too late to set off to-day, father."

"It is entirely too late for *me* to place myself in any such a position. I am in no mood to face successful people. *I*, who have been so pushed off, so foiled, so hindered and cast out ! I will not thrust myself where the contrast will be so marked that he who runs might read what a failure my life has been. We started fair—Champlin and I. He won ! I lost !"

"But you still own all things, father. The things which are withheld are doubly yours. You observe I retain your profitable instructions. I really cannot believe you will let this chance slip, when a slight exertion on your part will secure——"

"If it depends on my visiting Toptown, be assured that I shall," answered he doggedly. "Where is my fine broadcloth coat ? Where are my gloves ? Where is my glossy hat ? Do *I* look like walking into a wholesale store owned by Dick Champlin, whose Latin I used to construe for him ? Why, I should be flouted and scorned by the very porters."

"But, father——"

"I will not be urged ! If you care enough for the worldly

advancement of the lad to go with him, well and good. If you don't, then the matter drops."

"Oh, that is your object in confiding in me! You wish to push an inexperienced girl into a situation you shrink from yourself!"

"*You* are a rich man's wife, Perdita. You meet the wealthy gentleman on an equal footing; you can afford it."

"I will go, father. My brother shall never lose such a good prospect by any cowardice of mine. Mr. Slaughton is in Toptown, and will render me all the service I need, and I believe he will approve my action, bold and presuming as it looks to me, I *hope*, as soon as I can explain it. Have Malcolm ready for the noon train. Fortunately, there are five on the road, and I can get back by midnight if—in case——"

She was thinking about her husband; but she did not finish her sentence aloud, and the old man left her, feeling that his "daughter, Mrs. Slaughton, was a smart woman, apt for business, able to grasp a situation, and act promptly in the premises."

CHAPTER LIX.

"LOVE SAILED A MATCH WITH TIME."

HERE had been a heavy shower the night before, and every leaf and grass-blade was washed fresh and green, and the air, freed from dust, was delightfully clear and cool.

With a suitable escort, her first journey would have afforded pleasure to this inexperienced traveller; but a certain tremor of anxiety as to her capacity to get successfully through the untried necessities before her agitated her so much that she could scarcely lend an ear to her brother's ecstatic interest in all he saw. Earlier in her married life Mr. Slaughton's opinion of the proceeding would have weighed lightly with her; but now all her motives of action were changed. She had found a master whom she desired to please. Amidst her worries as to how she should find a hotel, what she should say to Mr. Champlin, and so on, came a dread of her husband's disapproval. Ought she not to have waited his return and placed the affair in his hands?

Then came a new set of feelings to the surface. She was about to meet the man whose name she bore, among strangers. How would she compare with others? What would be his judgment when he found her in this untried position?

It was evening when they arrived. Perdita veiled carefully her trepidation from Malcolm, as she tripped up the hotel steps, and really, she seemed entirely composed and steady, though she did give a little nervous laugh as she caught her foot in the stair-rod, and came near tumbling upon her nose.

"I hope there is no truth in signs, Mat," said she; "if there is, I shall see trouble before I go down these steps. Won't it be a pity if Mr. Champlin is out of town!"

"It will be too blabed bad," replied Malcolm (as the lad had a cold in his head, his utterance was rather thick).

A smart chambermaid was the first person they met.

"I want a room," said Perdita, stopping her.

"A room, mum! and why don't you ring the bell and call the clerk then? There's the parlor straight before you."

Hasting to obey this curt advice, the traveller stepped to the door and looked about her, expecting to see a bell on the table or mantle, but none was to be found.

"Where do you suppose they keep their bell, Mat?" asked she after a puzzled survey.

"And is it the bell that ye's after wanting?" asked a grinning boy who was watching the pair; "sure it's there upon the wall.   Pull that green tossel and 'twill ring for ye ; but I'm the boy that'll come anyhow, so ye may as well be after tellin' me what yer wanting, till I fetch it ? "

"Oh ! and is it the clerk ! " said he, eyeing the young people over his shoulder as he disappeared.

Presently, a prematurely bald man, with a pen behind each ear and his forehead full of scowls, presented himself at the door.   He scanned them hurriedly, and it seemed that their plain dress and unassuming appearance found little favor in his eyes.

"What do you wish ? "

"Can I have a room ? " asked Perdita in a faint voice.

"A room, miss ? I don't know if we have one vacant.   Any luggage ? "

"No.   I am only up on business for a day."

" I don't think I can give you a room, miss, we're quite full ; I've turned away sixteen this morning."

" Is not Mr. Slaughton stopping here ? "

"Mr. Slaughton, miss ?   Did you wish to see Mr. Slaughton, miss ? "

"Yes."   She began to see her way so hedged in, and so full of lions, that she hesitated and faltered, before she pronounced the word.

"On, you wish to see Mr. Slaughton.   Very well, I'll inquire whether there's such a gentleman stopping here."

The look he threw at her said, " I'll find out whether Mr. Slaughton wishes to see *you*."

Soon he came back.   " The gentleman is out ; don't know when he will return."

" Very well ; you may show me a place to wash, and I will get ready for supper.   I dare say he will be back for that."

"Does the gentleman expect you, miss ? "

"I am Mrs. Slaughton.   I am not *miss*," replied Perdita, blushing violently under the fellow's gaze.

"Oh, Mrs. Slaughton! very well ; here Pat, take this lady to Mr. Slaughton's room, No. 40."

"But I desire a room to myself, and one for this lad, who is my brother."

Perdita's confusion and blushes caused the clerk to look at her still more suspiciously. "I'll call the *head*," said he retreating.

The "head" appeared in half a minute.

"Is not this a hotel?" demanded Perdita.

"Yes, ma'am, the Toptown House," replied he, smiling.

"Well, sir! being a hotel, I suppose your business is to accommodate travellers ; therefore you will please give me two rooms ; one for my brother, this boy, and one for myself. And as I have been asked impertinent questions about my luggage, which I suppose implies doubt of my honesty, or ability to pay, I shall settle my bill now! how much will it be till to-morrow morning?"

She took out a roll of money from her purse, and looked with haughty anger in his face, waiting for his answer.

"No offence, miss, I hope ; but, you see, we have so many adventurers."

"Do I look like an adventurer?"

"No, miss! certainly not," answered the head clerk, deprecating her proud wrath ; "come with me, and I'll make you as comfortable as possible. I suppose you want adjoining rooms, you and the boy?"

"Of course!"

"Here we are, ma'am. Please to ring your bell for anything you wish ; tea at seven."

Perdita was dreadfully disturbed by her first attempt to push her own way ; but she tried to forget all annoyances, and hurriedly making herself tidy, she rejoined Malcolm, who was industriously kicking his heels in the hall, and whistling to a mocking-bird which hung in a cage at the far end.

"There's forty!" said he, as they walked down the long passage ; "that's his room."

Perdita knocked boldly at the door, and her heart answered each appeal with a quick throb. No answer. "We shall find Mr. Slaughton in the parlor, I dare say, or at supper," said she, as they passed on.

"Let's stop just one minute in this beautiful place," begged Malcolm; "tea isn't ready yet—a boy told me so. I never saw such handsome things!"

He was gazing rapturously around the rotunda, which filled his imagination with pictures. It seemed to him like some old Moorish palace, or the fabled wonders of one of his surreptitiously read story-books.

The wide gallery which ran around three sides of the great square was supported by Corinthian pillars reaching from the floor below to the vaulted roof; and as he leaned over the railing, he could look down into the vast office, occupying the wide central space, as well as that beneath the corridor; while fronting him was a conservatory filled with blooming plants; the walls behind and around him were hung with pictures, and open doors led in all directions to parlors and reading-rooms. The sofas and arm-chairs which were conveniently placed here and there were filled with chatting groups, who were looking down at the moving panorama below.

At the far end, in a corner near the conservatory, were a company of gayly dressed children sporting and enjoying themselves.

Before the lad had half finished his study of the paintings, the flowers, and the people, a band of harpers began to play in the office, and he left all to lean over the rail and listen; and soon the children, taking partners, waltzed easily about like butterflies. It seemed to the country boy that they might be fairies or angels, they were so light and graceful.

A stout, gray-haired man sat beside a little carriage, in which lay a pale girl, a cripple, with a lovely face, to whom he was talking in soft, loving tones; and a couple of ladies not far off on a sofa discussed them.

The mother of the cripple was dead.   Somehow, this child had gotten a fall, which so injured her spine that she could not stand ; and she passed all her days lying in her carriage, drawn hither and thither by a stout attendant.

While the ladies talked, and Malcolm eagerly swallowed their words, filling in the outlines which his fancy sketched, a beautiful little boy came with his nurse, and stood by his father, timidly waiting for a welcome.

"'There! look, Electra!" said one of the dames ; "all that man's love is for the girl ; he has not a word or smile for his only son, and he is as handsome as a cherub, too."

Such pity filled Malcolm's heart, that it nearly welled over at his eyes, and the music, which had sounded so joyous, changed to a minor mournfulness, which was like a continuation to the sad story.

Perdita had followed her brother, looking eagerly among the comers and goers for the man she wished but almost dreaded to see ; and she, as well as Malcolm, had heard the talk about the motherless children, and when she sighed softly, he turned and laid a hand on her arm.

" Here is a father who *can* love, and who leaves one of his children out in the cold, to dote on the other.   I think it is better to be as we are—none of us cared for, don't you, Perdita."

Almost before he had finished his question his attention was fastened on a small Bohemian in the court below, who began to dance with a tambourine ; and Perdita lost consciousness of everything around her, because her ears caught the tones of a familiar voice, and her eyes saw a sight which she never in her whole life forgot.

A couple sat a little way in front of her, whom she could plainly see, but who could not look at her, unless she leaned forward from behind the great pillar which concealed her.

The lady was tall and superbly handsome, and had rich masses of dark red hair twined about her head.   The gentleman was Samuel Slaughton, whose back was turned towards Perdita, but so close that she might have touched him with her hand.

They were talking earnestly, and in louder tones than they would have used in a silent room, because of the noise of the children, and of the music below them.

A sudden lull in the waltz left their words distinctly audible to Perdita's quickened sense, which was painfully alert, without being conscious of any effort to overhear them.

"More than handsome, Sabrina; enthralling, entrancing, I find my every sense satisfied. I feel bewitched, led in chains; to live is to love, to love is heaven! It is true, however deeply enamored a man may be, however madly he may worship a *goddess*, he can love a woman but once."

He was looking full in her eyes, so that the profiles of both were offered to the listener. Though he spoke lightly, and with bright animation, he was in deep earnest.

"You make me smile, old friend," said Sabrina, "and yet I am very glad, very happy, for I see plainly that the years we have passed have not cooled your youthful fervor. What you say is true—to live is to love, to love is heaven. I found it out long ago."

As she finished her confession, a deep blush suffused her face, and she turned away her eyes. A minute's silence followed, in which both seemed deeply thinking, and then Mr. Slaughton resumed the conversation, as if continuing an interrupted theme.

"This girl!" Perdita started. Of whom could he be speaking, in that cool business tone? "This girl is proud and delicate; she ought to be independent, she ought to have freedom of action, and I am determined she shall have all I can help her to. It is quite evident that her parents' notions were mercenary in pushing on the match, and they ought not to reap any benefit from their unworthy conduct; *her* discretion is perfect, and she will make a good use of the fortune which will be settled upon her."

"But are you certain that the husband's conduct has been entirely blameless?" asked Sabrina, turning a meaning look on him.

"It is of no use to discuss that now, Sabrina; the past cannot be altered, and we have only to deal with the present and the future——"

Here the music recommenced so noisily that their voices were lost in the clamor. He leaned eagerly forward, and then they both spoke earnestly, and with very sober faces.

In the next lull, she plainly heard *this* from the man to whom she had given her whole heart.

"Yes, Sabrina, you are right; divorces as a rule are wicked, monstrous! But when a man has done his best to win a woman's love and gets only sour disdain and cold repulse, what shall he do? Must he give his life for nothing? shall he drag on a horrible existence, tied to a wife, like a living body bound to a dead corpse? I say no! let the law set him free, that he may mate with another who is willing to make him happy."

"I find it a subject too difficult and delicate for discussion," said Sabrina.

"I do not ask you to discuss it; only promise me, when it is over, you will be kind——"

He took her hand and looked beseechingly in her face. Perdita did not hear any more of his words, because the music burst into a jubilant uproar of all the instruments, which effectually drowned his voice.

She had heard enough. All her fond dreams vanished. All her hopes of happiness faded and died; the world looked cold, and a dim darkness floated before her vision. She seemed to live a long life in the few seconds which followed, and she knew that she must lift her burdens from day to day as the galley-slave does his task—without hope or cheer. But what of it? What right had she to complain? Her duty in her place was not altered. It was a bold stand which she took on that far-off wedding-day, " I shall be your housekeeper. I shall not miss what you call love."

She had grown wiser now, but none the happier, as it appeared, with her knowledge.

The full-orbed woman who was his first love was still the idol of her husband's soul ; she was not able to doubt it. It seemed that his passion for her kindled his whole being ; it shimmered all over him as heat and light radiate from fire. Even if she had heard no words, the looks, the attitudes of the pair, their very silence, proclaimed that they were lovers. His eyes drank at hers deep draughts of bliss ; while hers were lustrous, still brimming over ; it was the giving which impoverisheth not, the receiving which maketh rich. Although the poor wife saw but dimly through a blur of unshed tears, she felt what his gaze was worth, for had she not sunned herself in those friendly warm glances? and she felt how bitter-hard was her fate.

As she moved to go stealthily away, something inclined the golden-haired lady to turn and look in her direction—their eyes met. Such dazzling beauty as Perdita saw made her drop her lids hopelessly ; no man could withstand such wondrous charms.

"Malcolm !" said Perdita, softly, " come, let us get some supper ; then we will go to our rooms. I am very tired."

" Won't you wait a little longer for him. I like this so much."

" No, no !" answered she, frowning. " I will go now ! this minute."

The lad was full of talk, to which she listened as well as she could, of " the great big dining-room,—beefsteak and coffee ! and chickens ! Perdita, say, Perdita, don't you wish mother could have some of this supper ? When I am clerk at Champlin's, she shall come here and stay ever so long. Perdita, Perdita, will they let me have some more meat ? I'm hungry yet."

When he had eaten till he could eat no more, and she had

18

dismissed him and locked herself into her room, how heavy was the night ! how desolate the darkness !

Even in her first despair she never thought of abandoning her post, of leaving the house she had learned to love as her home.   When he desired to send her away, he should say so—this man, who had tried to be indulgent and agreeable to the awkward thing thrust upon him by a couple of old women. He had sometimes pitied her loneliness, compassionated her isolation ; but he also resented her natural struggles in her hard place, her indignation at the insults he had begun by offering her.   She had been so foolish and weak as to mistake his friendly indifference for love, but it was still true, he had never seen but one woman worth loving ; and the time was coming— must be close at hand, when he would set himself free from a marriage which was no marriage.   Till then her duty lay straight before her—housekeeper and governess.

There were many points in their talk which she could not comprehend, but turn and turn it about as she would, the divorce was a thing certain ; she had heard him say so, and he asked his first love to be kind to him when it was over, and she *would* be kind.

What dreadful feelings fought within her ! What regret for her shattered life, all settling into hard resentment, bitter anger. What right had he to speak such words to any woman, no matter how much he worshipped her, while he had a lawful wife ? It was despicable ! it was wicked ! nothing could make it just or right, nothing could excuse it ! He had proved, in her hearing, in her sight, that he was not a man fit for the love of a pure girl ; he was a man to despise ! to hate ! And only yesterday, she had hoped to win a place in his heart, a good home for her soul.

When the stars were paled out by the day dawn, poor Perdita looked colorless and wan ; her eyes, yesterday so brilliant, were cheated of their brightness, and set in circles of purple ; her very lips were faded, and life seemed a burden too hard to pick up again. She turned her face to the wall wishing that the struggle was ended, that she could die there and be forgotten.

She was aroused to the need of action by Malcolm's impatient voice calling her to come to breakfast—he was hungry. Oh, yes ! hunger and thirst, labor and fatigue, were still her portion, and it was necessary for her to arise and stand in her place among others.

She cast fearful and perturbed glances along the gallery and down into the office beneath, as she walked to the breakfast-room, and questioned the faces at the table. *He* was not there, and his golden-haired beauty was nowhere to be seen.

Malcolm hurried her with the restlessness of eager boyhood, to the completion of her mission.

It was high noon when she returned to the hotel, leaving the lad to his first trial of business in his new place.

The only person she met after she ascended the stairs was Samuel Slaughton, who came with hasty strides, with hands extended, and his handsome face aglow with astonished pleasure.

"This is indeed a surprise, Perdita !" he exclaimed in a glad voice. "You have come up to town to see *me !* You missed my presence in the old house ; you found it lonely, dull, without *me*, clumsy as I am?"

"I came on business, sir. I was sent by my father to introduce Malcolm to Mr. Champlin."

"Oh, indeed ! Champlin & Everts. Has he a chance in that firm ? Well, that *is* a stroke of luck. Shall we go directly and see the parties, or will you choose to rest awhile ?"

"I have already completed the business, and I left my brother at his post."

"Already, Perdita? and you did not consult me—did not let me know of your arrival ? I have found out that you like helping yourself, but really I call that defrauding me of a pleasure—I might say of a right."

" I did ask for you. I was told that you were out, and that
no one knew when you would return."

" How stupid ! what a lonely little child you must have been
in this great city I why couldn't I have found out your presence
so near me I I ought to have felt it. Why, I sat here
in this very chair last night till past midnight, thinking about
you ! "

Perdita blanched to the hue of a white lily as he spoke.
" What a pity that your busiest meditations were bent on a plan
to separate from me, that you might be free to marry another
woman whom you have already in my hearing entreated to be
kind ! " she thought.

Mr. Slaughton looked anxiously at his wife, trying to understand her and the emotion which was shivering through her.

" You are ill," said he ; " you are suffering I You have
attempted too much."

" No, I am quite well. I attempt nothing. My strength is
only equal to that which is thrust upon me, and which I must
not shrink from."

" I don't see at all why this affair of Malcolm's should have
been, as you say, ' thrust upon you.' I could have done it just
as well. I wonder your father did not ask me ; too proud, I
suppose—he'd rather tire out his daughter. I will have no more
of it ! Ah, now you are blooming again, Perdita ; now I can
believe you are, as you say, well. We'll have a nice lunch,
that will rest you. What a curious thing it is to find you here.
Like a little runaway frolic. I like it vastly. And now that
you are here, I shall keep you. You shall visit the art gallery,
and see how my pictures are hung. We will go to the Shaugh-
raun this evening, and to-morrow we will drive out to the lake,
and the aqueduct. Oh, there are lots of places worth our
time. Do you know, Perdita, I have wished a thousand times
for you. Now you shall fold your wings close by me, till I
please to let you free, and when you go I shall go with you.
I had a long talk about you with an old friend, since I came

here, of all things past, present, and to come. My friend gave me some good advice."

Perdita started, as if from a dream. His voice, his eager manner and cordial *empressement* had almost lulled her into forgetfulness of her real condition, and she came near feeling happy in his presence. The bitter outrage of the shameless announcement he made with such an unclouded, unabashed countenance, stung her to the quick.

" You meet many friends in your travels," she replied, significantly. She could not keep the scorn out of her face, but she tried to speak carelessly. She waited for him to speak. She hoped he would honorably touch the fatal subject, and plainly mention Sabrina Bradshaw's name. She felt as if she could respect him more if he did, and she was prepared to hate him as soon as it passed his lips ; so consistent is passion. She waited in vain ; he disclosed none of his intentions, as how could he at such a time, in such a place ? And while he seemed disagreeably puzzled by her manner, he appeared also determined to ignore its sarcastic sharpness, and bent on urging her stay in Toptown.

" Come, Perdita, you must want to shop a little. I never went into buying-places with you. It will be a new experience ; will you beat down the clerks and flout them as my mother does ? I don't think I have forgotten how to carry ladies' parcels. I used to be quite *au fait*."

" Very likely you have refreshed yourself with recent practice," replied she. " You will never carry any parcels of mine, however. I am going back to your house by the next train."

Perdita spoke faintly. She was bewildered, dizzy. How could she reconcile what she had so plainly heard with her own ears, and seen with her own eyes, with the looks and actions she now studied. He wore such a semblance of truth and affection.

" He temporizes with the miserable wife till his plans are

ripe.   He is civil, he smiles and speaks her fair.   'After it is over, Sabrina, promise me that you will be kind.'"

The words seemed hissed into her ears, and her breast heaved with wild rage.   Only the evening before she had seen this pleasant-spoken, sweet-voiced gentleman holding his first love's hand (she had pulled *hers* away from his grasp almost before he touched them).   All unskilled in the ways of men, all unlearned in passion's signs, she knew that while he cajoled her with cheering phrases he was a wicked mocker, treacherously deceiving her ; so dark grew her face, such intense, disdainful contempt flashed from her eyes, that Mr. Slaughton started back blushing and frowning.

"What is the matter, Perdita?   What has gone wrong?"

"Everything! everything!   Stand out of my path.   I shall be too late for the train."

"Perdita, if you will not remain, or explain your conduct, you cannot prevent my accompanying you home."

"No, I cannot prevent you," cried she, all composure forsaking her, and her bosom heaving with jealous fury.   "No, I cannot prevent your going where you choose ; but you cannot compel me to look at you or speak to you ; and if you will have me say it, I despise you, Samuel Slaughton !   I know you to-day for just what you are, and all the gratitude and kindness I have been cultivating for you has turned sour.   I think before long I shall hate you."

He stood aside from her vehemence and overwhelming scorn, without another word.

When she returned with her travelling-bag on her arm to the spot where she had left him, he was nowhere to be seen.

CHAPTER LX.

"DAUGHTER, BE OF GOOD CHEER."

NCE events begin to march, the rate at which they post is sometimes marvellous. You may lead the life of a cabbage in your own native village, day succeeding day, week following week, without circumstance or change ; but should you cut loose for a holiday, and turn your back on the fixtures as fast in their places as stumps in a clearing, people will commence directly to make quarrels, get married, or die with most surprising facility and dispatch ; so that when you return, all the ancient land-marks are uprooted, and old familiar faces shuffled out of sight.

Mr. Slaughton's visit to Toptown seemed to be the pivot on which turned the signal for "Presto! change!" And when Perdita reached the Blithebeck station, half dead of fatigue and the devouring emotions which had torn at her heart and kept her brain whirling with giddy amaze and fright and anger, sorrowful anger all the way, she found Stephen waiting full of flurry and excitement. He scarcely waited for her to reach the platform when he blurted out the news that Dame Slaughton had been stricken down with typhoid pneumonia.

Despair and heart-sickness were swallowed in the necessity for immediate action, and she hastened to the bedside of her mother-in-law, to do with her might the work which lay right under her hand.

So ill was the poor old lady that her breath came already in sobs, and Perdita never forgot the regretful, hopeless gaze she fixed on her as soon as she appeared.

"Oh ! you've come," gasped she. "I was afraid I should have to die alone. I've had my warning at last—the white horse !   His eyes were wild and staring, and his chest was covered with foam, and he plunged into the black water and sank out of my sight ; and I knew that my time had come. Where is Samuel ? "

" He has not returned," whispered she, half shrinking from what seemed to her the ravings of a diseased brain.

"Send for him !   Send for Sammy !   Don't you see I'm dying ! send this instant ! "

Perdita dispatched a telegram, bidding Stephen wait for the midnight train.   When at last she heard the horses' quick trot up the road, she stepped to the door to forewarn the son, and prepare him for the sad sight he must see ; and she felt so much pity for his sorrow, that she ruled all reproach and anger from her face.

Stephen had returned alone.

She dreaded to take such doleful news to the sick woman, and could not bear to meet the eyes which fastened upon hers so filled with yearning and expectancy.   No words were needed.   The messenger brought her message of disappointment in her face, and the poor old creature shook her head, and closed the faded, wrinkled lids, through which a couple of tears slowly filtered.

" I shall never see Samuel again in this world ; I shall have to die without a kiss from my son," she moaned.   " Old, alone, forsaken ! forgotten ! "

When the Doctor came in the morning, she asked him plainly, " How long have I to live ? " and, although he parried her question with hopeful words, she had gotten so near to eternity that she was nearly able to read thoughts.

" To-night.   I shall die to-night ; can't you fetch my Samuel before dark ? "

Seeing the young wife without counsellors in her inexperience, the Doctor advised her to dispatch a messenger to Toptown. "Your father will go," said he; "let him start immediately."

Old Parson Hethwaite's pride had kept him aloof from the prosperous rich; but he was quite willing to go in search of this man coming into a heritage of sorrow. That was in his line of business, and he set about his preparations with alacrity. And I think he ran over, in his mind, the various texts of his best funeral discourses; and I know he hummed Windham and China while he packed his old valise.

All day Perdita watched the sufferer, applying the prescribed remedies; and so intense were her hope and dread, that her heart stood still when she heard approaching footsteps at evening.

Only one! her father had returned alone. Mr. Slaughton was not in Toptown. He had left the hotel on Friday, and nobody knew whither he was gone.

Another long night of watching! Two o'clock had struck when the sick woman roused from the heavy torpor which had shut in her senses for hours—insomuch that her labored breathing was the only sign of life in the nearly worn-out body—and looked eagerly around her.

"Not come yet?", she whispered with difficulty. "Old! alone! neglected! forgotten!" A spasm of grief convulsed her wrinkled features as she moaned out her desolation, so dreary! so pitiful!

It was unutterably dreadful to the young watcher, who sat a little way off quietly weeping, to witness her joyless departure. To know that she was surely going out of the world, where she had been so busy, so energetic, so full of will, into silence mute and soundless. Going, not of her own desire, as one sets out on a journey, but dragged by a power she could not resist or dispute; that she would not be permitted to linger for a farewell to the only being she truly loved; that the hand she

18*

had held fondly clasped in hers, when, in his beautiful infancy, she pressed her baby to her breast and he mirrored himself in her eyes, could not reach the cold fingers lying helplessly above the throbbing heart, through which the chilling life-blood coursed ever more feebly and fitfully.

An awful terror seized upon Perdita—knowing that the relentless messenger, Death! was grimly watching with her for the appointed moment when his fatal touch should still that panting heart, and stop for ever that laboring breath.

Superadded to all she was enduring was the sickening certainty that this poor mother's longed-for son was a man utterly unworthy and that he held *her* whole soul in his keeping.

Suddenly she found a pair of glassy eyes fastened upon her, and the dying creature's lips moved. She drew nearer to catch what she felt were the last words she would ever utter.

"Perdita, I made a great mistake. I thought too much about myself, and I did not think enough about you. I wanted a good, honest girl to help me—a stout, willing pair of hands to lift the burdens which I felt too heavy for mine. I have deeply sinned besides ; for after I got you here, I hated to see that you could take his love from me, and I was angry to know that he gave it of his own accord ; and you had to try no arts to win it. I felt bitter to see how soon he loved you, how you grew into his heart. It is your own place, Perdita—your own! You are so good and my Samuel is so true, that it could not have been otherwise. What short-sighted, selfish creatures we are ! I wanted an heir to my property. I hoped to live to see little Sammy trotting around the old rooms ; and I did hope to hold my dear boy's child in my arms, which cradled him. I shall not live for that joy. I am punished for my wicked hardness, terribly punished. The Lord did not count me worthy. Try to do your duty as you have always done, my daughter."

She reached out her hand, clammy with the death-sweat, and tried to touch Perdita's ; the girl made a strong effort and shudderingly laid her fingers on the cold ones, which sent an icy chill through her as she felt their clutch.

"Promise me to stay at your post here in the homestead, and keep the children together.   Have patience with my poor Cicely, and may the Lord open her heart to goodness and truth ; and as you do by mine so may He do by yours.   Give my love to Samuel, and don't forget right away the poor old woman who blesses you with her latest breath.   I think I shall be there in the room when you awake to mother-joy.   I can't see your face, Perdita.   I'm going fast.   I shall not see day dawn.   I am truly thankful that it is so well between you and your good husband.   I should hate to die, knowing I had spoiled two lives."

Perdita withdrew hastily from the bed, and pressed her hands upon her breast.   She felt that she must cry aloud—she knew with such bitter knowledge that her life was marred past mending.

The birds were beginning their morning concert, and still the watcher sat listening to the labored breathing, whose throbbing throes counted themselves in the stillness.   She listened till her heart seemed a part of the one whose uncertain strokes were about to cease.   She felt weary with the unconscious effort to keep time with those panting breaths.   All at once there came a gurgle in the throat, a faint gasp, and—such silence, as if all human life was stopped.   Even the bird-songs ceased, mute silence ! sudden ! profound.   She waited motionless, watching the stark form ; dreading, expecting the next breath ; her straining ears could catch no sound ; she seemed to see the hand stir ; she rose and looked fearfully in the palid face.   The half open eyes were glozed, the lower jaw had dropped ; she put her ear close to the pillow.   Silence profound ! terrible ! She fled swiftly, but with noiseless footsteps, lest she might awake the sleeper, whom nothing could arouse till the arch-angel's trump calls forth the dead.   On the threshold she paused an instant, sending a glance over her shoulder.   A bird had alighted on the rose-bush close to the open window, and with its bright eyes fixed on the poor, worn-out old body, it burst into a rapture of melodious song, which filled the whole place with triumphant rejoicing.

CHAPTER LXI.

"WHITHER GOEST THOU, PILGRIM STRANGER?"

AMUEL SLAUGHTON left Toptown. He took the first train which met his sight when he reached the depot. On a great placard he read, "Through for Chicago, St. Louis and the West." He entered a car and sat down. After a while a man came along with a lantern, and touched his shoulder. He pushed off his hat, which had been slouched over his face, unfolded his arms, and looked up at the intruder, who was shouting in his ear above the rac-a-tac of the wheels:

"Want a berth, sir?"

Of course he wanted a berth. What so good to pass away time as sleep? He gave his name, received his number, and relapsed into thought. Presently he was disturbed again.

"Ticket, sir."

He turned fretfully. There stood the conductor, inspecting his hat-band by the light of his lantern; he put up his hand, and finding no check, he remembered that he had not purchased a ticket, and he pulled out his wallet.

"How much?"

"Where to?"

He stopped to think where he was going, and the conductor

commenced impatiently running over the main points of his route.   Chicago—St. Louis, etc."

" Yes, Chicago ! how much ? "

" You can pay me to Redwing ; we get there at five o'clock. There you can buy through ; I get off there to-night ; you ought to have bought at Toptown ; saves considerable to get a through. Here's your change, and your check," he called out, as loud as he could scream. He saw that his passenger was not attending.

As the sleeping-car man passed the other, he tapped his forehead, and winked significantly at Mr. Slaughton, who had forgotten them both.

" Queer street," said he ; " fifth story ; nobody to home."

The heavy hours clattered by, but they brought no rest for tumultuous thoughts, which were scarcely thoughts, so disjointed, aimless, and distracting were they.   All at once the thread of noise which had been bearing them along was snapped. The cars stood still.

" Redwing ! twenty minutes for refreshments ! "

He followed the crowd, being disturbed, nearly deafened by the clamor of a great bell, which a fellow on the platform was swinging back and forth with all the strength of his arms, while he bellowed out the name and attractions of his house. He walked into a hotel.   An officious waiter bowed him in.

" Room, sir !   Breakfast, sir ! "

" Yes ! a quiet room."

Mr. Slaughton lay down, and a heavy slumber fell on him—a stupor of forgetfulness.

When he awoke the day was far advanced. He sat up and looked about him.   He slowly recalled the late events, and his first impulse was to go home and look in Perdita's face. He felt hungry for a sight of her.   A dreary flood of memories which beat over him—of her parting words, her bitter scorn, her disgust, her hate, engulfed him—sweeping away hope and joy, and happiness, and he was stranded on an arid shore of unrest. Before him stretched a boundless desert of barren unprofitable-

ness.   No use in living; no motive for action; as well here as
anywhere; better anywhere than there.   He let the day go by
without arriving at any resolution.   He did not note the
wasting of the hours, but just allowed them to drip—and drip,
without caring for their flight.   If he had known that his last
one was counted, he would not have lifted a finger, or breathed
a sigh of regret.

When the waiter came and asked him to dine or sup, he
followed him, eating what was fetched for him, and rising with
the others when they left the table, careless of the eyes which
were watching him with compassion or curiosity, and of the
busy tongues which were wagging over his condition and
affairs.

As he was walking slowly down the hall, his hands were
suddenly seized, and a familiar voice shouted out with a glad
accost, " Sam ! my dear fellow, I have found you at last ! "

" And what do you want with me ? " asked he, nervously
resisting the strong grasp with which Chandy Goldsmith had
laid hold of him.   He lifted his sad, troubled eyes to the great
loving ones, full of sympathy and sorrow, and added, " What
has happened, Chandos ?   Why are you here ? "

" I've terrible news for you, Sam ; terrible news !   You must
brace yourself to meet an affliction—a bereavement, Sam, old
fellow."

" Has—has Perdita gone away ? has she left my house ? "

" Perdita ! no.   Sam, come up to your room," added
Chandos, seeing a curious crowd gathering around them.   " I
must speak to you alone."

" Tell me, Chandy ! " said his friend, as Mr. Goldsmith linked
his arm in his, and they ascended the stairs together.   " Tell
me !   You can't hurt me more than she did."

" Your mother is very ill !   Your mother, I fear, is dying."

" My mother ! " exclaimed Mr. Slaughton, stopping short ;
" ill ! and I, her only son, away from her !   I must return immediately ! immediately ! do you hear, Chandos ? "

He passed his hand across his forehead as if trying to recall his scattered senses, and he threw a quick, suspicious look at his friend, who was intently observing him.

"I see you think strange of my vagabondizing; but a sudden fancy took me to run up here. I didn't think to stop so long. Dying, did you say? God grant I be not too late!"

"I trust not," answered Chandos. "They telegraphed to you from Toptown, and Mr. Hethwaite himself went after you; but you started in too much haste, it seems, to leave a line or post a letter. As they could get no clue to you, your wife sent to me! Of course I started instantly. I got your name from the sleeping-car list, and here you are. Now, Sam, shan't I go on home with you? You are likely to need a friend?"

Mr. Slaughton felt the delicacy, which, in face of his late revelations (meagre though they were, yet sufficient to let his friend know that his relations with his wife were not happy), hesitated to thrust itself into his troubles. He sent a thought among his home situations, and he felt averse to unveiling them afresh to this happy man, blessed with a fond companion who clung to him, comforted and helped him. He felt it easier to go alone.

"No! thanks, Chandos, I will send, if there is anything you can do. I trust I shall find my mother better. I must set off at once. You are kind—always kind, old friend. You can afford to be kind, for your life is rich in blessings."

Mr. Slaughton staggered under the sudden blow, which effectually aroused him, and sent his thoughts into their wonted channels. All his faculties centered instantly in his mother and the duty he owed her.

CHAPTER LXII.

GOOD-BY, SWEETHEART!

HO can tell the thoughts of the silent man, over the casket dressed with flowers, over the open grave, in the lonely rooms? The voice he had first heard there was hushed forever ; the woman who reared him, planned for him, worked for him, bewailed his absence, rejoiced in his presence, was dead ! She had died alone !

Was he mourning her loss? Was he sorrowing over his lost love ? Was he planning a prosperous future ? Was he despairing ? Was he angry ? Was he calculating his chances of happiness ? Was he indifferent ? He made no sign. He went soberly about his duties, answering decorously all calls upon his time, all demands upon his attention. He saw the undertaker, he conversed with the grave-digger ; he gave a concise and particular order to the monument man ; he selected a turfer and graveyard gardener, and paid him a bonus on future wages. He smoked a good many cigars, and he walked miles and miles. He visited the oak wood where he and Chandy had intruded on the picnic, and the old mill where he had saved the setter, Sam ; and the garden where he had helped his wife plant the bulbs ; the studio where he had given her lessons ; the old house under the hill where he had accompanied her when she went to fetch home Cicely Vance ; all the places which had the least reminiscence of or association with his wife Perdita, he haunted and lingered over. He even went down to the old parsonage, that he might sit in the room where he had first seen the dark-browed girl who withdrew so pointedly from his neighborhood; and he went and stood in the precise spot in the darkened parlor, where he had taken her hand and promised to love and cherish her.

Perdita did not intrude upon his occupations, but went resolutely about *her* duties and preparations. She gathered the children together, keeping them out of his way. She sat at his table; she got them all measured for their mourning; she put on hers, and the regulation crape veil; and she locked up the lavender muslin, with its flounces—poor muslin! After all the joy, and hope, and bliss, which had been trimmed into its trimming, it had turned out such a desolate failure. Never seeing its heyday of happiness, a dungeon with a locked door, darkness and obscurity are its proper meed. Good-by, pretty dress! pretty to no good; useless, out of time and place, hide yourself in secret; be ashamed! fade! and drop to pieces!

All the outward signs and forms at the mansion house were correct; the funeral was large and solemn, the bearers stout, respectable men—old neighbors, who looked and behaved with decorum and reverence; the singing good; Parson Hethwaite's sermon solid and heavy—his address to the mourners in the front pew, who stood up to attend, was orthodox and dreary.

After it was all over, and the air and light of heaven was once more admitted to the house, and the living, having left their dead behind them, were moving on as if no vacancy had been made, no chair empty, Samuel Slaughton came for the first time into the library where Perdita was sitting.

"I shall leave this country for a while," said he. "I trust you will remain in this house!"

"Assuredly!" she replied, with great outward composure. "I promised your mother to stay among the children, and I shall keep my word till I am removed."

"Perdita!" said he, looking piteously at her, "it is of no use going back into the past any more, I suppose, and there is nothing in the future for you and me!"

"Yes! to live apart, as you feel, since you are about to

quit this place. When you are ready to take the necessary
steps to set you free in the eyes of the law, as you have always
been in fact, you may rest assured that I shall not lay a straw
in your road."

"And you will rejoice in *your* freedom!" exclaimed he
bitterly.

"There is no question of me! There was none in the beginning; there is none in the ending."

He looked at her with aching eyes; proud, cold, every look
and attitude full of alienation and dislike.

Suddenly she turned her face towards him, though her eyes
still sought the ground—the black, intense eyes, with their
brows arched by nature into such disdain that they needed the
bright smiles her red lips were so capable of, to soften their
pride. What a pity she had not lifted her glance to his, instead
of veiling it beneath her dropped lids till her long, curling
lashes touched her cheek.

"I wish to ask you a question before you go, just to please
and satisfy myself. You are at liberty to answer or not, as you
choose."

"Ask it!" exclaimed he eagerly, and yet, as it seemed to
her, with curious trepidation. She saw, without looking at him,
that he was deeply discomposed, he turned his mourning ring
about and about on his shrunken finger, and his gaze fastened
fixedly on her. The deep line between his eyes deepened, and
the faint red flickered and changed in his haggard face—such
alteration had the few days effected in his appearance. It
might be sorrow; it might be remorse.

"If the words were revoked which tie you in this most un-
fortunate marriage, and you were free to choose again, do you
know the woman whom you would marry?"

"No! a thousand times no!"

His manner was violent, his face splashed with blushes, his
eyes sparkling, his voice hoarse with emotion.

"One word more! Have you ever spoken words of love

to any other woman since you took my hand in the old parsonage—that blessed day the sun shone on?"

Oh, how bitter was her tone! how repellant her manner!

"You wish to insult me, Perdita! You do insult me!"

"That is all, and more than enough," said she, rising. The good time for meeting his glance had passed now; his glowed and beamed with anger, which burned up all its tenderness.

"I shall not be up to-morrow morning when you leave. I will say good-by now."

"Good-by, Perdita. God bless you!"

"God *forgive* you!" she said, in a hard, resonant voice, as she passed out of his sight.

CHAPTER LXIII.

"THE GOOD MEN DO LIVE AFTER THEM."

HE autumn passed away quietly—the gorgeous time of ripened leaves, so rich with memories.

The many-tinted beauties with which Perdita had decked the old library, and which her husband had praised and admired a thousand times, had withered and faded, and been gathered and swept out as rubbish.

The hopes which she had slowly and fearfully garnered while they were aglow, were dead also, and buried out of sight; and though she plodded through the daily tasks, faithfully teaching the children, ordering Slowgo, drawing, studying, everything about her was so full of the man who left her to lead her desolate life, that she felt often that she must flee away from their heart-breaking associations and give herself rest.

One good had come to her out of her wreck. She had learned that her father was able to be a valuable counsellor ; and there were times when she almost opened her heart enough to feel him a friend. The disasters in her life, which he could not help seeing, had much shaken him out of his apathy, thawed his ice-crust, and ameliorated the sternness which years of disappointment and poverty had built up around him ; and in his first outgo of benevolence, his earnest endeavor to comfort his child, he also opened his eyes to his faded wife's need of cherishing, his children's want of a father instead of a tyrant.

As the poor, stricken lady, once pretty Violet Wemple, expanded in the unwonted and most unexpected kindness which came to her like rain on the mown grass, she lifted her head a little, and nearly felt as if she might bloom afresh.

The first gust of natural tenderness among them was when Perdita brought down to the parsonage a bundle of papers she had found in her desk directed to her. They were among the documents which she was obliged to read, informing her of the money arrangements which her husband had made for her when he left home.

They were the legal forms of adoption, executed and signed, bestowing the child Bettine upon her, making her darling the joint property of Mr. and Mrs. Slaughton, and an heir of the Slaughton estates, in default of legal successors to the same.

It bore a date immediately after the Thanksgiving dinner, and had been kept back by poor Sam for a *bonne bouche* to accompany the talk he promised himself and his wife on his return from the fateful Toptown journey.

Such tears of mingled happiness and misery as were showered upon the tiny darling, made all her own by this noble, disinterested action ; such broken thanks, such tender kisses ; tears from the woman who had shed so many that her beauty was dimmed and faded; tears from the little fairy in her soft muslin, gay ribbons, and floating curls, who wept because Perdita sobbed so dreadfully that she could not choose but droop her sweet lips in sympathetic sorrow; tears from rosy-cheeked, careless Dolly, who palpitated beneath her mother's caress, and got no rebuke for the folly.

Tears also from the sere fountains long unused to flow, which rained down in torrents, when Perdita went over to her father, and throwing her arms around his neck, kissed his withered cheek.

"Father, I thank God and you for your goodness! and I shall pray to him every day on my knees to forgive all the hard and bitter feelings I have cherished against you. Bettine is mine!"

That night, when the Parson was left alone with his wife, he told her for the first time in his life that he was sorry. She could hardly take in the wondrous announcement; and when he followed that by saying he meant to do different, she just settled down into a tired little heap and moaned and sobbed at his feet.

"David," said she in a broken voice, full of tenderness and love, "I always felt that if you had had good times you would have been different. I don't mind. I won't ever think of the past again if you will be soft to me. Kiss me, husband! Kiss your faded Violet. I was fresh and blooming when you married me."

The old man raised her up, straining her to his heart, and calling Heaven to witness that he took her in good faith.

"Great God! if I could but bring back thy sweet youth again!" exclaimed he in such bitterness of self-reproach as made her pity him.

"No, David, that cannot be!" said she solemnly. "See here! My black hair has bleached to snow, and yours has fallen; we are old and worn; there is only the evening of life left us. Pray that our sun may set in glory, that we may fall

asleep together. Only, be gentle to me, David. There is
still time to keep your promise :

> "'If friends to thee have proved untrue,
>   I will be all they should have been,
> If fortune frown upon thy view,
>   I'll give thee smiles thou shouldst have seen,
> Thou shalt not want for anything
> That he who loveth thee can bring ;
> And love makes all things to be had—
> Prythee, Sweetheart, be not sad !'

You see, I remember well, because I loved well, David."

" Don't, wife ! every word you say hurts me like a blow."

" Then I will talk no more, and we will begin to be truly
happy."

" Dolly," said Mrs. Hethwaite, one day soon after, " I am
afraid your father is going to die."

" I hope not, mother, just as he is getting bearable and
decent."

" Yes, Dolly, I think he must be ; he is getting dying grace."

CHAPTER LXV.

"FOR THEE WAS A HOUSE MADE ERE THOU WAST BORN."

HE winter was marked by two events;
Randy Teazle was taken ill, and Cicely,
after telling lies enough to ensure per-
dition (unforgiven), trumping up excuses
to visit him stealthily, finally begged with
tears to be allowed to go and stay with
him " one long, long day."

" I'm sure it will be so sweet to nurse Randy, aunty."

Ignoring the sentimental leer with which Cicely delivered

this opinion, Perdita consented, after some consideration. She really pitied the loneliness of the boy. He was such a gentle creature. And she hoped to keep the would-be nurse in good faith with her by consenting. So she put up a basket of jellies and other delicacies, and started her off full of rosy satisfaction.

In the afternoon she thought she would herself pay the sick lad a visit.

She found Cicely and Sal in a high game of romps; laughing, and jumping, squalling like cats, and all the plates and bowls were empty.

"So this is the way you nurse Randy, is it?" said Perdita severely to the abashed frolickers." "It is a wonder you haven't killed him outright."

"Oh, Mrs. Slaughton!" implored the boy, holding the soft, cool hand she extended to him, in his burned and parched with fever. "Oh, do take her away! I'm fit to die! They ate up all the nice things you sent to me, and they most split my head with tearing round; and when I asked them to stop, they made up faces at me, and they called me 'cry-baby cupsey.'"

"Upon my word, Cicely, you come out strong in your new vocation. I'm not sure a hospital would not be your true sphere," remarked Perdita.

"I don't care. It wasn't any fun to sit still and do nothing; and Randy was so cross and pokey, he said he wished I'd stayed at home. I don't want to nurse him any more."

"Mrs. Slaughton," whispered the sick lad, as she was taking leave of him, careful to send Cicely on before her, "will Dolly come to see me, do you suppose? I love Dolly; she is so dear, and so nice, and so handsome. Will you ask her?"

"Indeed I will, Randy. I know she will be glad to visit you; and she will read to you, and take care of you. Dolly can be very pleasant in a sick-room; she has a kind heart. I'll tell her to bring down the dominoes she got for Christmas, and show you how to play; that will amuse you, won't it?"

"If I can lie still and look at Dolly, I shall be content," answered the lad with a satisfied smile.

So, in the old cottage under the hill, red-cheeked Dolly did her first bit of mission-work, and she did it well, for her charge slowly recovered. Whether the working in her life with his, as she did day after day, was a good thing for her patient, is a point which we will debate some other time, when we have got all the bearings of the case. He got up quite well and strong, at any rate, with his soul full of new impulses, and his mind stirring with new ambitions.

At the spring examination of the district school in Blithebeck Centre, Randy Teazle shone so brightly in geography and arithmetic as to receive honorable mention from the committee, and a new silver dollar with a hole in it as a medal, which adornment he wore with more honest pride than any knight ever felt in his crosses or garters.

Before he left his bed, Cicely came to Perdita, her face crimson with excitement and pleasure.

"Randy is worse to-day, aunty," exclaimed she. "If he dies may I have on my best black clothes, that I wore to grandma's burying, and go to his funeral? Black is very becoming to me; the dressmaker said so."

The second event of the winter was one which wrought a radical change in the Parson's family.

An old uncle died and left Mrs. Hethwaite a legacy, which was to her a large fortune. She received the news with a burst of joy and gratitude, and carried it to her husband.

"There, David! It is all yours; do with it as you will."

Strangely enough, the words were the very same she had used when she bestowed upon him her bank stock, soon after her marriage. He needed a minister's library, and suggested that her money might buy it; trustingly and meekly she resigned her all in his hands, saying:

"Take it, David! It is yours! do with it as you will."

Perhaps something in her voice or manner kindled his

memory, so that the coincidence struck him. He brooded over it, and it rankled, till he tortured her goodness into a taunt—a fling at his incompetency.

Since that day of amazing confession and contrition, the old man had been gradually and surely settling into a state of morbid moroseness. He never resumed his former high-mightiness of behavior towards his family, but he was sourer if possible than before—more bitter, and he became suspicious of them. If they spoke low, they were discussing him; if they laughed, they were ridiculing him; and he would fly into a sudden and most unseemly rage, and storm and scold, belaboring the one who happened to be nearest him with violent, sarcastic abuse, bringing into use sundry words which had long been vanished from his vocabulary.

He would shut himself up whole days, refusing to see anybody. If he fell asleep in his chair of an evening, they found it best to let him alone, for when they awakened him he was furious enough to drive them all crazy. For weeks at a time they carried his food to his study, and left it there, to be devoured in solitude.

He was already far gone in this state when the fortune came. There was a terrible scene that day in the old parsonage, and he never spoke a pleasant word, even to his wife, again, and obstinately refused to touch or taste any of the luxuries purchased with the money. He would have hindered the others from enjoying the good things; but Mrs. Slaughton set his conduct before him in a strong light. After that he was doggedly silent in her presence, and paid no more attention to what was transpiring around him.

In February he was taken seriously ill. When the doctor arrived, he insisted on knowing his opinion of his case. Very reluctantly the doctor answered his close questions; but he finally wormed out the verdict that his life was only a question of vitality and endurance. The next day he called the other physician, who tacitly confirmed his medical brother's statement.

19

From that time he refused all nourishment, and shut his lips in persevering silence.

When the fatal moment approached, he watched his nails growing purple, as the life-current flowed more and more feebly, and wiped the death-damp from his forehead, and turning his face away from them all, he closed his eyes and breathed his last without a farewell, even to the wife of his youth.

Poor Mrs. Hethwaite wept some natural tears over his body, and felt that she ought to be sorry for his loss. She struggled against the sense of relief which would possess her, as against a sin. She sat alone with his corpse, trying to recall all his generous actions, conscientiously endeavoring to bring back the love she had felt for her young minister. But it was of no use; her trials and crosses and hardships under his dominion were and would be paramount.

When he was laid in his grave, and she was free to plan and work, to come and go, and order her life, to embellish it, even, without any more dread, any more mortifications, any more secret tears, she began to grow fresher and brighter, her face rounded, and the light came back to her eyes, and Violet Hethwaite smiled almost as often and as pleasantly upon her children as Violet Wemple had done upon her lover.

She religiously visited his grave, and made it a duty to pray over the mound; and she returned home afterwards with brisk step, and full of the new life which was spreading and blooming before her.

Ease, plenty, and comfort for her old age! *Her* sun was setting with mild radiance. Every day she had moments of trying not to be too peaceful and happy, knowing in her secret soul that her life-trouble was turning to dust, and worms were devouring his body.

CHAPTER LXV.

"WHEN SHE WILL, SHE WILL, YOU MAY DEPEND ON'T."

M R. and Mrs. Philip Penhurst went up to Roaring River to celebrate the anniversary of their wedding-day, a festivity which occurred, you may remember, in the month of March.

All the dearest companions of Sabrina's youth being gathered together, she had a very delightful week. Of course she met Chandos Goldsmith, and of course, also, they talked of their mutual friend, Samuel Slaughton. Sabrina listened attentively to all she heard, and then she fell into deep meditation.

"And you say he left Toptown hurriedly?"

"Hurriedly? I should say so! And the most mysterious thing altogether, Sam sat with me one night till nearly morning talking about his wife. You know how queerly they were married? Well, I happened to be in his house when he brought home his bride, and I was struck with her beauty, and I stayed long enough with them to find out that she had plenty of attractions, mental and spiritual, and I told Sam he was dead sure to fall in love with the girl. She was such a rare creature, every way—uncommon, I assure you. Why, if I had not been head and ears with my Bertha, I shouldn't have escaped, myself! Well, Sabrina, all the while he was running on, rhapsodizing in such high style, I was chuckling over my sharpness. I had to bite my tongue to keep it from telling him 'I told you so!' You never saw such a mad lover!"

"I saw *him* that very time," replied Sabrina, smiling. "He opened his heart to me. It did me a world of good to hear him talk ; I felt so very happy in the happiness of my old friend."

" Indeed ! Well, now, listen. The very next day, as I was going up the hotel steps, whom should I meet but Mrs. Slaughton coming down. She had a travelling-bag on her arm, and I was struck at once with her woful face. I stopped to shake hands and say a few little things ; but she could hardly speak, and she positively declined to let me accompany her to the station—said she had rather go alone. I never was so snubbed in all my life ! I wilted like a cabbage-plant in the hot sun, and I positively came as near sneaking off as a man of my figure and carriage could, under the look she burned into me when I inquired where I could find Sam. While I was looking after her, Otho came up, and I had to go down to the Medical College with him, so that I didn't get back to the hotel till night, and Sam was gone. You know the rest : how he sailed for Europe without a good-by to anybody, and nothing has since been heard from him. I get news once in a while from Blithebeck in a roundabout way. I know his wife is there ; but I have not felt like intruding on the strict privacy she maintains among the children."

" Chandos ! " exclaimed Sabrina, " I understand it all. I saw that girl ! I know I did ! I feel it ! I was advising with Sam about poor Cousin Phil. You know he had trouble with his wife, and was getting a divorce from her. Sam advocated his doing so, and talked very earnestly ; we sat close together in the corridor. She was jealous of me ! We *must* have looked mighty confidential. You know Sam's fashion with those he is fond of. I can recall the strange glance she gave me, full of glowing fire, and proud, indignant, sorrowful anger. I remember I was minded to call Sam's attention to the beautiful fury behind us ; but before he came to a pause she was gone. Chandos, I have something to do in this business. I'm going over to Blithebeck before I return to Canadasset."

" I believe you are right, Sabrina," replied Chandy, musing.

"Sam had the Ruth he painted from your sittings up at Cragen-
fels, in his studio; and stay! Yes, it is as clear as moonshine.
She overheard a rhapsody about you, which Sam was fool
enough to pour forth on his wedding-day, which it was impossible she could ever forget. In fact, he told me, with the queer-
est sort of face, how he had been made to pay for his incautious
words; how she had tossed them back at him; and how resplendent she had been while she did so; how bewildering!"

"Pooh!" said Mrs. Penhurst, loftily. "Sam's little nonsense over me died a natural death long ago—a mere fancy."

"It is dead now, at any rate; his wife fills the bill at present. I wish to gracious he would come home and mind his
business."

Mrs. Penhurst carried out her intention of visiting the recluse. Her husband did not enter heartily into the project;
he rather considered it impossible romance, and, to speak
plainly, "none of their business."

For one less self-centered, straightforward and candid than
Sabrina, it would have been a difficult undertaking to bring to
a successful issue. It needed a good deal of right-minded
earnestness, as well as tact, to force herself into the presence of
a deserted wife, believing herself the cause of the husband's
defection, knowing beforehand how proud and shy and reserved the poor girl was to all strangers, and how bitter and
angry she might be with her.

But she dashed fearlessly into her mission, forgetful of self,
thinking only of the best interests of two noble natures so
unhappily sundered.

Perdita was busy in her conservatory, when Hannah came to
tell her a lady waited in the parlor, who desired to see her on
business.

She had just finished cutting a bunch of roses, and she
approached with them in her hand. Her long, jetty braids
were fastened with their crimson ribbons; her dress was short
and simple. (She had always shrunk from making any change

in it, clinging to the fashion she brought with her to the
mansion house, and which had been hers through her short life
in the companionship of her husband. The black robes which
she was obliged to don for the dame's funeral were immediately
laid aside after it was over ; and her isolated life did not make
it necessary for her to resume them when her father died.
There was a lilac muslin folded in her chest upstairs which she
sometimes dreamed over, and which she felt it possible she
might yet assume ; but this was a rare dream, when youth and
love and hope would get the mastery, and it always ended in
tears of despair.)   As she stepped forward, her visitor noticed
the low shoes and red stockings and the remarkably pretty feet
Chandy had described to her.

The regular life and constant occupation of the recluse kept
her health perfect, notwithstanding her trials ; but though the
bloom of her face was resplendent, her eyes looked sorrowful,
and she had taken a habit of half veiling them beneath their
long lashes, as if the world held nothing worth looking at.   So
that the sudden start, the vivid blush which swept into her
cheeks, and the dazzling light which flooded those wonderful
eyes when she opened them full on her visitor, almost electrified
her, and it was half a moment before she found a word to say.

Once entered on her business, however, she pushed right
forward from point to point in a clear, decided, honest way,
which carried conviction with her.

What ever-varying emotions they were which played over the
expressive countenance of the listener, and what a look it was
which Sabrina got when she finished !—perfect trust, unwavering
confidence ; and all unused and unskilled as was Perdita in
concealments, she never thought of trying to hide the joy which
enveloped her like an atmosphere when she once more knew
her husband for a true man.

But when Sabrina proposed that she should write and recall
him, or at least let him know how she had found out her mistake, she turned proud and firm in an instant.

"No!" said she, "he weakly forsook the plain path of his duty; he adopted his usual habit of letting things arrange themselves. He is my husband. He ought to have remained at home; he ought to have made me understand him, and insisted on my obedience, duty, and respect. He ought to have told me he loved me. I shall not take a step towards him; it is his business to come back to me. I have not deserted him; he has deserted me!"

"But did not you speak some unpleasant words to him?"

"Yes, I did; but what are woman's words to man's strength? I should have as easily turned towards him as the Clytie turns to her sun-god, if he had taken the trouble to talk and explain."

"But you forget he was shrouded in a maze of doubt. He did not in the least understand why you flouted him so dreadfully, when he was full of fondness for you."

"I asked him if he had ever made love to any woman since he married me, and he said 'No!' I should suppose he would have recalled his talk with you such a short while before. I should think he must have read what was in my mind."

"But he did not make love to me," answered Sabrina, smiling. "He magnified the perfections of his wife to his old friend, who was delighted with his enthusiasm."

"Quite true," replied Perdita, dryly; "but you must recollect how I had heard him *enthuse* over the very lady to whom he was talking, and you will not wonder at my error."

"But that was boyish nonsense."

"I hope it was—I believe he loved me when he left me."

"Besides, he had a confidential conversation with Chandos Goldsmith after I left him; they sat up till nearly morning."

"Oh!" said Perdita, "indeed!"

It was of no use, she could not, would not try to get back her rover, though she shyly owned that she should rejoice to see his face again; and therefore Mrs. Penhurst took a fresh resolution, which she lost no time in carrying out as soon as she returned to Canadasset. She wrote a letter, copies of which she dispatched to all the principal banking houses of Europe, hoping that some one of them might reach the wanderer and bring him home.

———◆———

CHAPTER LXVI.

CICELY VANCE FINDS HER VOCATION.

PRING opened early that year, and by the middle of April the leaves began to shoot, and the roads were quite settled.

The children were full of excitement. A grand menagerie and circus was coming to Blithebeck village, which they were all eagerness to attend.

Fortunately, Malcolm was home on a visit, and volunteered to take care of the party ; and Mrs. Richard Pritchard begged an invitation to stop all night at the mansion house, so that her young ones could partake the wonderful pleasure.   Perdita was as flushed and animated as the children ; the real live beasts, the vaulting and the riding, were as wondrous to her as to them.

When it was over and the party were ready to go home, Cicely was nowhere to be found.   After much search she was discovered behind one of the booths, with the clown and the bareback rider, giggling and chatting, all alive with antics and excitement, her face as gorgeous as a carnation, her blue eyes blazing and her curls flying, as she danced and flitted about, encouraged by the applause of her audience.

"My gracious !" exclaimed Malcolm, much put out by the heat of the hunt and the delay, " I should think that girl had better go along with the gang at once. What a lot of shapes she can put her broom-sticks into !"

The next morning Cicely got leave to ride down to Blithe-beck village with Stephen, who was sent for groceries. While he was busy about his errands, he heard the circus band, who were advertising their entertainment through the streets, and feeling uncertain of his horses (he had left them hitched, and had entreated Miss Cicely to remain in the wagon and keep quiet), he made haste back. The horses were all right ; but Cicely had disappeared.

She was not able to resist the music, and the clatter, and had slipped away to take just one look at the flags and the gilded wagon, and the gold-laced jackets of the band, and so had followed the crowd quite to the tents. There she found her friend, the bold-faced clown, and the trainer, who winked at each other and exchanged a few low-voiced words, as soon as they espied her ; and then Mr. Clown, who was a rosy-cheeked, merry-looking fellow enough, quite calculated to take the fancy of such a girl as Cicely Vance, went up and said how pleased and proud he was to see the handsome little lady again, and offered her tickets for the show.

Of course she heedlessly accepted, unmindful of consequen-ces ; and the result was she was easily cajoled into joining the company, her head being full of the spangles and finery of the riders. Such dresses and such a gay life seemed absolute bliss, especially when Mr. Clown treated her to a paper of can-dies and a couple of glasses of ginger-pop ; and her bright com-plexion and agile movements made her a desirable prey. She told them she had no father or mother, nor much of any friends—only a cross old aunt, whom she hated ; and she promised to steal away the next night, and she exulted in the assurance given her by the trainer, that she should have a fine new name, and he would teach her to be the best bareback rider in the known world.

She ran as fast as she could after parting with her fascinating

19*

new friends, and Stephen found her at last sitting on the steps of a church. She told him she had been inside hearing mass, which was only just over. He grumbled a good deal over the trouble she gave him ; but he was in such fume and hurry to get home, that he gave little heed to her talk, and nothing was said about it after their return.

All that day she carried about with her the secret of her intended flight.

The next morning Hannah came to her mistress with a disturbed countenance.

" I hate to complain of Miss Cicely, ma'am, but I had seven dollars in my wallet, and I am afraid she's took 'em. She was in my room yesterday afternoon, when I was looking over my things, and she saw my money, and got it into her hands ; she pestered me to let her count it. She is always poking her nose everywhere—a meddlesome plague as ever lived. This morning I found my old wallet empty, and tossed under the bed."

" How very shocking, Hannah ! I do hope you are mistaken ! "

" I'm not, then, ma'am ! " replied the maid positively. " It was there ; it isn't there now ; that girl has got it."

" Tell Cicely to come to me directly, Hannah."

Pretty soon the servant hurried back. " She hain't in her room, Miss Perdita ; her best dress, and all her sashes, and trinkets, are gone too ; her bed is touzled, but I don't believe she lay in it at all ! "

Terror and confusion filled the house. Perdita started immediately for the station.

" Yes," said the ticket man in answer to her inquiries. " Oh, yes ; the young miss bought a ticket for Toptown on the early train this morning."

She followed thither ; but, though assisted by Malcolm and the police, they failed to find any further traces of the fugitive. Those who had her in charge understood their business too well.

It was a fearful experience for Perdita, and helped to sadden her days. Oh! how desperately, *then*, she bewailed the hard fate which had set her alone with such a responsibility, and apart from her natural support and counsellor.

———◆———

CHAPTER LXVII.

CINCINNATUS RETURNS TO HIS PLOUGH.

R. SAMUEL SLAUGHTON, a passenger of the steamship *Restless*, was very ill on the voyage, and was carried on a bed up to the hotel in Liverpool, where he lay for weeks betwixt life and death. His nervous system was completely disordered, and the strangers around him considered him doomed.

His good constitution prevailed, however, and he arose at length; but such a ghastly, pale, emaciated wreck of himself, that his best friend would not have recognized him. His head had been shaved in the access of his fever, and his flowing beard and mustache were gone, his eye's fire was burned out, and his step was as feeble and tottering as the gait of age.

The first place he visited on getting out was his banker's, in the dim hope of finding letters. Of course there were none, and being interested in nothing, he drifted aimlessly towards the south, so that autumn found him settled at Rome—if it could be called settling to forever roam about without object, sitting on old palace-steps, hovering around churches, loitering in hotels, and walking miles and miles only to retrace his profitless wanderings when half dead of fatigue and *ennui*.

At length he took a studio, and began to paint. Always brooding over one face, he repeated its features in every picture he made, Madonnas or Magdalenes, again and again Perdita.

When the Italian sun began to pour down its summer beams, and lassitude and languor prostrated him, he experienced intense home-sickness. As soon as the necessity of moving forced itself upon him, a vision of his native hills arose continually before his imagination—their green pines, spicy hemlocks, cool water-brooks. He saw the old mill where he had given Scamp to Perdita, the wood where she had cooked the fish, the shady lanes and grassy roads where he had ridden by her side ; even the calf-pen under the great, spreading apple-tree, where they had taken shelter from the infuriated bull—and he longed to go home.

Once the idea was admitted among his reflections as a possibility, it became a necessity—immediate, arbitrary, absorbing, which hurried his preparations and sent him flying by the swiftest route.

At whatever cost, under whatever hindrances or obstacles, he must have his wife ; and before long it became, " I *will* have her. She shall listen to me ! She shall love me !" Then Mr. Samuel Slaughton's face looked strong and earnest, able to conquer and keep.

CHAPTER LXVIII.

" God send us pleasant dreams,
And make them all come true."

 UT of the morning land the royal sun-god approached with stately steps, and the lowly earth blushed beneath his ardent gaze. He darted his bright rays upon the hilltops, which glowed crimson, he touched the leaves into glory, illumined the lakes, glinted in the water-brooks, kissed into bloom all the flowers in Perdita's garden, and sent an arrowy beam upon the young girl-wife's eye-lids and a dream of hope into her heart, which so warmed and cheered it that she awoke with a smile on her red lips, and a sweet, pleasant thought of her rover, so interesting and inspiring that she watched and courted and cuddled it, and hated to let it go.

" I believe he has been near me in that land where soul meets soul," said she, half aloud. " Ah ! if he might but come once more in real presence."

She sprang up eagerly ; she felt an exaltation, abuoyancy of spirit which sent the blood leaping joyously through her veins —an undefined but sufficient expectation of a good to come, worth the effort of living her life in the best and fullest manner.

She had a busy day before her, too. Mrs. Richard Pritchard, who would persist in dropping in occasionally, though without much encouragement, had sent over word that she and the children were coming to tea, which of course meant to spend the night, and it was more than likely that the Brandegees would accompany them.

Teddy and Malcolm were at home, and their sister meant to have all her family up for the evening; and while she hurried her preparations, she ran up and down the house humming a certain reel she was fond of, and which seemed to bring with it many pleasant associations, for she stopped working twice or thrice and laughed aloud.

CHAPTER LXIX.

MR. SLAUGHTON DECLINES TO PLAY THE FOOL.

HEN our traveller descended from the cab at the St. James, the first person he saw in the office was Chandos Goldsmith, and he made great haste to get to his private room, that he might receive the latest news of his home.

" I rather dread the first meeting," said he ruefully, after the breathless silence in which he had drank in all his friend had to impart. " I feel tremendously foolish, now that I am so near meeting poor Perdita. She can set a fellow down so sharp; and of course she is indignant at me—how can she help it? Lord ! I wish it was over, and I was smoking my pipe by that wood fire she fixed up for me. Oh I you needn't laugh, Chandy ! I was not born with your impudence. *You'd* squirm right into the right spot, say the right thing, and make a success out of this fix. But I'm such a slow chap."

" It is lucky that you are not likely to go by the historical axiom that dark-skinned races are only fit for military government, and attempt to rule your high-spirited wife by the strong hand of power."

"Rule her! Rule Perdita!"

"Why don't you begin by serenading her first—a very excellent, good, conceited thing, after a wonderful sweet air, with admirable words to it, and then let her consider?"

"Humph! you must take me for a conceited thing!"

"I've hit it, Sam! I've hit the very thing!" exclaimed his friend; "the precise idea. Save all demonstrations and explanations, you know! Open the door for your easy entrance like a blast of wind, and in you go! You must carry the fort by stratagem," continued he, sinking his voice to a whisper, and drawing up close enough to the traveller to pat his knee and look in his eyes. "Do something funny! something to make her laugh!"

"Something funny?" replied Sam, with a ghastly smile. "Something funny! when you haven't seen your wife for a whole year, haven't written her a word; when you parted from her in such a spirit that you did not suppose it possible that you could ever look in her face again. Something funny!"

"It is your best card, however," persisted Chandos. "Listen now, till I tell you," he went on, volubly unfolding his idea, dressing it up with his best skill. "You may as well make a frolic of your return, if you don't want some terrific scenes. I assure you it will be a perfect success; you will carry off the situation with a laugh, and save yourself a vast deal of heart-rending excitement."

"I won't, Chandos. I won't make a fool of myself!"

"Of course not, Sam!" replied Chandy, who was projecting a good time for somebody, certainly. "I am to go with you, you know, and help you out. It'll be a capital thing; she'll like it, you'll see she will. She has excellent sense, and she will thank you for sparing her a trial full of vows and tears and repentings, and you can just sail right in and carry matters with a high hand; and what between surprise at your audacity and joy to get you safe back, you'll find it will end in a grand *feu de joie* and a royal good time. Take your choice, Samuel ! follow my advice, or give her the whip-hand of you by asking, begging to be received into your own house by your own wife."

I suppose there never lived a man who could be so easily led by his friends as Samuel Slaughton, especially when the alternative forced him to face a disagreeably obstinate fact. There was no getting around the certainty that he must make his peace with Perdita. Therefore he was unwillingly willing to permit Chandy Goldsmith to help him, and glad to get all the comfort to be found in talking over probabilities and particulars in the interim.

CHAPTER LXX.

A POSSE AD ESSE.

T was a warm evening in July, when two gentlemen got out of a Toptown car at Blithebeck, and started on the two-mile walk up the hill; and twilight had fallen, and the stars were out, before they reached the mansion house.

A glimmer of lights in the library, and a murmur of childish voices, reached them as they stepped noiselessly upon the piazza. Suddenly the soft strains of a flute rose on the silent night, thrillingly sweet.

Like all people who love music inartistically, Mr. Slaughton had the intuition of attaching certain strains to particular passages of his life, so that they seemed part and parcel of himself, as one sets words to a song; and joy or sadness swayed his sensibilities, as his memories were sweet or bitter.

So full of pathos seemed the familiar reel, which the player was weaving in threads of melody, and so many thoughts twined among them, that he stood breathless till she had finished, and laying down her flute, arose and went over to a corner alone, while the children chatted merrily together.

The lamp shone full upon her where she sat. A little paler, he thought, than he had known her, full of dignity, ravishingly beautiful! The same simple dress, long braids of raven hair, but her expression was changed; her face was glorified by suffering, matured by her year of trial, so that there was gentle sweetness, as well as conscious power, underlying her earnest, steady truth.

When she put up her hand and dashed off the tears which had gathered in her eyes, the man who watched her was not surprised; he felt a like moisture filling his own, and he knew she was thinking of him. He had come home on purpose to find out; but with such an array of doubts to quell, before his happiness could be certain, and such an overwhelming sense of his unworthiness to possess so much beauty and goodness, he hesitated, and felt his heart faint within him.

A jubilant burst of waltz-music from the piano in the long drawing-room caused a quick shifting of the figures before him; and Perdita came to the window almost close enough to touch his hand, before she lifted Betty in her arms, pillowing the child's golden head on her breast, and moved away among the others. A soft, sweet smile lighted her wonderful eyes, and just parted her lips, as they all trooped through the door, leaving silence behind them.

"Come away, Sam!" whispered Chandos. "You really must put off your revelation a little longer. Such a sudden surprise might be dangerous, fatal! But listen to me! You have no idea what frail creatures these tender women are; take a married man's advice, I entreat you; let me go first and break the news of your coming; let me do it gently."

Mr. Slaughton twisted impatiently away from the friend who was shaking with internal laughter.

"Leave me alone, Chandos! If you wait another minute, I'll pull off this cursed stuff and leave you and your plan in the lurch entirely."

"Don't, Samuel, I beg of you; be discreet, be wise, be patient. There, they are going to waltz, and we shall have an admirable chance to enter quietly; now then!

The young people were hardly afloat in the dance, whose music Mrs. Richard Pritchard was playing with admirable time and emphasis, when Hannah entered and whispered in her mistress's ear: "Two gentlemen in the library, wanting to see you."

Mr. Goldsmith and a brother artist, who asked a few hours' hospitality; "Belated, out sketching; great liberty, and so on."

The brother artist was a tall, broad-shouldered fellow, with blue eyes, full rolling lips, which were shaded by a black mustache, curled up like a brigand's at the ends, and a shock of thick black hair covering his head; his eyebrows met in the middle, and were long and bushy. He did not seem to have much to say for himself, leaving Chandy to do the talking.

Perdita received them courteously. "Most happy, Mr. Goldsmith,—pleasant surprise—always welcome. Stop all night, of course; never shut our gates on benighted strangers."

She showed Chandos to his old room, that he might refresh his travelling toilet; and she made his friend comfortable in her husband's apartment.

She did this on a second thought; the first words the brother artist uttered, she lifted her head, turned on him the full radiance of her illumined face, and flashed into his a burning glance from her intense eyes, and when she laid her fingers on his for the American hand-shake, she used all her force to steady them, so that no tremor should be felt by him.

After they were bestowed, she ran and called Dolly, begging her to remain and keep her company while the gentlemen were in the house.

"It is not proper, you know, Dolly," said she, with a strange, excited laugh, "for me to keep them here by myself. I might entertain angels unawares."

"Of course, Perdita, I'll stay. But why are you so merry?"

"I feel flurried, Dolly, dreadfully flurried. It is so long since I have had any such guests! It is such a wonderful thing to happen to me! I can scarcely believe my senses! Oh, Dolly, I am so happy!" ,

When the artists descended, the young hostess had regained her composure, though her eyes were shining through wet lashes, and her crimson cheeks outvied the rose. She was dignified and hospitable, however, and conversed easily with the strangers.

"As a painter," said she, addressing the black-haired one, "you must take great interest in pictures. I shall enjoy showing you some which Mr.. Slaughton finished before he went abroad. Perhaps you do not know that my husband is in Europe. When he returns I think the world may prepare to be astonished."

Taking up a lamp, she led the way to the studio, while Chandos studied her curiously. Did she know the man, or did she not? She seemed clear-faced and candid, and her voice sounded as smooth as the tones of her flute.

"This," said she, pausing before the Ruth, "this fair crea-ture is a portrait of Miss Bradshaw, a friend of Mr. Slaughton's early youth; it is a much better finished picture, you perceive, than this one of me, and I believe it is a striking likeness; but I'm told he painted that in the first blush of life's best illusions —painted it *con amore*. It is quite a romantic story; would you like to hear it, sir?"

"No! yes! of course, any tale would come gracefully from such eloquent lips," stammered the guest.

"You flatter me, I am afraid. Now this same Sabrina has a tongue of silver. Perhaps I weary you; you are not attending. I dare say I was premature in my exhibition, and I forgot that artists are apt to be jealous—are they not, Mr. Goldsmith?"

" Of each other, you mean ? "

" Of course, what else could I mean, sir ? Come, let us descend, though it does seem a pity to leave that gorgeous creature shut up in darkness. I think if you will lend the help of your strength to-morrow, I'll hang it in the parlor."

" *I* think you won't do anything of the sort," muttered the brother artist, as he followed the lamp like its slave down the stairs, and the tripping steps of·the handsome girl who held it.

As soon as she had placed her light on the table and seen her guest seated in a safe corner, she followed Mr. Goldsmith out upon the piazza, whither he seemed to have gone for a safe and solitary chuckle ; at any rate he interrupted himself in an exercise which sounded amazingly like it when he saw his hostess approaching him.

" Look here, Mr. Goldsmith, is this fair ? " said she angrily.

" What fair, Mrs. Slaughton ? "

" To expose me, a weak, trembling, suffering woman, to such a trial of her fortitude and self-command. How did you know but I should be surprised into throwing myself into that man's arms, or at his feet ? "

" Well, why didn't you ? that would have ended the masquerade *en règle*, and I could go home to my Bertha."

" No ! oh, no, sir ! I was spared that. He left me ; he must sue for pardon. Thank heaven ! I was mistress of myself. Now, tell me, what does this ridiculous farce mean ? Why does Samuel Slaughton come to his house in a black wig and false whiskers? "

" Well, you see, they shaved off his hair in a fever he had, and it has not grown out much yet; and he has never let his beard grow since. I think he made a vow not to, till he had accomplished a certain adventure and won a certain great prize which he infinitely desires. I'll tell you what he said to me, vebatim et literatim, and then you can judge for yourself: I must see my wife ; I must hear her talk ; I must find out whether she loves me, before I venture my happiness."

.

" And how does he expect to find out ? "

"It is my full and positive belief that he knows already."

" It is not mine then," replied she, leaving him in a hurry.

She found the brother artist waiting for her when she entered the door—in fact, she nearly ran into his arms.

" Come out into the conservatory with me," said he authoritatively."

" There is nothing there to look at," replied she, trying to push past him. " All the plants are in the borders."

" There will be something, when you are in there," was his reply.

" Oh, well, if you will, I suppose I must," said Perdita ; " but I must say you take a good deal of liberty for a stranger."

" I am not a stranger, Perdita ; I am your husband ! "

She took the arm he offered her, palpitating, and she stepped by his side without another word.

" Tell me now, and tell me truly, " said he, placing himself in front of her, and seizing both her hands in a firm grip. " How long had you been in the Toptown House, when I met you in the corridor ? "

" I can't exactly tell you ; don't crush my hands. I had spent some of my time at Champlin's. I arrived there the night before at half past six o'clock."

" And you saw me talking with Sabrina Penhurst ? "

" Yes, sir, I did ! and I heard enough to convince me that my hopes were dead."

" Then you did not hear all, and you heard wrong."

" So I found out afterwards, when she hunted me up and most nobly insisted on explaining everything. I was terribly rude to her, too, before I gave her a chance."

" And yet, after you had found out your mistake, you still kept silence. You never wrote to me a word."

" No ! you left me. I did not leave you."

" But you did ! you forbade me to accompany you."

" You ought to have known better than to have minded that."

" Perdita, if you were not bound to me by law, would you be my wife ? "

" Would you ask me ? "

" I do ask you now. Will you pardon the past, and truly love me in the future ? "

" Till death us do part," answered she solemnly.

There was a moment's silence between the pair, who heard each other's hearts beat in their first warm, close embrace, and then Perdita broke away from him.

" Sam," said she, " please take off that horrid black stuff from your face (I never could bear black-haired men), and tell me when you first began to love me."

" I think ever since I first touched your hand, and you so coolly said, ' I will.' "

" That is quite a long while ; well, I couldn't tell you when I began to love you. It certainly was not when I heard myself styled an Ethiop by a gentleman who ought to have known that the old Greek word means sun-burned ; and yet you see I am not darker then a Hellene, and if you will look, you will observe there is no lotus-bud, meaning south, on my halter," said she archly, showing him the end of her snood.

The tears would come, in spite of her running on, and she was forced to wipe them away.

" You love me now, and I am satisfied," replied he, obeying her and flinging his disguise away.

" Then let's go in and dance this waltz."

" I thought you told me you couldn't dance."

" But I never told you I could not learn with proper effort and attention. There is an excellent master in Toptown, and as I had to take the children there for their lessons, I thought it would be a pity to waste valuable time sitting about, when I could as well be tripping. So I got myself taught as a child ; and I have not put away childish things."

"Humph! while my young wife has been growing young, I, her old husband, have been losing all the tricks of my youth. I am afraid my old-time capers are out of fashion. However, we'll tread a measure, if it were only to give me a chance to get my arm around your waist. Ah! what a slender little waist has my nut-brown maid."

After the waltz was over, and they two stood apart in a corner, Perdita turned to her partner with a smile which had a little dash of trouble over it.

"I must ask you a question!"

"I am all ears!"

"Not quite; and still, yes, speaking after the manner of men." She critically examined his auricles, which were truly of generous proportions. "You remember, I dare say the pictures I so politely showed you this evening, upstairs?"

"I seem to think I do. I will owe you one for that performance."

"Oh, no, you owe me nothing. I have forgiven all your trespasses. Tell me, and tell me truly, am I as beautiful in your eyes as your golden-haired Ruth—as your first love?"

"Perdita, my dear—no, no, don't shrink away from me. I will not forget that the room is full of curious people still exclaiming over my advent. I will be decorous, for is not Dickey Pritchard watching us? Rest assured, that my standard of beauty is entirely changed. I admire brunettes, and I dote on the brownest of them all—my wife Perdita. Have I made it strong enough? If not, I'll swear!"

"Oh, yes; don't swear. Remember I am a parson's daughter, and I don't approve of profanity. Well! we were married in haste to repent at leisure, were we not?"

"I never repented; but if you say so, we will go and stand up in your father's old parlor and let him tie us over again—so that we can say 'I will' with vim, and mean it."

"No, oh, no," replied she in a soft voice, remembering how

the hand which joined theirs that day was turning to dust. " I am satisfied with the knot as it is."

" Well, then, I'll espouse you as Joseph espoused Mary. ' If thou consentest to be my wife, accept this token.' We are told by the fathers that that was the love-making of the carpenter to his bride, and she agreed to the contract and took his offering ; will you have mine ? "

He pulled a golden eagle from his pocket and placed it in her hand.

"Ah, yes ! I do remember, you long ago promised to pay my housekeeper's wages in gold. I suppose this is the first installment of that bargain. I'll have a hole bored in it and wear it around my neck for luck."

" I expect and intend to be in myself and mine all the good luck you can ever wish for, or dream of. I suppose you are still up in your Latin, and will be able to interpret an old proverb, ' A posse ad esse.' "

THE END.

www.ingramcontent.com/pod-product-compliance
Lightning Source LLC
Chambersburg PA
CBHW022027110726
47901CB00006B/1672